Golden Light

Praise for The Creations Saga

"Undoubtedly fascinating and complex. 5 Stars"

— *Readers' Favorite*

"The characters feel very real and very raw."
"A fascinating fantasy world."
"No matter how many adaptations are made, Red Sand is one of those stories you can't fully experience unless you read it."

— *NINA Productions*

"Epic adventure. Powerful and beautiful. Love this book. Love Lilith and the journey she travels. Can't wait for more!"

— *iBooks Review*

"Red Sand is the best book I've read in years!! Absolutely vivid and beautiful prose and such a gripping story."

— *Instagram Review*

"Wonderful and heartfelt story. I look forward to the next book."

— *Goodreads Review*

"Beautiful. Adventurous. Mystical. An amazing adventure and journey. Could not put the book down."

— *Goodreads Review*

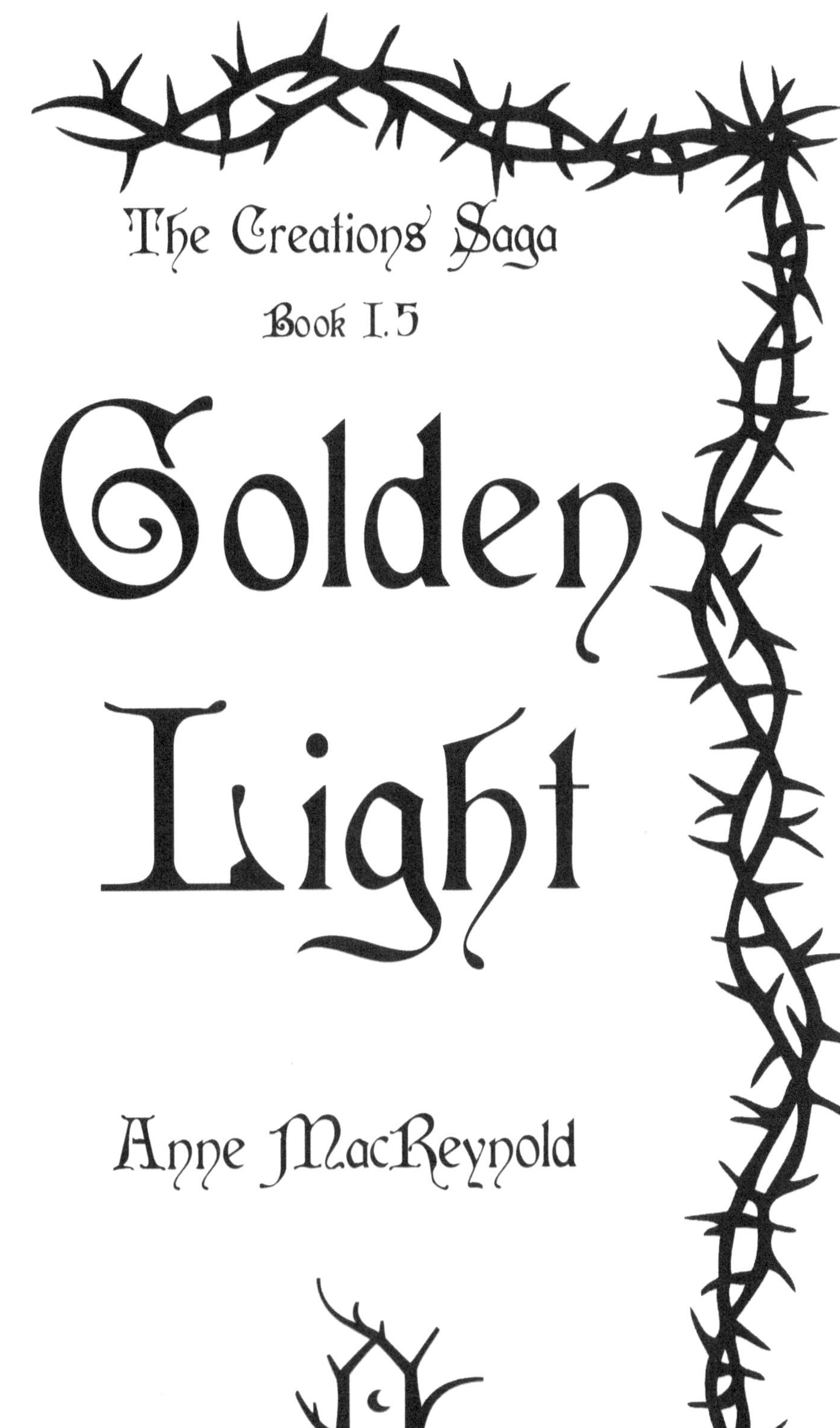

The Creations Saga
Book I.5
Golden Light
Anne MacReynold
Enchanted Publishing House

Enchanted Publishing House

Golden Light Copyright © 2021 Anne MacReynold

Book Design by Brandon Rice

Manuscript Editing by Enchanted Edits
www.EnchantedEdits.com

Original Cover Image: ©Liliya Sudakova/Dreamstime.com

LCCN: 2021909307

Paperback ISBN: 978-1-73712-180-0
E-Book ISBN: 978-1-73712-182-4
Hardback ISBN: 978-1-73712-181-7

Printed in the United States of America

Dedicated to my father.

An incarnation of darkness.
Darkness that both inspires fear and swathes those in need of solace.

Contents

Introduction

The Creations Saga is all about perception. Though you will read from Lilith's view throughout most of the series, this book will be from the antagonist's perspective, Lucifer. I plucked Lilith and Lucifer from mythology where they were seen as dreadful people, gods, demons, angels, etc. But like every story, there are multiple sides. And when we view someone as "evil" we don't stop to consider why they did such horrible things or what their intentions were to begin with. Though the result is what matters in the end, it's still worth hearing the full story. This way, we can form an opinion of our own.

If you read *Red Sand*, Book 1 of *The Creations Saga*, you've probably already developed your own opinion of Lucifer. But there was much that Lilith didn't know and much that you did not read.

Why did he do such terrible things?

Why did he insist on possessing her?

Golden Light is meant to fill in those gaps and answer some of the questions we all had. I felt it was important to tell Lucifer's side of the story before we continued with Lilith's tale. You, the reader, and I needed to know him better before their story developed further. Lilith has a long journey ahead of her, and Lucifer is a vital thread in her ancient tapestry.

It's choices that shape the person. So, enjoy this novel and discover what choices Lucifer will make and what kind of world they will create.

Sincerely,
A Creator of Choices

Prologue
Before

She was gone. In anger, I released part of my fury upon a little vermilion planet, and the life there was extinguished. Before I could realize what I had done, a red spark of light caught my gaze. Beside the vermilion sphere, there was a blue planet I had overlooked in my haste, and it cast a strange, familiar glow.

I found you.

Part I
The Child

Innocent child

Young eyes to see the old

Young ears to hear the wisdom

Old guides and inspires

Creates and molds

But there is no old

I

Woman

Follow the light.
-S

Prehistory

My body burned, but it didn't hurt. The warmth covered my form and expelled the negative emotions that coursed through me. I couldn't remember why I had felt so sad. So lost. But now it didn't matter. The golden light that danced behind my eyelids calmed me. My senses awoke and I could smell the sunbaked plants beside me. I felt a cold breeze pass through my hair, though the warmth from above quickly snuffed out the chill. My mouth was dry and begged to be moistened, but the sound I heard quickly distracted me. I opened my eyes to the noise.

The heat that radiated overhead was bright, and it took my eyes a moment to adjust, but I was soon able to see what had disrupted my rest. A dark gold creature stalked along the tree line. It hadn't seen me yet. Instinctually I kept low, only moving so I could keep the creature in my line of sight. The breeze drifted past me to the dangerous-looking animal. It lifted its head at the new scent. It was unsure, and scanned the clearing I hid in. The grass was tall enough to conceal me so long as I didn't move.

Satisfied with its solitude, the lion chuffed and disappeared into the dense undergrowth beneath the towering trees. Curious, I stood and followed silently. The grass crunched beneath my feet, and gold strands fell into my eyes. I was wary entering the dark forest, but I hoped that whatever I found would answer the question on my mind.

Why was I here?

The lion stalked quietly beneath the vast emerald canopy. The leaves were gentle as they swayed to and fro, the breeze teasing. I listened to the steady *thud…thud…thud* of the cat's heartbeat while we followed the invisible path. The creature knew exactly where it was going, lifting its nose to the scent that beckoned. I traversed the path effortlessly, concentrating solely on being silent. Unaware of my place in this world, I thought it best to merely watch.

Hours later, the cat stopped at the edge of a great clearing. It crouched low with its tail twitching, still unaware of my presence. The sun had moved overhead, and the heat had grown. I sat upon a tree branch overlooking the field. The lion stiffened, even its breath ceased, just moments before it sprang out of the shadows and into the sun. Its speed was daunting, the grass parted before the lithe creature on command. I was prepared to follow, but then I realized what it was doing—hunting. Instinctually my body tensed, ready for a fight.

I looked farther ahead, seeing only tall, sun-kissed grass, but the grass parted into trails as the buffalo fled from the predator. Their massive bodies moved both heavily and with grace. The thick brown fur that grew from their skin was matted with dirt, the heady scent wafted to me even at this far distance.

The herd protected each other with numbers and sheer size, but a lone youngling separated from the herd, and I knew immediately this was the easiest target. I waited for the lion to follow its trail, but the cat merely glanced at the small creature before turning toward the herd again. Confused, I climbed high into a tree, hoping for a better view.

What was the lion's purpose?

The lion continued to harass the herd, causing one buffalo to separate and attack the cat. The lion maneuvered with ease as the creature charged at it, leading it farther and farther away from its kind.

Finally alone, and exhausted from chasing the lion across the field, the buffalo stopped. Its breathing hitched. I couldn't imagine the heat the creature was absorbing with the thick fur and determined light from above.

The lion hid in the tall grass once again, and the buffalo, too tired to search for its attacker, walked slowly to the edge of the forest where it could rest in the shade. By the time it had, the lion had been forgotten.

I smiled in anticipation.

The lion leapt from its hiding place and locked onto the buffalo's throat, its strong teeth unyielding. It wasn't long before the massive creature could not breathe, allowing the cat to release its grip. The lion stood proudly over its kill, red liquid dripping from its jaw.

The lion let out a rough cry. I could not understand what it said, but more of its kind exited the woodland moments later, still unaware of the watcher hiding in the tree. They greeted the hunter with chuffs and fur rubs before tearing into the beast that lay before them. The fur was ripped away. Pieces of the animal was consumed. The rest of the buffalo's herd departed, unknowing of their kin's sacrifice or simply indifferent to it.

I took this opportunity to disappear as well.

Could these creatures tear me apart too?

My feet were moving before the creatures could answer the question. I leapt from tree to tree until I was sure I was far away from the beasts. I landed softly on the moss-covered ground, enjoying its strange texture. While the field had been dry and hot, the forest was moist and cool. Bumps raised on my skin, disappearing when I laid my hand over them.

Soft groans sounded from a wall of thorn-covered brush. I parted them only to prick my skin. I watched the small wounds close immediately, but not before strange red particles appeared and fell to the ground below.

The groans continued. Frustrated with the pricks and stabs of the brush, I jumped over the wall, landing quietly. In doing so, I startled a creature so white, it was blinding. The horse stood tall, two ivory horns protruding from its forehead. They glimmered in the sunrays that peered through the canopy. I was wary of the sharp points, comparing them to the lion's teeth.

My suspicion was replaced with curiosity when the horse didn't attack but groaned again. I could see now that the creature was in pain. Its violet eyes spoke another peculiar language, one that I was able to partially understand.

I raised my hands and spoke with my eyes as well, hoping that whatever the horse saw in them would be enough to tell it that I meant no harm. Overly trusting, or in too much pain to care, the horse bowed its head and allowed me to place a hand on its soft fur. The hair mirrored the light around us as its muscles rippled beneath my palm.

I was entranced by the strange beast, so I was startled when the horse let out a painstaking cry. What followed was the strangest thing I had yet seen. A small horse was birthed onto the ground, the moss creating a soft landing for the child. It looked the same as its mother: white fur, violet eyes, and small stubs protruded where its horns would be.

I took a step toward the foal when its mother huffed. I looked into the horse's eyes again and understood. Retreating only a few steps, the submission allowed the mother to turn and care for the child. The horse began to lick the foal's wet fur, and the newborn took a breath. I stood still for a long while, just watching the interactions between the two animals.

Life.

My chest ached in that moment. Something was missing.

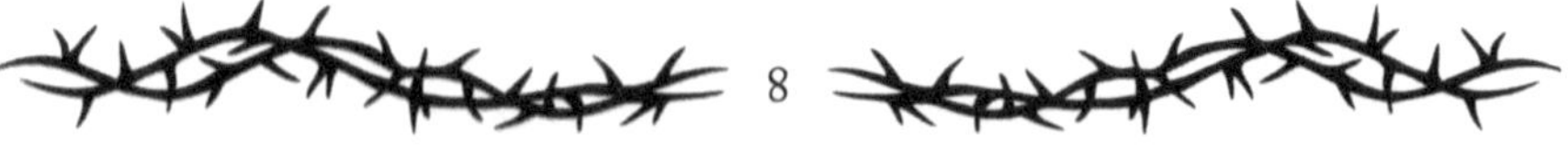

My thoughts returned to the lions. I stepped toward the foal, now standing, but still very much weak. I thought of wrapping my hands around its throat.

Was that what I was supposed to do?

Removing my gaze from the foal, I looked to the mother. Its bright eyes were locked on me. The horse rose from its resting place on the ground, standing between the foal and the threat.

A strange sense overcame me, and I bowed my head, speaking the only language we both knew, and disappeared behind the shrubbery. The farther away I was from the horse and foal, the clearer this existence became. There were predators and prey. There were the strong and the weak.

And I would not be the weak.

At that moment, I promised myself I would not cower again. I would be as the lion had been and take what was mine.

Just don't look them in the eyes.

I awakened in a strange and confusing world. All day, I traversed the woodlands and fields, learning much about the land in that time, but the purpose of this existence was still unknown, which caused a feeling of emptiness.

Nothing else to guide me, I hunted as they did, using what little skills I possessed to chase and overcome my prey. Though, tired from my efforts, I sought something to quench my growing thirst.

By the time the sun disappeared and darkness came into being, I found it—water.

The water fell over a sharp hill and into the pond below. I dove in and drank my fill, knowing instinctually this was what would sustain me. However, the life in the water unnerved me. The fish poked at my sides, nibbling on my skin.

Could I trust them?

Once my thirst was satisfied, I looked upward, where the dark sky loomed. There were tiny facets of light scattered throughout the menacing ether, but I couldn't keep the cold from seeping into my bones upon the sight. I brought my attention back to the water and focused on its surface. What gazed back was a creature I hadn't yet seen—a man—me. My hair was gold like the sun, skin was the color of warm sand, and my eyes glowed ice blue in the reflection of the mysterious white light above. I touched my cheek, curious of the form.

My body tensed.

I smelled her before I saw her. It was a sweet, intoxicating scent that filled my head with unfamiliar thoughts. My lungs were bursting because I refused to let any of the delicate scent escape me. The pollen from the night flowers smelled like her, but there was something completely unique about hers. It beckoned me as the animals beckoned me to hunt, but the hunt I had in mind didn't end with her death.

I dove for her hiding spot behind the waterfall, but the creature escaped me. She swam expertly through the water, and once she had her feet planted on land, the woman ran faster than anything I had yet seen. I followed.

I heard her faint footsteps in the distance. I passed by a red flower on my chase. It distracted me for only a moment—the color was so similar. I didn't know why the woman was running from me, but I enjoyed it just the same.

The steps suddenly stopped. I listened carefully for the sound of her soft breaths or the words that would summon me. I wondered what she would sound like. Surely her voice would be just as beautiful as her aroma or the grace with which she moved. But what I heard next was far from beautiful. A low growl rumbled in the direction of the woman I chased.

I ran faster.

The red of her hair, and the ivory glow of her skin was easy to see through the trees. I had assumed she was waiting for me until I saw the shape beside her. It put its muzzle against her scalp, scenting my prey. Upon my approach, the predator turned from the woman and posed to challenge me. Though my eyes were no longer on the woman, I could still see her. She held her left side protectively and trembled. *Did this creature hurt her? Was she afraid?*

I didn't know how to defeat such a predator. I hadn't attempted to yet, but my instincts said it was something I had to do. I had to protect the woman and claim this land as my own—it was the only way. I was considering leading it away from the woman when she shifted. Though the woman returned to her defensive position when she realized she wasn't strong enough to stand. The small movement caused the saber-toothed cat to turn and look at her.

Angered by the cat's territorial claim on my prey, I ran at it. But it was quicker than I thought. I was barely able to avoid its long incisors while I jumped onto its back. I wrapped my arms around the creature's neck and squeezed, assuming it would submit.

It did not.

It wriggled and fought to throw me off. Unable to find a grip, I locked my legs against the cat's sides. I felt the vibration of whatever I broke inside the beast. The sounds were satisfying, but I was quickly distracted by another sound. The woman called out in fright.

I looked to the woman to see if she was hurt, but also to make sure she hadn't run away again. Her eyes locked with mine, and the green of the forest was what stared back. They were wide and full of terror, but I could see a challenge hiding behind them. And I wanted desperately to find out what kind of thrill she could give me.

The thrashing animal distracted me from her trance, and I was irritated because of it. The saber-toothed cat snapped its jaws at my leg. Then it was over. My hand instinctually reached out and grabbed the fang. I pulled back with little force and its neck snapped. I heard the beating of its erratic heart cease, and its limbs went limp. I could have escaped before the creature took me down with it, but the woman diverted me yet again. I saw her crimson curls flying behind her as she ran from me. Confusion washed away my other senses.

Why was she running? The beast was dead.

I struggled to get the cat off me. I would return to consume it later. I had more important things to do.

The woman was fast. I couldn't catch her, but I could track her. That intoxicating aroma would never elude me. It was etched into my memory. No matter how far she went I would follow, even if I never caught her. My entire being told me to do so.

A loud ripping noise thundered against the forest's walls. I followed the sound. I couldn't hear her delicate steps anymore, and I stopped. Her scent was all around me. It was hard to focus. *Where was she?* I treaded carefully through the crunchy leaves, hoping to stay silent. I didn't want to frighten her away. I was too close.

I smelled harrowed earth. I looked down to find a tree's limb had been uprooted. Dirt and moss hung from it, and some continued to fall into the new crevice below. This was the noise I had heard. *She was close.* The night's small creatures had stopped scuttling when I entered the area, but I could still hear their tiny, frantic heartbeats and rapid breaths.

I closed my eyes and concentrated. All the sounds of the world disappeared as I honed in on one. A gasp from above. I looked up in time to see the woman lose her grip on the high branch of a tree. She fell through the rest. It looked painful, but she didn't call out as I expected her to. Her red tresses flailed in the wind and blocked out the sight of the pale moon.

I barely had to move to catch her. It was as if she'd planned it—maybe she had. There were easier ways to get my attention, but I had a feeling she was going to challenge me in more ways than one. Her emerald eyes looked up at me once she landed safely in my arms. I realized then what had attracted me to her.

Like me, she had no heartbeat.

That could have meant only one thing.

II

Hunt

Take life and be given life.
-G

The forest came alive as night became day. Creatures began to wander and flowers turned to face the light above us. The woman I captured had struggled in my arms at first, but now rested comfortably against my chest. She gazed into the rising sun as I did. Looking at the light, I felt a sense of relief. I was unsure if I would ever see the daylight again, while the darkness seized the sky only hours ago. But of course, the darkness couldn't be as terrible as I assumed.

I found her in it, didn't I?

The woman raised her hand. I thought it was to fight against me again, but she simply shifted the gold strands of hair that blocked my sight. Intrigued, I risked a glance toward her. Her green eyes shimmered in the light, and the crimson that colored her wild curls were set aflame. I was intensely aware of how close we were and how soft her skin was against mine.

I looked away quickly. She was already frightened of me. I couldn't push her too far or I'd have to track the fleeing woman again. Though I would follow, I wasn't sure I would ever be able to catch her.

I let out a silent breath in hope to calm my nerves. Nerves that were completely new to me. Both terrible and wonderful. *Did she feel the same?*

I prolonged the trek as long as I could, but eventually, we reached the waterfall where our journey began—the place I attacked her. Although the act was merely an instinct, it had frightened my only chance of finding answers to the questions I kept asking myself.

Where was I? Who was I? Why was I here?

I had enough knowledge to name what surrounded me but not enough to tell me why I needed to. The creature in my arms shifted slightly. "Comfortable?" I asked the woman. She made no move to remove herself from my hold, and for a moment I allowed myself to hope. To hope she didn't fear me anymore.

However, what came next caused those hopes to crumble. The woman's elbow met my rib, and I hated to admit, it hurt more than anything I'd experienced in this existence so far. My reaction wasn't much better, and I regretted it as soon as she slipped from my hands and into the pond below. Because once she was no longer touching me, I could feel that emptiness in my chest again.

I felt alone again.

The woman rose from the water, and I heard her true voice for the first time. "You moron! Why would you throw me in the water? I'm injured, and I thought you wanted to help?"

I had expected something soft, delicate, and mesmerizing. And it was in a way, but her words were unexpected. I hadn't yet experienced laughter, and it disabled me. I fell to my knees, unable to control myself. She wouldn't stop shouting at me. I understood that she was upset from being dropped into the water without warning, but she's the one who attacked first.

"Why did you chase me if you were going to treat me this way?" she demanded.

I quelled my laughter. "Well, because you ran from me, of course.

And it's clear you can't defend yourself. That cat would have eaten you for dinner if it wasn't for me." *Wasn't it obvious?*

"I can defend myself just fine. If you wouldn't have shown up I would have parted ways with the creature, neither of us harmed. You are the one who startled him and crossed onto his territory." Her anger was rising, and it was difficult not to answer it with my own.

"I doubt that, but in any case, it's my territory now, isn't it?" I hadn't acknowledged the possibility until I said it aloud, but I was one of the creatures here too, better even. I had a right to the land we walked upon. My wits were more refined than any animal I had encountered.

Except her.

"The land may be yours, but I'm not." She made a move to flee again.

"Oh no you don't. You're not running off again. I need answers, and you're the closest thing I have."

"Why would you think I have answers? I just woke up last night," she said, irritated.

As I suspected, she was as naive as I was. Still, there was a small part of me that had hoped. Though, I was learning quickly that hope was useless and led only to a path of disappointment. "Well, I guess we need each other then, don't we?"

Reluctant, she nodded and descended deeper into the water. "What now?"

"Now we look at your injuries." I remembered how she'd clutched her side when the saber-toothed cat attacked. The woman had been coated in red dust. Then, after running from me again, she fell from a tree, hitting every branch on the way down. *She must have been in pain.* I shouldn't have taken so long on the journey back. My own selfish desire to hold her made it so she was in pain longer than she needed to be.

Maybe I deserved her anger.

I took a step forward, and she shouted, "No!"

Confused, I asked, "And why not?"

"I don't want you touching me."

The words felt like another blow to the rib. "Afraid you won't be able to keep your hands off me?" I attempted a friendly smile, in hopes to earn her trust with humor. *I enjoyed the emotion, maybe she would too?*

The woman's cheeks turned pink, piquing my curiosity. "No! I just don't want you near me right now. I don't know you, and you've been chasing me through the woods the entire night. I'm tired."

It was clear she was unsure, and I wanted to be with her longer. *I didn't want to feel empty anymore.* "I only want to help."

Before I could finish my sentence, she splashed water toward me. By the time I wiped the pond droplets from my eyes she had vanished behind the falls.

I left the woman alone at the waterfall. If I wanted her trust, I'd have to be patient.

I went back to where I defeated the saber-toothed cat, planning to bring it to her for nourishment. I grabbed the massive leg of the predator and pulled, discovering that it wasn't as heavy as it appeared. Smiling, I turned toward the waterfall, knowing this would prove to the woman that I only wished to protect and care for her. The birds' songs ceased. The winds grew angry. The trees groaned from the pressure. Leaves clapped frantically. Soon, I could only hear breathing. Heavy, slow, hot breaths warmed the air around me.

I dropped my kill and looked upward.

A creature, the size of the monstrous trees, lowered itself slowly to the ground where I stood, uncaring of the canopy that obstructed its landing. The trees were no match for this beast.

The dragon exhaled blue fire. The angry flames caught the greenery in its grasp, turning it black until it crumbled to the ground below, though the horrifying power didn't spread due to the wind coming from the dragon's massive wings.

Despite the heat the dragon created, I was frozen. My core was as cold as the night, and my body refused to move. *What was happening to me?*

The dragon let out a roar, so loud, I was sure even the woman could hear it. The vibrations of the mighty sound carried through the air and reverberated through my body, waking me from my trance—from my terror. I abandoned the meal and leapt away, barely avoiding the creature as it landed its massive claws on the earth.

For as slow as it had been to land, it was gone before I could blink, rising high in the sky with the cat's corpse in its tight hold. One of its claws had impaled the cat's body, and its blood slowly dripped toward the earth, the color nearly black.

Staying where I hid in the thicket, I listened to the beast fly through the calm sky, toward the north where the mountains rested. Branches dangled from the gaping hole in the canopy. The sunlight was free to shine down onto the dark woods. I reached a shaky hand toward the rays of warmth, comforted by their presence.

The creature claimed what was mine.

Lesson learned: Do not trust the animals.

I pushed the new emotion down deep into myself, unwilling to acknowledge the terrifying realization that there was something to fear in this world.

Once I was able to stand, I returned to the meadow where I first woke, remembering the small accomplishment I'd made the previous day. The lion taught me how to hunt in the short time I had watched it.

Stalk. Chase. Kill. Devour.

I did not expect for the lion to win, not when its prey was so much stronger, but skill and patience were the answers to winning such a fight. I had doubted the reason for killing such a dangerous creature to begin with, thinking it unnecessary, but I understood now, recalling how the rest of the pride came to share the meal.

It wasn't just for one.

I kneeled and dug into the earth where I hid the squirrel and shrew. *My first kills.* When I found them, the smell wafting upward had me gagging. I drew away from the hole in the ground and laid down in defeat.

Another lesson learned: Do not trust the earth.

I looked to my lost meal, studying the bloated bodies and feasting insects. The eyes were already gone, and the fur was dull and listless. I lifted my gaze to the sun and wondered if it had a factor in this process as well.

I reburied the small creatures and stood with new determination.

I was going to have to hunt something new. But it couldn't be as pathetic as a rodent. It would have to be great enough to demonstrate my strength and prove that I could care for another. I needed to show the woman that she didn't have to be afraid of this world.

She didn't have to be afraid of me.

The hunt drew me south. I followed scent after scent, unsure of the new sense. Then I came across the strongest yet. *It was close.* I could hear the soft footsteps of the beast wading through the brush. I stayed quiet and low. I forced my breath to slow and the shake in my hands to still.

An animal from above suddenly started chattering. I looked up to find an oversized rodent with a long fur tail fearlessly shrieking at me. I glared into its dark eyes and cursed the life that dwelled here. The soft footfalls stopped. I stood to my full height and peered over the brush. My gaze met long, twisting antlers before they rested on black eyes. The stag tensed, but before I could react, the creature ran.

Why did everything run from me?

My feet responded naturally. *I was hunting.* The faster I ran the more

I understood my purpose. The power was exhilarating. I ran faster than I did last night when the woman fled. I realized now that I had chosen to slow my speed. I chose to enjoy the chase. Which was what I continued to do.

The buck knew its fate. I sped and slowed, not only testing myself, but taunting the docile animal. Quickly, my prey grew tired. The stag stopped and turned to face its hunter. It angled its neck to attack with the deadly weapons growing from its head. I circled the beast, waiting.

The stag flew forward, and I could almost feel the sting of the protruding bones. But just before the buck reached me, I swung myself onto its back, using its own weapons to guide me up and over. I defeated the saber-toothed cat from this position, perhaps I could do it again. I held onto those natural weapons as the creature bucked and fought beneath me.

Why do these creatures fight me?

I knew the answer as soon as I caught sight of the animal's terrified gaze. *To live.*

The thought overtook my mind and my grip loosened. That was all the stag needed to fling me forward and off its back. I turned in the air so only my left side would take the impact of the fall. The rocks beneath me ripped the skin open, and crimson sand poured out.

Too startled by my wound, I didn't look up as the stag disappeared and ran so far, I could no longer hear its frantic heartbeat.

I spent the remainder of the day and into the night honing my senses. I listened to the sound of the forest and the creatures that dwelled in it. I memorized the scents of each animal that I came across. I felt the vibrations in the ground, and soon, I knew if there was beast or rodent near me with only the soles of my feet and the palms of my hands.

I watched as the sky darkened. I never felt more alone than when the light was absent. I thought of the woman waiting for me at the waterfall, and it eased the pain. *I'd kept her waiting long enough.*

I quieted the panic that planted itself in my thoughts and concentrated. I rested my palm on the soil below and listened for any sound that would indicate a meal. The moss released evening moisture as little feet stepped upon the greenery. *Squish...squish...squish.*

I followed the sound until I found what I was looking for. The small animal was bright in the darkness. Its white fur glowed in the moonlight, and its eyes gleamed red, reflecting green as it turned its gaze to and fro. The rabbit was nibbling on a small piece of red fruit. The stem fell from the top as the animal's teeth buried deep into the fruit's core.

The creature hopped close to the dense greenery. I nearly lunged in panic of losing it, but it only paused to lay the remains of its meal on a protruding root. The root glowed as bright as the being's fur. The rabbit blended perfectly into the strange wood. My prey was small and not what I had planned to bring back to the woman, but day would soon be upon us, and I couldn't keep her waiting any longer.

I took a small step. Red irises locked with my blue ones, and I understood it was going to be a chase. But from what I discovered about myself today, I knew nothing would escape me again. I broke our stare, ready for the challenge.

III

Spite

Give your trust and take your poison.
-D

The sun rose just as I entered the meadow. The waterfall was quiet while it cascaded into the pond below. I could see red hair between the gaps in the falls. I smiled to myself. *She waited for me.*

I laid the rabbit beside the pond. I looked to my soiled hand and the dirt it had left behind on the animal's white fur. The rest of my body was the same. I cringed, realizing how I must have looked. *Like one of the animals.*

I dove into the water, hoping to rid myself of the dirt before the woman woke. But she roused, and her green gaze found mine. "Oh good, you're awake! That means you can help me," I said to distract her from my appearance. I didn't need her help, but I did want her to see the meal I brought her. If I was hungry she would be, too.

The woman came out from behind the waterfall, and my breath caught. The sunlight glinted against her wet ivory skin. My eyes followed the water trickling down her body, lower and lower as she gradually rose from the pond and reached the shallow depths beside the mossy bank. Her pink lips lifted into a smile when she saw the rabbit, and I couldn't help but be pleased with myself.

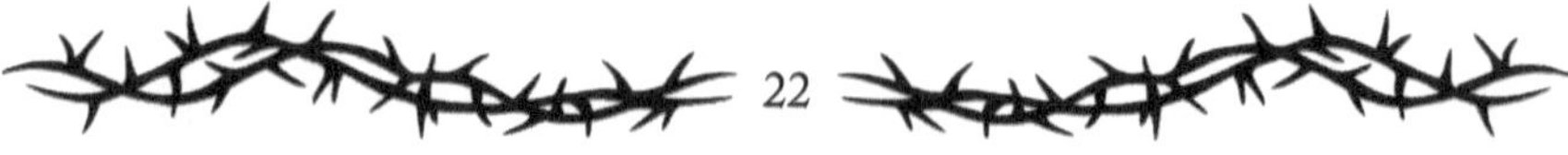

She pulled herself onto the grass hill beside our meal and stroked its fur. "What's wrong with him?" she asked.

Confused, I stopped washing and explained, "Nothing's wrong with it. I broke its neck so we could eat it. It took me a while, though. It was very hard to catch." My voice disappeared, recalling the stag I'd allowed to escape.

Quicker than I could comprehend, the woman stood and ran to the closest bush. The noises she made were unpleasant, and I didn't know what to do besides stay in the water and wait.

What was wrong with her? Was this a symptom of hunger?

Did I return too late?

The woman stopped heaving and turned toward me. "How could you do that? What made you even think to? That's horrible. This rabbit was my friend. He helped me find food yesterday after you left me here." Her hands shook. I had hoped I saw the last of her anger yesterday, but clearly I had been wrong.

I had no words to give her. *What did I do? We needed to eat.*

The woman stepped forward and I tensed, preparing to fight, but she collapsed beside the rabbit's corpse instead. Water poured from her eyes.

Sadness.

I climbed out of the pond and sat next to her. I tentatively placed my palm on her shoulder, fully expecting her to bite my hand. I wanted her to look at me, but her beautiful green was reserved only for the rabbit.

I stood and entered the dense forest, remembering the flower I had seen the night before—the flower that reminded me so much of *her*. I plucked the lone crimson lily from its place in the ground. Not finding any more, I stole a rose too. Its thorns pricked me as I pulled, and red sand seeped from my finger. I cringed.

The woman was still sitting in the grass beside the animal when I returned. Kneeling, I laid the red rose on top of the rabbit in hopes to appease her. The color of the rose beckoned me in a way I didn't think it would. Red was a powerful shade.

Offering the lily to the woman, I said, "I am sorry for your friend. I would have chosen another animal if I had known that. Will you forgive me?" Though her reaction to my hard work hurt me, I desperately wanted to make amends with this woman. She was the only other of my kind, and being alone wasn't an option.

She finally looked up and met my gaze. The tears stopped, and she took the lily from my hand, her fingers brushing against my own. As she smelled the flower, I glanced to the dead rabbit. A new emotion overwhelmed me, and I suddenly hated the creature.

Why did this docile animal deserve her attention more than me?

I tore my gaze away from the rabbit. "I saw this flower soon after we met that night. The brightness of it stood out in the dark. It reminded me of you. The crimson for your obvious anger toward me," I forced a smile, "and for the color of your hair. Though the beauty of it does not compare to you, it is the prettiest flower I have seen."

The woman's skin flushed pink.

Was this another reaction to me? "Do you not like it?" I asked.

"No, it's beautiful. Thank you," she whispered.

A good reaction this time.

I couldn't help but see the rabbit in the corner of my eye. I had claimed this creature in death, and I could do so with the rest of the life around us. But not *her*. She was something different and something more. But my instinct was to claim. I had the same feeling when I first saw her. Even after she ran, even after she showed affection for nature instead of me, her own species, *I wanted her.*

The woman removed her gaze from the lily and looked to the rabbit.

"What do I call you?" I asked.

"What do you mean?" Her eyes returned to me.

"A name. The creatures around us and the plant life have names. Shouldn't we?"

She twirled the lily nervously as she considered what I said. "I suppose so, but I thought we did already. You're Man and I am Woman?"

"Yes, that is what I see, too, but we seem to be different from the rest. Don't you think? We should name ourselves," I encouraged.

"If you would like. What do you want to call yourself?" I had her full attention now.

"I can't think of anything. Would you name me? Mostly because I have the perfect one for you." My excitement grew the longer she looked at me.

"What is it you have chosen for me then?" she asked. I could see she was nervous, and it only made me happier. The more we spoke the clearer it became that she needed a guide. It explained her rash behavior before.

"Because you are so much like the lily you hold in your hand, I thought Lilith would be your name. Do you like it?" The woman couldn't seem to answer. "Yes! That is your name. Lilith is perfect for you. Now, what name do you have for me?"

Lilith couldn't create a name for me yet, unable to decide. Though I was disappointed, my theory had been proven right. The woman merely needed someone to lead her. She was delicate, and I feared for her safety.

But I would care for her from now until the end.

We left the waterfall, and I soon found myself inspecting mushrooms. Lilith was beside me and had insisted I eat the vegetation instead of meat. Although I agreed to try it, I doubted I would ever survive on so little. I would have eaten the apple she'd found, but the woman had refused to share. Despite the fact that I hadn't wanted the fruit, it hurt that she didn't feel the need to care for me as I did her.

It's my responsibility. Not hers.

The scent of the mushrooms Lilith pointed to were unpleasant, and I looked to her with suspicion. "You don't have to. Try what you want. That one tasted good to me is all," she said. The woman's face was kind and open.

Maybe she did care.

I plucked the plant from the ground and swallowed it whole, unwilling to taste it. "That wasn't terrible I suppose. Meat is still much better," I said, remembering the bite I had taken from the squirrel before I buried it, unaware it would rot. I should have taken the time to eat the entire animal, but I was eager to hunt again. I thought on the possibilities for our meals as the mushroom slid down my throat. We could create something that suited both of our tastes, using both animal and plant. I swallowed another.

The woman burst with laughter.

I turned and saw the wicked gleam in her eye. "What did you do?"

"Have fun with that. Those mushrooms made me very ill. Consider this vengeance for my rabbit friend. Enjoy!" Lilith ran from me. Though this action had a playful twist, it revealed she still feared me. That thought alone was enough to make me sick, and the mushrooms returned to their home.

Fully emptied, I lay on the damp ground.

How could I make her trust me?

The woman's reactions to me were timid at best. Vindictive at worst. There had to be a way to control her responses. She needed my help. We couldn't coexist if Lilith wasn't willing to follow my lead. I was the strongest both in body and mind from what I'd seen.

Our survival was my responsibility.

The birds flew from branch to branch in the canopy. I listened to their song with appreciation, and my thoughts calmed.

I allowed my senses to focus. The soil below shifted slowly, revealing the small beings that lived in the earth. I concentrated my hearing downward. An underground stream weaved its way through the rocks and roots.

Then the tree's roots were all I could hear. Achingly slow and terrifyingly strong. They grew with purpose—*they reached for one another.*

Distracted, I heard quiet chewing followed by a whisper of hair gliding across a smooth surface. I turned my head and my eye caught sunrays gleaming against fine thread. Still weak from the mushrooms, I crawled toward the strange sight. Creatures the size of my hand worked tirelessly to weave an intricate design from the material they produced. Their long legs were well practiced in the artistic movements. And the eyes… So many eyes stared at me, the sky, the ground, everywhere. These beings witnessed everything without the slightest pause in their work.

Beautiful.

My breath paused at the thought. The only thing I found beautiful since waking into this existence was *her.* Thinking of Lilith filled the hollowness that plagued me constantly. Even if all she offered me was pain, it was preferable to being alone.

But perhaps the woman had been right? Nature was beautiful in its own strange way. Maybe there was more to Earth than I assumed. I observed the spiders a few moments more.

Just as I was standing to leave, a grey moth flew down from the canopy, and in attempt to avoid me, landed on the spiders' intricate web. I expected it to leave once it discovered it was in the presence of predators, but its feet were attached to the thread somehow. The more it struggled to free itself, the more entangled it became. The spiders moved toward the moth quickly and began wrapping it in the same glimmering thread they used to make their artwork.

I sighed. *Carnage disguised as beauty.*

The woman was wrong. Nature had only one goal: Survive. It was simple and pure. No hatred was involved, but killing was the only way to live. I thought about how Lilith deceived me: not to survive, but solely because she wanted revenge for my actions against the rabbit.

Reaching for the spider, I allowed it to crawl into my hand willingly. The creature's sable body was surprisingly soft and its feet painfully delicate. I turned away from the masterpiece trapping the moth, knowing I had to do something about Lilith before her beauty trapped me as well.

The woman had gathered fruit after she abandoned me. I watched her from the tree line as she carefully organized them on a large leaf. Yes, she needed guidance. The woman was selfish and spiteful. She left me to suffer in the woods only to find food for herself. This would be her first lesson.

Lilith avoided my stare as I approached. Once I was close, I said, "Thank you for that wonderful experience. I will be sure to return the favor."

The woman's gaze found mine, and her eyes widened in fear. "Now, wait, I only deceived you because you killed that innocent rabbit. We're even now." She stood and slowly backed toward the pond. I could feel the small creature twitch in my hand, hidden behind my back. It wanted to be freed. The legs moved frantically in attempt to escape its prison, but I was too strong.

Smiling, I said, "Oh no. That isn't right. I only killed him to eat. There was no malice involved, unlike your little deception. I don't think we're quite even yet." Before she could respond, I took the spider that clung to my palm and threw it toward Lilith.

Unsure of what I had unleashed upon her, she rushed to the water's reflective surface and found the spider tangled in her crimson curls. In her panic, she flung the creature into the pond to drown.

"What's wrong? Is that one not your friend? Is that why you killed it?" I mocked. Perhaps this lesson would teach her why spite was unwelcome in this world, and my way of existing was best for everyone. But Lilith didn't even look at me. She dove into the water to save the creature, however, she needed to learn that she couldn't take back her actions once they were done. My stomach rolled as another wave of nausea hit me. I sat and reached for one of the pears she gathered. But I paused. *What if this was another trick?*

Lilith pulled herself onto the emerald bank. The spider was nowhere to be seen. I thought about saying, "Regret your actions now?" But I held my tongue. From the look on her face, she'd realized it already. My breath ceased when I heard the beast from before passing high above us. Wide wings manipulated the wind, and it soared effortlessly, the sun shining through the thinner layers of skin. The tough, scaled body was marred with scars, and I wondered what could have harmed such a creature. My gaze stayed on those scars until the dragon disappeared behind the mountains, refusing to lower my guard until I was certain it had gone.

Still unsure of the fruit in front of me, I concentrated on Lilith instead. Her smooth ivory skin was drying slowly in the sunlight, and I followed its shimmering path from her face, past her breasts, along her torso, and down her long legs.

Carnage disguised as beauty.

She stood, and I returned my gaze to the fruit. Despite what had happened between us, she sat close to my side. The woman must have realized I was her only option if she wanted to survive.

She reached for a pear and took a bite. I followed her example, eager to fill my belly. "These don't taste as bad as I thought they were going to. Thank you for gathering them. It has ebbed the pain in my stomach." I knew she hadn't gathered them for me, but I still felt the need to thank her. I didn't want to attempt hunting again while I was so weak.

"The hunger you mean?" she asked.

Did she not know what she did to me? "No, the sensitivity left from the mushrooms," I corrected.

She smiled.

As the pain reduced in my middle, I grew excited for the meat that beckoned me from beside the pond. I had been so focused on Lilith's actions, I had forgotten to check if the rabbit was still there. I expected the other animals to steal yet another meal from me, but there it was in the grass, waiting to be devoured.

"I know you won't like this, but we must eat the rabbit before it spoils." Lilith's horrified expression caused me to check my own. I replaced my eagerness with concern. I wanted her submission, not fear.

"Is that what happens after death?" she asked.

"Yes, after a day the body begins to rot and is no longer edible," I explained.

"How long have you been awake?"

"I believe two and a half suns. I observed the lions on the first and was able to catch a few small critters before the day was done. Then I found you." The emerald of her eyes captured my attention, and I became the moth in the spider's web. I forced myself to look at the dead rabbit. The breeze teased its fur enough that I thought life had returned to the carcass. But I could hear no heartbeat. *From any of us.*

"Why is it you woke during the day, and I woke during the night?" she asked. The question had already crossed my mind, and I decided that whatever brought us into existence gave me more time, so I could prepare and care for the woman.

Though Lilith's questions raised ones of my own. What was life? What was death? I supposed only exploration would tell. "I don't have an answer for you," I replied. *Best to let her come to the conclusion on her own.*

Once Lilith returned to her meal, I rose and dove into the water. I groped the bottom of the pond until I found what I was looking for; a tapered rock. Quickly, I lifted myself from the pond and bent to retrieve my meal. My hand grasped the rabbit's feet before I remembered to warn Lilith. "I understand that you won't want to see this, so I will cut the meat from it elsewhere."

As I turned to leave, she shouted, "Wait! What are you going to do with the rest of him?" Despite Lilith's timid nature, she held my gaze.

"What do you mean? No other part of it can feed us," I clarified. Did she have the same idea? Use the rabbit to learn more about life and death?

"His fur can be of use. It would be a shame to waste it," she said quietly.

Perhaps Lilith would be more helpful than I thought. "Yes, I suppose it does get a bit cold at night. Though it is not much, it will help us keep warm."

"Just do your best not to waste any of him, please," she whispered.

Lilith saw the potential as I did, so why did she choose to fight it?

I left the waterfall and found myself in the meadow where I woke. I took the edged stone in my hand and tore into the rabbit's fur and flesh, hoping to find the answers I sought.

IV

Life

Don't fear being needed,
fear being unwanted.

-S

The pain was intense. I ripped into my chest, hoping to find a heart. The rabbit had been cut and studied as much as it could. And one thing was painstakingly clear. Life needed a heart. It needed the heart to beat and pump blood through the body. But there was no such sound coming from my chest and no blood coursing through me.

Dry red sand was all that poured from my wounds, and they healed as quickly as they were given. *It wasn't right. It wasn't natural.* Even the plants had water flowing through them, and I could hear vibrations pulsing from their roots to stems. A constant mysterious beat. All life had some form of a heart.

I dropped the rabbit bone, that was now used as a carving tool, and began pulling at the flesh with my own hands. I cried out, begging for an answer. Just as the opening was made, I reached part of my hand inside the chest cavity and paused. The wound was closing, I had to hurry unless I wanted to tear myself apart again. My fingers inched closer to the space inside.

The bone, muscle, and skin were closing around my fingers, and I removed my hand before it was trapped. I stared at the ground where grains

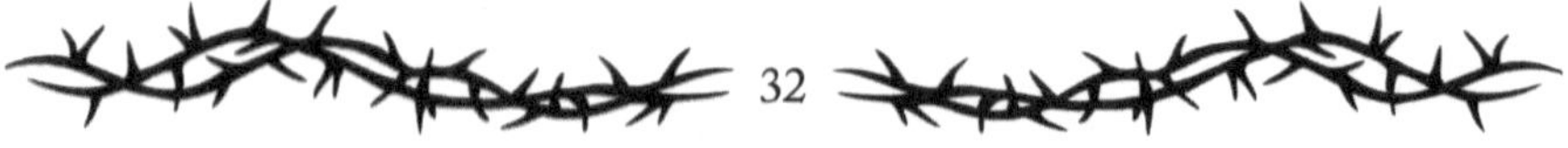

of red sand lay, covering the evening-chilled grass. The granules slowly filtered down until they became a part of the earth below.

I listened instead, and heard nothing but a stag grazing on the other side of the meadow. I was unsure if it was the same one that escaped me, but I knew I was being mocked just the same.

I was weak.

I was alone.

Was I even alive?

I didn't want to know the answer.

Slowly, I reached for the vital piece of life that rested within the rabbit's remains. It no longer beat, but the power it gave these creatures was unmistakable. I brought the organ to my lips. It slid down my throat easily, and the metallic taste was almost enjoyable. I wiped my face clean with the damp moss, discarding the dead greenery after I was finished.

I wrapped what was left of my kill in large leaves, intending to share the rest with Lilith. I ran, knowing she would chase away the emptiness that afflicted me.

I realized it had become night while weaving between the dense trees. The darkness nearly suffocated me. But I was determined to be strong. *For her.* She would see the progress I made and know I would care for her. Rose thorns grabbed my legs as I ran. The tiny rips hurt, but I was satisfied knowing I had broken most of their branches.

Lilith was floating on the pond's surface when I broke the tree line. I felt relieved knowing she'd waited for me. I hadn't realized how frightened I was knowing she might have run away again. But she was there, with a worried expression on her face.

Putting down the rabbit-filled leaf first, I jumped into the water. Lilith would know I had triumphed and learned as much as possible for her. I thought on my now healed injuries and cringed.

She didn't have to know everything.

We discussed the various parts of the rabbit, and to my surprise, the names she spoke matched the ones that came to me. Bones, organs, muscles, skin, and blood. We worked together, separating what we wanted from what we didn't. After storing the meat beside the woman's other findings, I tossed the innards into the pond for the fish to devour. I was glad Lilith had not shown interest in any of the organs because I was worried she might have noticed the one that was missing.

I looked around at the tree's that circled us and studied the carvings Lilith created, wondering what they were for. I turned to ask and found Lilith leaning down to lay the rabbit bones on the grass to dry. The moon fell downward and lit my path to her. I was entranced by her beauty, but this time, I didn't want to break it. I stood closer than I should have since I didn't want to frighten her, but I couldn't stop myself. It took all the strength I had not to reach out and touch her.

The woman's arm brushed against my leg as she stood, making her realize how close I had come. Lilith's green eyes found a way to glimmer in the darkness and her lips parted in exhale. My breath stopped. I didn't dare move as she reached up and used her gentle fingers to trace my face. The path she created moved down and across my shoulders and chest. When her touch teased the top of my hips, I raised my hand toward her so I could feel what she was feeling.

The breeze played with her curls, and the curve of her neck was exposed. I imagined running my fingers along her soft skin. Just as I was about to experience the most pleasurable emotion yet, Lilith dropped her hands and stepped away from me. I lowered my hand in resignation. I didn't miss the emotion in her eyes as I reached for her.

She was still afraid of me.

I wanted to tell her that I would never harm her, but before I could, she asked, "Do you think we look the same underneath as well?"

"What?" The silence had been a heavy thing between us. No words were needed in the brief moment we had together. The noise that came with speaking was uncomfortable.

"The same as the animals I mean," Lilith explained.

Had it just been me who felt the new emotion?

Despite my confusion, I responded, "I was curious about that, as well. I cut myself to see, and it wasn't the liquid that came out of the other creatures. It was more like the sand that lies at the bottom of the pond, but red. We have bones and muscles that are similar though." I paused a moment, debating how much to tell her. "It hurt quite a bit, but the wound healed quickly. Actually, I had to keep reopening the wounds I gave myself to keep going deeper." The memory of opening my chest came suddenly, and I found myself fearing she would discover what I did.

"Yes, my wounds healed quickly from the night we met." Lilith pondered a moment. "Still, I didn't get a very good look at the inside."

The woman was clearly interested about our anatomy, but I couldn't have her digging into herself and discovering what I feared was true. I picked up the jagged bone from where it lay drying on the ground and gripped Lilith's forearm. The cut happened fast. She didn't even comprehend what I was doing until she felt the pain.

"Why? I could have done that!"

"You would have taken forever considering if it was worth the pain. We would have been here for days. Besides, it heals fast." My excuse seemed to quell her anger, and she looked to the crimson sand pouring from her wound, mesmerized. I could see from the expression on her face that she found it just as beautiful as the life around us. But the sand we bled wasn't life. I continued to stare at the sand with her, expecting it to close as mine had.

It didn't.

The woman realized this and tried closing the wound with her other hand. The granules forced themselves through the cracks in her grip, refusing to be contained. Panicked, I searched our surroundings for a solution. The rabbit's fur hung from a branch beside me. The fur was wrapped tightly around her forearm before I could consider if it would work. The sand stopped flowing.

My hands refused to part from her skin once they were there. I told myself it was to keep her wound closed, but it was because she wouldn't let me touch her otherwise. I had to take advantage of every chance I had. "Apparently you don't heal quickly," I said.

"No, I do, because whenever I get scratched by the bushes or branches the wounds disappear almost instantly," the woman explained.

If that was true, then there was only one factor that differed. "Maybe it's because I'm the one who cut you," I said.

"Maybe." Lilith reached down and picked up the mutilated bone that wounded her. With assertiveness I hadn't yet seen, she grabbed my forearm and did as I had, but much gentler. The scratch barely broke the skin, yet this small wound did not heal.

"You were right," she whispered.

In that moment I realized why we could only harm each other, why I felt so complete when she was near, and why we had no life inside us.

We were meant to be one. We were each other's weakness and strength. Each other's heart and life.

Man and Woman were not created alive, but not dead either. We were somewhere in between, and the only way we could truly experience life was together. Lilith was the *life* I craved. The heart that belonged inside me. I clutched my chest tight, unable to claim my own heart for fear of losing it.

I held Lilith's hand firmly, met her gaze, and said, "I will protect you." But there was only one thing she needed to be protected from, and that one thing refused to let her go.

V

Truth

Neither dead nor alive.

-S

10 Years Gone

The days had been long, so we decided to rest for the evening. I set out to hunt, leaving Lilith behind to build our fire. I smiled as I thought of the power. Fire was a force only the dragons and sky wielded. *Until me.* I realized quickly that if I wished to conquer something, I merely had to try.

Before, I watched as lightning lashed out from its place in the sky and struck an unknowing tree. I then replicated the motion with wood and stone, forming our own fire. I made many discoveries since then. The most obvious being: Humans were one of the strongest of Earth's creatures. Our strength, speed, and cunning were vastly advanced. And on the rare occasion I was harmed, I could heal instantly.

I had but one weakness: Lilith. She was the only one who could lethally harm me as far as I knew. She was the one who occupied my thoughts at all times of the day and night, and though she didn't know it yet, she would give me life.

That was why I continued to care for her. She was too weak to do what had to be done. She refused to kill any animals and survived solely on the vegetation, which I didn't understand because the greenery was alive too. I've known since we first met that it was my responsibility to give us life. To give us hope.

I continued to do so even now. From my position high in the tree branches, I watched as a moose passed by. The spear in my hand was ready and aimed when another creature came tumbling out of the brush. A calf clumsily followed its mother through the thicket. The earthy tones of its fur caused it to blend with its surroundings.

The calf tripped and tumbled into a patch of thorns. It called out in distress, but its mother had traveled too far, unknowing of the predator stalking its child. The spear left my hand before I thought to command it. No sound escaped the calf's lips as the weapon wedged itself deep in its brown belly. Though the meal was lesser, I saved a life by taking the calf. If I had taken the mother, the calf would have died without its guide. *Lilith didn't know what I did for her every day.*

Leaping down from my place in the trees, the smell of blood wafted up to me, and my mouth watered. I removed my spear from the calf and knelt beside the creature, avoiding its dead gaze. I plunged my hand deep into its chest and pulled. Though it was small, it would quell the need I'd developed for the life-giving organ. My body thrummed in appreciation, and I carefully wiped the blood from my mouth. *Lilith didn't need to know. This burden was mine to bear.*

Returning to Lilith, I dragged the calf behind me, but I remembered to pluck a peach from a fruit tree on my way so the woman could eat as well.

I couldn't help but notice the birds had stopped singing.

Once I reached the river, I tossed the peach to Lilith where she waited patiently beside the fire. Sunset had passed, and we were now swathed in a mock imitation of the glorious daytime blue. The sky was nearly black, but there was a shimmer of color that kept us from blindness.

Lilith devoured the peach. *The woman ate too little.* How could she expect to be strong when she didn't do anything to strengthen herself? I turned away from her to skin my meal. I knew it bothered her, and I didn't want her to see the fist-sized hole in the calf's chest.

"Let me help," she said.

I laughed to distract her while I peeled the fur from the animal's chest. The knife I always kept strapped to my side worked quickly to relieve the corpse of its skin. "No. You can't handle it." The rabbit bone that was my blade was proof of that.

"Yes, I can. Now face me like the man you claim to be and show me how it's done," she argued.

My laughter seized. I hurriedly cut open the carcass's chest and stomach, letting the organs fall out and onto the ground where she wouldn't notice anything missing. My panic was then replaced with surprise. "Finally, ready then?"

"I have been ready. I just wanted you to do all the work is all." Though she spoke with confidence, she couldn't hide her hands from trembling. But I played along anyway.

"Deceitful as ever, I see. Punishing me for something I didn't know I did? It's the mushrooms all over again." I smiled while I said this, but the pain of the deception was still there. *Could I ever truly trust her?*

"Of course. How could you think otherwise?" the woman laughed.

I placed my knife in her hands and watched in delight as she cut the meat from the youngling's corpse.

After our shared meal, we lay under the stars. Lilith enjoyed the nighttime immensely because of them, but they seemed too distant. Too unearthly. And I had enough problems to deal with on our world, let alone think about what was beyond it.

We've searched for others of our kind for years. But there was nothing but the animals and plant life living on this mass of land in the middle of one giant body of water. *It was just us.* Lilith hadn't wanted to accept it, and I'd indulged her, but tonight something changed. *She* changed. Whatever thought or realization she had come to, it gave me hope for our future.

"Lilith, are you ready to go home? There's nothing out here," I started.

The woman tensed as she said, "We haven't checked everywhere. We can't be the only ones." A rehearsed line.

Didn't she see? The only way there could be more of us was if she accepted it was just us. "But what if we are?" I could wait for Lilith to be ready, but it didn't make it any less painful. Lilith's face fell, and a little piece of myself broke knowing she was so unhappy with me. Still, I asked, "Would it be so terrible if it was just us?"

Lilith continued to stare at the stars, wishing for something more than me.

"Lilith, I know it's been hard for you, adapting to this life. You have such a caring nature. It keeps you from making tough decisions. That's why I've done it for you." I stumbled over my words, unable to express how I felt about her. Maybe if I did she would realize she felt the same. "Today, you showed me that you can make those decisions…"

Still staring at the stars, she asked, "What are you trying to say?"

Wasn't it obvious? "I want us to be together," I nearly shouted.

"But we are together. All the time." Lilith still refused to look at me.

"Yes, but I want more…" The frustration was building inside me. All the patience I'd practiced over the years shattered.

"More what?" she asked.

Hands shaking, I said, "I want more of you!" My lips were on hers before she had time to reject the declaration. The urge to hold her—to *feel* her—was insatiable. But I held myself back. She had only begun to open to me. *And if she still feared me…*

The woman pushed against my chest, and I fell backward. The rocks that rested in the grass dug into my skin, but that pain wasn't nearly as bad as what I felt on the inside. Even with Lilith at my side, the hollowness widened knowing she didn't love me.

Then the unexpected happened. Timid, frightened Lilith straddled my waist. I could feel her warmth through the fur covering I wore, and I cursed myself for even thinking of the idea of clothing. Her lips closed over mine, and the night pollen scent of her surrounded me. My hands couldn't get enough of the woman. One was tangled in her hair, and the other pulled at the furs covering her chest.

Soon, her hands became as greedy as mine, and though I enjoyed the thought of being wanted, I did not enjoy her dominance. For the first time, I was at her mercy, and it unnerved me enough that I rested her on her back, placing myself between her legs. She pushed back against the motion at first but succumbed when I gently bit her lip.

"Wait," she moaned.

"Why?" I whispered, I pressed my body harder against her thighs and listened to her sharp intake of breath.

"I don't want to do this here," she said.

I regretfully stopped what I was doing and lifted myself to meet her gaze. "What? You don't want…" *Did I push too far? Was she truly that frightened of me?*

Smiling, she said, "I didn't say I don't want to. I said I don't want to do it here." She paused a moment, and I thought I was going to lose my mind. "I want to go home."

Once I realized she was answering my previous question, I kissed her and said, "Let's go then."

I leapt up, pulling Lilith with me, and ran. There was no longer a need to continue our search. We could go home, back to the beginning.

Lilith was happy with just me.

Finally, after all this time, we could be together. The woman's strength had grown, and before long, we could both have what we wanted.

A family. Life.

She had been desperate to find other humans, but she could create them with me. They could bring life into our existence. Life that we surely lacked. I listened to Lilith as we ran toward the falls. *No heartbeat.* Maybe uniting would change that.

I ran faster than I ever had before, and I hated to admit, it was a struggle to keep pace with Lilith. So, I gathered her in my arms and carried her home myself. Over lakes and across great fields, I held her. I only put her down when we reached the edge of the pond, and my spear was tossed aside instantly. We continued where we stopped at the riverside, hands and mouths starving for one another.

The air was cold, but the woman's warmth seeped into me, and the loneliness was made small and insignificant. But then her touch disappeared. "Why did you stop?" Lilith surprised me again. With my guard down, I was shoved into the water with only Lilith's mischievous smile as a clue. I returned to the surface, irritated, and asked, "What was that for?"

"You know you are more sensitive than you let on?" she teased.

Baffled, I said, "No, I'm not. I just live with a creature whose purpose is to torment me." *I should have known better than to trust her.*

"That may be so, but have you ever considered that you torment me, too?"

I scoffed in disbelief. *How could I ever torment her? I protected her.* "Are you going to tell me why you pushed me in here…at a very inopportune time I might add." The back and forth from pleasure to confusion was tiresome, and I didn't know how much longer I could handle it.

"Yes. Ever since we woke in this world, you have been nothing but frustrating. You constantly order me around. And I am done with it," she said confidently. But after seeing my confused expression she changed her tactic and said, "Or maybe it's just because you stink and needed to wash." Her confidence was gone as quickly as it had come. Now, there was uncertainty in her eyes. Her posture crumpled, and her breathing was uneven.

Despite her decision, she still wasn't strong enough. But with my guidance she could be enough. "Well, if the all mighty queen wants me clean, she'd better come do it herself." She sent me a glare. "That wasn't an order. It was a request." Lilith was weak, and I would continue to protect her, but she also needed to feel like she was in control. If that's what it took to gain her trust, then I would allow her to feel such power.

The woman smiled at me knowingly but sat and turned away. *Always a game with her.* I swam up to the bank where she rested and placed a hand on her leg, relishing the softness of her skin. "I think it's time you join me. I'm not the only one who needs to wash."

With little struggle, I pulled her into the water with me. I took my time with her, enjoying every moment of our union. The darkness slowly disappeared from the sky, and the sun greeted our skin kindly. The birds chirped cheerfully as they typically did in the mornings, though they quieted as the day grew, and I claimed what was rightfully mine.

The sun had set, and the cold night air returned. Lilith rested peacefully in my arms where we lay on the moist grass. I was happier than I had ever been. Lilith trusted me. She knew she couldn't survive on her own, and though I would give her the illusion of some control, she would follow my instruction. It was a small price to pay for *life*. The children she'd bear would certainly give us such a thing.

With our superior abilities *and* heart-pumping life, we would be unstoppable.

A spark of light lit up the night sky as a dragon passed overhead, its breathing pattern almost sounded like laughter, as if it was mocking my weakness. I ignored the hairs that raised on the back of my neck and forced myself to turn my back on the beast.

My stomach rumbled with hunger. I was exhausted, but food was necessary, and I was sure Lilith would appreciate a meal when she woke. I rose, careful not to disturb my mate.

I picked up my spear from the edge of the pond where I had dropped it in my lust-hazed confusion that morning. The blood from the calf had dried and stained the stone blade. I dipped the spear's tip into the water and scrubbed. Flecks of blood floated away, and the fish that dwelled in the darkness below rose to consume it.

Soon, I would have no reason to envy nature. I would be a part of it. Another life among them.

But I would also be above them.

The breeze flowed past my nose seductively, bringing with it the tantalizing scent of meat. My mouth watered. Soft thuds sounded against the forest floor. A large body pushed aside greenery as it walked. With one last glance at my mate, I ran in the direction of prey.

Despite my hunger, I slowed and enjoyed the hunt. I stalked the black bear that treaded through the woodland. It was a mighty predator, but compared to other creatures I had faced, it was merely a throw of the knife.

I knew I needed to challenge myself if I was to improve my skills, but I was hungry and fatigued, so I allowed myself this easy kill. The nocturnal creatures made themselves scarce as my scent invaded the forest. The bear knew something was wrong but was too focused on its own hunt to notice another predator.

My stomach rumbled, and my position in the trees was discovered. The bear looked up at me, its black eyes flashing green in the darkness. I leapt down, uncaring of the large paws that swatted at me. The claws raked across my chest, and red sand poured to the ground. I dropped my spear. I hadn't realized until I saw the sand that I had expected the union with Lilith to alter me somehow. I gripped my open chest, confused.

The wound was closed before the bear could take another swipe.

As the bear raised up on its haunches, I ran forward, unsheathed the knife at my side, and plunged the weapon up and through the base of its skull. The tip peeked out from the top, the blade now crimson. I ripped the knife out as the bear fell and watched its blood soak into the moss below.

Immediately, I began to cut into its chest, needing the sustenance it would give. Then I heard a small gasp. I removed my grip on the heart within the bear's chest. "What are you doing out here? I thought you would still be sleeping," I said to the woman.

Lilith's face was horrified.

Did she know? In need of a distraction, I asked, "Want to help?" I moved the blade downward so I could start skinning the creature.

The woman turned and ran.

"Lilith! Where are you going?" I called. I took a step in her direction but paused. *Did she run because of what I was about to do? Or simply because of the kill?* Either way, I decided to leave her be. I didn't know how to explain myself. Consuming hearts was the only thing I could do to be close to life—to feel like I had life in me. I clutched my empty chest, waiting for it to be filled, as blood dripped down my chin.

Carrying as much meat as I could, I made my way to the falls. The water was still, despite the stream that fell into its depths. Lilith was sitting at the edge of the pond, waiting for her mate.

"Why did you run from me?" I asked. I had already set aside the bear meat, hoping she would eat as she did the night before.

"Why didn't you chase me? Isn't that what you do?"

"Well, because I thought you didn't want that anymore." It was hard to understand what the woman was thinking, especially when she was turned away from me.

"No, I suppose I don't," she agreed.

"Was it the bear? I thought you were over this?" I asked, irritated.

"I thought I was. But I would have been only lying to myself despite what happened."

So, she had seen the heart. Still unsure, I asked, "And what happened?"

"When I woke last night, I discovered that I could see."

Worried, I took a step forward. "See what?"

She answered slowly, "Everything." She paused, watching the fish swim lazily in the pond. "I can see everything: how everything connects, where creatures go when they die, where they go when we kill them…" The woman's voice disappeared into her web of mysterious thoughts.

"What are you talking about, woman! Didn't we discuss this yesterday? Things need to change if we are to continue on." *She needed to be stronger. She needed to listen.*

"Yes, they are," she agreed. I breathed out a sigh of relief. The woman knew she needed The First Man. Then she stood, and the look on her face terrified me. "We are going to live differently. No more killing. We don't belong here. We don't have a right to take from it. Can't you see it, too?"

Lilith must have seen. Maybe she'd known for longer than just last night. She knew I was afraid and desperate. "Is this about us? Because if you changed your mind, then just tell me. Don't make up more excuses to keep us apart." I would not be lied to. I would not be seen as weak.

"Us? This is bigger than us! How could you think that?" she shouted. Lilith's back was straight, her face was angry but poised. Lilith was sure of herself, and I was the one being left behind.

"It's not hard to guess. It took this long for you to realize how I feel about you, and now you're spouting things that have nothing to do with us." My fists clenched and sand rubbed uncomfortably between my fingers. "I thought things were going to be different. Am I not enough for you?"

"Of course you are! I love you…" she sputtered. It was the first time she had ever expressed that emotion to me, and I could see that she didn't mean it.

I closed the distance between us, desperate to hold her, and gripped her face in my hands. "Then why are you doing this?" I whispered.

Lilith met my gaze, but the lust and submission from the day before wasn't there, only determination. "I need time to think." The woman turned and left. My hands fell. I managed to remove any hurt from my expression before she turned away, but it was too late. She had seen the weak, vulnerable thing I was.

How could I have let this happen? I was the one who protected us. I was the one who was going to give us life. But now… I don't know what happened. This *sight* she spoke of shook me to my core. How could she see where life went when it died? *What did she see when she looked at me?*

My stomach heaved knowing the bear's heart rested within.

I brushed the hair from my eyes and caught sight of the small white scar on my forearm instead. The one Lilith had given me in the beginning as an experiment to test if we could harm each other. Before, the knowledge hadn't bothered me. Now, I couldn't stop thinking about it.

I forced strength to fill my body. My mental barriers were reinforced. She would not make me cower. The *sight* was merely an excuse. My hands trembled as I followed her aroma to the meadow where we woke. The first thing I heard was muscle and skin ripping apart, then the snapping of bone. *Had she decided to hunt after all?*

Through the thicket I could see Lilith lying in the grass, and the wind sent her hair spiraling in the air. I crossed the tree line and watched as Lilith's hand entered her chest. A stream of water flowed steadily from each of her eyes. But she was utterly silent.

The woman removed her clenched fist, and it fell to the ground beside her. I slowly walked toward her, and just as I reached her side, I caught a glimpse of what rested within.

Nothing.

I nearly collapsed from the knowledge. A part of me had known, which was why I had tried so desperately to fix it. But there was always the comfort that I didn't know for certain. I had stopped my hand from reaching inside my own chest for fear of what I wouldn't find.

And Lilith just destroyed the sliver of hope I'd clung to all these years.

"We don't belong," she whispered. Her eyes were clouded. She didn't know I was there, yet she felt the need to say the truth aloud. I had yet to say the truth, even to myself. Realizing that, I learned another, even worse truth: I was not the strongest.

VI

Ashes

Ignite the wrathful flames within yourself.
-S

Furious, I set my sight on the mountains. I ran far, leaving *her* behind in the meadow. After watching what she'd done to herself—*to us*—I couldn't stay.

The forest passed by quickly as I ran north, but I saw every detail. Every leaf that hung from the branches, every protruding root, every part of the land was known to me. Yet, the knowledge about myself continued to evade.

Knowing what I know now, would I ever find peace?

The moss beneath my feet became rough, rocky terrain as I reached the base of a mountain. Lilith and I had explored here before, when the hope to find other humans still existed. But we had never climbed to the top, and my tattered mind wished desperately for a distraction.

I ran as far as I could upward, but soon, I had to grip the protruding rocks and climb the rest of the way. At times my grip was too strong, and the earth crumbled in my grasp, forcing me to move quickly and find another purchase. My spear was tucked safely in the furs I wore, the stem running along my spine. I repeated this dance with the mountain for hours until I came upon a ledge where I could easily lift myself onto its edge and stand.

A cave rested beyond the cliff, towering over me just as the trees did. Spruces grew abnormally around its opening. Many of their seeds lay on the ground, unable to take root because of the solid mineral. Though there were small patches of earth within cracks and hidden crevices where the lucky seedlings found a home. The spruce's pleasant smell, however, wasn't strong enough to mask the scent that seeped from the hollow; a strong odor that made my nostrils flare and the hairs raise on the back of my neck. *Power.*

For a moment I considered moving on.

No. I would not cower. I was the strongest being on this Earth. I quickly banished the memory of Lilith reaching into her chest and moved forward. The wind gusted around me, taking my scent into the cave I silently challenged.

The cavern was quiet. Once the wind was no longer rushing past my ears, I could hear it—breathing. I didn't dare make a sound as I prowled through the winding mountain tunnels. In this instance, I was grateful for the lack of heartbeat.

Moments later, I met a break in the tunnel. Three new pathways lay before me, each one's odor just as strong as the other's. I chose the middle, unable to decide between the right or left. Soon, I saw the remains of the monster's meals littered along the cave floor. Bones of every size and shape decorated its home. It required full concentration to keep my footing so I wouldn't snap a bone in two and alert the creature to its hunter's whereabouts. I gripped my spear tightly, comforted by its presence. I couldn't help but notice how dull the stone head had become.

The tunnel suddenly widened, revealing a mass grave. Aged bones lined the walls, being pushed out of the main space by new ones. The color difference was daunting, and I realized how even after the creatures were dead and gone they continued to age.

I leapt onto rocks that jutted from the cavern's walls, searching. A shadow shifted, surprising me. Its crimson scales shimmered as the dragon exhaled a sigh of fire in its sleep, lighting the dark hole momentarily. The darkness returned, smothering me. Though I had always been able to see well in the darkness, there was no trace of light to absorb in this cave, leaving me to rely on other senses. My hands shook.

The beast shifted its body, dragging its massive claws across the stone ground. The sound of rattling bones followed as a mound was knocked aside.

My muscles tightened, and my breath stilled. This moment in the hunt was my favorite—just before the kill. Time slowed, and a calm washed over me. It was a space in time when it was just me and the animal. A special moment only we shared. This beast was no different than the others I'd faced. I smiled as the spear left my hand and flew, deadly silent, toward the dragon's exposed throat. I imagined the feast I would have with such a mighty heart in my hands.

The spear fell and clattered to the cave floor, disturbing another hill of bones. They rattled loudly, and the weapon was buried in the avalanche of remains. My stomach sank. I had never hunted such a powerful creature, and my weapon didn't even scratch the scaled armor. The dragon's eyes opened upon the disruption, and my breath caught. *The eyes.* The fire they so commonly expelled glowed behind its golden irises, lighting the cavern with a mere glance. Its oval pupils were not the traditional dark, but pure white. And they were staring directly at me.

The beast's wings spread wide, revealing just how big the cave was. It stood on its haunches, rose high above me, and looked around its home, as if it expected more than just me. The creature's strange eyes met my own, and I couldn't help but get lost in them. I hadn't been this close to a dragon since it stole the saber-toothed cat from me all those years ago. They constantly flew through the skies, but none had landed in our home since.

The mountains were where they could be found, and I supposed that's why I came here.

For years I had wondered about them. Were they as strong as they looked? Was I as strong as I thought? None of Earth's creatures had defeated me. Lilith's face was all I saw in that moment. Her hair, the color of the dragon's scales, and the look of determination I saw only hours ago made my knees weaken, just as this dragon's stare did now.

I would not cower from a challenge. Not again.

I jumped. My strength allowed me to glide through the air until I reached the top of the cavern. Then, with all the agility and grace of a wild-cat, I flipped and pushed off one of the hanging mineral deposits. I could see the rock's gold tint due to the glow of the dragon's eyes. I landed on the beast's back, taking advantage of its confusion. Clinging to the horns that lined its spine, I crawled upward until I reached the area on its body where I would find it—the heart. Its beat thundered in the cavern. I would rip it out with my bear hands.

The dragon turned its head back and forth, snapping its long jaw in my direction. It came close to biting me a few times, but I was quick. And I was hungry. I brought my fist back and plunged it into the dragon's skin, only to make it through the first layer of armor. I removed a couple scales, but the layers of protection were vast, and each time I attacked, the sharp skin would nearly cut my hand off. I needed another way in.

Gripping the spine firm, with my hand still bleeding red sand, I climbed to the beast's head. The dragon let out a wail of pain as I used its open wound to steady my footing. I gripped one of the massive horns protruding from its skull and angled the light from the creature's eyes down to its chest and belly. The armor was weak there. The scales were fine, as if they were made of feather and not tough hide. I would have to time it carefully; the dragon's snapping jaw would have the perfect position to bite into me. Though I healed quickly, being devoured wasn't ideal. Doubt crept into my mind: *What if the dragon could fatally harm me, too? Just like Lilith.*

The dragon flapped its mighty wings, and the wind it created in the enclosed space nearly carried me away. I pulled the dragon's head backward as far as I could by the horn and quickly leapt down to its chest, clinging to the feather-like scales that layered its front. I tore one of my hands away from the beast, finding the fine armor was just as sharp, but it wasn't as strong.

Again, I brought my fist back and forced it through scales, skin, and bones. Crimson blood spilled out of the mighty creature—even dragons bled. I knew its gaze was upon me, the golden light shining down upon its destruction. The creature was in too much pain and perhaps too shocked to fight back anymore. My arm retreated and sank into the dragon's chest several more times before the noble beast collapsed. Its breathing was heavy, and the ground was now crimson. The light from its eyes dimmed gradually.

Satisfied, I released my grip on its scales, allowing myself to heal. Just as my mangled hands returned to normal, the beast's lungs filled. The dimly lit eyes were focused on me. With its last breath, the monster lit the cavern ablaze, exhaling a raging fire. The dragon wished death upon me, as well. It refused to die alone.

I closed my eyes.

Time was irrelevant as I lay under the debris of the collapsed cavern. Smoke clogged my newly formed lungs. My body stung as new skin was created and stretched over the sensitive muscles. *How much of myself had I lost?* There was no one to call out to. No one to help me. Lilith was far from here. The animals didn't care about me. I wasn't even sure if Lilith cared. All I could do was wait for my body to heal.

Fear had created doubt and distraction. I had feared what the dragon could do to me. I had been afraid to die. Yet, wasn't dying a part of be alive? A final step in the journey? The fact that I lay on the cavern ground, breathing, was further proof of my stagnant existence. An existence that wouldn't allow me to move forward.

I swallowed the fear but refused to forget it.

My legs tingled, and I was able to shift my position. I slowly crawled my way toward the tunnel's exit. The collection of bones had melted and melded to the rock below. I looked back and realized only the dragon's skeleton remained.

Changing my course, I crawled over the misshapen ground until I was able to caress its jawline; it was cold. I gripped a massive fang in my hand and pulled. This piece of the creature would stay with me as a reminder of my fear and my strength.

I rolled onto my back and grimaced when a protruding piece of ground scratched my newborn skin. I took the fang in both of my hands, breaking it in half. I knew how to get Lilith back. She had seen me at my weakest with the bear. This would show her how strong I truly was. Lilith would have no reason to create excuses when she knew I defeated the strongest of Earth's creatures.

I looked to the empty chest cavity of the beast, angered it had robbed me of my true trophy.

New weapons in hand, I ran down the great mountain. My body had healed. I had conquered my mind—my fear. *I was the strongest.* I would be respected and obeyed.

I approached the meadow where I left Lilith. Though it had been morning when I left her, and it was now morning again. I looked back to the mountain I came from and watched the sun rise over its peak. The breeze brought her scent to me, and I followed it to the white tree. Lilith sat, leaning against its snow-colored trunk, while staring at an apple dangling beside her on a branch.

"Lilith," I whispered. I came here to demand her respect, but I found it hard to disturb her when she was in this place.

The woman turned her sad, emerald gaze to mine. "You've been gone for months." There was no anger in her voice, just clarification.

Months? Perhaps I had healed from something worse than mere burns. "Yes." I closed the gap between us, kneeled, and placed my gift in her delicate hand. "For you."

The woman merely stared at the dragon-bone blade I had carved for her. I'd wrapped animal skin around the handle so she could better grip it. Her eyes were clouded in a strange way, as if she wasn't seeing the same thing I was. The woman's hand, holding the new weapon, began to tremble. A tear streamed down Lilith's cheek. "What have you done?"

"A dragon. I defeated it at the mountain." I paused. "Quite easily." I reached out my hand to pull her chin up. I needed her to look at me.

"No!" The woman refused my touch and stood. "Did you hear nothing of what I said before? You're not just killing the animals, which is terrible enough, you are killing the Earth itself." Another tear. "What is wrong with you?" she asked, still clutching the knife.

"I don't care."

"What?" the woman's eyes were no longer clouded. They peered right into my own, clear and full of fury.

"I am the strongest. This is my land, and I will do what I want with it." The woman refused to submit. But the longer we spoke the more I understood she truly believed what she said. *She hadn't discovered my weakness.* Lilith didn't know that I tore the hearts from my prey and devoured them. She didn't know I would do anything to feel alive.

Gripping the knife harder, she said, "This is my land, too." Lilith turned from me and walked into the tree line. I could hear her delicate footsteps on the moss, a slow, determined pace.

I stood, clutching the weapon I had created for myself. The spear-head was wrapped tightly at the end of the long piece of spruce wood. The dragon's fang gleamed in the sunlight, its tip menacingly sharpened to a fine point. And as my gaze roamed, I noticed there was no longer a scar on my forearm.

Lilith could believe what she wanted. It didn't matter. She would submit to me again. And then I would have what I so desperately craved.

Part II
The Warrior

The warrior fights

Battle after battle

He wields his weapon

He eradicates souls

He knows how to kill

But can he die?

VII

Lost

How can the human heart be broken if it does not exist?
-E

700 Years Gone

Distracted, I wandered the woodland, unaware and uncaring of the predators that skulked in the shadows. My thoughts were of Lilith as they often were. My instinct to take her had only grown with time. I craved the sensation I had centuries ago when we mated at the falls. The closeness. The possibility. The *hope*.

But Lilith kept herself from me. Something happened to her that night after I left her to hunt the black bear. I regretted my decision often, always wondering: If I hadn't left her, would things have been different? Would she have continued to submit? To accept my way of life? The only way as far as I could see. Why would she choose to stay in this stillness? This existence was not life. *We were not alive.*

But Man and Woman were not dead either, and that knowledge moved me forward.

Over the years, Lilith had gone to extreme measures to torture me. She refused to mate with me in fear of creating children. Though she claimed it was to spare the spirit's suffering from more of us, I had my doubts. Even if she did believe in this spirit world, why did she choose it over me?

After gaining the *sight*, she starved herself, unwilling to take from Earth. I brought her fruits and plants of every kind, but she wouldn't even drink the water. She was frail and vulnerable, unable to walk by herself.

Then came the day I dreaded most. "Please, just end it," she had said. The water-filled leaf trembled in my hands as I stood above Lilith. Her eyes were now rotted green like the dead plants at the bottom of the pond. Her crimson curls were listless and heavy with grime.

"What do you mean?" I asked. I had laid her beside a stream in hopes she would submit and drink from it. I brought her to a new place every day, wishing one of them would beckon her.

"Kill me. I can't stand this pain anymore." She turned her clouded gaze away from me and toward the grass beside her cheek.

"You don't have to be in pain, Lilith! Just drink!" I poured the water from the leaf over her mouth, but she turned away before one drop could hydrate her. I crumpled the leaf in my grip, and she gasped in pain. She watched the greenery fall from my hand, tears gathering in her eyes. But severe dehydration wouldn't allow them to fall.

"Please stop," she whispered.

"Why do you care?" I ripped the grass from the ground and held it close to her eyes. "It doesn't matter if you kill it or not. It doesn't care about you. It is incapable, and even if it did, it doesn't deserve your sacrifice, Lilith!" I ripped up more grass, letting them fly and then fall around us. "Live. If not for yourself, then for me." I cupped her delicate face gently, forcing her gaze to meet mine. Nothing but clouds looked back. No recognition for her mate was seen in the dark emerald forest of her eyes. "But perhaps you are simply too weak to do such a thing."

The clouds thinned.

I rose and left her beside the stream, hopeless and dreading the lifeless existence ahead of me. Unable to stray far, for fear of what Lilith might do to end her own existence, I rested against a mulberry's trunk and tried to sleep.

Rest seemed impossible for hours, but I soon found myself drifting toward a bright golden light of peace. A place where life was abundant, even in myself.

The dream morphed from contentment to curiosity as Lilith joined me there, holding a stray piece of grass. Smiling, she said something so soft even my acute ears could not register it. Then, the grass transformed into a red apple. She brought it to her lips, devouring the meat hidden beneath the skin.

Strange.

I suddenly woke and discovered I had moved in my sleep and now crouched behind a rose bush, watching Lilith as she washed herself in a stream. The grime disappeared, and her tongue ran along the freshly cleaned skin, desperate for the revitalizing liquid. Still addled from sleep, I allowed myself to hope again.

After washing, Lilith compelled herself to stand. I wanted to run to her, but she needed to do this on her own. She needed to prove that she was strong enough.

After a long while, she eventually stood on two feet. I rose and walked as slowly as I could into her line of sight. "Lilith," I purred, "I knew you were strong enough. Come, let's get you something to eat." I stepped toward my mate, knowing my future was not as dark as I feared.

"No." The woman's voice was weak, but stern.

"Enough Lilith. Join me in a meal. You will feel better. I have a dragon hide at the falls." My hand merely grazed her arm when I reached for her. Lilith jerked away from me so fast she nearly fell over, but her thin frame held its ground. Looking into her eyes for the first time since I left her hours earlier, I realized how much brighter and aware they had become.

"I. Said. No." The woman straightened her crooked back, the spine rippling under tight skin. "I discovered something new about this *sight*. I can alter what I see." Unable to bend to retrieve what she desired for fear of collapsing, she pointed at a disfigured piece of fruit lying in the torn up grass.

"Where did you find an apple?" The dream from earlier returned to the forefront of my mind.

"I didn't. I created it from the grass you stand on."

I chuckled. "Lilith, I think the lack of food and water has finally muddled your brain." My fist tightened in frustration, and I hid it behind my back.

"It's true," she stated calmly.

"Woman, don't create more excuses. If you don't want me around anymore, then just say it." I smiled, knowing she would submit. She wasn't strong enough on her own, and she knew it.

Deliberating for only moment, she said, "You stay in the north, and I will stay in the south. The falls will be neutral ground." She swallowed, fighting against her dry throat.

What was she saying? Was she actually leaving me?

"If you care for me at all, you will do this," she said. I started to argue when she stopped me with a mere raise of her hand. "If not, I will have to find another way to make you listen." Her eyes cleared completely, boring into my own and willing me to submit.

Lilith would rather abandon me then take what was rightfully ours. Refusing to answer, I left a weak, starved Lilith to fend for herself in the land she had claimed as her own.

Of course, this separation had been merely one of her tantrums. She never strayed far. But keeping herself from me in this way was a punishment in itself. After existing so long and realizing that we were truly not aging, her wishes left me bitter. But all I could do was wait.

Now, the memory dissipated as vibrations traveled along the forest floor. My feet were following the source before I had a chance to think. *They were running.* My instinct was to chase. To hunt. But another, much more intense, reason had me chasing after the cheetahs. *Lilith.*

The cats were quick, and the closer I came, the clearer I could hear Lilith's footsteps trailing behind them. *She would have made an excellent hunter.* Perhaps she still could.

I met them head on. Hiding behind a tree, I watched as the wildcats sensed me. They stopped only to pace around one another, sniffing the air for the source of the predator. One of the cheetahs cried out in fear, but my spear was through its flesh before the creature could take another step. The remaining two cheetahs ran. But I no longer had need of them, I'd found *her.*

"Didn't expect to see you here," Lilith said. Though she kept her voice from shaking, I could see the anger in her eyes. The fire drew me in, and it took all my will power to retrain my need and not force myself upon her.

"The hunt takes me where it wants." It did indeed, but I wasn't hunting when I crossed the borders onto her land.

"Stay on your land. That's the only way this is going to work," Lilith told me—it wasn't the first time she had.

"You think this is working? That's funny."

"Fine, I will leave this time." Lilith leapt down from where she had been perched in the tree observing the cats. She turned to leave.

No, it wasn't enough time. Quickly, I ran and blocked her path. "Stay with me tonight." The need to have her was suffocating. My hands begged to touch her skin, to feel what we once shared.

"You know why I can't," she whispered, placing a hand against my chest.

"Yes, I do. And I'm asking anyway." I didn't wish to hear any more about the spirits and how they were more important than creating life—how they were more important than *me*. I wound my fingers through hers, where they still rested against my chest. Lilith wanted me as much as I did her. I only had to push harder. This time, she would submit. *She had to.*

"You know why I can't. We can't risk creating more of us. They would destroy this place, and us along with it." Lilith's eyes left mine, and the clouded look I'd come to loathe returned. The woman wasn't with me when this happened. I could touch her, but she wouldn't feel it, not truly.

"We don't have to have children," I said. The clouds disappeared. "We can still be together. You didn't become pregnant the last time." My desperation was palpable, but I didn't care. *I needed her.*

"I can't risk that," she whispered.

"Please," I said just as quietly. Not letting go of our intertwined hands, I pulled her close. I wished to feel her skin against mine, but she had to close the small distance between us. I needed her to want me just as much. Her night pollen scent overwhelmed me, and I couldn't control how my body showed it.

"Do you believe me?" the woman sighed. The urge to have her was painful. I could not wait a moment more. The pleasure, the closeness, the companionship was all I wanted.

Slowly, I said, "Yes." Perhaps that's all she needed—my acknowledgment.

The woman moved closer, her lips a breath away from mine. "Are you willing to change for it?" Lilith let go of my hand and placed her arms around the back of my neck, her breasts brushed against my skin as she shifted.

My blue gaze locked with her emerald one. Her eyes were clear and giving me their full attention. Should I just give in? Could I exist without hunting? Only taking what was needed to survive? Never creating? *Never knowing life?*

"No."

Lilith released me.

The hollowness in my chest returned. "This isn't worth it, Lilith. None of it."

Furious, I stalked past her just as she turned away from me. I retrieved my kill, ripping the spear out of its abdomen. Its crimson blood poured over the thirsty moss.

Without another glance in her direction, I ran north. Toward the land the woman had designated as my immortal grave, darkness growing the closer I came.

No longer hungry, I tossed the cat's carcass into a velociraptor's nest. The dank pit in the ground was nauseating; rotted flesh and feces. The lizard creatures were obnoxious and irritating. They were merely half my size, but had horrid tempers. Being scavengers, they often stole my meals, so I often killed them. But tonight, I had no such distractions.

Walking aimlessly through the thicket, I listened as the beasts tore into their fresh meal. Jaws snapped toward each other, fighting for the remains. Their talons dug into the soil, ripping greenery from the roots and revealing the ancient bones beneath.

Lilith fought to save these disgusting creatures.

My fist found its way through a tree. I almost submitted, but Lilith was close to giving in, too. I could see it in her eyes. The woman needed me as much as I did her. She was just as lonely. I only had to wait for her to break.

Freeing my fist from the downed tree, I stared at the sky while the moon transformed from white into blood red.

The sun returned, and I had yet to sleep. The strange blood moon had only lasted a brief time, but it made the sand beneath my skin crawl. I did my best to forget the strange phenomenon.

Man and Woman's union was imminent. Something had changed. I could feel it in the air I breathed and the ground I walked upon. After centuries of stillness, of the same day after day, it was easy to sense change.

Thirsty, I walked to the waterfall. I never wandered far from the pond. The woman had said she wanted us separated but was never far from the falls either. *She wanted me to find her.*

I crossed the tree line, enjoying the sound of the waterfall. It was a peaceful sound, one I rarely appreciated. The air was warm, and the breeze caressed my skin gently. The woman sat in the grass beside the water, hands covered her face, and tears escaped between her fingers. Her silent sobs gave me hope that the change I felt was a good one.

Lilith was going to submit.

Quietly, I approached her from behind and lowered myself to hold her. The woman wasn't startled at all by my presence. Even in her hysteria, she was aware of me. I smiled, knowing it was hidden in her fiery curls. Her tears came faster, so I held her tighter, listening for the words I had been waiting centuries to hear.

Lilith turned to face me. I wasn't prepared for the sadness in her eyes, a deep misery that I had yet to see. *Could I really do this to her?* If taking from Earth caused her such grief, should I be the one to change instead?

Lilith opened her mouth to speak but stopped. She couldn't say the words, and though it would cause her great pain, I needed her to. I needed her to choose me. Perhaps if she did, I could choose her. I gave a small, encouraging smile.

Say the words.

Instead of speaking, the woman moved closer. Her lips were a breath away, and I lost my careful control. I gripped her beautiful face in my

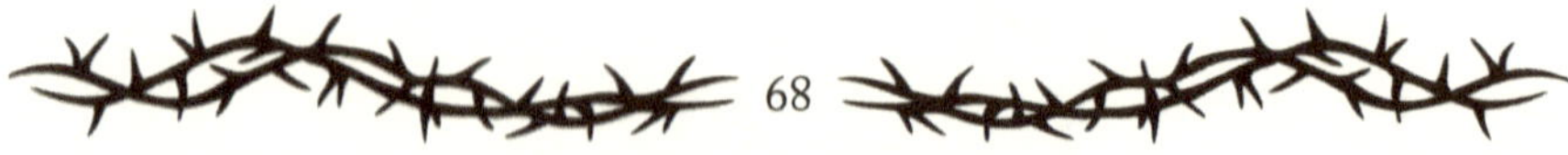

hands, forcing her to my lips. Hungry, they roamed her mouth, cheeks, and neck. I laid back, placing Lilith above me. I could give to her just as she was giving herself to me. I longed to hear the words she was about to speak, but the primal desire for her body overtook me.

My hands journeyed her body, the curves fitting into my grip naturally. She gasped, and I smiled, satisfied with her reaction. I could feel her defenses fall with each touch that we shared. Soon, she was just as greedy as I was, hands and tongue tracing the hard lines of my chest. She returned to explore my mouth. I gripped her hips and moved her against me, unable to withhold myself any longer.

I lifted her slightly, preparing for the most satisfying feeling I would ever experience in this existence. But the woman froze above me. Her soft lips touched mine one last time before she rolled to grass beside me. I didn't try to stop her. Lilith was a frustratingly complex being. She would only feel comfortable with me if her emotions were expressed through words. *I only had to wait until she said the words—the words that would set us free.*

"I'm sorry, Lucifer," she whispered.

Lucifer… "Me, too." Upon hearing my new name, I turned to face the woman. "Lucifer, huh? Does that mean you have finally named me?"

"Yes. It means 'bringer of light.' I thought it fitting since you are the sun in my life. The light to my darkness. You don't have to use it. I know it took me a long time to create it, and I am sorry. My indecisiveness is a curse, and you've been the one to suffer from it," Lilith explained.

The woman's tears returned, and I withheld my joy, knowing what was to come. My gaze never left her face. The happiness within me grew as she turned her full attention to me. She closed her eyes and said, "Lucifer, I need to tell you something. I've made another decision. One I've been avoiding." She stopped, unable to finish. I wound my fingers through hers.

Say it!

"I am leaving. What we have together isn't working, and I think we will both be happier if I am gone. But don't worry, you are not going to be alone. I am going to make you a partner, and she will make you happy, because I know I can't."

If I had a heart, if would have stopped. The absolute dread was a crippling, agonizing emotion, especially after following the pure joy I felt only moments before. This was different from last time. She didn't even look me in the eye as she said the deadening words. My grip tightened around her small hand. Finally Lilith opened her eyes, and a look I hadn't seen in centuries returned—fear. She forced her hand from mine, and I let her. She scrambled away from me. *Why was she running? Why was she afraid of me?*

"Did you hear me?" she asked. What an odd question to ask after completely destroying me.

As I stood, I said, "Yes, of course I heard you." I used the agony writhing inside me and transformed it into fury. Fury was something I could express.

"Are you sure? I said I am going to leave you a mate. You won't be alone anymore. She will make you happier than I ever could." The woman stood, and I couldn't help but take it as a challenge.

"Oh, yes. I heard that part. And you think that would make me happy?" My hands shook. I clenched my fist tight, hoping to disguise the weakness.

"Of course that would make you happy! Why would it not? I'll never be able to give you what you want! Don't you want children? A partner to be with whenever you want? Someone who doesn't reject you like I do? Why are you so angry?"

"I am angry because I thought you were finally going to give up this pointless fight of yours and finally be with me! But it seems that's not the case. You've just gone crazy! And yes, I want those things! But I want *you* to bear my children. I want *you* to make me happy. And if I can't have that

I'd rather continue on with the way things are than be with someone else. Don't you see that?" I looked away briefly, hiding the water that gathered in the corners of my eyes. "I love you, Lilith." *But Lilith didn't love me.*

"If you love me, then why do you continue to live the way you do? I've told you before, the light I see diminishes with every kill, with every pluck of the fruit even. If you love me, then why not change your ways?" Lilith challenged.

"Do you love me?" I asked.

Quietly, she said, "You know I do."

"Then why not change your ways for me?" Lilith's fury calmed. Mine only grew. "I have reasons for living the way I do, too. I don't do it out of spite for you. I just can't accept some invisible thing dictating my life and how I should live it. I won't give up my pride because of things that are uncertain and may not even pertain to us. Do you really not see my side of this?" I searched her emerald gaze, begging her to understand. I couldn't say it aloud. I would not say we lacked the most vital thing that existed. That we were not meant to be. That we were not alive. I shouldn't have to say that we needed each other like we needed air to breathe. I deserved her loyal devotion without having to ask for it.

The clouds returned, and her gaze was no longer mine. I closed the distance between us, wrapping my arm around her waist and holding her cheek with my hand. I pushed the loose curls from her eyes. *I needed her to see me.* I searched and searched for understanding. But the clouds would not leave. Knowing she didn't want me, I said, "I'm sorry, Lilith, but I won't give up my freedom. Not even for you."

Instead of clearing her gaze, my words clouded her eyes so much I was sure she was no longer aware of me. She merely stepped from my embrace and began gathering the food and furs scattered on the ground. *Supplies.* I should have seen this coming. But I had ignored what was happening, simply because it would hurt too much.

"No." I left Lilith by the waterfall. If I lingered, I didn't know what I would do to make her stay. All these years, I'd refused to lay a violent hand on her, but the more she hurt me, the less I cared about that rule.

After destroying parts of the forest, I calmed enough to return to the falls. I knew she would still be there. Her scent was strong, and though she spoke of leaving, she wouldn't be able to. *What kind of existence could we have alone?*

Another scent invaded the clearing—animal.

I stopped to stare at a woman. Not *The Woman*. A woman. Another woman. Another human. She was shorter than Lilith. Her skin was darker than ours. She had hair that waved down her back, the color of honey. And her eyes…amber orbs. Her pupils were thin in the bright light of day but widened upon seeing me. They were full of fear.

Just another frightened animal.

"What is this? What have you done?" I shouted. I hadn't believed her. Lilith said she possessed magic, but I thought it was just more excuses to keep us apart. I ran to *The Woman* and gripped her shoulders hard. "Why are you doing this?"

Without expression, she explained, "This is Eve. She will be with you after I am gone, and hopefully will produce children for you. She will make you happy."

Was Lilith lying to me all this time? Had she ever loved me? "Children? Doesn't that go against the whole reason you're leaving? Have you completely lost your mind? If you just don't want to be with me, then say it. Don't make up excuses and lie to me!" I released my grip on her and backed away, unable to understand.

"Lucifer, you're right. This whole thing has been an excuse. I didn't want to hurt you, but you leave me no choice." Lilith stepped forward and gripped my chin hard, forcing me to look up. I hadn't realized I'd bowed my head in shame. "I don't love you, and I want to leave. I'm only leaving you Eve because of the time we have spent together. I owe you some happiness for the pain I've caused you. Now please accept my offering so we can put an end to this."

I removed her grip on me and backed even farther away. "How did you create her?" Lilith had magic and power beyond anything I'd imagined. She had lied to me. What else was she lying about?

"I used a monkey and a snake to make Eve." I hated the name she had given the abomination; "life-giving" was not something this creature would ever be capable of. "Their combined personalities should make an ideal mate for you. The monkey being generous, wise and funny; and the snake being intelligent, cunning, and seductive." Lilith stuttered over the word seductive, and I took note of it. "The *sight* allowed me to change them. Like I tried to tell you before, magic is what holds the Earth together." Lilith's voice was monotone. She had removed herself from reality, the clouds in her eyes said as much.

Was she hiding pain? "I don't want her to be funny. I don't want her to be smart. All a woman is good for is her body. Just make it so she can function to take care of herself and remove everything else. I have had enough of women who can think for themselves. It seems an independent woman does nothing but destroy things. So fix it," I demanded. I needed to see what she was truly capable of.

She revealed her pain for only a moment before she wiped her face clean and turned to do what I asked. *Lilith would not leave. She needed me.* This facade was merely another attempt to change me. She was using fear to control me.

I refused to submit.

The creature ran to Lilith and clung to her side. I held myself back from attacking it. Its animal scent carried to me, and I withheld a gag. Lilith whispered, "I am sorry. Everything is going to be all right. I just need to make a few changes." The tenderness in her voice maddened me. She never used such a delicate tone with me.

My thoughts were interrupted by the shifting of skin and bone. The abomination transformed from an attractive, healthy woman to a smaller sickly-looking version. Her hair blackened and her structure narrowed. The slits of her eyes remained, and the amber color only brightened.

Lilith hadn't moved a muscle. She merely looked at the creature, and it transformed. The abomination's chest opened to reveal the ribcage beneath. The woman stepped forward and removed one rib. Before I could ask what she was doing, I saw what lay behind the bone barrier. Its beat was erratic but steadied as the rib bone was removed. *The heart.* My mouth watered out of habit. The wound closed, leaving only pale white flesh.

Startling me, Lilith said, "Is she acceptable to you now?"

"Yes. When are you leaving?" It was difficult to hide the panic in my voice.

"As soon as I know you're going to be okay," she answered.

"Well, you can rest easy. I have an obedient woman to be with now. I'm happy, so you are released from me." My bluff was well delivered. She discreetly clenched her fists in anger.

"She is made from the animals, so I don't know how long she will live, but the children she will bear for you should be fine if they come from us. Though I can't be certain because—"

"I get it."

Lilith placed the rib she had taken from the creature into her lion-skin bag. The skin I had killed so she could exist comfortably. She didn't realize how much I gave up for her. How much I sacrificed for her.

The woman reached for me in what I knew was going to be a farewell embrace, but I refused to allow it. I turned my back on Lilith and marched back into the woodland.

Lilith would not leave. She needed me. This farce would end upon my return.

It had to.

I forced my way through the dense brush. I didn't care as the thorns sliced my skin open. I would heal as quickly as they were given anyway, and I caused more damage than they did. It gave me a feeling of satisfaction to know that.

I was blinded by rage. I was blinded by the red of her hair, the rosiness of her cheeks, and the pinkness of her lips. The fire would fade as I thought about kissing those lips, but then I would remember what she said to me, and the flames would engulf me again.

She couldn't have meant those words. She knew they would destroy me if they were true. *I don't love you, and I want to leave.* The words echoed in my head, fueling the growing anger. I tore through the trees that blocked my path. A bird's nest fell to the ground, its eggs cracked, and the fluids spilled onto the moss.

Lilith couldn't have meant what she said. I had given my all to her. I had given everything to her. I kept her safe. Not only from the beasts that lived among us but herself. Lilith had always been unwilling to do what needed to be done, harming herself before she would harm another.

Crossing paths with a stream, I reached my hand into the cold water and plucked a fish from its shallow depths. Bringing it up, I watched it gasp for breath before ending its suffering in my tight fist. The fish's bones pierced my hand, and its scales filled my wound. Still, I felt nothing but hatred.

A bear wandered tentatively out of the greenery, smelling the dead salmon. I threw the remains to it. It looked nervously in my direction, scooped as much as it could carry of the scattered meat into its mouth, and backed away. Even the predators of the land knew not to disturb me. I had claimed this territory, and I was not one to be challenged.

There had been only one who didn't back down from my authority, and she continued to be the bane of my existence. Still, I loved her. I would until the day I died. Which wouldn't be until she decided to kill me. But I knew she wouldn't. Lilith wasn't strong enough to kill a butterfly, let alone her own mate.

So much wasted time. So many years gone.

Still seething with fury, I came across a lone tiger, antagonizing it so it would attack. It grumbled but refused and jumped into the strong trees for cover. Its lean muscles tensed as it strove for balance, thinking the high ground could save it. I nearly laughed.

I paused my rampage to look back at the trail of destruction I'd caused. Trees were unnaturally fallen, flowers were crushed, and I could see the stream where the fish's remains lay scattered. My reckless footsteps had caused a blockage, so it could no longer flow down its natural path. I heard light thudding then. I turned quickly, fully intending to attack whatever dared to disturb me.

I saw a twitchy nose first, whiskers, then long ears. A rabbit hopped out of the brush. It didn't even know I was there. I stood as still as a mountain so I wouldn't be discovered. I watched as the brown creature hopped from plant to plant, pulling up the roots to find food. I remembered the first time I had killed a rabbit, and my anger calmed. My body relaxed, and the rabbit finally saw me and hurriedly hopped away.

What would Lilith think of me now?

The need to destroy dissipated the more I thought of her, and I ran. I needed to go back to her. She would be waiting for me. I was sure of it. Lilith may have been stubborn and misguided, but she wasn't strong enough to leave on her own. She knew that. *She needed me.*

I raced through the trees, knowing that my mate would be waiting for me at the waterfall where I left her.

I entered the clearing confidently. I was prepared to reprimand my mate for her threats. She would stop the lies and come back to me—where she belonged. My mind was ready for the fight, but my body was not. I felt it. In my chest. An emptiness.

A lack of heart.

I had always known we didn't have one, even before Lilith proved it by opening herself up. I knew we didn't have the organ to pump the blood that would age us. But I had never felt so utterly empty, like I did now.

"Lilith?" I called out.

Silence.

"Lilith!" I felt a strange sense of panic, an emotion I rarely felt.

"She's not here," a slithering voice said from the pond. I hadn't noticed when I entered the clearing, but the creature Lilith claimed was a woman lounged comfortably against the grassy bank, her body waist deep in the water. I couldn't help but notice the differences between her and my mate: whereas Lilith's body had been tall and strong, this creature's was small and delicate. I could have snapped her in half if I wanted to. This new woman's face was narrow, and her snake eyes darted toward the slightest movement. Her irises were nowhere near the enchanting green of my mate's. I moved my gaze down and noticed her breasts weren't as full, and her ribs protruded prominently against her pallid skin.

"When is she coming back?" I questioned the strange creature. Her straight, black hair blew into her amber eyes.

"Oh, she's not coming back." The snake-woman feigned concern, but quickly changed her tactic. "You don't need her anyway. Lilith seemed like a bore." An unusually long tongue licked her lips instinctually. Clearly, she wasn't *all* human.

"Don't you dare speak her name." I strode toward the creature and stood above her on the damp bank. "Why do you say she isn't coming back? Surely that's not true." My voice was steady and sure, but my lack of completeness said something different. The hole in my chest seemed to grow the longer I considered it.

Completely unfazed by my presence, she responded, "Oh it is. She told me, 'I won't be needing Lucifer anymore. I hope you have a wonderful life together.' Then she ran off." I took a shaky step back. My body trembled. I thought it was because of the anger I felt, but the red never overtook my vision. I collapsed onto my knees, unsure of the emotion that weakened me.

Seeing my fragile state, the snake woman slithered out of the water to embrace me. She whispered in my ear, "What's wrong? You don't miss her, do you? I am here now."

Confused, I said, "I love her. She can't be gone." I understood then what I was feeling. For the first time in my long existence, I was truly weak. *I was alone.*

The strange woman cupped my face and lifted it, so I was forced to look at her. Concern in her eyes, she said, "But she is. She left you. She doesn't love you and never did." The yellow-orange color of the woman's irises mesmerized me.

"But she is my mate. She is my…heart." I clutched my chest while staring into the snake's eyes, begging for an explanation. My breath refused to come, and I admitted, "It feels broken."

Her thin pupils grew wide, and she whispered seductively, "How can the human heart be broken if it does not exist?" She wrapped herself around me and tightened her grip. "You have me now, and you can call me Eve."

I let the creature hold me. I was in shock, and for the first time, I didn't know what to do. Even with all of Lilith's self-destroying ventures and questionable ideals, she was still with me. She always stayed near enough I could find her. She never left me, and I never left her. We were meant to be together. That, I never questioned. *Clearly, she had.*

Realizing my vulnerable state, I shoved the abomination named *Eve* away from me. "Don't think you can take her place. You are nothing, *snake.* Lilith will be back. I am sure of it." I forced myself to believe the words and ignored the nagging sense of emptiness.

The snake was startled and slithered back into the water. A look of realization passed across her darting eyes, and she knew then that she was not supposed to exist. Recovering, she stated, "What you think of me doesn't matter. This *Lilith*," she acted as if the name left a bad taste on her tongue, "stole me from my comfortable life for a reason. You heard her as well as I did. She *doesn't love you.* She left you here to breed without her." Eve looked nauseated. "So, I am your mate, whether you like it or not, *human.*"

Eve's persona changed. The delicate woman lifted herself onto the pond's edge, stood, and slowly made her way toward me. She caught my gaze, and her eyes entranced me. I stood still, waiting for her approach. It was as if I had no control over myself; the weakness I felt from Lilith's departure affected me more than I thought. I was lost, and this new woman was offering me a safe place to rest.

Eve never removed her eyes from mine. I could hear the water as it dripped from her body and landed in the soft grass. I didn't have to look down to know her nipples puckered from the chill. I felt a tightness in my hips while she moved her hand along the sinews of my chest and arms. Her light touch was moving downward when I woke from my stupor.

"Do not touch me!" I pushed her harder than I should have, and she fell to the ground. I was used to Lilith's rival strength and speed, not this weak creature before me. "Do not put your hands on me again. Unless you would like your meaningless life to end."

I wasn't fond of Eve, but I was mostly angry with myself. I had allowed her to prey on my weakness. *No more.* She would see none of it.

Looking to where the heart beat frantically in her chest, I could almost feel the slick organ in my hands and imagined how it would be to consume her life, albeit an unnatural one.

"Fight all you want, *Lucifer*." It was the first instance she had spoken my new given name, and I wished desperately it had come from someone else's lips. "You will give in eventually. You will realize soon enough that your precious lily is gone for good, and I am your only hope for happiness."

The words were low and threatening as I said, "Leave. Now." Eve only showed she was frightened for a moment before she stood and strolled casually into the darkness of the forest. I was relieved she was gone, but I would have to deal with her at some point. Either she would have to leave and live on her own or be put down. The latter was more likely. What kind of life could she have as a human when she clearly wished to be an ignorant animal again? She was merely reaching out to me because she had nothing else.

Lilith would come back soon.

I wouldn't be alone forever.

VIII

Alone

I Year Gone

I paced the pond's edge for the countless time, looking toward the forest. It was a habit now. The movement was second nature. I only noticed when Eve began complaining—which was often. "Sit down, Lucifer. There's no use torturing the grass over your anxiety." I looked down and saw that I had flattened a path next to the sunlit water.

The sun usually calmed me. The warmth on my skin and the blinding brilliance of the star felt right when it shone down on Earth. The sun's rays revealed the truth and removed the lies that hid in the darkness.

But not today.

Today wasn't different from any other day. I woke after a restless sleep, hunted, ate my fill, then came to the waterfall to wait for Lilith. But my "anxiety," as Eve called it, did torture me. I knew something was wrong. It wasn't like Lilith to disappear, and it was especially out of character for her to stay away so long without finding me. Even when she said she wanted to split our home, she would always let me know she was safe. I was always able to follow her scent. But she had been gone too long, and her scent was now untraceable; the rain had washed it away. Sometimes, when the wind was strong, I would think I could, but it was gone as quickly as it had come. And I was alone once again.

"I don't care about the grass. I care about Lilith. She must be hurt. That's why she hasn't come back," I explained, excuses swarming my mind.

Annoyed, Eve responded, "Whatever you say." The snake perked up then. "Why don't you go look for her and see for yourself?"

Also annoyed, I said, "No, she needs to learn that she can't threaten me. She needs to learn I won't run after her every time she has a tantrum." I continued to pace, flattening more of the emerald grass.

Eve rose from her place behind the waterfall where she enjoyed the resting rock—Lilith's resting rock— and swam to me. "But if she's hurt, how can she return to you? If you truly love her, won't you try to save her? Even if it's from herself?"

Eve's words made sense, but why was she trying to help me? She had been nothing but a huge pain since Lilith left her here. If she wasn't complaining, she was trying to seduce me. And that wasn't going to happen. Not only because Lilith was my mate, but because Eve smelled like one of them—the animals. My instinct was to kill, not mate with her. It disgusted me that Lilith had been so thoughtless.

"Why? Do you know something?" I asked. Eve had learned to control her expressions. She was careful about what she said to me, but I could detect a hidden motive.

"How would I?" the snake smiled. It wasn't a pleasant grin. It said, *Trust me if you dare.*

I did.

Accepting her answer, I said, "I suppose you're right. You stay here in case she returns before I do. Keep her here. Do you understand?"

"Of course." Eve grinned again. That was enough motivation for me. It made it that much more tempting to search for Lilith, knowing I

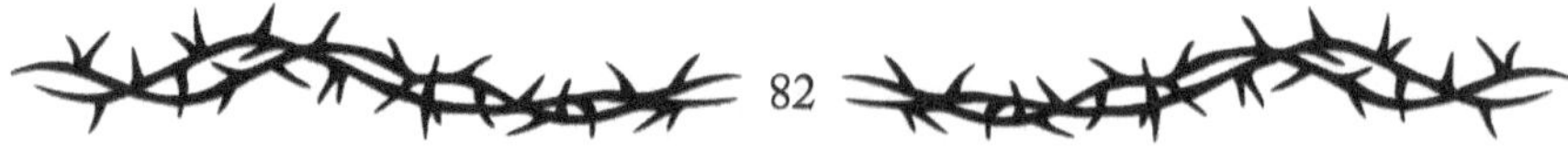

wouldn't be around Eve anymore. I approached the southern tree line and placed my palm on a tree's trunk. The markings Lilith had carved in the beginning remained, but they rested much higher than where they used to; my head tilted upward to find the rabbit-shaped lines. Inhaling a breath of strength, I began the hunt.

I stopped constantly on my journey, begging the winds to bring me her sweet scent. But there was nothing for weeks. I could only smell the beasts that roamed the land, and the greenery that darkened my path. Lilith and I had explored these lands long ago in search of other humans, but I hadn't paid much attention to it.

I was busy watching her.

The graceful way she floated between the trees. The delicate touches as she smoothed her fingers over flower petals, as if she wished to speak with them. I would follow and watch as her long, curled hair blew softly behind her while she walked, hiding the outline of her shape. I wished to run my fingers through the thick strands, just to see if my hand would be lost in its depths. It would have been okay if it had. *We were meant to be one.* She had to realize that, too.

The sun had set, and the little light that peeked through the canopy was no more. I lay to rest for the night and watched as a snow-white owl dipped and snatched a scurrying rodent from the ground. It carried it up and into a tree, then tore into its meal. The mouse didn't make a sound as it was consumed, but I did see its tail twitch as it slid down the bird's gullet. The bird then turned its deep golden eyes on me.

Our eyes made contact for a moment before the owl hooted and flew deeper into the woodland. It was rare to see a white creature; most were darkened so they blended into the environment. I realized then that the only white creatures I had seen were the owl, the horse, and the rabbit I killed all those years ago.

The breeze blew by me, whipping golden strands into my eyes. I stiffened. *I was being hunted.* I leapt into the nearest tree for cover. I had strayed far from my territory, and these animals were not yet aware of my command. I listened carefully, waiting for my pursuer to reveal themselves.

I was dealing with a well-experienced hunter. There was no sound, no movement, but the scent of power was there. Whatever creature stalked me was careful not to make a false step—predators could sense other predators. I threw my spear to the ground across from me. The wooden instrument made a *whoosh* sound as it glided through the air, and the bone spearhead clanked against a hidden rock in the earth when it landed.

The hunter was prepared for a chase and was surprised when it ran out of the dense brush to find a piece of wood instead of a meal. The ebony panther circled the weapon, confused. That's when I pounced. But right as I leapt from my perch, the wind passed by again, taking my scent with it. The panther turned its sapphire eyes on me and yowled aggressively. I changed my course and avoided the sharp claws by pushing against a nearby branch, landing gracefully on the ground in front of the cat.

We circled slowly, waiting for the other to attack. The panther's eyes followed my every move, every twitch of muscle. This hunter was careful, but confident. It knew what it was doing. The scarring on its hide had taught it well: Do not trust your back to an opponent. Despite my instinct to challenge and rule, I had a simple respect for the predators. They were not unlike me in our quest to survive. Though my battle for survival wasn't physical, it was mental.

The panther was nearly invisible in the blackened night, all but its bright, shimmering eyes. They caught and reflected what little light there was, but so could mine. We danced behind tree limbs and around sharp thorns. Its claws nearly grazed my face, but I was too fast. I just needed the right position to grab it and end its life. It would be quick—merciful.

I positioned myself in a tree above the cat. The panther had lost me.

I stared down at its vulnerable stance. It would have been easy to trap and twist its neck; I found it was the easiest way to end a creature's life. No need for suffering. No need to get injured killing them. Quick and clean. But there were times I wanted to make them suffer, if only to relieve some of the anger that festered inside me.

My muscles tensed to jump when I heard a voice in the distance. I paused and waited. It was small, delicate, and far away. The panther's ears perked up too. Its tail twitched, irritated with the conflict. The cat wanted to continue its hunt, but there was somewhere else it needed to be.

Resolved in its decision to abandon the challenger, the panther ran toward the voice. I followed quietly behind in the blackness. Though I often lost sight of the creature, its scent was easy to follow. Soon, that scent evolved; sweet night flower pollen that had been bathed in moonlight. Only one thing on Earth could exude such an intoxicating aroma.

I ran faster.

The tinkling sound of her voice grew clearer. "Where are you?" she called.

She was looking for me. I knew she couldn't stay away.

I was about to call out a response when I came upon a clearing at the bottom of a hill. The river water crashed into the lake beside me. I had yet to leave the protection of the greenery and watched as the sable panther, that challenged me just moments before, ran to the center of the flowered clearing.

A red-headed woman was lounging among the perfumed petals, turned away from me. She twirled a rose in her hand despite the thorns that stabbed her fingertips. Red sand disappeared with the breeze. I stiffened upon seeing the panther stride confidently up to my mate. But as I was about to charge forward to defend her, Lilith reached out her hand and stroked the creature's back. The moon was overhead. Its light reflected against the cat's shining black fur, and illuminated my mate's ivory skin.

She was even more beautiful than I remembered.

My chest filled with anticipation. *I had found my heart.*

Lost in the trance, I hadn't realized Lilith's breathing hitched, and her body tensed. A hand supported her frame as she sat back, and the other held her stomach. She dropped the rose, and the petals fell loose, scattering across the clearing. I still couldn't see her face. Was she in pain? Was this why she couldn't find her way back to me?

The panther growled gently. *What did that sound mean?* I had never heard such a gentle sound come from an animal before. The panther willingly let Lilith lean upon it for support as she stood. Once upright, she turned to face the lake. This gave me a detailed view of her bare profile. Lilith's face was pinched in pain but it smoothed as her body relaxed. I moved my gaze down, taking in every inch of her form. I had missed her so much.

How could I have willingly let my heart run from me?

I absorbed the sight of her slowly: from her beautiful face, to her slender neck, to her delicate shoulders. I noticed her breasts had grown in size. Then, I saw her stomach—it bulged painfully from her frame. Her small hand cupped it protectively, as if she could hold the entirety of it in her grasp.

Realizing what this meant instinctually, I rejoiced. I relaxed my fighting stance and smiled. Lilith was pregnant. This was why she had failed to come home. She was too weak to travel. She was too weak to seek out the father of her child. My hands balled into fists as I reprimanded myself for waiting so long to search for her. I hated that we had been apart for this most natural and long-awaited experience. But I was here now.

I took a determined step forward when I heard footsteps coming from across the clearing. "Lilith?"

"I'm here," my mate called out.

From the forest's edge, opposite of where I hid in the trees, a man stepped from the undergrowth carrying all manner of fruit in his arms.

Lilith's laughter filled the clearing and echoed within the surrounding trees. "Adam, you didn't have to bring so much! Silly man."

"We have more to think of than ourselves now, my love." Approaching my mate, the man dropped his findings at her feet and embraced her. My body tensed, and my vision blurred with rage. It took all the self-control I had to stay where I was. I wanted, no I *needed* to kill this man. Lilith was *my* mate. *How dare he put his hands on her.*

I watched as they kissed, and his hands gripped her hips. I was seething. Not only was there another man touching her, but the way she responded to him was unfamiliar. Lilith welcomed his touch and moved farther into him. Her hands found their way into his hair and gently brushed through the strands with her soft touch.

Lilith had never been that way with me. Even when we mated, it was not calm and trusting. It was a whirlwind of desire. We became animals who were intent on one purpose—mate. I saw what we could have been when Lilith and this man embraced.

Human. More.

This man wasn't even human. His monkey tail twitched eagerly. He was merely an animal. *An animal who made her happy.* I swallowed the bile that rose up.

Of course, it's not mine. The one time centuries ago was all we had. The rest of the years, she either cowered from my touch or avoided me completely. Instead, she created a man in her image, one who would follow her direction without question, just as she created Eve for me. How ironic it was that Lilith was my image of a perfect woman, yet she didn't see me as her perfect man. She barely saw me at all.

Was I so hard to accept? Was it too much to ask that she loved me?
Only me?

My rage died down, but my vision was still unclear. Confused, I wiped at my eyes. Water was what blocked the view of my traitorous mate. I had seen Lilith cry more than once but had never experienced it for myself.

I wiped the remaining water aggressively from my eyes and forced them to stop. They did. But I felt heavy. Like the weight of the world was crashing down on me, and no matter how strong I was, I would never be able to hold the heaviness of it. I fell silently to my knees. I couldn't make myself leave, but the last thing I wanted was to let Lilith see me in such a weak state, especially when she was in such a strong one.

The woman may have been weakened by pregnancy, but I could see that she had become stronger. She held herself straighter, she was sure of her movements, and she was smiling. *She never smiled that way around me.* The situation was made so much worse because I could still feel her where my heart should have rested. But she no longer wanted a claim to the space I made for her. And the life I strove for was no more.

I couldn't move from my position in the trees. Lilith and Adam had gone to rest in a small shelter across the clearing. *So much for not harming Earth.* Didn't creating go against everything she believed? Everything that she had fought against me for? But that was it, wasn't it? It had never really been about saving Earth or the creatures in it. It had been about us. She had meant what she said when she abandoned me.

Lilith never wanted to be with me.

I collapsed to the ground. The soil was soft, and I sunk into it upon landing. It absorbed my form as if Earth recognized me as one of the dead. No matter how much I tried, I couldn't breathe. The very air had abandoned me.

Right as I was about to close my tear-filled eyes, a spark of light flashed across my vision. It was only one at first, but it quickly became hundreds. Then thousands. Then millions. What was happening? *Was I truly dying?* The thought didn't sound terrible. I looked closer, hoping to find what I wished for.

A flower, resting beside me, exuded a pink hue. I could still see the flower and that it was white and had a yellow core, but I could now see past it, like I had grown an extra lens. I reached out and stroked the pinkness of it. The light shone from the flower even in the dead of night. The moon had shifted behind the clouds, and I was trapped in a blanket of unknowing terror. The lights I now saw were my only reprieve. I gravitated toward them as I did the sun. I took a much needed breath.

Upon the petal's touch, a new sense overwhelmed me. I could not only see the flower, but I could *feel* it. I felt the life pulsating from it. This was what Lilith had seen. But knowing that she hadn't lied didn't placate my anger. It only grew. *She chose these spirits over me.*

I heard a newborn's cries from across the clearing.

Gold blocked out the rest of the colors, and I plucked the flower violently from the ground, crushing it in my palm. I ignored the silent cry of it, and the instinct that I shouldn't be doing such a thing. This *sight* came with a new awareness, but I was determined to fight against it. I was the fiercest predator that stalked the forests of this world. I was a creature that feared nothing. I was a being that could not die.

I was Man.

IX

Power

Magic weaves and manipulates until
there is nothing left to wrought.
-E

Acknowledging my newfound *sight* and wanting to block out the wails of Lilith's newborn abomination, I forced myself to stand and run. I ran fast and far, making sure to retrieve my spear on the way back.

I had thoughtlessly left it behind in my rush to follow her voice. I cringed, recognizing how pathetic I was.

For days my muscles didn't tire, but my mind was exhausted. The strong emotions that overwhelmed me were new and very unpleasant.

Death would have probably been better.

I slowed my pace, the spirits of the forest beckoning. I found myself stroking the leaves of the trees as I passed by, just to feel the life that they shared. I lost all sense of time. Before I knew it, home was near, but I didn't want to see Eve.

I found myself in a place that was special to Lilith. Though I hated what she did, the need I had for her was permanent. The white tree stood sure and true in its placement. The sun was high in the sky, and its golden light cascaded through the canopy. The orange and pink colors of the butterflies' fluttering wings decorated the unsoiled tree. They disappeared when they relaxed their wings, the white camouflage on their backs hiding them in the foliage.

I placed my hand against the smooth trunk and let the cool temperature seep into my skin. I didn't know what to do. I was always the dominant. I was always sure that I had a place in this world. I stayed my destructive hand for Lilith's sake. I only killed to eat and gain land, just as the natural creatures did. So, Lilith had no right to say I had to change because we didn't belong.

But she did anyway.

Feeling lost, I reached for a dangling apple. *What's so special about you?* I silently asked the fruit. I plucked it from its home and took a bite. I had never particularly enjoyed the taste of fruit, but the juices seemed to refresh me, and I felt stronger than I did before.

After taking another bite, I witnessed the apple's white spirit seep into me. The golden light that shone from me grew brighter. I felt a mix of pride and disgust at the sight of my own soul. I ate more and more until the spirit was nearly gone, and I could no longer eat any other part of it. I threw it to the ground and watched as Earth's insects attacked and took it for their own. Their little spirits didn't grow in power, and the apple's didn't diminish.

Lilith had spoken truth: We were separate.

The lines that connected those to others were entangled in a massive web. I looked around to find that I was not a part of it. But I had known this before the *sight*, unlike Lilith. I had known we were not alive. The only way we could ever be, was if we were together.

But she had chosen someone else, something else, over me.

I ripped another apple from the tree's branch and crushed the tough fruit in my grasp. The juice dripped down my arm, and the soft insides were reduced to pulp on the ground. I had fought for so long to keep my emotions in check so I wouldn't hurt her, or the horrid nature she cared about. But the hurt she caused me forced those feelings to the surface, and I reveled in the power I felt. I would no longer be tied down by her meaningless grievances.

I was free.

The red that obstructed my vision before the *sight* was no more. It was now golden light. It was me. The anger I felt transformed into something greater. Absolute fury. My breath became heavy. My soul was hungry. A heart should have been pounding in my chest. Suddenly, the white tree that Lilith treasured lit with red flame, and that flame soon became the deepest blue I had ever seen.

I expected it to be hot like other fires, but this one was ice cold. I reached my hand out to it and felt its icy burn. I slowly withdrew my hand and stared down at the wound. My skin hadn't charred or blackened. The skin was pale and coated in ice. I couldn't feel the sun from above anymore.

Anger still ruled my actions, and confusion for the strange fire led me to recklessness. I willed the fire to burn hot. I wanted Lilith's beloved tree to burn. But the harder I tried, the colder the tree became. The ice that coated my hand melted. My flesh was hot, and I watched as my once frozen appendage puckered and blistered from the unnatural heat I produced. The surroundings rose in temperature.

Why couldn't I control it?

The butterflies fell from the tree, frozen solid. And when they touched the ground, they caught fire and turned to ash.

My anger was nowhere near exhausted, but my body, for the first time since awaking in this world, felt tired. I released my grip on the flame, and the blue fire disappeared. The gold light that choked my vision dissipated.

I reached out to the trunk and felt the coolness of it. *I'm weak. I couldn't even burn a tree.* While my hand still rested on the side of the snowy trunk, I watched the charred skin fall from my hand and new skin regrow, healthy and pink.

Besides the blackened grass, it looked as if the fire had never existed.

I walked the forest. The light from the sun had long retired for the night, and I was swathed in darkness once again. Perhaps it didn't matter. The light didn't offer comfort anymore. I realized that it wasn't the sun that had kept me strong all these years. *It was Lilith.* My other half. My mate. My heart. And she had ripped the organ from me. There was no warning. No reason. Just cruelty.

I should have known. I should have seen.

If I had, I chose to ignore it. I chose to ignore her withdrawn touches. I ignored the fact that she wouldn't look me in the eye when I spoke to her, as if she was hiding the secrets of her heart from me.

I was supposed to be her heart.

I had refused to see her as she was. A cruel creature, whose only purpose was to torment. I fell to the cold, damp ground. I could hear the small creatures scatter and the predators come in for closer inspection. They were wondering why the dominator of the forest was on the ground begging death to take him. I was wondering the same.

Why was I so weak? What kind of creature could bring the master of this world to his knees? *The woman.* The woman could strip me of my power and dangle the mangled heart in front of me. *And I let her.*

I curled in on myself, ashamed. Tears ran down my face, and pathetic sobs echoed against the woodland's walls. No animal bothered me, though. Their fear of me was greater than their curiosity. That thought usually gave me a sense of pride, but now, it only made me feel more alone. *I wasn't wanted. I wasn't loved.*

I could hear the rain from above, but the canopy was dense enough that only a few drops reached me. I heard soft footfalls. They were delicate and barely made a sound. *Lilith?* No. Those weren't my beloved's footsteps. I would know. These footfalls were subtle and quiet, but they slid across the ground. Almost slithered.

"What are you doing?" a honeyed voice asked.

I didn't bother responding. No one cared what I did. *No one ever had.*

"Get up! What kind of man are you?" Her sweet voice turned vile.

"Leave me be, snake," I begged.

"No."

"No?" I repeated.

"No, I am not going to let you wallow because some pathetic creature doesn't want to mate with you." Eve kneeled to look at me. The rain was harder now, and we were drenched. Even the canopy couldn't protect me from sadness.

"Lil...*She* doesn't love me," I whispered, unable to speak or even think *her* name.

The snake-woman took my damp face in her hands and gazed deep into my eyes. The amber burned my soul. My golden aura glowed dimly in the darkness. Eve's was almost nonexistent. I strained to see it, and when I did I understood why. Eve's spirit was as black as the dark night around us.

"Listen to me, *human*. You are going to get up, wipe the muck off yourself, and come back to the waterfall with me. *I* am your mate now." Whether it was due to my weak will or her hypnotic eyes, I did as she said. However, I didn't move toward the falls.

"Come," Eve commanded. I stood strong, an unmovable force. Confused, she stopped pulling my hand and returned her gaze to my own. I gripped her small arms forcefully, but not so much it would break them. She was much more delicate than The First Woman, I had to remember that. I pulled her against me and looked down at her from my tall height. I crushed my lips against Eve's and forced the repulsion down deep into my stomach. *She* wanted to be with an animal. *She* wanted to protect Earth. Then I wouldn't hold myself back any longer.

I pushed Eve to the ground and climbed on top of her. Surprise crossed her face, but she quickly hid the weak emotion. She may have been mostly human now, but her animalistic instincts were still there. Eve moved to wrap her arms around me, but I twisted her, so the woman's stomach was crushed into the moss. I didn't want to see her face. I didn't want to smell the reptilian odor coming from her skin. But this was the only way.

Eve cried out in pain when I entered her, but I didn't care. She wasn't my equal. She wasn't even fully human. *Stop.* I had to see her as human. It was the only way I was going to get through this. This was what I had wanted for so long. Nearly every minute of the day this natural act infiltrated my thoughts, but I held back. For *her*. I never wanted to hurt The First Woman or force her to love me. I wanted it to be her choice. But in the end, she chose Earth over me. *Perhaps it wasn't even a choice for her.*

Despite her reasons, I didn't accept her decision. She was going to love *me*. No one else. I was the only one worthy of her love. She had to see that eventually, and I was going to be the one to show her. The more I thought of *her*, the easier it was to mate. I pushed Eve farther into the ground. I cringed when the wind blew her black hair into my face.

The First Woman and I were separate from the rest of the world. And I knew it was because we were special. We were meant to reshape Earth in our own image and start anew with our own kind. It was the only logical explanation. The knowledge that I would be with her again reignited something in me. The loneliness was pushed down and replaced with blinding determination. I pumped harder and faster until I was able to release my new desires and intentions for the world into Eve.

I crawled off the snake-woman, leaving her to lay in the crushed moss. I started walking toward the falls. My idea was growing, and it became clearer the more I thought on it. For the first time in seven hundred years, I had something to look forward to.

The waterfall was quiet, but the life that dwelled in the water was active. I could see the fish swarming one another, their colors reflecting against the light of the waning moon. And I hated them. When I first woke, I was indifferent toward the pond-life; much like I was with everything else. They were merely food. But *she* made me see that there was more to them. *She* made me see the beauty behind their ignorant faces.

Curious, I kneeled and placed my hand on the still pond. I remembered the moment when I realized her belly did not hold my child, and the feeling that came after. I was empty. Alone. *Cold.* Starting where my skin touched the surface, ice began to form. I could feel the sting of it, but I didn't mind. I was in control.

The ice went deeper and deeper, until every fish in the pond was staring up at me in fright. *Funny. I didn't know animals had facial expressions.* I removed my hand and marveled at my power. But nagging thoughts ruined my good mood: Why did I develop these powers now? Was it because of *her*? Could she have somehow repressed my power? Possible, but I didn't think that was it.

My head ached from the pressure of remembering. Of finding any commonality or trigger. Perhaps the grief I felt was what released this power. I had never allowed myself to truly feel my emotions. That would explain why she received her power so early in our existence. *She allowed herself to feel.*

Without needing to touch the water, it began to melt. I allowed the burning anger to consume me and everything that dared to be nearby. I couldn't burn the white tree, but I could burn everything else. The moon had fled, and I felt the rising sun hit my skin and feed my inner fire. The sky was doused in saffron and scarlet hues, reminding me of *her* flaming hair.

The ice melted and steamed. The point in between where there was water and then nothing, I saw the fish flail and flop, gasping for breath. I smiled down at them before they burst into vengeful flame. I smelled the heated flesh and my mouth watered. I was considering having a fish feast when they all disintegrated into ash.

I drew the anger inward, and the flames died down. All that was left was an empty hole in the ground. The surrounding trees were singed due to their closeness, but the water from above the falls trickled down to the vacant pond, refusing to die. That was okay for now. I enjoyed the refreshing water just as much as The First Woman had. At least now I wouldn't have to be bothered by the life that pestered me while I swam.

A small bramble bush still burned, and the flame was slowly traveling. *I couldn't burn the forest down just yet, could I?* I allowed the frost to overtake the small bush, extinguishing the stubborn flame. I smiled as Eve stepped through the trees. Her face was wiped clean of weakness, and she confidently strode up to me. However, she didn't stand as close as she once had.

This was going to be fun.

X
Family

Sand before blood.
-S

5 Years Gone

I watched as she danced and played with the children. She was so gentle with her son as she lifted him up and twirled the child through the air. She was being overly cautious with him because of her strength. The children didn't possess such force and not only because they were young. They were weakened by the blood that flowed through their veins. They were weak because of *him*. Because of Adam. The woman's face lined with worry when she thought no one was looking. She knew these creatures were not meant to be.

Even so, I often found myself entranced by her offspring. Their round faces, green eyes, and red hair would lead me into a fantasy realm where The First Woman and I raised our own family. Then I would see the brown eyes, wide jaws, and dirt-blonde hair. And I would remember that these *animals* were not my own. My chest would ache, and my stomach would heave. *No, these children were not mine.* I forced myself to hate them because of it so I could continue. So, I could survive.

Of course, I had my own offspring, but I couldn't find it in my missing heart to look at them. To really see them. To acknowledge that they had my golden hair and blue eyes. No, I couldn't allow myself to care. Not when I knew their fate.

"Naavah, take Kun and gather fresh water from the river," Adam instructed, the smile a permanent fixture on his face. It made it that much worse to stay hidden. Every instinct I had told me to kill her creation.

Naavah and Kun did as their father said. I noticed how protective Naavah was of her younger brother; she gripped his hand fiercely and led them where they needed to go, and Kun was content just being by her side. The rest were too small to take orders and ran toward the family's hut, their mother chasing them the whole way. I hated how her stomach swelled with yet another unborn child, but the young children's laughter was hard to ignore. The joy was contagious, and I found an unwilling smile on my face.

Distracted, I hadn't realized how close Adam had come to the tree line where I hid. I lowered my stance and halted my breath. I knew Adam didn't have the enhanced senses The First Woman and I did, but he seemed to be suspicious of the greenery, and I took precautions because of it.

The monkey's tail twitched back and forth anxiously. *What was he doing?* Suddenly, he froze. I looked to *her* out of habit; she was carefully wrestling one of her toddlers into the lake for a bath. I looked back to Adam, and he was gone. I searched the foliage. Seeing nothing, I listened. The animals were quiet, which was normal when I was in the area. There was no crunching of twigs or squishing of moss. Concentrating, I heard a heavy heartbeat from above.

My instinct was to attack, but I thought better of it and ran deeper into the woodland, toward my own land. I slowed my pace so I could hear if he followed.

Nothing.

I stopped. *That was too close.* The First Woman could not know that I'd been watching her. She couldn't find out about my plan. Another weak thought manifested: What if she'd been watching me too? I smiled. *Stop! She doesn't care about you—not yet.*

Suddenly, I was on the ground with a body weighing me down. A pair of hands pinned my arms above against my head, and a knee was in my back. My face was shoved into the damp moss. I coughed up dirt only to breathe it in again.

"What are you doing here?" the attacker demanded.

"Remove yourself," I said, my voice muffled by the ground.

"Not until you tell me why you're here."

Frustrated and embarrassed at my weak position, I forced my hands free and reached behind to grab Adam's lowered head. *Shouldn't have left yourself vulnerable.* I threw him forward, my face still in the moss. Adam may have caught me by surprise, but I was much stronger and faster than he would ever be.

I stood quickly and assessed my opponent. He was built strong, and he was brave if he thought he could challenge me, but I could see in his eyes that he feared what would come of it. "Not as strong as you thought you were?" I taunted. The rush I felt was addictive. I never had a true male challenger before, and I couldn't wait for the outcome.

"I knew I wasn't as strong, but I had to try anyway," Adam explained. "Why?"

Quickly, he replied, "Because it's my job to protect my family, and you are a threat to it."

I nearly growled. "Me? A threat?" Adam nodded once, never relaxing his defensive pose. "Why would I be a threat? Have I done something to hurt you or your children?" I questioned.

"Not yet," the monkey bluntly replied.

I stiffened. *Maybe both of them had been watching me.*

"You've hurt Lilith enough. You've had several lifetimes to do so. She's happy now. Can't you see that? Surely you do, you visit often enough."

Flinching at the sound of *her* name, I said. "I don't know what you're talking about—"

Adam interrupted my argument, "You may think you're the ultimate predator. One that no other can challenge, and maybe you are. But you forget that I was once one of the naturals. I learned in my last life how to detect beings such as you. I know when I'm being watched." Adam took a step toward me. "I can smell the rancid odor you ooze, and it surrounds my family's land." Another step. "Lilith may deny it, but she can smell it too, and it makes her unhappy to be reminded of you every day. Stop coming here. Stay on your land, and we will stay on ours."

My fingers twitched with the urge to grab his neck. "That's not going to work forever. She will realize soon enough that she's made a mistake and come back to me. You know she will."

The look of worry that crossed Adam's face gave me hope that I was right, but he quickly erased it. "No, she won't. Lilith is stronger than you give her credit for, and she deserves better than you."

"Oh, and that's you?"

Shoulders tense, he replied, "No." Thinking I won the battle of wills, I moved to leave, but the monkey continued, "But its most definitely *not* you."

Unwilling to acknowledge his spiteful words, I asked, "What did you mean you can smell me? Your senses are not as powerful as ours."

Confused by the change in topic, Adam answered, "No, but the senses from my past life remain." Scrutinizing my expression, he asked a question of his own, "Did Eve say she lacked such abilities?" The monkey laughed. "She's lying. And I can't blame her. I wouldn't trust you either."

My hands balled into fists. *Not yet. You can't kill him yet.* "You've insulted me enough. I am done with you." I moved to walk around him, but he blocked me. "No. We are done with *you*. Don't come back here again."

"Or what?" I stepped forward, so we were nose to nose. The monkey was slightly shorter, but he stood his ground. I was accustomed to animals submitting, but this creation did not.

"I'll die."

I took a step back. "What?"

"Well, that's what would happen, right?" The determined glimmer in Adam's eye confused me.

"Yes," I answered, unsure now.

"Because you'll kill me," Adam stated.

"Yes."

"And then Lilith will hate you even more than she does now."

I swallowed. *Would she hate me?* I knew the answer but refused to accept it. "No, she wouldn't. She doesn't hate me."

"No, she doesn't." I looked up to meet his gaze. I hadn't realized I was looking down. Adam wasn't smiling now, but I could still see the laugh lines etched around his mouth. A constant reminder of the happiness *I* was supposed to have. "But she will."

"You couldn't possibly know what she feels," I argued.

"I do. Because unlike you, I take the time to listen to her and care for her. I do what she wants. Not what I want. You have never done that for her."

"And what do *you* want?"

Adam looked startled by the question but recovered quickly enough. "I want her to be happy."

I closed the distance between us and spoke slowly, so even he could understand. "Good. Because she'll be happy with *me*." I pushed past him, quick enough that he didn't have time to block me. Then I ran. I ran faster than I ever had before and reached my own family sooner than I wanted to.

I heard the waterfall first. It didn't take long for the pond to recover after burning it, but the life never came back. I smiled at that fact. I smiled because of the power I had over this pathetic Earth. *I had the power to make her love me.*

I recalled the day I lost her. The rain had soaked my furs, icing my skin. And the sheer coldness that dwelled deep inside me was vivid and etched into my memory. I'd crumpled and nearly died from the pain she caused. But really, I had to thank her. I wouldn't have uncovered these skills of mine if she hadn't left.

The punishment she gave me for loving her was what unleashed my power. I would not waste it.

I begrudgingly stepped through the tree line and into the small clearing where they waited. My *family*. If they could really be called such a thing. Their purpose in life was to make me happy, so I suppose they earned the title, no matter the modified intentions.

"Father!" My eldest ran to me. She should have known better, but time after time she fought for my affections. Her silver aura danced excitedly, and I had to block out the *sight* before I saw too much. I didn't want to know her. It would only make what I was doing more difficult.

Just as she was about to embrace me, I held a stiff arm out to hold her back. "Cainadra, what have I told you?" Her heart beat frantically.

The child moved her familiar icy gaze down and whispered, "No touching. Only speak when spoken to."

I couldn't help but feel a tug of pain in my gut, but I continued anyway, "That's right. Now, take your brother and check our traps."

Cainadra immediately obeyed. She grabbed her twin brother's hand and ran into the woods, their dark, curled hair bouncing as they did so. I had to admit, they were useful when it came to tasks. Of course, I had to wait at least four years before they were competent enough to carry them out, but they learned quick enough.

I couldn't fight against the strange feeling that overcame me when I thought of such things. I had yet to name the emotion.

I looked to my temporary mate. Eve was swollen with child. Its blue soul was barely able to shine through her black one. Her delicate frame was so small and fragile I hadn't thought she was strong enough to carry any offspring. But she had. The one that grew in her now was our sixth child. One every year except for our eldest twins, Cainadra and Abel.

"Lucifer," Eve greeted numbly. Despite her original *enthusiasm*, she had become a cold, unpredictable woman. Adam's words were loud and clear then: *She's lying. But I can't blame her. I wouldn't trust you either.*

If Eve had indeed kept her natural senses through the transformation, why was it that my children's senses were so weak? They could not see, hear, smell, feel, or taste the same things I could. The hybrids were weaker than I meant them to be. But they would do, nonetheless.

I nodded my head in response to Eve and dove into the icy pond water, unable to look at the twisted life I had created. The falls used to fill me with warmth. It used to absorb the rays of the day's sun, but not since I burned it away. It was just a puddle of lifeless water now.

The First Woman's voice echoed in my head again and again as I floated: *It's because you're selfish. Nature doesn't give unless you have something to give in return.* I submerged my head under the water's surface, hoping to drown out the unrelenting torment.

15 Years' Gone

"Cainadra, you are more than old enough now to have children. You have to contribute to our kind or else we won't be strong enough." I had berated my firstborn several times before. When she was young, she was eager to please me, always following my commands. But when she reached her tenth year something changed—she started thinking for herself.

I hadn't had that problem with any of my other children. Her twin, Abel, may have defended his sister on occasion but quickly retreated when I grew angry. No one wanted me angry. I was The King of this land. No one else. And soon, only *my* offspring would be occupying this world. It was only a matter of time, and I had an endless amount of it.

"Father, I don't want to be with anyone, and I don't want to have children. I see how unhappy it makes Mother," she finished quietly.

Cainadra's concern for her mother only fueled the flames that scorched my insides. "Your mother doesn't know how lucky she is. She is contributing to our race by giving birth to my children. You are my child, and it is your duty to obey me."

"Why?"

The flames died down, and the green of the forest reappeared. "What did you say?"

"Why do I have to obey you? What gives you power over me?"

"You know the answer to that. Don't test my patience, girl." Instead of the rageful heat, I was becoming cold. The drop in temperature meant that it was beyond the point of anger. Cainadra felt it to. The branch that brushed softly against my shoulder snapped due to its newfound frailty. Frost overtook the trees around us. Cainadra exhaled white puffs.

"Father," my daughter took a bold step toward me and placed her delicate hand where my heart should have been. "I don't know what happened to you, but I know you're hurting. I know your *heart* is hurting." My child's touch allowed the frost to dissipate. "Let me help you, and maybe then you'll understand."

Understand? What could she mean by that? This infant—this abomination. "What have I told you?" I said under my breath. I looked down to where her hand rested, unable to look into the blue eyes I knew so well. The blue eyes I had come to loathe because they weren't the eyes that *she* loved.

Hesitantly, my daughter removed her hand, but she continued to fight for my gaze. "No touching. Only speak when spoken to."

Gruffly, I responded, "That's right. Follow those rules, and you will be happy." I was tired of the fight, and didn't yet have the will to force my wishes upon her.

As I turned to leave Cainadra said, "No, I won't."

The forest was the outlet for my rage. The greenery, the animals, even the water was not safe when I was near. *How could I make her obey?* I had to find a way, because if she didn't listen then she would have no purpose, and no place in my plan. I had to create as many hybrids as I could so they would outnumber *hers*. But that was hard when I had so many sons and so few daughters. I needed more females, and Cainadra was not helping the cause by refusing to take a mate.

Eve was aging rapidly. I didn't think she had the strength to birth any more children. Perhaps it was time to choose another mate. One that was strong enough to help me in my cause. *Could I really do that though?* I banished the weak thought away. My children were nothing but weapons in the grand war I was fighting. Though it went against my instincts, I would have to soon. Eve would no longer be needed, but perhaps she could continue to serve as a caretaker for the newborns. Yes, she would be content with that role. I laughed aloud while I leapt high above the trees to snatch a young dragon mid-flight. *It mattered not if she was content. Eve would obey regardless.*

The young dragon had just learned to fly and had gone out on its own without its mother's protection. *How convenient for me.* As I landed back on the ground, with the fledgling fighting me the whole way, puffs of fire escaped its lips. I had to give the species credit: they fought until the end.

The creature was dead with a quick jerk of my wrist. I looked down at the limp body and admired its exceptional coloring. Each dragon was utterly unique and beautiful. Though I strove to kill as many as I could, I still admired. Their meat was the most delicious of all Earth's creatures, and my mouth watered in anticipation.

I sat by a creek and willed a small fire to light. The trick to roasting a dragon was a hot flame. A flame only I could produce. I ignored the inward reminder that I *wasn't* the only one and continued. The dragon was skinned by the time the fire was blue, and I threw the meat on top of it. The creature's blood burned away slowly.

Dragons produced a hot enough flame to appreciate, and that was the reason it was so difficult to roast them. But their heat was nothing compared to my own. I cleansed the tough skin in the creek and added it to my coverings; even after death their hide was warm. I had come to appreciate it in the cold season, which was new to me. The changing of seasons began only a short while ago, and I wondered often if I was the cause of it.

I smiled at the notion.

Happy with the new skin and my belly full, I made my way back to the waterfall. The small clearing had become cramped with too many children, so they lived among the forest. Our shelters were built in the earth or high in the trees. This was a freedom I gifted them. Something to occupy their minds and time so long as they accomplished what I wanted.

My space was placed above the waterfall. There was just enough room for a small tent. Just enough room for *me*. Eve had her own tent, but she chose to sleep on The First Woman's rock behind the falls most often. I assumed she enjoyed the security and darkness it provided, or perhaps it was because she didn't have to look at me or her children. As long as she was available to me, I didn't care where she slept. Though the nagging thought that it was *her* space taunted my empty chest.

I was just about to crawl into my tent for a nap when I heard a cry, "Lucifer!" Immediately, I dove over the side and fell with the cascading water into the cold pond. Faster than any fish could have, I swam beneath the waves and under the falls to Eve.

The water had become dark, and it was difficult to see. Returning to the surface, I discovered Eve lying on her back on the large, flattened rock. Her body trembled, and her face was contorted in pain. I reached for her hand and realized her body was slick with sweat. I gripped harder and asked, "What's wrong?" Eve's stomach was just beginning to swell with my twenty-second child.

"Your child…" then her hand went limp in my own, unconscious. She was bleeding. *But how? It wasn't time yet.* I swam to the other side of the rock and discovered her dilated birthing canal. But my instincts said she wasn't giving birth. Something was wrong.

Unsure of what to do, I called out for Cainadra; she'd helped with her mother's births since she was small. Once she arrived, I demanded, "What's wrong with your mother? It's too soon for the child to come." My daughter swam to Eve's side and sucked in a breath.

The blood was everywhere now. It was dripping down the rock and into the water, darkening the pond. I cringed knowing that we were standing in her blood. *Strange. Blood never bothered me before.*

"She's losing the baby," Cainadra whispered.

"Why?" I questioned.

Finally, she moved her clouded gaze to my own, wakened from her shocked stupor. "She's too weak and too old to carry any more. If you keep trying, you'll only kill her."

"What of the child?" I demanded.

"The baby is already lost. It's Mother we have to save now."

Enraged, I left my daughter to tend to Eve. I knew Cainadra was hurt by this, but I didn't care about Eve, and I didn't know how to help her anyway.

I waited until my daughter exited the cove. She was covered in her

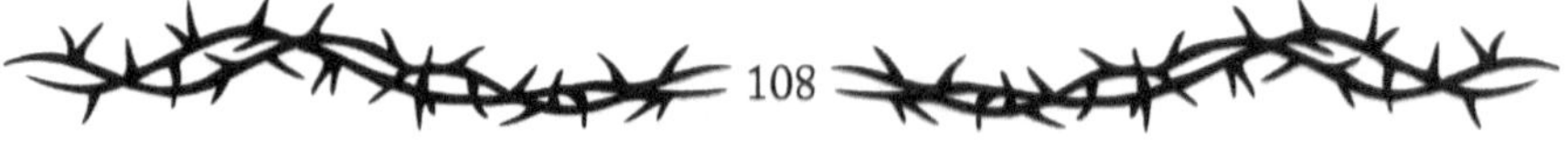

mother's blood. Some of it washed away as she swam toward me, one arm hovering above the water's surface. She cradled something small in her hand, but I couldn't comprehend what it was—it was hidden in red.

Wading now, her face was grim when she said, "Mother is going to live." She held the object in her hand out to me. It was as small as an apple and colored as such, no light shone from it. Reality became clear then. This was my child.

I took the tiny dead creature from my daughter's gentle hold. It fit in the palm of my hand. All the power in the world, and I suddenly felt powerless. I couldn't even save an unborn infant. *My* unborn child. Hot water pricked my eyes, but I held it back. I couldn't show weakness. Not now. I refused to take my eyes off the lump of flesh in my hand. "This is *her* fault. She shouldn't be allowed to exist," I said through tight lips.

I didn't have to look to know a horrified expression lay upon Cainadra's face. "How can you say that?"

"It's fairly easy." My daughter thought I spoke of Eve, but I didn't feel the need to correct her. Without warning, the child burst into flames. Cainadra fell back into the water, while I watched my never-to-be-born child become ash in my hand. The breeze stole away the evidence, and I was left with a charred palm. I placed it in the water, and when I lifted it back up it was completely healed, as if nothing happened.

"Father? Cain? What's wrong?" Abel walked hesitantly to the pond's edge, taking in Cainadra's blood covered skin and my numb face.

"Help Cainadra carry Eve to her tent." Abel didn't question my command; he was the perfect son, and the perfect warrior for the army I was building.

I watched Abel and Cainadra carefully float their mother across the water's surface and lift her onto land. Abel struggled to lift his portion, but Cainadra did it with ease. Her shocked and helpless expression was gone, and a determined one replaced it. She questioned my authority at every turn, but she was strong.

She reminded me of someone else.

Eve's incident was long forgotten and replaced with a new resolve.

XI
Father

Eve recovered within a few weeks to my dismay. It would have been one less thing for me to worry about if she wasn't around. Cainadra was with her every waking second, and even the non-waking ones. She slept in her mother's tent, taking care of her every need.

They had never been particularly close, but this experience brought them together somehow. I caught Eve smiling when I checked for an update on her recovery. The smile quickly disappeared upon seeing my face, but my daughter's remained. *At least there was one person who didn't hate me.* I returned what I thought was a warm smile and quickly departed. I hadn't been able to look my daughter in the eye since the loss of the fetus, but I was going to have to speak with her eventually. I just didn't know when.

Abel approached as I stepped out of the tent. "Father, can I speak with you?" he stuttered.

Irritated by his hesitant demeanor but reminding myself that this was how I wanted him to be, I said, "Of course." He led us away from anyone in earshot and turned to face me. His heart pounded, and his hands trembled. "What is it you want, Son?"

Mumbling, he said, "I have always followed your orders, and I've nev-

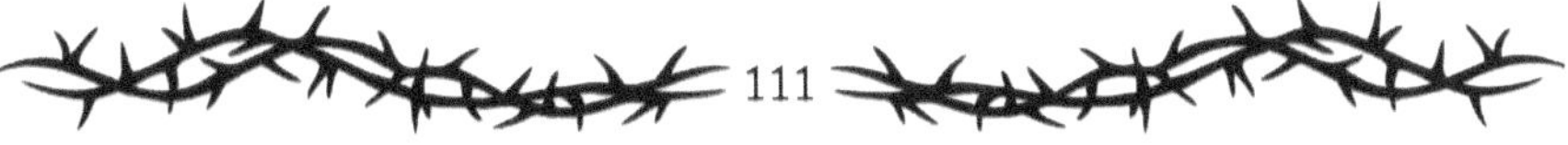

er questioned you." Abel wound his hands together.

"Stop fidgeting, and spit it out," I demanded.

"We almost lost Mother. She can't have any more children. So, I am asking, no begging you to leave her be. Please. If not for her sake, for ours—your children." Though Abel was shaking, I could see he was determined in his cause. Abel never defied his father, so Eve must have meant a lot to him if he was approaching me about it.

I hesitantly put a hand on his shoulder. "Son, you have nothing to worry about. Your mother is indeed too old and frail to carry any more of my children. I will leave her to care for the new generation as a grandmother."

Abel exhaled a sigh of relief, but I could see in his marigold spirit that he was surprised by my answer. "And I am sure you will make a magnificent grandfather."

"Yes, but my fathering days are not yet over, Abel." I removed my firm hold on his shoulder, and he discreetly rolled it back to stretch out the tight muscles.

Abel was stunned, but he hid it quickly. "How so?"

"Your sister, Cainadra, is well into her adult years and has yet to choose a mate. I am now making that choice for her. She will replace Lil… Eve and our numbers will continue to grow."

"Does she know?"

"Not yet. I was waiting until she recovered from the shock of her mother's incident. But she will soon."

Desperate, my son reached out to me, but thought better of it and balled his hands into fists at his side. "Father, please allow me to take your place. The rest of my sisters have already chosen their mate. I am still one of the few of my brothers who don't have a match. Please let me have Cain. You know she doesn't want one, but she trusts me and will concede if I push her."

I took a moment to consider my son's words and said, "I understand that not all of my sons have a mate or even the opportunity to pick one. But you have had years to convince her, and she has not budged. Cainadra needs a stronger hand to guide her, and that is not you."

"But Father—" I stopped his words with a look.

"You will have a mate soon, Abel. I have daughters that are still too young, but they will age quickly, don't you worry. Time passes all too quickly for a mortal."

I woke with resolve the next day and left to retrieve Cainadra. I knew it was going to be a fight, but I strangely craved the conflict. I had grown bored with my obedient children and needed stimulation. I hadn't realized until after *she* left how much excitement she brought into my existence. Without her, I was nothing but an animal.

I made my way to Eve's tent; it was hidden in an uprooted tree. The roots provided a nice shelter, but it was too dark for my taste. Moving the fur door aside, I looked in to find both mother and daughter sleeping.

I started to speak but found myself studying Cainadra instead. The stubborn set of her jaw was nowhere to be seen. Her eyes weren't open, so I didn't have to look at the pity she reserved for me. My daughter's dark curls were splayed around her. Moving my gaze down, I noticed that the blanket she donned didn't cover one of her legs. I was appreciating the smoothness of her skin when I heard a noise.

Eve had shifted and was now staring at me. I couldn't determine her expression, but I suddenly felt the need to get away. I thought only *she* could make me feel that way. Perhaps Eve was more influential than I wanted to admit.

"Cainadra, wake up," I whispered. She breathed out a sigh but kept dozing. Seeing I was going to reach out to my daughter, Eve gently shook Cainadra. Her eyes cracked open, and the ice-blue I loathed shone even in the darkness of Eve's burrow.

"Come," I ordered.

My daughter responded immediately, so I withdrew from the doorway, but not before I caught Eve's reassuring gesture; she took her child's hand and squeezed it gently. My chest boiled with heat. My territorial instincts were strong. Especially now.

With a grunt, Cainadra stepped out and into the light. "Why do you always shrink away from the light?" I asked.

"It's too warm," she quickly responded.

"The shelter was warmer."

Evading an answer, she asked, "Was there a reason you woke me?"

I answered by turning and leading her to the falls. No one was there in the early mornings. My children preferred to watch the stars and sleep during the day.

No one enjoyed the sun like me.

Banishing the lonely thought from my mind, I sat down on the grassy bank and lowered my feet into the pond. The cold water cleansed my grief-filled mind. "Sit with me," I said.

Cainadra did the same procession but sat farther away than she should have. Sighing, I started, "Do you fear me?"

My daughter didn't seem surprised by this question. "Yes."

"Why?"

"Because it's what you want, isn't it?" she said.

Taken aback by her bluntness, I took a moment to respond. "No, it's not what I want. But it is what I need."

"Why do you need it? I know you don't enjoy being alone. I see the hurt on your face whenever you approach us and the laughter stops. I see it when one of my siblings refuses to look you in the eye." She paused. "Yes, Father. I do fear you, but I also love you. Even if you may not be capable of such an emotion."

"Of course, I'm capable. You don't know me as well as you think, girl." I looked away from her piercing gaze. *Was this how everyone felt when I looked at them?* I didn't like it; the sense that she was looking past the man and into the soul. But that couldn't be. The First Woman and I were the only ones. Then I thought back to my last visit in the south—it wasn't that long ago.

I caught The First Woman's daughter, Naavah, roaming the forest alone. I didn't approach her, but I did see how her pupils dilated strangely. I knew that look well. *She* had the same gaze whenever she looked past our physical plane and into the spirit realm. I remembered because I was always trying to get that gaze to focus on me.

From of the corner of my eye, I saw Cainadra's spirit twitch. *She was waiting for me to explain.* Instead, I asked, "Is there anything you want to tell me?"

This time, she was surprised. "What do you mean?"

"You know what I mean." *How could I have been so blind?* I always knew Cainadra was different. I had explained her stubborn attitude as a genetic side effect, but it was because she thought she didn't need to follow me. *Because she was powerful, too.*

My daughter's expression became blank, and her spirit calmed. "No."

"Don't lie to me."

"I am not. There's nothing I want to tell you."

We stared into each other's blue eyes. Challenging. Waiting. Then I was unsure. *Maybe I was wrong.* My gaze moved to the water. I was distracting myself to prolong the conversation I brought her here for. "Fine," I grunted. I shifted my position to face her. I needed to be firm. I needed to be in control. "I don't want to fight with you, Cainadra. But if you continue to disobey me, there will be consequences."

"Is this about choosing a mate again? We've been over this. I don't want any of my siblings." Her shimmering spirit danced angrily, but she quickly contained it.

"You don't have to pick one of your siblings," I explained. My next words were so much harder to say because I saw how her face lit up with delight at what she thought was her granted freedom. "You don't have a choice anymore. I'm choosing for you." Before she could open her mouth to argue, I said, "I am your mate now."

My daughter recoiled. "What?"

"It's as you said before, your mother is too old and weak to birth any more of my children. I need someone young and strong. That is you, Cainadra."

My child stood and stumbled backward. "No. You can't do this."

"I can and will." She was about to run, but before she could take another step, I said, "Have I ever hurt you or your siblings? Have I not given you a comfortable life? Why is it so hard to love…be with me?" I stood so she wasn't looking down on me.

Cainadra straightened her back. "You asked earlier why I didn't like the sun?"

I nodded.

"It's because it reminds me of you. Sure, it offers gentle warmth when it pleases, but ultimately its purpose is to burn. And it's only a matter of time before it no longer wants us and sends out a flare." My daughter turned on her heel and ran into the protective blackness of the forest. Her curls blew angrily behind her, and I couldn't help but remember the last time a woman ran from me.

XII

Flare

Hidden sins often create the most captivating stories.

-E

I let Cainadra have her time away from us. I hadn't seen her since she ran into the woods, however, it was normal for her to disappear at times. The knowledge that she would be my mate spread among the children. They said nothing to counter me, but I could see they weren't happy. I caught many staring, and once I raised my eyes to theirs they would look away, as if my mere appearance singed their eye sockets.

"Don't you have enough already?" Eve asked. I was floating in the pond water, my eyes piercing the sun and wishing that it would turn me to ash. But Eve interrupted this fantasy, and I tore my blinded eyes away. Once the pupils recovered, I looked to the animal-woman. Eve still moved as graceful as a snake, but the skin around her eyes had wrinkled, and her mouth was lined from her constant frowning. Some of her black hair had turned silver.

"Enough what?" I mumbled. I was in no mood to speak with the snake, but there wasn't a moment that I ever was.

From her position above me on the water's edge, she said, "Enough control. Enough power." Eve took a long breath. I could hear the loud pumping of her heart. "I know you only had children so you could use them against Lilith. You have done so. Now let them do the rest of the work for you. You don't need to be with Cainadra."

Sighing, I lowered myself under the water and waited a few minutes before resurfacing. "You're still here?" I asked, my golden hair heavy with ice-water.

"Yes," Eve said calmly.

"Nothing I say will make you happy. I don't know why you bother."

"Because they're my children, too. They don't belong solely to you, despite what you think." The snake-woman crossed her arms as if to protect herself.

Numbly, I said, "Of course they are. I created them. And as for your part in it, you aren't even fully human. The First Woman *created* you. You are nothing. To me or your children."

Eve's expression remained neutral, but I could see the wet shine in her eyes. "You're right. I was created. But I was *something* before you. I was happy before you. And regardless of what I am now, I still have the instinct to protect my children."

"I protect them. Nothing and no one has harmed my children. Ever. So, what exactly are protecting them from?" I asked.

"You." Her heart pumped harder.

I never told Eve my intentions for the children or Earth for that matter. But she had learned much over the years, and the most important thing she realized was that I didn't do anything for nothing. There was always a reason.

Attaining my power, I became overwhelmed. I could do so much with it, but I was just one man. Then Eve came to comfort me that dark night in the woodland, and that's when I knew what I had to do. I could still have *her* unconditional love. A love that was reserved only for me. Because there would be nothing left to love once I was done.

"Leave me." Eve didn't move, but once I finally made eye contact, she felt the power in my words and walked away. Eve was right when she said I was using my children against The First Woman. The more numbers I had the sooner Earth would die. I needed the numbers to conquer her children. But most of all, I needed them to suck the life from this planet. I wasn't sure until Cainadra and Abel were born, but if they were anything like me, they would help me with this. And I was right.

They absorbed the energy around them into themselves with or without consumption, which was something I did not foretell. But the quicker the planet died, the sooner I'd get *her*. We may die along with Earth. That was certainly a possibility. But whether we did or not, I would have The First Woman. In life or death. This existence was meaningless without her. I would only have happiness again when she was with me. I just had to be patient.

The guilty thoughts that Eve planted in my head were discarded. I would not feel fault over beings that were never meant to be. Beings that only existed to fight for The First Man. Cainadra may not want a mate, she may even hate me, but freedom was never an option for her. Weak emotions slipped past my barriers at times and made me question myself. But all I had to do was think of *her* and they would disappear.

Tired of my family's presence, I left to hunt. Hunting always allowed me a release. It freed me in a way. I didn't have to think. I didn't have to feel.

I caught the prey's trail and weaved quietly through the dense forest. My footsteps were so quick I barely had a chance to make an impression on the moss. I floated across the terrain, an invisible predator on the hunt for living flesh.

The scent led me to a clearing. A large lizard was grazing in the middle of the flowered ground. Its armor was dry and cracked in the sunlight, though it was fused together to make one impenetrable defense. The thick plates of bone that coated the beast were well used, each disc was large enough for me to lounge on. Many had tried to claim this creature as their prey, but none had succeeded. Until now.

I kept low and to the shadows. The clearing was vast, but the trees towered above us and provided plenty of cover. I breathed in the mouth-watering scent of the large animal, continuing to appreciate its body armor. I would wish for something similar if I didn't have such power of my own.

Like me, animals had an oversensitivity to being watched. The beast grunted and thumped its massive tail as a warning to whatever being stalked it. Its beady eyes darted in and out of the tree line, waiting for me to make a move. I stilled and waited. I waited so long that the sun shifted and shone down on me through the canopy. The rays glinted against my golden hair. That was what disturbed my carefully timed hunt.

The lizard turned my way, seeing the reflected light. It reared its rugged tail and slammed it down several times before calling out in frustration. The ground shook upon impact and sent vibrations my way. *Come to me.*

Upon request, the bony creature charged. It reminded me of the first time an animal charged at me—a stag. I recalled its long, furred antlers and how they nearly impaled me. It was right after I found *her.* I was challenging myself. I wanted to bring down a creature worthy of The First Woman. But I had hesitated, questioning myself, and it escaped. Though that was before I discovered she didn't eat meat. *Before I discovered it didn't matter.*

I leapt on top of the raging lizard. It tried to throw me off, but I only used the momentum to jump higher. Descending, I landed on the armor of its right side so it was crushed into the ground, and its left side was tipped upward. There, I was able to impale its soft underbelly with my spear. The spear was an extension of my body. I wasn't even aware I had brought it with me until it was deep in the beast's flesh.

The stem of my spear was stained with the blood of many animals. The lizard was only contributing to it as it slowly bled out and died. After *she* left, I didn't care whether the deaths of animals were quick or not. I tried to be compassionate for her. I tried to be what she wanted. But this was what I was. *Human.*

I plunged my hand into its thick chest and ripped out its heart. The pulse was faint, but it was there on my tongue as it slid down my throat. The creature's eyes were closed, unable to haunt me. My spirit hummed in delight.

I used the creature's shell to transport the meat I'd carved from it. The intestines were forced to pull the once mighty armor through the thick brush, and the rest was left to rot. I lost my grip often, as I was trying not to crush the delicate flesh in my grasp, but the blood didn't allow a stable hold. I could have used my magic for aid, but I took pride in doing things on my own—most of the time.

Either way, this kill would feed my children for a long while.

I was thinking of other ways I could have transported my kill when I reached the waterfall. Frustrated, I threw the intestines down. Angered voices sounded from the north, and I traveled the short distance to the meadow I'd woken in so many centuries ago, curious about the commotion. I paused and hid behind a tree along the clearing's edge to listen.

"It's true! Please believe me, we must go to them," Cainadra pleaded.

When did she return?

"Father says we are the only people on this land," my son, Seth, defended. He was merely fourteen, but he had a sharpness about him that always surprised me.

"Father has lied to us. If he lied about this, then what else is he keeping from us?" Cainadra said.

"We all know what Father wants from you. We understand. But you cannot escape it, no matter how many stories you tell. True or otherwise," Abel explained to his sister. The rest of her siblings murmured their agreements.

"Don't you see? We can all escape him. There is another like him. She is just as powerful as he, if not more. She will protect us," my daughter reasoned.

"You spoke to this woman?" Abel asked.

Pausing for only a moment, Cainadra answered, "No, I did not. But I saw her power and saw her family. She cares about them, which is more than Lucifer has ever done for us."

The children were silent. They were considering my daughter's words.

Cainadra continued, "We can all have happy lives. All we have to do is leave."

"We do lead happy lives, Cain," Abel commented.

"How can we be happy if we are not free?" Cainadra retaliated. I heard Abel take a few steps away from the group. His heart was racing. My eldest son was contemplating what his life had become and what it could be.

I stepped out from behind the tree and walked into the sunlight. I hated this place. It always begged the question, *Why did we exist?* Cainadra's face paled, and her heart nearly stopped when she saw me. "What is the meaning of this?" I demanded. The only answer I received were averted glances and labored breathing. They were frightened of me. I couldn't help but feel hurt, but I ignored the weak emotion and continued, "Don't make me repeat myself."

Cainadra stepped forward, as expected. "We know you've been lying to us. We aren't the only ones here, and you are not the only one with power."

"Is that so?" The tree beside me lit with fire. The blue flames licked the entire being until it crumbled beside me; its neighbors were left unharmed.

My children stepped back. All except the twins. "You don't frighten us anymore. We will not be your slaves, and we are leaving. Now," Cainadra said. Abel turned and ushered his siblings to the northern side of the clearing. It was the long way back to the waterfall where they would retrieve Eve, but they didn't want to be anywhere near me.

Cainadra had a confused expression on her face. I didn't know for sure, but I must have been smiling. I remembered how much *she* hated my smile. "Aren't you angry?" she asked.

Confident, I answered, "No."

"Why? What game are you playing?"

"There is no game. I simply know that they aren't going anywhere. That includes you."

"Watch me," my daughter threatened.

Just as she turned, I appeared in front of her; my speed was greater than she had ever seen it before. Startled, she stumbled back and ran the direction I had come from. Quick as lightening, I caught her arm and spun her around. "How do you expect to leave my land if you can't even escape the meadow?" I dragged her in the direction of the falls, but the earth crumbled beneath my feet. Soon, I couldn't take a step. I looked down to find that the soil had trapped my legs.

I ripped my limbs from the firm hold, but I had to let go of Cainadra to do so. She ran. Once freed, I chased after her again, but this time an earth wall as tall as a mammoth blocked my path. Angered, I forced my way through the rocks and grime. Reaching the other side, I discovered my firstborn waiting for me. She didn't look frightened anymore. Her face was hard and sure. I recognized that look. It was the same expression *she* had when she left—determination. "Angry now, Father?"

Gold was what I saw when I charged at her. My spirit thrashed in anger, but she surprisingly evaded my attack. Cainadra threw herself to the side. I watched as she fell into the earth, and it swallowed her whole. The surface closed around her, and I could no longer see my opponent. *I was right before. She did have power.* I forced myself to calm and listen. The longer I waited, the clearer the sounds of the world became.

I raced for the southern tree line and sent my hand into the hard soil. I pulled up dark hair, and my daughter's body followed. I threw her down, and she raised her hands up to protect herself. But I wasn't going to strike her like she thought I was.

Why did everyone assume the worst of me?

I felt for the moisture in the grass and air. The plants shriveled as the life-giving water abandoned them, and the dry air made my mouth feel like cotton. I formed the water around my daughter, leaving small openings so she could take shallow breaths. And right as she moved her gaze to me, the water froze, trapping her in a cage of my own creation.

I let myself stare into the pale blue eyes that were so much like mine. I allowed myself to acknowledge the fact that those eyes were staring at me with hatred. I waited for a long while, unsure if she could free herself. But it seemed she could not, and I finally lay down to rest. Not to rest my mind, but my body. I felt tired. A different tired. I looked to my golden spirit and discovered how dim it had become. It had been shining bright that morning. Now, it dulled as if a piece of it had been burned away.

The sun had set, and I closed my eyes to block out the inevitable darkness. Though there was little difference, I still preferred the darkness I could control. In my personal world I could look into emerald eyes and run my hands along soft ivory skin.

Footsteps on dry grass were what disrupted my pleasant dream. "Cain? Where are you?" Abel called. He stumbled across the meadow, tripping over the disturbed earth.

"She's here, boy." Startled, Abel slowly made his way to where Cain-adra and I dwelled at the edge of the forest.

"What have you done?" Abel's body trembled, and he collapsed onto his knees. His hands reached out and felt the ice that encased his twin.

"I have done nothing. She is merely trapped. Do not worry," I explained. But it didn't stop my son from getting up and attacking me. I let him throw his weak punches. Sand leaked from my nose and lips, but I healed as quickly as the wounds were given. Unperturbed, I subdued his flailing arms and rolled us over so that he was eating dirt, and I was sitting on his back.

"Calm down, Son. There is no reason to fight me."

His words muffled by the soil, Abel said, "There is every reason to fight! You have lied to us! You discarded Mother like you do the animals!" Abel quieted as he said his last accusation, "You killed Cain." His struggles stopped, but he continued to talk into the dirt. "How could you do it? How could you kill your own daughter?"

I breathed out a tired sigh. "I did no such thing. Her heartbeat is weak, but it is there. I just wanted to teach her lesson. One that she won't ever forget." I stood and lifted my son to his feet as I did so. "Now, where are the rest of your siblings?" Tears were streaming down my son's face. *How could I have created such a weak creature?*

"What? She's not dead?" Abel whimpered.

Impatient, I demanded, "Where are they?"

Slowly, he answered, "They're at the falls, waiting for Cain."

Good. They wouldn't leave without their eldest. "Go to them. Keep them there until we return." Abel was reluctant to leave but leave he did. I turned back to my daughter and checked for any weakness in the ice. There were a few cracks, but I chose to ignore them. I willed Cainadra's ice cell to travel alongside me in the forest. I was sweating from the effort, but rest wasn't an option.

Finally reaching the falls, I moved Cainadra into the pond and froze the surrounding water. Eve was at the peak of the waterfall, near my tent. I turned to the rest of my children.

"My children, none of you are going to be harmed by me. Physically or mentally, despite your sister's words. She is confused and knows not what she says. There are certain plants in the woodland that, if eaten, will cause hallucinations and illness. I suspect she has ingested one of these species." I sent a concerned look Cainadra's way. "She merely needs to rest, and my ice dome will allow her to do so." It was obvious that Abel did not believe me, but the rest of my offspring nodded and sent Cainadra concerned glances of their own.

"How long must she be in there?" Seth voiced.

"Only through the night, my son. There is no need to worry for your sister. She is safe." I heard a soft chuckle from above the falls.

"Safe? How can you say that when she is freezing to death? I suspect that Cain is not the one who is unwell." Abel had stepped forward, far enough away from the rest that they couldn't stop him if he decided to attack their father.

In a voice only he could hear, I said, "Ready to challenge me again so soon, Abel?"

The boy lowered his eyes, but he still stood apart from the rest, undecided in his decision. While he deliberated his next move, I went to reassure my children again. But before I could, there was resounding crack. It echoed against the trees, filling the small space with its obnoxious noise.

I turned just in time to take an ice shard to the chest, right where my heart should have been. The impact made me take a step back, but I recovered quickly and removed the weapon. However, the heat from my growing fury was quickly melting it. I dropped the shrunken shard to the grass. The ice dome had exploded. Cainadra freed herself and was making her way to me through the frozen pond. The ice didn't melt like it would have for me, instead it shattered with each step she took through the waist-deep water. Blood dripped from her thighs as she forced her way through.

Cainadra's expression was fierce. She was angry but in complete control. *This was a true challenger.* But that formidable persona dissipated once she reached the shoreline. I looked to where her shocked gaze lingered. Abel was on his knees. The young man faced his twin, clutching his middle. The moss below him quickly absorbed the blood that dripped from his body.

"Abel!" Cainadra cried. She dropped down in front of him. They mimicked each other perfectly. Their dark curls danced in the wind that gusted through the small clearing, and their delicate faces held the same hurt expression, though for entirely different reasons.

"Cain?" Abel asked. What he was asking, I didn't know, but Cainadra did it seemed. "I'm here. I'm so sorry. I didn't mean…" My daughter's hands were shaking as she placed them over Abel's. They were pressed against the fatal wound, willing it to close, but the ice shard was melting quickly.

I didn't know what compelled me, but I looked up. Eve was still at the peak. Her feet were dangling over the side while she stared down at us. There was not a hint of concern or surprise at what was transpiring. I looked to the rest of my children: some stood frozen in shock, and some collapsed to their knees as their eldest siblings had. There were ones too young to understand what happened and looked to the eldest for guidance. But none approached. They feared the same fate as their brother.

I continued to stand where I was. I wasn't in shock. I wasn't scared. I wasn't angry. I wasn't anything. Yet, this couldn't have worked out better for me. My eldest children were the only ones who challenged me, and in turn a threat to my cause.

So why did I feel…lost?

"Father, do something!" Cainadra begged.

I took a step toward them but stopped. My resolve came quick as well as my reply. "There is nothing I can do, Cainadra."

"You know that is a lie," my daughter spat at me.

"Abel," Seth whimpered. It was so faint none of my children heard him. But I could.

"You did this. Now you have to suffer the consequences." I strode up to my daughter and took her by the arm. Putting as much anguish as I could behind the next words, I said, "You have killed your brother and my son." I paused. "You are not worthy of our family." I pulled her with me as I made my way to the nearest tree. Her hands were ripped from Abel's, and he fell to the ground, grasping at his bleeding stomach. Cainadra struggled, but it was clear the determination she had moments before was dying along with her twin.

She's weak. This is the time.

I willed the half-rotted intestines from my hunt that occurred only hours ago to my waiting hands. I held Cainadra against the trunk of a tree and wrapped her tightly in the slimy organs. Soon her struggle was nonexistent. She'd lost the battle before it had truly begun. *And all due to her weak emotions.*

My daughter looked to the top of the waterfall. "Mother, please help," Cainadra begged. Eve didn't even glance at her pleading daughter. The snake-woman's eyes were on me, waiting for something. Cainadra's head slumped in anguish. Her mother would not come to her aid. And in that moment, I knew why.

Abandoning my previous excuses, I said, "My children, it is clear your sister, Cainadra, is not well. First, she refused to take a mate. Then to further this wish of hers, she claimed there are others like us. This is false." I took a moment to look each one of my children in the eye. "Now she has killed your brother. All for her selfish desires. But no one is above contributing to this family."

I looked to my crestfallen daughter now. The pungent smell from the decomposing intestines infiltrated my nostrils, and I nearly gagged. But I swallowed the bile, along with everything else. "If you are not going to help this family, you don't have a place in it."

"Father, please, leave Cain be," a small voice from the pond's edge cried.

I left Cainadra, trusting that she wasn't strong enough to break free from the constraints, and went to Abel. I kneeled beside him. Only Seth was brave enough to approach his dying brother. His young fingers clasped Abel's free hand; the blood dripped down his arm and onto the sable wolf fur he wore.

"Father, please do not punish Cain for this. It was an accident." Abel coughed, and the blood that escaped dripped down my cheek, but I did not flinch.

"My dear son, you are blinded by your love for her, and I cannot blame you for that. Your heart is full of love for your family. I am only sorry that you will not live to share it with your own children." I raised my voice so everyone could hear clearly. "Cainadra has taken your life from you, but do not worry, she will atone for her sins." I brushed a curl away from Abel's sweaty forehead and kissed his hairline. "You have been a dedicated son, Abel. You will not be forgotten." I surprised myself by meaning what I spoke. For once, I met the eyes of my prey, and they were full of sadness. My son's neck snapped cleanly in experienced hands.

This brought my defeated daughter back to life. "No!" she screamed. The wrapped organs tore from her, which caused partially digested food and blood to spray outward. Cainadra ran at me, and I looked into her eyes for the last time. They burned me with their cold hatred, and I knew there was no time to waste.

Right before my daughter reached me, she fell to the soiled ground. Saffron and then blue flames licked her once ivory skin. The dark curls that she shared with her dead brother became ash. But not once did she scream. Not once did she remove her gaze from mine, willing me to watch her as she died. Still, I couldn't help but look down and inward where her heart slowly burnt away. Where her *life* burnt away.

As my daughter turned to dust, and her spirit joined with mine, I breathed out a sigh.

There's only one left.

Part III
The King

Great is the king

Sagely and just is the king

There is but one who can bring him to his knees

This one is comely and delicate

This one is strong and definite

This one is The Queen

XIII
Secrets

Freedom is not found in dust.
-E

My children wanted to bury Abel, but that was the way The First Woman would have done it. So, I made a decree that the dead would be burned. The hybrid's spirits could not give to Earth and their corpses wouldn't either. Cainadra and Abel's souls thrashed against my golden light, trapped for the remainder of my days.

I took my time walking through the trees. I was doing what I did every day; guarding my territory. Making certain *her* children had not crossed onto it. Though, I secretly wished I would catch her sweet scent on the wind; it would prove that she still cared for me. But her scent had not blessed this land since she left.

"She won't come," a sickly sweet voice said from behind.

"What do you want? Shouldn't you be grieving for your lost children? I saw how distraught you were when they died," I turned and sneered at Eve. Even with my acute hearing, I had not heard her approach. Her snake-like stealth stayed with her through the transformation, and it irritated me.

"I could say the same," she responded with a sneer of her own.

I continued walking, but I allowed her to follow behind. "Did you come all this way because you enjoy my company, or did you have a reason?" I asked, though I didn't really care about the answer.

"Hmmm…"

"What?"

"The children's deaths affected you less than I thought they would, but of course, you are very good at hiding your emotions." Eve slithered gracefully over a protruding root.

"Oh, did you think you would live long enough to see it? If it wasn't for the circumstances, you would have been long dead before you watched them die of old age," I clarified.

"I doubt any of our children are going to die of natural causes with you around."

I glanced back to catch her gaze, and what I saw was unsettling. "What is that supposed to mean?" It was taking all the willpower I had to keep myself from striking her. *Why did I feel so angry?*

"Don't pretend. You've had the same thoughts. Human beings are complex creatures. They need stimulation. They need to create. They need to be *free*." Eve stopped walking. "And they're never going to have it. You won't let them."

I stared at the forest's ground, realizing I had stopped walking, too. The moss was so many different shades of green: jade, olive, mint, and *emerald*. "They are not human. They don't *need* anything."

"Yes, they are. A part of you is in every child. It makes it that much more entertaining to watch you literally destroy yourself." Eve chuckled. "I have to admit, when Cainadra burned away, your face was precious. Knowing that you were turning a piece of yourself into ash. That must have hurt."

"Why are you saying this?" Gold was licking the edges of my vision, and my hands trembled. Emotions that I'd been repressing were coming to the surface, and I didn't know if I was going to be able to contain them.

"Didn't you wonder why Cainadra was so eager to leave you? Why she left on her own all the time? Why she rebelled against you?" I turned and lifted my gaze to Eve. Her amber irises were burning bright with anticipation. "She's known about Lilith's children for some time now. Though, I am unsure of her relationship with them." Eve pondered for a moment before continuing. "Forcing her to be your mate was what lit her rebellious fire, but that was the purpose all along."

"Purpose?" My hand itched to reach out and grip her small neck, but I waited. This was just like any other hunt. I had to bide my time and strike when the time was right. *She was just like any other animal. Limited and mortal.*

"You thought I was just going to stand back and let you control me for the rest of my life? The spell Lilith put on me was extremely specific and limited what I could do, but I found a way."

My body stopped shaking. *A spell? Was that how she did it?* The thought left the sand beneath my skin scratchy and irritating.

"Shall I reiterate it for you? Oh yes, I remember every word. Not that you would. You were gone, having another one of your tantrums while my life was taken from me!" Eve's usual composed persona was gone, and she spoke the words that transformed a snake into the woman standing before me.

Thank you for your sacrifice
You will now become something different
Something more
A being of beauty and intelligence and generosity
You will be a mate
A mother
A brand new being on this Earth
You will be Eve

Eve was the one shaking now. Her body trembled with anger and loss. "I have been trapped in that spell for too long. She cursed me to be human. She cursed me to want choice and freedom, yet didn't allow me to have it. She made me a slave." The snake-woman balled up her tiny fist as if she was going to hit me but thought better of it and relaxed her grip. "I can't leave you. I can't kill myself. I must be at your beckon call whenever you feel like satisfying your disgusting desires and take care of the resulting offspring. And you know the worst part? I *want* to do all those things because that's what the spell makes me feel. It makes me want to *be Eve.*" Eve's bright gaze bore into mine. "But I'm not."

The gold no longer lined my vision. I almost felt sorry for Eve. *She* had betrayed both of us. Though, I couldn't speak. Eve may have been forced into this life, but she was still beneath me. *Still an animal.*

"So, I found other ways to rebel against you. If I couldn't, then your children would do it for me." Eve had control of herself once again. Her slippery smile reappeared.

"What did you do?" I knew where this was headed, but I still felt the need to ask.

"I encouraged our children to be free. An inspiring phrase there, a discreet nod there." Eve stepped closer. The breeze blew through her blackened hair, and a few strands grazed me, along with her even blacker spirit. "I only truly had luck with Cainadra, but a few of the young ones show potential." Eve lifted her hand and traced a bony finger down my chest. "You and Lilith will pay for taking my life from me. And it begins here." Her index finger halted, and she pressed her nail into my chest where a heart should have been. "You will never be happy. I only just realized that I never had to do a thing. You will destroy yourselves."

The snake-woman licked her lips and continued to put pressure on my missing heart. I raised my hand and traced her collarbone. "If that's how you feel, allow me to free you." The snake-woman stiffened in surprise but forced herself to fight the instinct to run. My other hand caressed her cheek, and she leaned into it with a relieved sigh.

With one quick movement, Eve's heart was removed from her chest, and my created mate was gone. I viewed myself as kind—her death was quick. Eve's body fell from my grasp. She lay on the ground, and I stared into her amber eyes, seeing they were wet with unshed tears. Their glassy appearance gave the illusion she was still living.

I didn't remove my gaze from hers as I lifted her heart to my lips and bit into the muscle. But I could only take one bite before I discarded the unnatural life. It landed beside the gaping hole above her breast. I felt the thick blood seep down my arm and onto the earth. This death was something I promised her when we first met.

I warned Eve not to put her hands on me.

Though she had hated me, I hated her more, so I burned her remains. Not even Eve's body would contribute to *her* precious Earth. Still, I saw how Eve's ebony aura raced for Earth's light, desperate for freedom. I laughed when I pulled her unwilling spirit into my golden light—she hadn't known everything. I watched the crumbling face of Eve until there was nothing left of her except dust. But even after she had gone, Eve's words were on my mind: *You will do it to yourselves.*

I could feel Eve's blood on my hands even after thoroughly washing them in a stream. Despite my intense dislike for the abomination, I found myself missing her. She had been a placeholder. I didn't feel so alone when Eve was around because I knew she was just as miserable as I was.

I banished the weak and self-destructive thoughts. Eve was an obstacle, so I removed her. My creations were weapons for me to wield, nothing more. Freedom was not an option, and with Eve around, I would have had nothing but rebels to snuff. I couldn't have that. I needed numbers.

I wiped my hands on the furs until they were raw.

The breeze brought a familiar scent to me. I held my head up and took it in. It was not the aroma I longed for, but it was similar. It didn't remind me of the dead of night so much as it did the beginning of dawn—chilled moss and blooming buds. Silently, I hunted the being that trespassed on my land.

A few miles south, I found what I sought. A young woman stalked through the trees. Her emerald aura startled me. It was nearly the same shade as *her* eyes.

She meandered about, waiting for something. Or someone. *But why here?* Surely The First Woman must have told her children to stay in the south? Why would the third eldest disobey her mother. If I recalled correctly, this hybrid's name was Verbena. I hadn't been able to visit *her* as much as I wanted to. The months quickly turned into years. The proof of that was in front of me; Verbena was no longer a little girl.

I felt a strange emotion in my gut then. *Jealousy?* Why would I feel jealous of a creature such as her? A moment's consideration revealed it was her aging that caused this useless emotion. Yet, I should have been grateful that time was meaningless to me; there were many things I had yet to accomplish. Dismissing the distraction, I followed the young woman's movements. She paced back and forth, nibbling on her fingernails. She was nervous. I stepped out from the tree I hid behind.

"What are you doing on my land?" Startled, the girl turned swiftly. "Answer me," I threatened.

"This is not your land," she responded weakly.

"Of course it is." Quicker than her naked eye could see, I ran forward, so we stood only a sliver apart. To my surprise, she didn't back down. *She didn't cower like she should have.*

"Where is Cain?"

I took a step back. "My daughter is none of your concern."

"Did you hurt Cain?" Verbena's weak voice was getting stronger the more she spoke Cainadra's name.

Avoiding the question, I asked, "How do you know my daughter?"

"She's my friend." Verbena's aura danced while she said these words.

"Does your mother know about this friendship?"

Verbena looked away and shook her head. Her jaw tensed with frustration. "I don't want to hurt Mother. Telling her about Cain would do so."

Confused, I asked, "Why?"

"She already sees her children as abominations. I don't want to show her another flaw." The girl's fists clenched.

"She said you and your siblings are abominations?" I smiled, and Verbena displayed her anger.

"Of course not. She would never. It's something she doesn't have to say. It's the way she looks at us when she thinks we're not paying attention." The hybrid paused. "With regret and fear."

I was right! The First Woman was unhappy. She regretted leaving me. Claiming her was going to be easier than I thought.

"Cain says your smile is like death. I wish I wasn't seeing it for myself," Verbena interrupted the daydream, and her gaze filled with absolute loathing.

Knowing Cainadra hated me that much iced my core. The air bit at our skin, and our breath was exposed by small clouds, but Verbena didn't seem afraid. Realizing all that she said, I asked, "What flaws do you mean? What was your relationship with my daughter?"

"I love her." The girl's eyes shimmered. Everything made sense then. Cainadra's aversion to pick a mate. Why she was gone for days at a time. Why she hadn't wanted to be with me.

"You were mates," I stated.

Verbena nodded. "We *are* mates."

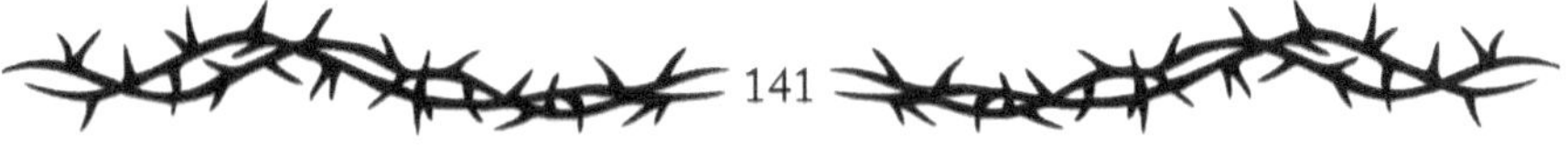

These abominations were flawed indeed. Something was broken inside of them. Not only were their senses dimmed to less than an animal, but some didn't even have the necessary instinct to mate with the opposite gender. How could a species grow if it didn't?

Perhaps this was nature's way of removing an unwanted creation.

My creation.

Eve had known. The way she chuckled when we spoke of Cainadra, and the vague description of my daughter's relationship with The First Woman's children. She knew this was the ultimate revenge on me. *I encouraged our children to be free*, she'd said. I regretted not making Eve's death last longer.

"No, you're not. Cainadra is gone. Leave now unless you want to disappear, too."

"What do you mean she's gone? Where are you keeping her?" Verbena accused. The girl was trembling now. She knew she was no challenger, but she still felt the need to defend her mate.

"Nowhere. I burned her to ash. She's nothing but dust now."

Verbena collapsed. Her heart was pounding an irregular beat. "She said you were a monster, but to kill your own child…"

I sighed. I didn't have to deal with this. "I know what you must think of me, but it hardly matters. You hybrids are merely a means to an end." As she raised her tear-streaked face to glare at me, I raised my hand and struck her temple. Not hard enough to kill her, but if I predicted right, she wouldn't be remembering much of anything.

I carried Verbena to her home beside the river, but it was still far enough away that they had to search for her if they wanted their daughter back. As I laid her to rest near the water, I thought, *She merely fell while crossing the river and hit her head.*

Though many days had passed while we traveled through the dense forest, she did not wake once in my arms, and I worried that I'd caused more damage than I meant to. *Why did I care?*

As I released Verbena and stood, I felt a sharp pain in the back of my calf. A black panther had my leg in its mouth. The sapphire eyes looked up at me with ferocity, and I recognized the creature instantly. "Let me go, and I will not harm the child." I could have destroyed the panther with just one movement, but I didn't want *her* to know I was here. Killing her domain's guardian would assuredly reveal me. Observing the dim coat and clouded eyes of the cat, I determined it didn't have much life left anyway.

The cat bit down hard before finally releasing my limb. "You can care for her now." *Strange how such a wild creature could come to care for these hybrids. I hadn't realized they were capable.*

I ran the opposite direction, hoping the coming rain would wash away my scent.

XIV

Empire

I was days away from reaching my children. *Not children—warriors.* I would no longer think of them as my offspring. They were my *creations.*

I ran quickly, but my acute sight couldn't help but catch random details in the greenery. The leaves were filled with moisture from the constant rain, and water dripped from the towering trees. The copper poppies and indigo bluebells were prominent against the emerald landscape. Wild roses and their hazardous vines seemed to grow over everything. There were barely any spaces devoid of sharp thorns.

My speed grew. *I was being hunted.* This was the first moment that the instinct to flee had come to me. It had always been to fight. But this time felt different. If I stopped, something terrible was going to happen. I halted and turned.

I listened and heard nothing. I raised my nose to the breeze and scented nothing. But I *felt* something coming. I waited, never relaxing my defensive pose. The ground was cold on my bare feet, and my worn furs bristled against the ever-increasing wind. An emerald shape appeared. It was floating toward me. The body that held the spirit was no longer attached to it.

What had I done?

I couldn't run, and I couldn't fight. My only choice was to wait and accept what I had done. Verbena's spirit took its time entering me, as if she wanted me to suffer that much longer. Once she was absorbed, I took a deep breath. I let it out on my way to the ground where I now rested. I couldn't go back to my warriors now. This needed my immediate attention. *But how could I fix it?*

I hadn't thought I hit Verbena hard enough to kill her. Clearly, I was wrong. I had just wanted her to forget about me. About Cainadra. But instead, I had made her suffer a slow death. *She* could not find out. It wasn't time yet. I wasn't prepared.

First thing's first. Hide the evidence.

I didn't stop running until I reached her. I was surprised no one had found her yet. There, she lay on the wet ground. The plant life was already trying to claim her corpse. The dewy leaves and vines crept along her limbs, hoping to entangle her, and time permitting, bring her down into the ground where their roots called for nourishment. Panther tracks surrounded Verbena's body, as if it had circled her, poking and prodding, only to find that there was no way to rouse its ward.

I gripped the vines tight and ripped them from Verbena. I couldn't help but pause and look at the deceased child. Her hair was the same crimson color of her mother's. She had Adam's eyes and nose, though I could see that she had *her* shapely lips. An emotion washed over me that I couldn't quite identify. *Regret?*

Still, I couldn't waste the very thing that had given her life. Easy as reaching into water, I reached into her chest and plucked out her heart. Though it no longer beat, it made my soul thrum in pleasure as my stomach was filled. The emptiness in my chest grew, and a tear escaped the corner of my eye before it was burned away.

I didn't have time for such emotions. I willed the gritty soil below us to rise and scrub Verbena's corpse, starting at the skin and moving inward until there was not even bones left behind; she was a part of the soil itself now. I had been experimenting with fire and water, but not earth and air. Cainadra had proven to me that I needed to. I *needed* to be the one in control.

With nothing remaining of Verbena, not even a strand of hair, I was free to do my work. I distanced myself from the riverside. I couldn't risk the panther leading The First Woman to me. That would not have been a productive encounter. Once I deemed my location far enough away, I sat and observed. I remained as still as the mountains in the distance, and as quiet as a tiger just before it pounced. Many creatures walked past me, unaware of my presence, but none that I needed.

A day had passed when I finally found what I sought. A doe grazed on the greenery, lazily walking my way. Its black nose twitched, and its small tail flicked back and forth. But most importantly, its emerald-green spirit glowed in the blackness of the night. The soul was a near replica.

Just as the doe went to take another bite of its meal, I grabbed hold of it, but not as I normally did. I was accustomed to using my strength and speed to overpower creatures, but I needed to hone the magic I possessed. My golden soul reached out and held down the doe. It was comforting to know that only those with the *sight* could see what actions my spirit took, but it was also unnerving, because I wouldn't know which descendants inherited such *sight*. The animal's wails were ear piercing, but it wouldn't last for long. Hopefully.

I didn't move a muscle. Concentrating my mind, I focused on Verbena's appearance, her smell, her speech, everything that I knew about her, which wasn't much. I hadn't seen how *she* transformed the monkey and snake into Adam and Eve, so I had no knowledge to help me in this endeavor. It was made even worse because I wasn't just creating a new being, I was trying to replicate another exactly. But the most important ingredient was the spirit. The emerald-green color of this doe was a close match for the lost child.

I could have sworn Verbena was pounding against my impenetrable golden barrier, breaking my concentration. My mind felt like it was going to burst. The mental restraints on the doe-girl loosened, and the creature was able to crawl away a few steps, but I grabbed hold of it before it was completely free. Sweat was dripping into my eyes, and my lungs were raw from harsh inhales. I had never felt so exhausted. *So weak.*

Hours passed.

Why couldn't I do this? The First Woman had done it in mere moments. *What was different?* It was hard to imagine that *she* would have forced these animals to transform. Eve said that she was trapped by the spell cast on her, but Adam seemed happy enough. Though there were times that I saw a sadness in his eyes. He knew he didn't belong. But perhaps the spell placed on him had been stronger than Eve's.

That was it! A spell!

Despite her intentions, Eve continued to be useful.

Focusing the remains of my magic, I spoke aloud to my creation:

Creature of Earth
Animal of the forest
I bid you to change and bend to my will
You will imitate one that was before you
A child of The First Woman
Verbena

I poured my thoughts and memories of Verbena into this last burst of energy so the creation could come to be—a changeling. This imitator would become what was Verbena, at least some of her. There was no way to give her the real girl's memories, but that's what I had wanted from the beginning, for Verbena to forget.

I collapsed on the ground and slept.

I roused with a start. The sun was rising and heated the chilled ground, where I lay shivering. *The magic weakened my body.* I would have to keep that in mind for the future. I forced myself into a sitting position and realized that I was not alone. The doe rested near me, or rather, Verbena did.

I took the time to scrutinize my work. Her red waves moved gently with the breeze, which brought her scent to me. It smelled exactly like the child. I looked for any sign of a flaw—I saw none. There was no tail or elongated ears or anything that would betray her as an animal. But I had yet to see her eyes. I thought of Eve's thin pupils and unnatural amber irises. Yes, there could be a problem.

With stiff muscles, I rose and stood above the sleeping imitator. I nudged her with my foot, and that's all it took to startle her awake. Her eyes shot open to reveal the earthy brown color of Adam, though her pupils were a little larger than they were supposed to be. After deliberating a moment, I decided it wasn't worth the trouble to try and change them. It could be blamed on her head injury and coincide with her memory loss.

"Speak," I demanded.

"What would you like me to say?" Verbena asked.

My mind blossomed. Handing her the furs I'd taken from the true Verbena, I replied, "I can tell you exactly what to say."

The next few hours, I worked with Verbena and told her about her life. Verbena was crossing the river when she slipped and hit her head. She woke with no memory, but still had the knowledge to get home. Of course, that was just for the sake of her family. My instructions were far more intricate. The changeling would report to me every six months. She would tell me how many children were born, any new knowledge the family learned about the world, and *her* state of mind. This time, I made sure to leave only a minor wound upon the new Verbena's head, just to quell any suspicions.

This couldn't have worked out better for me. It was impossible to hide my scent from Adam, so my visits were dwindling. I needed someone to infiltrate *her* family. This changeling was perfect. However, her submissive spirit worried me. Surely The First Woman would notice such a change in her child?

No. She wouldn't. I may not have visited her as often as I liked, but I saw from the few times I had that she looked away from her children as much as she could, unable to accept them; Verbena had said as much. *She* knew her children were not meant to be. She knew she would come back to me.

It was only a matter of time.

I entered the clearing to the waterfall confidently. The past several days had shown me what I was truly capable of, and there was only more to discover. But my stomach and soul cried for sustenance. I passed by the charred remains of my first son, the fire long dead.

"Father," a voice said from the behind the falls.

"Seth?"

"Yes. You've been gone a long while. Where have you been?"

My happy mood dissipated the more I spoke with my son. "That is no concern of yours."

"Of course, Father. Have you seen Mother?" The boy refused to come out from behind the falls, and his voice sounded strange. Perhaps it was just his age; the timber of it sounded rough.

"Your mother has gone. She will not be returning," I said numbly.

"I see."

"Come out from behind the falls. I never taught you to behave in such a way. When you speak to me, it will be face to face." I heard a rustle in the brush.

"I'm sorry, Father. But I'm weak. I was injured after you left." The forest was quiet, except for the rapid beating of several hearts. The sources of the heartbeats were nowhere to be seen.

"What happened?" I gave away none of the suspicions I felt, keeping my voice even.

"It's a long story. Could you help me swim across, Father?"

"Of course, Son." Placing my spear in the ground, I stepped into the familiar water. I treaded until it became too deep, and I had to swim across the pond to the falls.

As soon as I passed the wall of freezing water, I was forced beneath the surface. Something solid hit my head, and several hands pulled me under as well as pushed me down. I was pinned to the bottom of the pond. I could feel the recovering plant life tangle around my limbs and rocks dig into my stomach and chest. I couldn't feel my head anymore, but the gritty blood-colored sand was floating into my eyes, seeping from the deep opening in my skull. I closed them and felt the granules rub against my pupils. More weight was added to me. My children were burying me with rocks, and others were just beating me with them. Something sharp pierced my spine.

Everything went black.

I woke to intense pain. My eyes opened only to be scratched by sand. I breathed in and found no air. I twisted in the water, but I was buried underneath rock and debris. The pain increased as I moved. *I needed air.*

I let out a groan as I lifted myself, and the weight tumbled down to the pond floor. I swam for the surface, and when I broke it the night air bit my skin. I shuddered, releasing the water trapped in my chest. The crisp air only added to the raw pain as I breathed in an out. Swimming for shore, I realized why the pain in my back still lingered. I dragged myself up and over the mossy bank and reached for my spine. In my lower back rested the head of my spear, the dragon's fang. The wooden stem attached to it had been broken in half and now floated in the pond.

With a grunt I removed the beloved weapon from my spine. I lay there, with the shaped bone in my hand, and waited for my body to recover. *How many days had I been under water?* My spine snapped into place, muscles were regrown and connected, and red sand filled my veins once again. But fury was what made me stand.

I lifted my nose to find the traitorous children. Except there was no wind, it was still and silent, as if it was afraid. I felt for the air, this was harder than the other elements. Air had the lightest shade of spirit, so pale I couldn't see it. But I could feel it. By the time I learned how to grasp it, I was able to create a gentle breeze. That was enough.

My children were headed south. They were going to *her*.

I followed their fading scent. There were many emotions mixed with their hybrid odor. Fear, sadness, but most of all relief. *They thought I was dead.* I was only too glad to surprise them.

Though I was weak and needed nourishment, I coerced the wind to carry me as I ran. Three days passed, but it was the fastest I had ever gone, I nearly floated in between strides. It took weeks to travel between the two lands, but no longer. I passed by a horse on the way. The sunlight shone down through the canopy at the perfect angle and reflected against its horns. The glint of them drew me toward the creature. It had no time to react due to my increased speed. I was starving for what the meat and spirit could give, but I continued down my original path instead.

It didn't take much longer to find the runaway warriors. Their pace was surprisingly slow; more evidence they thought I was no longer able to hurt them. My fury dimmed upon seeing the children in the distance. To survive, my missing heart grew cold and hard. *They killed me.*

It was time for a different approach.

I went deep underground. Though I couldn't see, I could feel the vibrations of those above. I also found that I could sense their spirits. *They were light and joyful.* I felt a sharp twinge in my empty chest. The soil moved my body where it wanted to be. I reached upward and grabbed hold of a limb mid-step.

I heard a scream, but I pulled him down anyway. My fourth son, Jacob was soon buried alive. He was not strong enough to dig his way out of the heavy, damp soil. I moved positions and went for another limb, though this one was prepared—Seth.

"Father! Why are you doing this?" My son knew what creature came to collect their souls.

I answered by pulling another one of my sons underground. His lungs quickly filled with soil and ceased movement. I repeated this until I had buried four of my own male warriors, and there was nothing but sobbing above ground. That was when I revealed myself. The soil shifted and made space for me to exit. *I could see why Cainadra had loved to manipulate earth.*

"Kneel," I commanded, thorns and roots falling from me, "or you will join your brothers." Some of the females had climbed into the trees to avoid being taken. The males had not been quick enough to realize that their sisters were not the targets. The moist earth clung to my skin, but I felt oddly comforted by the mask I now wore.

Seth stood tall despite having to hold his injured brother upright; I had tried to take the boy down, but he fought me, and his leg had been broken. I noticed a slight tremble in Seth's hands. Breathing hard, my rebellious son replied, "No."

"Anyone else want to challenge me?" I asked, meeting the eyes of my ungrateful warriors. These twisted, unnatural creatures had both spirit manipulation and hearts—both power and life. Yet they squandered it. Too weak to rise to their potential. Not that I would let them.

There were a few who stood, and it was clear they were afraid. But soon those who kneeled were able to convince the rebels to join them on the ground where they belonged. I made sure to remember which ones kneeled first and which ones had to be convinced.

Seth remained, releasing his injured sibling.

"You killed our brothers and sister. You killed our mother. You are nothing but a monster. I will *never* follow you." Seth took one glance at his siblings. *A last farewell.*

"So be it."

Seth inhaled one last time, unable to exhale due to the spearhead that now rested in his heart. It only took one movement to throw that piece of bone across the gap between us and into his flesh. My son staggered and fell. His heart no longer beat, and I kept my gaze on it. I willed the dragon's fang back into my hand, and blood spilled out from the fatal wound and onto the forest floor. My face was numb, though I knew I was smiling because of the horrified expressions on my warriors' faces. I barely registered Seth's soul as it was confined to its immortal cage.

"Come," I instructed.

I waited for the remainder of my damaged warriors to start walking home before I lit Seth's corpse ablaze. Though I craved life, I could not make myself consume the warrior's heart—my descendant's lives weren't what I sought. My gaze turned from the melting flesh to look south. I could hear the river's falls emptying into the lake and smelled the sweet night flower aroma I desired.

I walked north without another glance at my smoldering son.

XV

Humble

Those who should rule do not wish to rule.
-C

500 Years Gone

Sunset, indigo, scarlet, emerald, and sapphire colors swam lazily in the pond water. Predators and prey. I stared at them, amazed. *Life always found a way. No matter how many times it was snuffed.*

I clutched my own chest out of habit and felt no such life emanating from it. But soon, I would have it. I'm coming for you, *Lilith.* There was no need to fight against it any longer. I let the name fill me with power.

"Asher, report," I said to my son as he strode past.

Asher immediately stopped. "We will be ready by the next sunrise, Father."

"Good." With that, my son continued with his task.

Almost there.

I had spent the last five hundred years building my army. Not only would they wipe out Lilith's small group of children, but the planet as well. Earth would take longer to destroy, but it would happen. My children were taught to take. To indulge in what nature had to offer, and with their succubus dispositions, it wouldn't be too long.

I observed one of my other sons, Alon, as he carried in his fresh kill. The sunset-orange spirit absorbed into his bronze one. He didn't even have to try. The buck's spirit was snipped and separated from the natural world and was now a part of the unnatural one. *The human world.*

I smiled.

I was happy knowing that I had done this. I had *created* this. Even if it was meant to end everything, it was beautiful. *Lilith and I would be together.* We were immortal. The only things that could kill us were each other—we couldn't end our own existence if we tried. If I was to truly die, it would have to be at the hands of Lilith.

At the far part of the clearing, a circle of men gathered. Two were in the center. They held no weapons, but of course, my children had trained their bodies to be weapons. The two men stalked one another. One had already been bloodied. His nose sat crooked above his lips and a bruise was forming along the jaw. The lion fur he wore had fallen from him during the struggle. The one who'd damaged him lunged again, seeing how his rival stood unbalanced. *Strike while your opponent was weak.* That was what I had taught my children—my warriors.

I watched the dominant warrior beat my weakened son until he could no longer stand. The men who watched cheered for the triumph of their brother and dragged the one who lost out of the fighting circle and threw him in the thicket.

My descendant's spirits were even more aggressive than their physical forms. Souls of every color attempted to take from their neighbor. Sometimes this would reduce the submissive hybrid to illness. For them, it was a natural instinct to take from one another, as well as the natural world. And they couldn't even see what they were doing.

Even if they all had the *sight*, it wouldn't matter.

Hybrids would always take.

The tamed mammoths fidgeted in the trees. They were restless. The paths we created for them were nearly perfect now. Three hundred years was long enough to flatten the terrain so they could pass easily across the land I ruled over. They only had one more stop. I could see from their dancing spirits that they were just as excited as me for the next venture.

I jumped to the top of the falls where my tent resided, along with my weapons. I sat and dangled my feet over the edge as I mended my overused spear. I still used the dragon fang from long ago. Though it had dwindled in size from sharpening it over and over, I wasn't ready to let go of it yet. It was from my first dragon kill. And despite her intense aversion to killing, Lilith had kept the knife I created for her, the weapon that held the other half of the bone. Deep down, she loved that I killed for her.

Over the years, I had changelings report to me from her ranks. At least once a generation I would catch her offspring exploring too far north for my liking. So, I would replace them with my own creations; ones that would follow my commands, just as Verbena did. But I did visit from time to time, just so I could see *her* face. I knew it wasn't wise. I couldn't risk her discovering my plans. Still, I couldn't resist.

From what the changelings reported, Lilith was all too keen on keeping to her restricted existence. Her children weren't allowed to hunt, build, or create. If they did, then Earth's spirit would be harmed. But I knew she could see the dwindling spirit of the world, despite her efforts. She knew my family had grown.

Why didn't she approach me?

Perhaps she wanted me to save her from the existence she hated, yet was too proud to leave. *Yes, I would save her from herself.*

The females on my land gathered medicinal and edible greenery and assisted in building the homes for us. But the most vital role they had was this: Birth children. Guide them in the world that I shaped. Teach them what their purpose was and follow it exactly, for if they didn't, they would be without purpose. And no one wanted that. I heard the whispers among both women and men of those who lacked purpose—they disappeared.

I chuckled. Fear was a useful weapon.

A toddler ran along the pond's edge. The small creature flailed its arms and laughed as if it hadn't a care in the world. I found myself envious. *I never had a chance to be a child—to be happy.*

The child slipped on the damp grass and tumbled into the freezing water below. The splash was quiet and went unnoticed by the rest. Only I saw the child fight to swim. Only I felt the distress from the creature as its tiny lungs begged for air.

Only when the small arms and legs slowed, and its heartbeat calmed, did I will the pond to rise and deposit the careless being onto the grass. The toddler coughed, and when it had expelled everything it could, it began to wail. Finally, one of the mothers, loading the mammoths with supplies, heard its cries and ran to the child.

She cradled the distressed being in her arms and looked up at my placement above her. The mother bowed her head in acknowledgment, but she couldn't mask her fear. She took the traumatized toddler to one of the tents to rest.

Moving my attention elsewhere, I watched the warriors prepare for travel. I reveled at the sheer number I had. It was easy to make my family cooperate after the initial cleansing of rebels. Cainadra, Abel, Seth, and many others had challenged me, so they were eliminated. Despite this setback, my family had taken over the entirety of the land. Lilith was nothing but a mere speck on the terrain. An easy win.

Yet, I felt unnerved. Logically, I knew this was going to go my way, but something in my chest taunted me, as if sand was scraping against my missing heart. *Against the emptiness.*

"Father," a soft voice said. I turned my gaze to the left, and in the tree line stood one of my daughters. She held a circular creation, woven together with branches, vines, and sunflowers. It was thick enough that two small horns were tied to each side.

Asher approached the girl, smiling. Beside her, he turned to face the clearing. "Brothers and sisters, gather around." My children didn't hesitate, Asher being second in command. The women carried the younglings in their arms, the men stopped fighting, even the mammoths seemed to calm, curious to see what my son had planned. I was curious myself.

Looking to me for approval, I nodded, and Asher said, "Today, we leave to a new part of the land. A part of the land with others like us. But they are weak, and it is our responsibility to rid our land of weakness. And we will prevail for one reason." He paused and glanced in my direction. "Our father has given us life, a home, and a purpose. To follow him, is to follow the sun itself." Asher nudged his young sister in my direction. I leapt down from my perch on the falls, landing softly beside her on the grass. Asher continued, "We thank our father, God of the forest, of the hunt, of fertility, of life." Surprised by this show of submission, I kneeled, and allowed the young girl to place the crown atop my head. I expected the thorns to pierce my skin, but she had masterfully crafted it, so the inside was as smooth as the clear sky above. "Thank you," she whispered in my ear. Her name came to me then, Aine.

I granted her a slight smile and stood to say, "All of you are necessary for the world I am building. With your help, we can change Earth, a land without purpose, into a thriving home for our kind. Create and expand my children. Follow my guidance, and you will soon live in a land full of wonder and magic."

Aine placed her head on the ground before me, Asher followed, then one by one, my descendants bowed to worship their God and Creator. I smiled, thinking of the potential. I wasn't the one who created the word *God*. It wasn't in my vocabulary, yet somehow my children managed to create something I never could.

Earth would feed these hybrids until it had nothing left to give.

Satisfied, I said, "Rise. I will leave now to prepare. Follow me when the sun has risen over the mountain." The people returned to their tasks, excited for the change to come.

Spear in hand, I disappeared. The wind carried me past the tents, warriors, mammoths, and trees, even past the quiet sniffles of the nearly-drowned infant. My power had only grown, and I basked in the elation I felt when I used it.

I was sure to avoid the meadow with the white tree. I only relived unpleasant memories in its presence, and the fact that I couldn't harm it made me feel something I didn't want to—fear.

I barely felt the ground between my long strides; the weight that plagued me was no longer an obstacle. The smell of the upturned earth caressed my nose. The sky was growing dark, but I made myself enjoy the journey anyway.

The warriors would take at least a week to reach Lilith's home; they had been rigorously trained. They would run or ride. For me, with my already superior pace and additional assistance from the wind, it was merely until the sun rose over the mountains again. I wanted to spend these last few days alone with Lilith and her children.

I would free her from her abominations. She didn't have to ask.

The horned crown tangled in my gold hair, and I couldn't help but feel a warmth blossom in my chest when it shifted. Just as Lilith was The Queen, I was The King.

XVI

Execute

An empty chest craves to fill its hollow void,
even if that means emptying another's.

-A

The days passed slowly. I watched and waited for my forces to arrive. *It would be any moment now.* I sauntered toward Lilith's current dwelling; a place kept far from her children's village. It was a small shelter made from bamboo, moss, and mud. The roof was lined with flowers of every variety, and the pear tree that protected the shelter was greatly cared for, though I didn't think it needed extra caring; nature had a way of providing for itself. The sun slowly faded between the dense trees of the forest.

I walked into their sad hovel and took a deep breath. I was expecting it to smell of Lilith's night pollen, but all I inhaled was Adam's wet-earth smell—his animal smell—and despair. I coughed after inhaling the strong odor. I went to the corner of the hut and picked up a patch of withered white fur. Realizing what it was, I opened the small bag. There, rested remnants of some red petals and golden hair.

I lifted the gold strands to my nose and pulled away smiling. *It was mine.* I placed the strands back into the ancient rabbit skin and laid it gently in the corner next to the dragon-bone knife I had carved for her. I turned and felt the bedding along the cold ground. A jaguar's fur. I knew from my changelings' reports that the furs came from animals that died by the will of their own natural family or old age. Despite this, it was promising that she wanted the furs at all.

Lilith wanted freedom.

My mood was joyful, but I couldn't ignore the stench of despair anymore. The last light from the sunset abandoned me, plunging the small space into darkness.

I stepped out of the entrance and willed the breeze to me. *Adam.* Without meaning to, the air around me grew hot, and the herbs that Lilith cared for singed from my close proximity. I reached the opposite tree line just as Adam stepped into sight.

The despair from the tent made sense to me then. Adam looked as if he embodied the entire emotion unto himself. His eyes and cheekbones were sunken, wrinkles plagued his face, and his dark gold hair hung limply on his shoulders. The streaks of white hair that colored his strands were bright. I was strangely curious of such features.

Lilith appeared beside him. Not a day of our long existence beset her beautiful face. But her eyes were tired. She reached for her lover's hand, and when he turned to look at her, his face lit up with joy. It was as if the age and suffering he endured disappeared for that one moment, and he was happy again.

Lilith let go of Adam's hand, and his face returned to what it was. *He was pretending to be happy for her.* Adam wanted freedom, too, but the type of freedom he wanted wasn't going to be with Lilith. Because she couldn't go where he could.

"What happened to my herbs?" Lilith interrupted my musing with her enchanting voice.

Adam crouched to inspect them. "Looks like they got too much sun."

Confused, Lilith said, "I'm going to find more to replace them. I'll be back soon." Lilith leaned over and kissed Adam's withered cheek, then disappeared into the darkness of the forest.

I only stayed long enough to watch Adam limp into the hut and collapse onto his bedding. The heavy thump of his heart was prominent against the quiet woodland. His body couldn't hold any more spirits. The fact that Lilith's children had enough control of their souls to share them with their ancestor and extend his life was unnerving. *Another reason to remove them.*

I didn't have to do anything about Adam. Nature would take care of itself.

The ground began to shake. The heavy steps of mammoths were disturbing the soil. *It was time.* Careful of Lilith's location, I leapt from tree to tree. The darkness was suffocating and heavy. I moved as quickly as I could through the thick blanket of black, wishing the sun a swift return. I returned to the spot where I hid the crown. I placed the symbol upon my head; it was just as comfortable as before.

I found my warriors easily. The mammoths had traveled to the end of their paths, and the men were setting up camp to rest for the night. The women were left behind of course. They were too important to lose in battle. I needed them creating children and training them for my empire.

"Father," Asher greeted.

"You traveled fast. I hope you aren't too tired for the morning?"

"Of course not, Father. A few hours of rest and we will be battle ready."

I smiled.

The sun rose as it always did. I raised my face to the warmth it provided, just enjoying the peace I felt upon its touch. I waited for the sounds of the forest to fill my ears, but there was only silence. That was happening more often as the years passed. As if the forest didn't want me to hear it.

"On your command, Father," Asher said as he approached, though he kept his distance.

Letting out a breath I didn't know I held, I said, "It's time." That was all Asher needed to start shouting commands to his brothers. Instinctually grabbing my spear, I led the path my army would take. The mammoths would clear the way and announce our arrival, but it would be too late to stop us anyway. Lilith was in her hut with the decaying Adam. Though if she was nearby, Asher knew what to do.

I forced my speed to slow so Asher could see the path he needed to follow. The well-trained mammoths ran after me with warriors on their backs as well as their flanks. My sons were equipped with spears and bow and arrows. Unlike Lilith, we were busy creating these past five hundred years. The heavy wool of the mighty creatures wafted to me as the wind carried us forward. Trees cracked and moaned as they fell in our wake. The yellow leaves of the changing season swarmed us. It was beautiful. Only when hybrids were born did the planet have to start hibernating for half the year just to keep up with our demand. Soon, snow would fall.

I saw the edge of the river where the falls tumbled down. I heard two distinct splashes in the water below it. I paused and let Asher take the lead into the feeble village. At ease, I sauntered forward where I could watch at the edge of the river. I would let my creations do the work for me.

But no one was there. *Where did Lilith's children disappear to?*

I knew as soon as I saw her. Lilith challenged Asher's mammoth and climbed up its front, only to find my son controlling the beast. I enjoyed the look of shock on her face when she realized who it was. Her red hair blew angrily as the mammoth tried to relieve her of her position, but she didn't even notice. Then Asher took control of the situation. He knocked her off his mammoth and let it crush her.

I cringed, knowing the pain she was in, but it was the only way. I needed her weakened if I was to kill her children. She would stop at nothing to defend them, despite the deep-seated regret for them.

I leapt from the falls' edge and landed in the field that lay below. I proceeded to walk across the chilled grass to Lilith. Asher abandoned his seat on the mammoth and met me beside the crushed body of my beloved. "Is she dead?" Asher asked. Though he knew the answer, it was hard for a mortal to understand the concept.

"No. She will wake again." I paused to look at Lilith's face. It was as if she was sleeping, but the agony she endured was intense. I rejoiced at the thought. I may have loved her, but knowing that she was being punished as I had was satisfying. "Just throw her in the lake. That will keep her down for a time."

I gently lifted Lilith's shoulders while Asher attempted to carry what was left of her legs. I could have carried her myself, but Asher was in need of approval. He wanted to help me in my quest. So, I gave him his moments. Reward and punishment. That was the best way to train hybrids.

Reaching the lake's edge, I said, "All right, toss her."

Lilith slowly sank beneath the surface. Her beautiful ivory skin was bright against the darkness of the water, like the moon against the obsidian sky. Her scarlet curls were the last thing I saw before she descended to the lake's floor.

She didn't need to see what came next.

"Follow them. They went south." I lifted my nose to the air. "The monkey is with them, but he is no threat. Leave him to me. Kill the rest."

"The women as well, Father? Should we waste the resource?"

I smiled. He was indeed my son. "Take only the young ones. The rest are too old to change their ways." Also, I couldn't have Lilith noticing her absent children. I couldn't take too many, but with the chaos ensuing, she wouldn't notice a few young girls missing from the corpses.

Asher nodded once and climbed up his massive ride to lead the rest of the warriors through the trees. The mammoths could not fit in the small clearing, so the housing was reduced to rubble under their footsteps. Even the animals that clung to Lilith's children had fled in fear.

So much for loyalty. But what could one expect from animals?

I went to the tree that rested in the center of the clearing, its green leaves rustling. It had managed to survive the tromping of the beasts and stand tall. The apples hanging from the strong branches were ripe and deep scarlet. I looked to the roots below and felt the ever-growing life and how it fed from the deceased buried below. One of the vines shifted in the crown on my head, and a thorn pierced my skin. Then the tree's roots were on fire. The azure flames licked the trunk, the branches, the leaves, and the apples until they were nothing, and the tree was a blackened husk.

It was the end of Lilith's era.

I came upon the last moments of battle if it could be called such a thing. I knew Lilith had never taught her children to fight, but I would have thought some instinctual need to protect themselves would have surfaced. There was none.

Lilith's children lay strewn across the forest floor, embedded in the moss and soil due to the trampling mammoths. Some evaded the beasts but were struck down by spears and arrows. Blood was the prominent aroma in the woodland now. It had soaked into the natural life and nourished it so.

"No!" The guttural sound of pain in the voice that called out made me cringe. There was a lone survivor amongst the dead. *Adam.* The grieving man's eyes found me then. "You! Why did you do this?" Adam wailed. My sons restrained the monkey before he could attack. I gave the signal to release him, and Adam did as I expected. The man punched and beat on me, but he could not harm me. *I was too powerful.* From what I could tell, Adam grew weaker by the moment. The death of his descendants was the last fatal blow to his unnatural life.

The man's strikes slowed until he had to hold onto me to stay upright, his head hanging. "What have you done to Lilith?"

It was unlike me, but I felt pity, almost respect for Lilith's creation. He had fought well, even knowing he was weak. That counted for something. My sons had obeyed my order and not killed him, but he was badly beaten. "Lilith is unharmed. She will be with you soon enough."

Adam raised his eyes to mine and asked, "Why?" A tear streaked down his face, though it disappeared quickly onto the blood-soaked ground. No birds sounded in the canopy. Even the rodents beneath our feet had stopped scuttling.

"You're a smart man. I'm sure you can come to your own conclusion." I gently laid him beside one of his lost sons, a spear protruding from the child's stomach. "Asher, did you collect the items we wanted?"

Discreetly, my son nodded. They had grabbed the young females while Adam was distracted. There was no chance of Lilith knowing.

Perhaps I could gift them to her once she returned to me.

Satisfied, I commanded, "We are done here. Leave us."

The sound of the mammoth's heavy steps departing echoed against the trees, and the wood moaned sorrowfully. I turned to Adam. His spirit was fading; the myriad of colors that shared his body needed something stronger to hold them. They needed an immortal. Natural beings were not meant to take without giving something in return. If their world became unbalanced, everything was thrown into chaos. *An unfortunate disposition.*

"This is goodbye, Adam." It was the first time I had said his name aloud.

Before the wind could rush me away, Adam said, "She will never be with you. Not after this."

Instinctually, I responded, "Our love is strong. She will forgive me as I will her." I said it more for myself than I did the monkey. *Why was I doubting myself now?*

Adam glanced to the crumbling crown that rested on my head. "No. She won't. If you think different, then you're more delusional than I thought."

"Our love is not an illusion!" My hands balled into fists, and the air was biting cold.

"Don't you realize? It's not love. It's obsession." He paused and waited for me to meet his stare. "You are obsessed with her, Lucifer. True love demands nothing. It gives without worry of consequence and without expectation. All *you* do is take and destroy." Adam's heart was beating hard and fast. He squeezed his eyes shut and held his chest. "Let her go. It's the only way either of you will be happy."

Numbly, I replied, "It sounds like you need to follow your own advice." I left Adam to die and waited patiently for the prize I'd been fighting for all these years.

XVII

Children

Obsession is easily mistaken as love,
at least for those who are obsessed.

-A

It was well into midday when I heard her delicate footsteps running toward me. *I knew she would follow the trail I left for her.* I removed the crown and placed it gently on the soft moss beside my spear, the horns falling from the circlet. Lilith's usual sure and steady run was now confused and hurried. I even heard the snapping of branches. She was desperate to find her family.

I took a step, and my beloved stopped in her tracks. "Lilith," I whispered. It felt wonderful to say her name—the name I had given her.

"Who's there?" she called out.

"Have you forgotten the sound of my voice already? That's disappointing."

"Lucifer. Why do you hide? Come out and talk to me." Lilith's voice shook as she demanded this.

I laughed. "Of course, *my love*." I couldn't help but be spiteful after what she had put me through. "My love" was what that monkey-abomination called her. But she was mine. I stepped out from my hiding place in the thicket.

"Why are you here? Where are my children? Where is Adam?" Her breathing was harsh. I wondered what she had done to escape the water prison; her skin was brand new.

"I guess you don't feel like catching up. I thought you would be happy to see me after all this time." Though her lack of excitement put a damper on my happy mood, I couldn't let it show. Her test was still to come.

"Catch up? If you wanted to talk to me all you had to do was ask! You didn't have to destroy my village and harass my children!" Lilith's soul flailed in anger, barely able to contain itself.

Seeing her soul's strength, I had to mask a surprised expression. And she hadn't yet realized what truly happened. "Oh, right, your children. How did that go? I remember you being so adamant against having *my* children, because it would harm the 'Earth's spirit.' Yet, you ran off and had children with—what was he before? A monkey?"

Lilith gasped.

Did she not realize how long I had been watching her? "The tail gave it away." I knew I was smiling, but my face felt numb. *Soon, I would know the truth.*

"Where is he?" she whispered. Her will was fading. Perhaps this was going to be easier than I thought. A tear bled from Lilith's eye, and I immediately removed it with my flame. It dissipated in a minuscule cloud of steam. *There would be no tears for Adam.*

Seeing her confusion, I said, "I never liked seeing you cry." I paused to let the knowledge sink in. "You're not the only one who commands the energy anymore. You should have stayed around longer."

"How? Did—"

I stopped her there, impatience ruling my response. "You did. The punishment you gave me for loving you is what did this to me." If I had a heart, it would have been pounding. Lilith had no idea how much she hurt me when she left, but I was going to make her feel it. "Knowing it was what you spoke of before, I began to experiment and found that I could do a lot with the light I saw." I remembered the first time I felt the power coursing through me; when I tried to burn the white tree and failed. But I forced a confident smile anyway.

"Then you see that the light wanes when you take life from it. Have you changed your ways?" Lilith asked.

I could see the hope in her eyes, and I relished the sight of it fleeing as I said, "Not even for a moment."

"Why? Do you not care what happens to your home? To my home?"

I couldn't say that I did. There was only *her* in my thoughts. Only one goal to achieve. "As I said before, I will not live by the rules you invented. There is no way of knowing if the light diminishing is a bad thing, and I honestly don't care if it is. I have lived a long life, and if my time ends with the light, then so be it." I made sure I didn't stutter over the word *life*. The most important test was coming, and I found myself dreading it. *What if she didn't pass my test?*

"What of your children? You may want death, but don't take them and everything with you. You're being selfish and monstrous." She blew out an angry breath the same time I did. "How could you?"

My careful control was lost. "How could *I*? How could *you*? *You* are the one who left me. *You* are the one who chose a life with an animal over me. *You* are the one who created these mutated children. And look at you now. Did it bring you happiness? Did you finally find what you were looking for?" I took a step toward my beloved, silently pleading with her to understand. "No, perhaps not. You don't even live among them anymore. Did you outgrow them like you did me? Did you discard them like you did me?"

Lilith fell to her knees; her spirit was weak and brittle.

Good.

Still, she managed to say, "You should realize that I left because I didn't want to create more of us. I thought that if we mated with ones who were part of the natural world, our children would be part of the light you see now, connected to it like the rest of the world is." Lilith tightened her small fists in frustration. "Clearly, I was wrong, but I didn't leave because I outgrew you, or I didn't love you. Leaving you was the hardest thing I ever had to do."

I sucked in a breath. *I was right. She regretted leaving me.* I suppressed a genuine smile.

Lilith continued, "You wouldn't change your ways, and if we had children you would have taught them wrong. Without your interference, I was able to guide my children to live the right way, despite the fact that they turned our worse than either of us." On the verge of tears, she asked, "Did Eve bring you any happiness? Any at all?"

I hadn't expected that question. *How could she think Eve would have replaced her? No one ever could.* My anger returned. *Time to finish this.* Avoiding her last question, I said, "Our children *are* worse than you hoped, but no worse than you. You brought this upon yourself, Lilith. There is no one to blame but you." I composed myself and continued to push her. "I will continue to suck the life from this planet, Lilith. There is nothing you can do to stop me. I have been busy these last five hundred years. My numbers are far greater than yours, and they have already spread across the entire land. You were our last stop, and I have accomplished what I came for."

"And what did you come for?" she asked.

"To see you in pain." I answered honestly, but there was more to it than those few simple words. I thought it would have made me feel happier knowing she suffered as I did, but it didn't. Perhaps it was not enough pain. "You hurt me, Lilith. No matter the reason, you still chose to leave me, and I will never forgive you for that." I turned to leave her and added, "Oh, and I couldn't have your children interfering. So, I got rid of them." *This was the ultimate test. Did she love me enough to let me exist?*

I heard a branch being wrenched from its home and the light footsteps of my beloved as she came to kill me. I turned just in time for the branch's end to pierce my empty chest, but it was nothing but a prick. I waited, noticing she no longer had the white scar on her forearm. The one I had given her so long ago.

Watching her inward turmoil, I said, "What are you waiting for? Do it. I took over this land to bleed it dry, and I killed your children. End me." For a moment, I thought she was going to, and I panicked. But I couldn't reveal how I felt. *I needed to know.* I gripped the rabbit-bone blade tight beneath my furs, waiting for her decision.

Lilith's spirit engulfed my golden light. All I could see was red, and the pure power disturbed me. "Why do you hesitate? Do I need to finish off your precious Adam as well before you will kill me? You are weak. I can't believe I ever loved you." I swatted the branch out of her hands, relieved to see that she didn't fight me. I watched as her crimson spirit calmed, and I let out a silent, relieved breath, releasing my hold on the hidden dagger.

Lilith recovered quickly from the murderous rage and asked, "Where is he?"

I was confused, but answered, "Mourning over your lost succubus children, I assume." Without another glance in my direction, she left to follow the mammoth's trail where she would find her grieving lover and dead descendants.

I wandered the forest at the pace of a mortal, the spear and crown in my possession once again. This part of the land was unfamiliar to me, but the mammoth's heady scent was easy to follow as well as their obvious trampled trail. The night flowers were blooming as I passed by. Their petals stretched toward me, begging for mercy. I ignored the pull I had toward such life.

I would give Lilith time to grieve and say goodbye to her lover. But ultimately, she would be relieved and grateful for the freedom she now had.

She would find me.

This was what I had been working toward, yet I felt strangely empty. Confused. *Weak.* There was a moment, however brief, when I thought I was going to die. The look in Lilith's eyes as she pressed the branch's tip against my missing heart... If I hadn't forced the branch out her hands, would she have done it?

No. She gave up the fight too easily for that to be true. I would just have to wait and see how she felt after seeing the corpses for herself.

But I was not dying alone.

Recalling the carnage, I had to admit, my children were ruthless. Not a single person they wanted dead survived. Small children were impaled as though they were the mightiest of foes. *I had created bloodthirsty creatures.*

I looked upward and searched for the white light that shone in the night, but a dread took over. One I hadn't felt in centuries. A blood moon stared back at me.

I quickly found my warriors, despite the dark sky and even darker forest. Sounds of a struggle, and a woman's whimpering was loud in the quiet woodland.

I strode over to a huddled group in the dense thicket. "What is this about?" I questioned, shifting the crown discreetly, as the thorns were coming undone.

Three sons of mine looked up from their place above a young woman. Two held her down while one placed himself above her. The woman looked up at me, pleading for help with her eyes. My son had a hand over her mouth to keep her silent.

They disobeyed my orders and took more than just children—they had taken women. Such greedy creations.

"This one would not cooperate. She needs to be taught the order of things." Aedan explained. I could not remember how many generations removed we were from each other or if he was my direct child. I tried not to pay too much attention, but I found myself curious anyway.

"You know each woman is assigned for a delegated period of time. You have no claim to her." I looked to the two men who restrained her. "None of you do."

Aedan stood and asked, "Father, did we not accomplish what we came for? Did we not please you?"

Considering, I said, "All of you did very well."

"Then don't we deserve a reward?" Aedan bowed his head in submission when he saw my irritated expression.

How did I handle this? I couldn't have my children running wild and disobeying me. I couldn't show weakness. But I did find decent results when rewarding and punishing accordingly. They wouldn't want to fight for me if I punished them afterward. Perhaps giving my warriors this allowance would quench their appetite for rebellion. *And I would be the one giving it to them.*

"Very well, but don't damage her. You know the importance of women." I turned to leave my sons to their task.

Upon my words, the young woman started fighting, desperate to be freed. She even managed to kick Aedan aside and pull away from the ones who trapped her, leaving them with bruised faces and egos. "Leave me be savages!" She ran deeper into the forest, not looking back at the men she'd left bloodied.

Shocked, my sons looked to me for guidance. At this, I laughed aloud. I laughed for so long that tears seeped from my eyes. I hadn't laughed in so many years. The feeling was almost foreign. "Be glad the enemy you fought today had no weapons or creatures to ride on, because clearly you are incapable of handling such encounters." I laughed some more. "If a mere young girl can defeat you, then how can you call yourself warriors, let alone men?"

I left my incompetent children to lick their wounds and went after the girl. She wasn't hard to find; her breathing alone woke the sleeping forest. I caught her by the arm and swung her around to face me. It was the first time I'd really looked at the hybrid. I had become accustomed to disregarding their faces and spirits, but now that I took the time, I could see Lilith in this young woman. Her face was a near replica: rounded in shape, a straight and delicate nose, shapely lips, and finally, the piercing emerald eyes. Though, the girl was quite a bit shorter and had dark golden locks, which belonged to Adam. But her hair was just as wild and untamed as *hers*.

"I thought Lilith's children had the fight bred out of them. But you are proof that there is still some of Lilith's rage coursing through her children's veins."

With a surprisingly strong voice, she said, "Who's Lilith? What do you want from me?"

Ah, yes. Lilith had removed herself from their lives a few centuries ago. They had no idea where they came from. "I want you to go back to camp, like the obedient woman you were meant to be. Explain to your sisters that if they don't cooperate, their fate will be the same as yours."

"And what is my fate?" The child pulled but found no give in my strong grip.

"It's your choice. You can keep fighting me, and I will allow my sons to have you, or you can listen and return to your sisters unharmed and tell them that my sons accomplished their task." I pulled her close. "Either way, you're going to be telling the same story." The defiant look in this woman's eye brought a smile to my lips. It reminded me of Lilith. *I missed her so much.*

Realizing this girl wasn't going to take my generous offer, I prompted, "Fight me, and you are violated and killed. I won't be able to quench my sons' thirst for it afterward. So, before you make a decision, consider what fate has planned for your sisters after you're gone."

At this, she stilled. However, she took more time to deliberate than I expected from a kind, selfless child of Lilith. "Fine." She yanked her arm back, and I released it willingly.

"Smart choice."

I escorted the feisty young woman to her tent and sisters, staying only long enough to hear her relay the message I wanted. *Fear would keep these women in line.*

I left to find Asher when Aedan approached, "Why do you let her go unpunished, Father? She needs to know her place." His eye was already swollen from the scuffle.

Irritated, I grabbed Aedan's furs and pulled him close. "*You* need to learn your place, boy." My son tried to back away in fear, but I held tight. I would not be challenged. "You will do nothing of the sort without my permission again. The fact that I granted you a reprieve should have you groveling at my feet. It's not my fault you wasted your reward by being weak and arrogant. Never underestimate your opponent, no matter who they are." I released my son, and he fell backward onto the hard ground. "Now, go collect more wood for the fires. They are burning low, and the chill is growing. Take your ungrateful brothers with you."

I watched my cowardly son scramble away and exhaled a tired sigh. "I'm sorry for their misdeeds, Father. I will keep a close watch on them from now on. You shouldn't be worrying about such things," Asher said.

I turned and walked the short distance to my loyal child. "You're a good son, Asher." I awkwardly patted the boy's shoulder, but quickly returned the hand to my side. *Don't show affection. It'd only be that much harder for them.*

I clung to the lies I fed myself and entered the tent the hybrids built for me. I laid my spear down on the soft bedding beside me, acknowledging how natural it felt in my hand. It was a part of me now. I placed the crown beside it, wondering if it would ever feel as natural as the weapon.

Confident in the work I had done today, I allowed myself to rest. But the emptiness in my chest still lingered, and I somehow knew it wouldn't be filled anytime soon.

XVIII

Pain

Broken bonds lead to broken empires.
-C

I woke to the horrid moaning of trees and thunder. However, the thunder wasn't coming from above, it was from below. The panicked voices of my children were nearly drowned out by Earth's cries, but I still heard them. I exited my tent just in time to watch it collapse into a hole in the ground. Earth had eaten much of the camp, and I could only see a few of my warriors. The rest had been lost to the ravenous soil.

I watched as the young woman from the night before led her sisters down a safe path. They disappeared into the forest and out of sight. I stepped forward to go after them out of instinct, but they meant nothing in comparison to what was happening now. I looked to the gaping crevice and down into the endless cavern. That's when I saw it. Or rather *her*. Lilith's spirit had hold of the land itself, ripping it apart piece by piece.

How had she become so strong?

I reached out to her with my own soul and tried to remove her crimson grip. I was immediately discarded. The momentary touch overwhelmed me with too much power. So many emotions were being weaved into this spell. I felt all her anger and sorrow, and I collapsed. I wanted to blame my weakness on the shaking ground, but it was the pain that she shared with me upon the unwanted touch. I had wanted her to feel *my* pain, but this was so far beyond anything I had ever felt before.

The sheer force of it could obliterate a planet.

Still, I would fight her. *She was not going to take them away from me.* I reached out once again, but she forced me away. I tried again and again to no avail, the crevice growing wider and deeper all the while. Until my concentration was disturbed by the scent of the ocean, which was supposed to be miles from here.

Just as I raised my head, an ocean wave of enormous proportion came crashing through the fallen forest. I looked to what children were left and how they clung to fallen cedars. Asher met my gaze, bravely clutching an unconscious brother to his chest, and I knew this was the last time I would see my dutiful son. A lost memory returned to me: a baby being birthed into the world, and the child being placed in my arms. Asher was covered in fluids and clearly shocked to be alive. But when our eyes met, he calmed, and I could have sworn a heart beat in my chest.

As the powerful water washed him away, a lone tear bled down my cheek, though I couldn't understand why.

I managed to climb to the top of a redwood where it continued to stand tall and watched as the land I claimed became nothing but an elapsed empire.

Long after the waves disappeared and the lands had settled, I clutched the top of the redwood tree, hiding like a lost child.

What had I done?

Since Lilith left me over five hundred years ago, I felt empty. Little had I known that it was filled by my creations. The sense of accomplishment for the life I was producing was all I had. It wasn't the love I felt for Lilith, but whatever the feeling, it was no longer there. It was banished to the very recesses of my mind and eradicated from my missing heart. Lilith had stolen it, along with my homeland.

A spark of emotion lit inside me. Lilith was not the victim as she claimed to be. *I was.*

Lilith fought me for years, tormenting me for existing the way I did. I took what I wanted, and that was only natural. Yet, it wasn't good enough for her. There were times when I thought she would finally give up the needless war, but that was only to confuse and hurt me further.

Then, the hardest time of my existence came when she abandoned me. My beloved left me with an animal for company and a cursed name as she did. I waited and waited for her to return only to discover she had moved on with another. The realization had been so painful, I was cursed with the *sight* that plagued me now. But I couldn't just see the life around me, I could *feel* it. It hurt each time I hunted an animal or drank from a stream. Each time I plunged my spear into a predator's heart, I nearly collapsed from the absorption of their soul. Before I was afflicted with the *sight*, I never felt such a thing.

My ignorance of the world was bliss compared to what I faced now.

Now, it was an endless fight just to be *me.*

I jumped down onto the damp ground, taking a tree limb as I did, and held back a cringe. I looked to the right and found my spear standing erect in the ocean-soaked soil. *My loyal weapon.* The crown was nowhere in sight. I relieved my spear from its placement and walked along the new forest's edge. The ocean spread far in front of me with no sign of where the other pieces of land were now.

Yes, Lilith had cursed me with this *sight*, but I had made use of it. For years I built my army; crushing rebels and training the obedient to fight for me. Somewhere along the way, I had come to care for them. Perhaps what I felt could have been called pride. Now, *she* cowered somewhere on Earth, hiding from me. But I would find Lilith regardless of how well she hid or how fast she ran.

I dipped my spear into the water and let the cursed power flow through me, into the wood, and through the dragon fang tip where the water touched. From there, the golden light carried the message through the ripples in the water. I found my spirit beguiling as it illuminated the darkness below. Finally, I was rewarded a few moments later with the washed-up corpses of my children. Their bloated bodies were willed onto shore. Lilith's spell had indeed been powerful. These were not the warriors I lost only days ago, but the women who I left behind. The female descendants of Lucifer and Eve.

The pungent smell was dreadful, and the greying skin was difficult to look at. Their eyes had been nibbled on by the ocean's creatures, and furs clung to their rotted bodies. I wondered how many souls Lilith collected upon this travesty. Though indirectly, she had killed them.

The waves had washed more than my children ashore. Corpses of sharks and sea snakes as well as others I didn't care to acknowledge came with them. This was followed by a realization I couldn't ignore. Possibly the reason I'd brought them to shore to begin with.

I could create more.

Hope returned, allowing me to weave a spell worthy of even Lilith:

Creatures of the deep
Children of Eve
You will be women and fish no more
But ones who will heed my call
And in turn call to me
My Sirens

With these words and my newfound intent, I created something completely new to the world. A creature of greater beauty than the sunrise and of greater song than the ocean. These sirens would search for Lilith in the world's water and call to me when they found her.

The bloated corpses no longer had souls attached to them, but I took from the surrounding light, feeding my own soul before granting my creations their own power. Alone with my grief, I realized I didn't need to kill to absorb the life force. *I was more like my succubus children than I'd thought.*

The sirens rose from their watery graves, blinking to moisten their pure white eyes. The grey skin of decay lightened, and blood now flowed through their new bodies. The multicolored, shimmering scales of fish decorated their womanly frames. Each scale pattern was unique to the siren, and these patterns ran down the body into a large, powerful fin. Delicate gills rested upon slender necks, and the darkest obsidian hair fell past their breasts, flowing freely as if it was already encased in water. When one spoke, it was as if the world was at peace; Lilith had never left me, and our children ran around us as we lazed by the waterfall.

A sharp pain broke me from this fantasy, and I looked down to find that the siren who spoke had crawled to where I stood and nibbled on my hand. Though what came out of her mouth was beautiful, it was filled with sharp, pointed teeth that craved men's flesh.

There was always something flawed about our creations.

"Release me." I didn't have to use force for the subservient creature to move away; she was shocked by her actions more so than I. "Now, you will scour the world's depths for Lilith. She is of red hair and emerald eyes. She has skin as bright as the moon itself, and a voice comparable to even your own." I clutched my spear tighter. "You will not attack her or attempt to bring her to me. You will alert me to her whereabouts, and that is all. You are my sirens."

The three sirens looked to one another, seemingly to communicate silently between themselves. "What of the other humans? We crave human flesh for we are missing our own," they said in unison.

Slightly disturbed, I said, "Feed as you wish, but only those who dwell in the water. Leave the ones on land be." The sirens seemed satisfied with my answer and crawled over the soaked soil, their too-thin arms pulling them toward the depths to search for Lilith.

I turned to the forest and snatched mockingbirds, one by one, as they flew past me. The spell was easier to weave this way, for I had their original souls to work with. The remaining bodies of my lost daughters prepared, I released the bird's fidgety forms into the air, only to trap them in the enchantment that called for them:

Souls of flight and mockery
Join those who are lost to me
For to become one
You must become mine
And to be mine, means to fly
Fly Sprites!

The bird's frantic chirps ceased once they joined with my daughters. For a moment, they merely lay upon the damp ground, but then the wings on their backs began to flutter, taking flight before they even opened their eyes.

The creatures were no bigger than my palm, and their delicate bodies were that of women, though I could see green and gold feathers inlaid in delicate patterns across their skin. Floating in the air at eye level, they slowly opened their eyelids and revealed the most startling blue. Though blue eyes were comely, these irises were clearly not human. Gone was sclera and pupil. It was all dead blue, and they stared into my own.

"What do you wish, Creator?" a sprite asked me.

I took my time finding the words, for their appearance startled me even more than the sirens, but I finally relayed the same message I gave the ocean creatures. However, these sprites would be searching by land, not water.

"And what of the humans?" the tiny beings said. "We have a need to mock and scheme. We need to summon the humans and feed from their souls. This is the only way to satisfy our ravenous spirits, for we are hungry for what we lack."

"Lack? You have souls, I can see them now."

"It is but the souls of animals. Not human, which is far different," a sprite explained.

"How so?"

My answer came in the form of giggles. The sprites looked to one another as if enjoying a private joke, holding tiny hands to their mouths, and dead eyes squinting in amusement.

Ignoring their deceiving nature, I said, "Very well, you may trick and deceive as you like, though only in the forest. The other parts of the world are forbidden." They smiled in delight, for there were many parts of the world that was forest.

My creations had their mission, and I took the time to rest my weary body. Sitting on the shoreline, I enjoyed the horizon, which betrayed the most beautiful orange and lilac hues. The sun was disappearing into the water's depths, though, logically I knew the star would return.

I thought on Lilith's actions and decided that if she had simply returned to me, I would have let her precious Earth live. *So long as she loved me.* I wouldn't have batted an eye at removing the disease that infested the planet. My children and hers. It could have been like it was in the beginning. When there was only The First Man and Woman.

The waves receded, and a soaked scrap of white fur appeared. The ocean dripped down my arm as I rescued the sad ancient bag from the sand. The rotted yellow and orange leaves of autumn floated along the shoreline. Pulling apart the teeth that had dutifully stitched the fur together, my suspicions were confirmed. The golden locks Lilith had kept all these centuries were encased in the soggy skin.

I rubbed the strands between my fingers until they were nothing but sand themselves. Wherever Lilith had gone, she hadn't taken her treasures with her. *She ran from me.*

Despite this, I couldn't help but hold on to the hope that she still loved me. She had stayed her murderous hand and refused to stab me. Even after discovering I had killed her children.

I clutched my heartless chest, reminding myself that she was my only hope.

I let the setting rays warm my skin until blackness overtook me, and the coldness of my soul bit the life that was unlucky enough to be nearby. The snow, which was usually reserved for the mountain peaks, landed gracefully upon my skin, unable to melt. I waited there, waited to see Lilith again. Still unsure if I was to embrace my beloved or condemn her to the same pain I endured.

Part IV
The Sun's Cycle

The angered searches

The searcher travels

The traveler hunts

The hunter follows

The follower wanders

The wanderer angers

XIX

Gone

If crimson does not fulfill you, perhaps gold will.

-S

3000 BCE

Everything was numb. Everything was black. I hadn't had skin or eyes for…I didn't know. The pain had been too much. The fury had consumed my every thought as I searched for Lilith. Century after century. Eons had come and gone, and I had not found one clue, one piece of Lilith to prove we walked the same Earth.

At first, I thought she was running from me, hiding even. But no. She had abandoned me completely. Not one whiff of her night pollen scent was on the winds, nor a stray strand of her hair lay on the earth beneath my immortal feet.

Lilith was gone.

My time was spent searching and hunting. The angrier I became, the hungrier I was. Hungry for fulfillment. For an end to the pain. For something *more*.

I hunted only dragons for millennia. Until there were none left, and I had nothing more to conquer. Those of my descendants who survived

Lilith's wrath were but weak creatures struggling to survive on their own. Without me, they would perish. But I no longer had the motivation to further my goal.

Hunger forced me to check every mountain top for the small chance a lone dragon would be hiding in its caves. Then, one day, I came across a new kind of mountain. One filled with fire so hot, no creature would dare come near its crown. Earth was constantly changing because of the unnatural life I had forced upon it. Hybrids were desperate to survive and unknowingly took the land's spirit to sustain themselves, though they would have taken it even if they had been aware; they were the embodiment of greed.

At the time, ice and snow were the dominant elements. The wildlife and hybrids fought for land at the base of the *volcano*—yes, that was the word—and only survived because of the warmth the rock radiated.

Embracing the intense heat, I had stood at its head and looked down into the fiery depths. The lava bubbled and stirred, looking as angry as I felt. And in just as much pain. I plunged my dragon-bone spear into the ground, splitting the rock. Refusing to think, I took one step forward. Then I was falling.

The air was thick and heavy with heat, yet painfully dry. I thought of the sun warming my skin as I plummeted into the deep hole. Looking upward, I allowed myself one last glimpse of the blue sky.

I didn't see anything again.

Now, though, after experiencing the intense heat of the volcano and then nothing at all as I became ash, the cold seeping into my body was a shock. If I could feel, it meant I was healing. I had predicted that if the lava didn't kill me, it would have at least trapped me in its depths for the rest of time. *I depended on it.* But it was foolish to think that something as fluid and ever-changing as Earth could contain me forever.

Nothing would outlive me. I was forever unchanging. Forever alone.

My fingers twitched with discomfort. The new skin was sensitive… unsettling. It felt tight and constricting. Though I could not *feel* in the traditional sense when I existed as ash—as nothing but a speck of dust— there was a sense of freedom in being detached from the physical realm. My soul was what was truly *me*. Even now, I sensed the lingering souls of those I had taken long ago, still confined within my golden light.

I smiled.

My new body moved easily, yet I shifted each part with care, adjusting to the foreign sensation. I inhaled the humid air, filling my new lungs. The moist oxygen was almost difficult to breathe, but the more I concentrated, the easier it became. It was a drastic change from the dry, frigid air of the age of ice. And even stranger after not being able to breathe at all. I shivered and, my skin prickled. I opened my eyes to the light that waited just behind the trembling lids.

High above me was a grey sky, filled with angry clouds. Their water poured down on me, washing away the earth and dust that coated my skin. My eyes slowly focused in and out, adjusting to the surrounding colors. A tall wall of rock circled me in a purposeful shape, but there was nothing above to protect me from Earth's tears.

Greenery adorned my body. Thornless vines wrapped around my limbs, the leaves gently brushing against my skin. Soft, pink rose petals rested lazily along my stomach, their scent overwhelming. I flinched, seeing the smoke that drifted above me, but I realized it was not from a fire but a small stick standing erect in a bowl of sand. The top smoldered, exuding a familiar scent, and reminding me of tree sap. There were several burning in the small space. Fruits were laid out before me, most of them were rotten, barely any spirit clung to their physical forms.

A woman gasped.

Quickly, I looked to the right, irritated that I had not seen the small opening leading to the outside. Green eyes met mine briefly before the woman turned and darted away with thick, red curls trailing behind her.

Lilith!

I forced myself up from the ground, not realizing I was a part of the earth I lay upon. Lifting one limb at a time, I struggled to relieve the ebony rock. I ripped the strange mineral from my body, and it took my skin in revenge. Red sand poured onto the black ground as I repeated the process, desperate to catch Lilith before she disappeared again.

Finally free, I looked down into the shallow grave I'd just been in. It had shaped to my form perfectly. I reached the door, and despite my panic, I was hesitant to step outside my small sanctuary.

How much had the world changed while I was in the volcano? Had Lilith found me while I was in the darkness? Had she waited all this time for me to heal?

I took the step I needed, knowing it was time to wake, regardless of the answers.

The rain outside of my stone housing was strangely gentle compared to the inside. The air was heavy with warmth and the aroma of spice was dominant. There were plants with large, edged leaves growing throughout the flat expanse. I lowered so I could run my finger across one, allowing myself the rare pleasure of enjoying its texture and calming spirit.

Sniffing where the plant had touched my skin, I discovered this was the source of the spicy scent. Life I had never come across before. One that had come into being while I was in the dark, and now thrived on the land I once called mine. The honey-colored spirit slowly drifted toward my golden soul. My spirit drank in the power greedily, despite its already intense glow. The emerald leaves wilted from its loss and collapsed.

I remembered who I was in that moment.

Abandoning the greenery, I searched the flatlands for movement, any sign that Lilith was truly here. But perhaps she had been a hallucination. *How could I be sure my body healed properly after being gone for so long? How could I trust my mind to function as it had?*

Thinking of my past, a stabbing sensation passed through my missing heart. I clutched my chest, realizing too late that it had been pain. *Regret.*

The crunching of grass and earth alerted me to their approach. I first saw a man, his skin tanned by generations of his ancestors living under the sun. It was marked with swirled designs, and at first, I thought it to be drawn on the surface with ash from the fire pits, as the hybrids had done during the age of ice. But these designs were flawless and smooth and permanent. They rested under the man's skin, forever a symbol of his status as a warrior and leader. Though time had passed, hybrids were ultimately predictable. The need to display their power was a part of who they were.

Still, even without the markings, it was easy to identify the warriors among hybrids. Strong and sure movements, even while walking. Scars were commonplace as well. But the leaders had but one natural sign of their skill—the eyes. A stare that contained answers. A stare that commanded respect. Not eyes that drifted in and out of reality, as ones with the *sight* often did. Leaders were rare, however, I could see this man was one of them.

My assessment was quick, and my gaze moved toward the small woman walking behind him. Green eyes peered over his shoulder, not frightened, but wary. Thick braids pulled the crimson hair back from her face, ending at the crown of her head and allowing the curls to fall down her back. Her skin was colored the same as the man she followed, but there was a glow that separated her from her kin.

A golden light. A golden soul.

Not once had I seen another with such a similar spirit to my own. It was hard to keep my composure, but I had control of myself by the time they crossed the vast field of emerald and black. They stopped a short distance away. The man seemed to be waiting for me to speak, but I stayed silent, unsure what my voice would sound like after all this time.

The woman spoke first, "Who are you?"

"Silence, Abha," the man ordered.

The woman did not speak again, but her expression was…annoyed? I couldn't think of another way to describe such a strange appearance.

"Forgive my daughter, she is frustratingly outspoken for a woman. She does not realize who we are in the presence of." Abha's father gripped her shoulder and lowered her down with him as he kneeled. Both their heads bowed, he said, "I am Nakon, Chief of the Maya people. As such, I thank you for your blessing upon our lands. Your visit is a great honor to us."

Confused, I asked, "You know of me?" My voice was strained, as if I had been screaming.

"Of course, you are our Sun God, you are *Kinich Ahau*, one who rules the daytime skies. Your return has long been foretold, and when my ancestors found you in the black rock, we knew you had at last come back to us. We have witnessed your transformation for years, since the time of the great fire, before my great grandfather's time." Chief Nakon took a breath before he continued. "My people have watched over your growth. We have made certain you were protected until you could wake."

"The great fire?" I whispered mostly to myself, but Nakon answered despite this.

"The mountain erupted generations ago, but since then has slept, leaving the ground before us black, as a reminder of your rebirth into this world."

Either, one of the hybrids from long ago had seen me jump into the volcano, or my offspring were far more creative than I gave them credit for. A man growing from rock. Only hybrids would give it any significance, let alone allow themselves to hope it was their salvation. I realized then what he had said, and that the rock under our feet was slumbering lava. The volcano had expelled me from its depths, allowing me to heal.

Even the fire had not wanted me.

I attempted to keep the pain from my expression, but the woman glanced up from her bow, studying me. She looked so much like Lilith, and my empty chest ached for her presence. Just a moment with my heart would have been a relief. To feel her body pressed against mine would have left me content. The rain fell harder, washing away the tears that ran silently down my face. I was sure Abha and Nakon could not see them, but the fact that I allowed such an emotion to surface revealed how weak I still was.

Chief Nakon finally raised his head. An expression of pure joy shown upon his face as he raised it to the sky. "You bless us Sun God, you've allowed the rain to fall at such a challenging time for our people. The drought has lasted for many seasons, but finally we have hope." Still kneeling in the black mud, he turned his gaze to me and said, "Thank you."

Surprised, I closed the distance between us and reached my hand out. "There is no need for your thanks. All I wish is to help, as you and your people have helped me." The chief clasped my hand and rose to his feet.

I offered the same to his daughter, Abha. The woman stared at my palm a moment before resting her delicate hand in mine and rising as well. The clothes she wore clung to her wet skin. The brown fibers laced with red and gold beads swirled along her neckline, around her breasts, until they plummeted down the center of her stomach, ending at the hem of her skirt, resting mid-thigh. Slits ran vertically along the sides of her legs allowing for easy movement. And I suspected to display more of her flawless sun-kissed skin.

I was aware I wore no such things, feeling every raindrop cascade down my form. Yet, with her hand in mine, I didn't feel so cold anymore.

The chief and his daughter led me to their home. As I strode through the

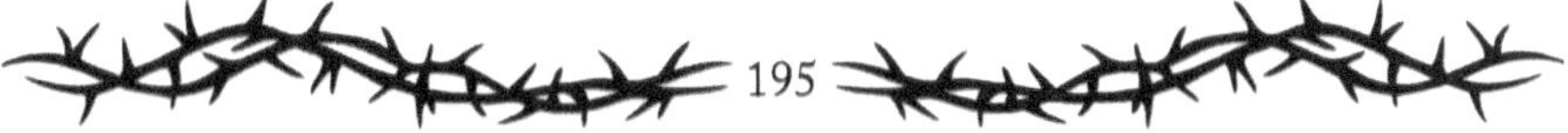

village, I was astounded by the vastness of it. The sheer size swallowed the base of the volcano. My sanctuary had been higher up the mountainside. Not as many trees and plants grew there due to my hunger. My spirit unknowingly did so. It also explained the rotted fruits the hybrids left as offerings. They had to replace them every day.

Nakon gave me his cloak, a black jaguar's skin. The fur, though weighed down by rainwater, was warm. I hadn't felt an animal's pelt in so long, the sensation was foreign as my fingers stroked the soft fur. The contrast of the fur to my sun-colored strands was startling. My hair hung lower than it had ever been, the damp waves brushing against my stomach. Running my fingers along its surface, it was hard to determine if it was the same shade it had been millennia ago, when I had sheared it to my shoulders every year to keep it from tangling in the trees as I ran.

I took notice that Nakon had coarse ebony hair along his lower cheeks and jawline. The hair was purposely shaped to his bone structure, the hair shortened. Raising my hand, I felt the same kind of hair on my own face. Glancing around, I noticed only the men had this feature.

Had I somehow changed along with the hybrids during my re-creation?

The age of ice was a hard one, even for me. Even more than I expected if our bodies had been forced to adapt. It made me wonder what else had altered about humanity. *About me.*

The Maya people stepped from their small houses as I passed, their mouths agape, before they threw themselves to the ground in a deep bow of submission. Clearly, they had all been to my resting place and gazed upon their Sun God's face before. They knew I was something different. Something more than they would ever be.

I studied this era's hybrids and noted the advances they had made. Their homes were not made of wood, but of reformed rock and earth; wood eventually rotted away but rock was nearly eternal. Their clothing was interesting as well. They didn't just use animal skins, but tiny threads woven together from plant fibers. In this warm climate, I was sure they wanted something lighter than pelts to wear. I wondered why they wore anything at all if it was too warm, but perhaps the age of ice had changed things. Perhaps that fear was still in their distant memories.

The ice was surely still inside me, as I shivered inconspicuously beneath the cloak. But perhaps it was because I'd become accustomed to the raging fire of the volcano, and had become weak in this new skin of mine.

I looked to the flatlands past the housing, and saw rows upon rows of vegetation. One field contained thousands of white, fluffy plants—cotton. The next field sprouted green bushes, which contained brown seeds. The breeze brought their scent to me; bitter, but it was nice to smell something new. The next field grew potatoes, recognizing the leaves protruding from the ground. The lands went on and on in this manner. Each vast field growing something that contributed to these people. Although, they were all wilted and smaller than they should have been. I now understood why Nakon had been happy to see it rain. I was sure the cause of it had not been me, but I allowed him to believe it was for one purpose.

The chief's home was at the center of the village. The stone house was surrounded by thirsty sunflowers. Swirling patterns were painted on the door, similar to those on the chief's skin. We entered and warmth wrapped intimately around my body. I dropped the wet cloak and allowed the air to comfort me. The floors were made from wood and soaked in the heat from the small fire pit in the center of the room. I leaned away from the fire instinctually.

"Please allow Abha to cleanse you. I will prepare for the feast tomorrow now that our fasting is over," Chief Nakon said.

Looking at my rain-washed skin, I argued, "The rain has cleansed the dirt from me."

Nakon opened his mouth, assuming to offer something else he thought I would want, when Abha spoke, "The rain has cleaned your skin, but the hot water will warm you." Abha looked to my shivering hands. "As well as calm you." The woman spoke with gentleness, but there was an edge to her voice that made me ponder her thoughts—something I rarely cared about. "Have you been in human form before?" she asked.

Probing her eyes, wishing to see what purpose she had in asking, I answered, "Not in a very long time."

Chief Nakon interceded, "I will leave my daughter to care for you. She will meet your every need. All you need is to ask, and it will be done." The man bowed slightly before exiting the shelter, but not before grabbing his cloak from the ground and sliding it onto his shoulders.

"I will prepare your cleanse," Abha stated before reaching for a large container filled with water. She placed it over the fire where it hung on a hook attached to the roof. She left me briefly, disappearing around a corner at the opposite side of the shelter and came back with a bundle of dried plants and two scented sticks, the same scent that had been burning in my sanctuary on the mountainside. After lighting the sticks in the fire, she blew the flame out softly and stood them upright in a jar of sand, their smoke filling the shelter. She placed a handful of the herbs in a stone bowl and proceeded to crush them with a rock until the plant was but dust. She placed two small pieces of fabric on the low table where she worked. She pinched the spicy herb dust into the fabric, tied them, and placed each in a clay cup.

Abha glanced to me, realizing I hadn't moved from my position by the doorway. The last drops of rainwater left wet imprints on the wood floor. "Tea," she said.

"Tea?" I repeated.

"Yes, it is the epazote plant. It cleanses the inner body." Abha fidgeted where she stood, waiting for the water to heat.

"The same plant on the mountainside." I remembered the intoxicating aroma, and the feel of its honey-colored soul feeding my own.

The woman nodded, surprised I had noticed.

"And the smoke?"

"Frankincense. Its scent calms the mind," she explained, with a small smile.

"Where does it come from?" I asked, curious of the familiar scent. It reminded me of the waterfall, the forest, of Lilith.

"It is made from the Boswellia Sacra Tree. It grows in a land far from here. My father gifted it to me after meeting a traveler at the port. He said she had many strange things in her possession. Things he had never seen before, weapons and medicines unknown to us." The woman turned toward the smoke, and it swirled in the opposite direction.

A glimmer of hope took root in my stomach, reaching upward to that empty space in my chest. "Where was this woman from?"

"Father said she didn't share much about herself, she was only interested in trade."

"Where is she now?" The desperation clawed at my insides.

"I don't know. She left as quickly as she came." Abha noticed my tense muscles. "Why? Do you know this woman, my Sun God?"

I shook my head in dismissal, and the chief's daughter wisely kept her mouth closed. She motioned for me to take a seat on a wooden stool beside the fire, and I angled myself so I wouldn't have to take my eyes off her. The comfort of her ancestor's features were too tempting to resist, as well as her aura. The gold was so like mine, but not nearly as bright. She hadn't had eons to collect souls as I had.

The chief's daughter poured hot water into the cups, offering one to me. I received it graciously and took advantage, allowing my fingers to graze hers longer than necessary. She didn't touch her own cup, instead she lowered the container of hot water to the floor beside me, then soaked a soft cloth in its heat.

"Drink," she said softly, placing the cloth on my arm. I tensed at the closeness of her, but relaxed as she used the cloth to warm my skin. I took a small drink of the tea. It tasted as strong as it smelled, a pungent flavor, though the hot water was calming, as she said it would be.

Abha dipped the cloth in the hot water repeatedly as she cleansed me, her emerald gaze following her own hand's movements up my arms, along my shoulders, down my chest and stomach. She paused for only a moment when she realized how my body reacted to her touch. But she continued, unfazed by my display of manhood, her caress moving down my legs.

Too soon, she pulled away, leaving to retrieve a flat, shining surface. She lifted it so the reflective side faced me. I would have flinched if Abha hadn't been there to witness such a weakness. She held a new creation before me—a mirror. Ice-blue eyes stared back at me, they took in the sharp angles of my face, the pale gold complexion of my skin, then settled on the new addition to my appearance—the beard. I somehow seemed…older.

Could it be true?

"Remove this." I motioned to my new facial hair. *I needed to know.*

Abha nodded, confused by the intense command in my voice. She left and returned quickly with a small knife, sharpened repeatedly until the mineral's edge shone. Wetting my cheeks, jaw, and neck with more warm water, she stood behind me and angled the knife at my throat. It took all the restraint I had to allow her to do so, but I needed the disguise gone.

A few skilled swipes of the blade had the hair falling to the floor, she was nearly finished when a flash of panic overtook me. Knowing I was so close to discovering the truth, I reached my hand up to stop her. The blade stumbled and cut into my skin. She gasped and moved to care for the wound.

Refusing to let go of her arm, I said, "Don't stop."

"But you're bleeding…" she started.

Nothing but red sand dusted my cheekbone, and the cut was healed in the same amount of time it took her to blink. Slowly, I released my grip on her and wiped away the sand. In what was either awe or disgust, she followed my orders and finished shaving the beard. Taking in a slow inconspicuous breath of courage, I raised the mirror up.

Glowing, immortal youth stared back. *Of course.*

I nodded to Abha, indicating I was done.

Curious, but unwilling to voice herself, Abha poured me more tea. "Rest now, let the tea do its work and sleep." Pulling my arm so I would stand, she led me into another room just big enough for a resting place, the wood floors layered in furs and cloth. She took the cup from my hands and placed it on the floor beside the furs and gestured for me to lie down.

I did as she asked, wishing for the soft caress of the fur; a drastic change from the cold, black rock I had slept on for several hybrid lifetimes. "Where will you rest?" I asked Abha.

"I will be staying in another shelter. This one is for you, my Sun God." The woman's full lips turned upward, beckoning. "Unless you need anything more of me?" Her green eyes roamed over my immortal body, a strange hunger in her eyes. I wasn't sure if it was strictly lust for my body.

Conflicted, I said, "No, I don't need anything from you." I listened to her leave the small shelter and step into the heavy rain, only to find myself cold once again.

XX
Feast

The sun offers gentle warmth when it pleases.
-C

Sunrays roused me from my sleep. A small opening in the stone wall allowed the light to shine through, and I couldn't help but be awed by the hybrid's creations—a race I thought would surely die after the land parted. But they were still here when the age of ice came and then when the volcanoes erupted. Not even Earth could rid itself of these pests, although, it wasn't for lack of trying. But neither ice nor fire could kill them. My children were resilient.

As were hers.

There was but thirteen females left of Lilith's children when I came for her all those eons ago. The ones she spawned with Adam were eradicated, and yet those women escaped me during Lilith's attack. They managed to survive the land-split and reproduce with my sons. Now Lilith was just as much a part of the hybrids as I was.

Abha was proof enough of that. But there was something different about the chief's daughter, something that separated her from her father's people. I would have to ask what land her mother hailed from, and perhaps there would be more of Lilith's kin to see there. But only after I hunted down the woman Abha spoke of, the one who had given her father the frankincense. *My father gifted it to me after meeting a traveler at the borders of our land. She had many strange things in her possession. Things he had never seen before, weapons and medicines unknown to us,* she had said. Lilith certainly fit the description. After eons of time, with peoples rising and falling, creations lost and remade, only an immortal could have such a collection. Yes, it *had* to be her.

"Kinich Ahau?"

Opening my eyes for the first time since I forcefully closed them the previous evening, I was relieved to see the colors and light the world had to offer. I had been afraid only darkness would greet me. It would take a long time to adjust after being trapped in the volcano for so long.

Would I ever truly recover?

"Abha," I whispered. The chief's daughter raised an eyebrow but smiled politely. I glanced around to find the furs had been tossed aside, so I laid on the hard flooring instead. *Another thing that would take time.*

"My people are preparing for the feast tonight. They are harvesting, and the hunters left early this morning." Abha bowed her head slightly. "Is there anything I can offer you until it is prepared?"

Remembering yesterday's conversation, I asked, "Your father said the people were fasting. Why?"

"The drought. We eat little because our fields have produced little. The rains have been absent, and the wildlife fled the heat. We have been starving." Abha choked on the word *starving*. "But you have risen, and the rain has returned." Her emerald gaze rose to mine, they sparkled in the sun's rays, her unshed tears making them even more so.

"You think the animals will return so quickly?" I pondered.

"We can only hope."

Rising to my feet, I realized she held clothing in her grasp. A long robe made from soft, delicate thread. The gold color was uncanny, as well as the harsh crimson design that lined the frame. I noticed Abha's clothing

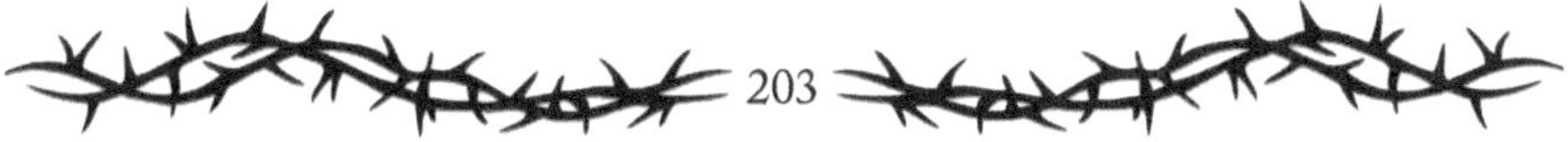

matched, except her design flowed seductively along her curves.

Donning the robe she offered me, I said, "There is no need for your hope. I will feed the Maya people."

The sun was shining, but clouds loomed in the distance, as if they were indeed at my beckon call. I smiled at the notion.

My fist tightened out of habit. I looked down to find there was no spear shaft to grip, and my smile disappeared. The dragon bone was long gone. It was strange how such a strong emotion such as sadness could be attached to an object, something that wasn't even alive.

But of course, I loved Lilith too, didn't I?

Masking my expression, I asked, "Where have your people hunted?"

"In the woodlands and on the flatlands. Nothing more than snakes have been found since the drought began," Abha explained. I heard her stomach rumble with hunger while she spoke. It was then that I noticed how unnaturally thin she was. Abha's collarbone protruded from her skin, and her cheekbones were sharp.

"Snakes?"

"Yes, they don't seem to mind the drought. It only makes their own prey weak and easier to catch," she said.

It was hard not to think of Eve in that moment; the snake-woman who birthed this hybrid race of humans. Her amber eyes and pale complexion were clear in my memory. As were her manipulations. The ones that poisoned the minds of my first generation of children, the manipulations that forced me to kill most of them so I could stay in control.

I didn't miss her at all.

I merely nodded to Abha and continued, "Have the hunters searched the mountain?"

"Past your temple, the land becomes treacherous. The ground crumbles beneath our feet and sends men down the hillside to their deaths.

Though, before the rains blessed us, many were debating whether it was worth the risk." The chief's daughter paused. "The air is cooler up there, and I have to believe it is where the animals have gone to." Abha looked toward the sleeping mountain, her eyes unfocused, and I knew exactly what she was seeing.

"Tell the hunters to stay away from the mountain. I will go."

I only took one step before Abha gripped my arm between her small hands and said, "My Sun God, it isn't safe." Her eyes were focused once again, and they pierced my own. She meant for the gesture to express concern, but there was a strange possession in her voice. Her spirit thrashed angrily, desperate even.

"There is only one thing on this Earth that can kill me, and it is not on that mountain." Abha blinked in surprise and reluctantly let go. I could see the question forming on her lips, but I was gone before she could speak it.

The rush of power I felt was invigorating. My body moved naturally, as it always had. My muscles flexed, filling with energy as I ran. I pulled in the life around me. The souls showed resistance, but they were not as strong as me. I reveled in the ecstasy of power that entered my soul. My golden light shone brighter and brighter until even the sun could not compare.

Sun God.

Perhaps the Maya people had been right.

For the first time in my existence, I stopped and looked to the sun, not to appreciate its warmth, but to take it. I reached my invisible hands toward the light in the sky, stretching as far as they would go. I came upon an icy touch at the edge of the world and my control faltered, my soul returning to its rightful place. The sun was too far.

Dark clouds drifted closer to where I stood on the mountainside. My soul reached out again, but this time the target wasn't so far. Gripping the floating water with my power, I took hold until I commanded every wisp of mist.

Water fell to the overheated ground. The black rock sizzled in surprise, and the clouds released their cry, no longer in control of itself. Lightning shot through the mist, hitting a tree beside me. It reminded me of Lilith in the beginning. She had feared lightning so much she had stayed hidden away, even as the tree she'd taken shelter in caught fire and tried to burn her alive. *Until I saved her.*

White hot lightening flew across the blue sky, a strange addition to the pleasant color. A roar of pain thundered through the land. The sky knew it had been conquered. It had only taken the creativity of the hybrids to give me the idea. I would have to reward them.

The sunlight shone once again, and the scent of blood drifted past me. Letting instincts guide me, I followed the odor until I found a tangle of trees nestled on the mountainside. The ground was unpredictable as I sank into hollow soil randomly above the sleeping lava. The slant of the mountain became steeper the higher I went. Plants penetrated the rock, reaching for sunlight. But I was careful not to misstep as I approached the feasting jaguar in the trees.

A small deer sagged over the thick tree branch; its beautiful red coat was ripped apart by fangs the length of my hand. The jaguar didn't hear me approach, and I willed the wind to change direction to mask my scent. I didn't have my spear, so I would have to get close and kill it the traditional way. Blood trickled from the branch and onto the black ground.

Once the hundredth drop fell, I sprang onto the branch right behind the jaguar. Its coat was ebony, but light enough that the spotted design was visible in the sunrays that peeked between the trees. It only had enough time to perk its ears before I plunged my hand through its back and chest, removing the life I would forever crave.

The blood wiped clean from my lips, I hauled the cat's carcass and what remained of the deer to the village. I dropped them at Abha's feet and said, "Prepare them, and put the meat on the fire. I will be back with more."

The look on Abha's face was a unique one; a strange mixture of appreciation and anger. But she didn't say anything to me as she bowed in thanks and shouted for someone to help her prepare the animals for dinner.

The rest of the day was spent hunting. I brought back enough meat to feed the village for weeks. The emotion I felt doing so was familiar to what it had felt like to care for my children in the beginning, when they were first born into this world. When they had a purpose.

When *I* had a purpose.

Maybe we could again.

The day was nearing its end, and I rested at the edge of the cotton field, allowing a few clouds to linger above the vegetation. The slightest of raindrops fell, enough to quench the plant's thirst, but not enough to bother me. Fires were crackling in the distance, and the smell of flesh blistering over the flames made my mouth water. *When was the last time I'd eaten?*

My stomach grumbled an answer that said, *Never.* Because this body had never eaten before. My old body was gone, and a new one had replaced it. The thought made me sad.

The breeze naturally floated through the vast fields. The cotton swayed back and forth, matching the rhythm of the air currents. Water droplets clung to the strange plant, and as the light peered through the clouds, they shimmered.

"May I join you, my Sun God?" Abha hovered behind me, her heartbeat steady. I turned to face the chief's daughter and noticed her spirit was calm, which matched my own soul's casual demeanor. Her eyes were unfocused as she gazed at her Sun God, seeing something most others could not.

I returned my gaze to the cotton field and said, "Of course." But before she could sit down, I continued, "But only if you promise to keep your gaze on the physical world and away from the one that distracts you."

Her heart stuttered. "What do you mean?"

Without looking toward the woman, I asked a question of my own, "Does your father know you are a Seer?"

She whispered, "A Seer?" I nodded once. Slowly, she lowered herself to the ground beside me and said, "I promise." She inched closer. "No, my father does not know. No one does. However, I suspect my mother did, but she died when I was a young girl." Abha's fists suddenly clenched and her soul thrashed out toward mine, as if she wished to challenge me. Shocked by her own outburst, she calmed herself, so her spirit merely twitched anxiously.

"Where did your mother come from?" I asked. The breeze was no longer natural as it blew our long hair to and fro.

"How did you know she wasn't from here?"

"You look different from the rest of your kin. Your mother must have been from another land for you to resemble..." catching myself, I finished, "...a foreigner." Although both Lilith's and my blood flowed in all the hybrids, people stayed on their own land for fear of the unknown. In turn, bloodlines were strengthened. Lilith's was strengthened somewhere on this planet. *Could she be with them?*

"My mother was born in a land of green grass and snow. One with rolling hills and magical, lush forests. She always told me about it. Even then, I knew she longed to go back." A tear slipped down Abha's sunkissed cheek. "I thought one day we would go together, but..."

"Why did she leave such a place?" I asked.

The red-headed woman wiped the tear from her face aggressively before answering. "She didn't want to. All I know is that someone wanted to hurt her. She ran and was eventually captured by slave traders, was put on a boat, and ended up here. My father saw her being…mistreated…and bought her for himself to save her." Abha's lips pinched in frustration. "My father is not perfect, but he has a good heart."

"Did your mother ever say what her land was named? Her people?"

Abha gazed into my eyes with curiosity and answered, "No, she didn't want to risk being found by them, and my father didn't force her to tell him. Why do you want to know?"

Unwilling to break our stare, I said, "You resemble someone from my past."

"Who?" Abha leaned closer, her sweet scent overwhelming.

"A woman," I whispered, unable to say anything more while her emerald gaze trapped mine.

"Was she special to you, my Sun God?" The woman's hand raised and gently brushed a strand of golden hair from my face, just as Lilith had once done. In the beginning.

"She means more to me than Earth itself," I answered, unaware my hand had found the curve of her leg, so near to me, and made soft circles on her skin.

Abha angled her face upward and asked, "The old stories say the Sun God, Kinich Ahau, had a lover—the Moon Goddess, Ixchel. They say she had power over the nighttime sky and the oceans. Some even say, the Earth was her plaything to wield as she saw fit. Did you give her such power, my Sun God?" Abha raised her lips to mine, her hands now gripping the front of my robes, but she stopped short, allowing me to decide if I wanted her.

Overwhelmed by her heavy scent of flowers and heat, I nearly said, "No, she was the one who gave me power." But instead, I responded by removing her hands and whispering, "I made her everything that she is." I willed the wind to carry away the distracting scents of want and hunger. My head cleared, and I forced myself to concentrate on all the differences between Abha and Lilith. Abha's hair was two shades too dark; her skin, while a beautiful, dark, earthy tone, was not Lilith's smooth ivory moonlight; her eyes were the same emerald green, but they did not sparkle with silver flecks of starlight.

Abha was not Lilith. Not my equal. Not my heart. Not the same.

All those centuries of reproducing with hybrids—with animals—I had a purpose. But I did not have the same goal. Now, it would only add to my suffering. I would not limit myself as Lilith had. Just as she sacrificed the delicious and fulfilling taste of meat for vegetation, I would not sacrifice the real thing for a poorly created imitation. The scent of animal was weak among the hybrids now, but I could still smell it. And I could not choke it down again.

Abha saw the disgust on my face and retreated, running back to her kin. I listened to the fires crackle and the blood from the meat drip onto the flames. Abha's distress forgotten, I thought of my Moon Goddess and all she meant to me.

The pain in my chest no longer bearable, I wandered back to the Maya people where the feast was being set out on low but long wooden tables. Over the fire pits hung my kills, and the skins lay in the shade where they could cool. The tusks, claws, and horns were collected as well, and a few children were making jewelry from them. Everyone had a smile on their face. I couldn't say the same.

"Sun God, please sit and enjoy the very first of our feast. It is because of you that we can have one at all." Chief Nakon approached and bowed as he said this. I nodded once, unable to return any pleasant words.

The chief led me to the end of the table where the grass was the softest and furs were placed for comfort. I accepted my place at the table, and young women set several plates of roasted meats, boiled potatoes, and greens in front of me. A strange brown drink was also offered, and I immediately recognized the scent. I gulped down the cold liquid, savoring the strange, bitter flavor of the cocoa beans. A new and wonderful creation. My cup was refilled with the savory drink as I tore into my meal. Millennia had come and gone without enjoying the simple pleasure of food. The most basic necessity to survive. And one of the most satisfying of desires.

No one even took a bite until I was completely satisfied, which was many helpings later. I laid back and listened to the hungry mouths devour the bounty. I shifted a stray cloud out of the way so the evening sun could shine its light on me. The warmth filled me as the food had, and the pain ebbed ever so slightly.

I hadn't realized I had gone to sleep until Abha's gentle voice said, "My Sun God, it is time to wake." Slowly, I rose to my feet. The long table had been cleared of food and drink. The people were nowhere in sight. Answering before I could ask, Abha said, "They are waiting for you."

She took my hand and led me out of the village, and up the mountainside where hundreds of Maya people stood outside the temple. I found myself unusually distracted by their spirits. All of them lunged and parried as they fought one another; challenging, wanting what the other had. For as long as I had been away from humanity, that part of them had not changed.

The hybrids parted, and I stepped through the small break in the wall. That was where I found Chief Nakon. He held a rope, and at the end was a small white goat. Blue paint coated its horns and fur. Blue flowers of every kind were braided in the creature's fur. The goat's eyes were ebony, round, and full of fear.

"What is this? Did you not have enough food?" I asked. I noticed that the creature was standing on top of my previous resting place. The shape of a man formed in the black rock; the soil was shattered due to my hasty escape. Frankincense was burning within the small space, and I followed the floating smoke up to the darkening sky above us.

"This goat is not for eating, Sun God. Every cycle we have sacrificed a living soul for you. Every year we have brought nourishment to your temple." Nakon's eyes filled with sorrow and pride. "Finally, you have woken. Finally, you have saved us. And we will keep you strong Sun God, Kinich Ahau."

"Oh? How are you going to do that?" I wondered. What could these mortals possibly do for something like me?

"Blue is the color of the daytime sky, a sacred color to us ever since you appeared and displayed your power. This was why we did not put a roof over you. We wanted your power to be freed." There were cries of admiration and prayers whispered beneath breaths among the people behind me. Abha stiffened. Nakon continued, "You wielded the skies even in your slumber. Every time you grew and changed into the man you are, a new sky would greet us. It was only when you could feed that you would you grant us with rain." I barely hid my shocked expression.

"So, we sacrificed what we could to you, and when we had no animals to give, we sacrificed our own." Chief Nakon moved his gaze from me to his daughter. "Now, you are awake. But our loyalty is strong. We will continue to give to you, just as you have given to us, Sun God. Please accept our humble offer." I watched Nakon kneel, followed by the rest. Abha was the last to bow, refusing to take her eyes from the goat.

Pondering only a moment, I said, "I accept your offer. You will be safe for another year."

Nakon exhaled in relief. Abha exhaled in disbelief. The goat bleated.

Looking to my golden soul, I allowed myself a peek beneath the surface, at the ones who existed within. They fought and clawed to escape, knowing another spirit was about to join them. But I was too strong, and they would continue to feed my ever-growing power.

I walked forward, so I stood directly in front of the animal. I reached out with my golden light, wrapping it around the goat's violet hue. The goat collapsed after only a moment, its heartbeat slow. The Maya people's gazes remained down, bowed in respect, knowing they were nourishing their God.

Only Abha watched as I absorbed its soul. Her heart pounded, and her emerald eyes were full of sorrow. I took so much of the goat's soul that nothing was left to linger in its form and nothing to hold the corpse together. By the time I finished, dust was all that remained, and the rope in the chief's hand hung limp in the air.

Above, the blue sky faded, and the clouds returned only to weep once again.

XXI
Faces

The enemy was not the one who defeated you.

-A

The night disappeared rapidly. Though I longed only to appreciate its beauty, the moon was eager to retreat from my gaze.

The Maya had left me at the temple. I sat on the black ground. Its surface was so strange with reflection and texture I wondered when it would come alive again and doom the temple to the bottom of the mountainside. The frankincense no longer burned, but the scent still lingered in the small space. Nature was silent. Even the wind seemed reluctant to disturb the unique tranquility the night had brought. I took advantage of the peace to absorb what had happened since waking.

Without even trying, I had an army of hybrids at my disposal. They worshipped me in a way even their ancestors had not. They knew nothing of what I truly was. These people did not know I was their creator—their father.

I thought of my firstborn, Cainadra. She had known how powerful I was. Known how dangerous it was to challenge me. But she did it anyway, knowing she was a part of me. Of course, it only made sense for her to think she could overthrow her leader. I was young and naive. I had not yet developed an understanding for my children.

If the hybrids believed they had power, they had power.

Even Abha, unknowing of her heritage, was beginning to show signs of rebellion. Simply because she could *see* we were similar in nature. I would have to fix that.

Black rock shattered. Up the mountainside, I could hear something clawing at the blackened soil. I was gone in an instant, following the sounds. The Maya people were wise not to traverse such unstable ground; the cooled lava was brittle, and cracks were everywhere.

I came upon a spot where the ground had turned from a crack into a small hollow. The trapped creature stilled upon my approach. Curious of an animal with hearing so sensitive, I peeked over the edge. Chuckling under my breath, I said, "Not as smart as you once were. Your kind was one of my greatest creations, yet you are now defeated by a mere fissure in the ground."

"Who speaks with such arrogance to a creature of the night?" the vampire hissed.

"Arrogance? Such nonsense coming from something made from the corpses of bats," I mocked.

While the vampire shrieked and clawed, I took the opportunity to sit and dangle my legs over the edge of the hollow. "Silence," I commanded.

The vampire quieted.

"Does your kind still stalk the humans? Do you still whisper into their minds?" I asked quietly.

Reluctantly it responded, "Yes." Its rough voice was both horrible and mesmerizing.

"Do you still search for Lilith? A woman with red hair and emerald eyes. A woman with great power. Do you still follow my command after all these centuries?" I could feel the creature staring at my dangling legs, knowing it would like nothing better than to suck the blood from my veins. *What a wonderful surprise it would be for the creature to find what truly lurked beneath my skin.*

"We follow no commands. We are the predators of this world. None can challenge us." Despite the grit of the vampire before, it said this as a question. I had no doubt the vampires made a name for themselves, though, watching it skulking on the mountainside looking half-starved, I had to assume the race was dying. The age of ice provided plenty of darkness, and in a time with so much light, the creatures were limited.

"That is disappointing." I rose to my feet and stretched my well-rested muscles. "I leave for a brief time, and you think that means you can run wild? You think you can feed as you wish without consequence?" I peered into the hollow again. "Well, your Creator has returned, and it is time to repay him for the power he so graciously shared."

The vampire snarled.

"Come." My light reached out and grabbed the grimy, mutilated spirit dwelling in the hollow. It struggled as it was lifted into the air and placed in front of me, but its efforts were in vain. "Kneel."

The vampire collapsed to its knees, no longer growling, as it realized my power.

"Where are the rest of you?" When I first created these creatures, they were mighty and powerful. Their strength was worth ten male hybrids, their senses were as refined as an animal's, and they could speak into a hybrid's mind to influence their thoughts. This was useful to me. The vampires would search the people's minds for signs of Lilith. But power always had a price.

The ugly creation had the audacity to smile as it said, "Everywhere."

"Good."

The creature's face wrinkled in confusion. Its wide flat nose and large pointed ears were startling against its chalky skin. Its body was similar to a hybrid's but was leaner and longer. Coarse white hair covered most of its body, and the eyes were large round orbs of nothing—nothing but blackness. Though, these creatures were not created for beauty.

"Can you still speak with your brethren? Can you hear them now?" I asked, hoping they had not lost this unique ability over time.

"Yes." Its smile grew wider, and I knew it was drinking some hybrid's blood through its kin's eyes. Drool dribbled from the corner of its mouth—it was thirsty.

The back of my hand met the vampire's face, just enough strength exerted to get its attention. "Focus." Its claws unsheathed and latched onto the ground, saving it from tumbling back into the hollow. "Now, tell your brethren this..." I waited to be sure the creature was listening before continuing. The look of fear on his bloodied face confirmed what I wanted. "Your Creator has returned. Oh, I am sure there are some of you old enough to remember me. Your kind was always resilient." I paused and allowed the vampire to share my face with the rest of its kind. "You have forgotten your mission. So, let me remind you."

The vampire cringed as I gripped its neck and stared into those empty eyes. Its body shook with fear and hunger.

"You are to search for a powerful woman. One with red hair, green eyes, and ivory skin. The humans may know her by different names, but it is Lilith. You are to search the minds of the humans for any sign of this woman. If you find her, you will come and tell me where she is. *That* is your purpose." I squeezed the vampire's throat tighter, knowing the rest could feel my grip. "Without purpose you are nothing to me and will become nothing in turn. Do you understand?" I smiled my friendliest smile, which I knew would frighten them into submission.

"Yes," the creature choked. I could almost hear all the voices of its people in that one word.

"Good."

"One of the others does recognize you, Creator." I released my hold on the vampire, and it slumped to the ground. "But you look different from before. Perhaps you are not as all-powerful as you make it seem? Then and now." A small tilt of the monster's lips told me he was hearing even worse things about me but was too smart to say them aloud.

I growled but felt my face. The hair had grown back. I knew I looked much older with the addition. Any sign of change was proof that I was not all-powerful, but weak and in need of adaptation. "You think this is a weakness?" I stood over the ungrateful vampire and pressed down on its leg with little force, breaking it in two. The scream echoed against the mountainside. So loud I was sure the hybrids heard it. "I am the embodiment of strength." The other leg was snapped. "You pitiless creatures are weak and only exist because of me." An arm was shattered.

The vampire fell to the ground, its eyes closed.

"Oh no, you are going to focus and tell your kin exactly what my response to their question is." I gripped its ugly face in my hand and forced its eyes open by pressing down on its now broken wrist with my free hand. I looked into its eyes, reaching out to all those bloodsuckers that were watching and said, "Get to work." With those last words I allowed the vampire to finally close its eyes before I crushed its skull in my hands, knowing the others would feel its pain.

The sun rose soon after. I dumped the vampire's remains into one of the volcano's tunnels where it would rot away, and I would not have to lay eyes on it again. I strolled along the cracks in the ground, all the way to the village where the people were waking.

There was a certain feeling in the air, one even I couldn't see. It was lighter, happier. I suspected it was the hybrids, joyous to have a god care for them at last. But it was me. My golden light was shining. *I had rediscovered my purpose.*

"Chief Nakon," I called. The man appeared quickly, emerging from his shelter.

"Sun God." Nakon bowed his head.

"Walk with me," I ordered. We made our way to the cotton fields. Their white puffs of texture matched the light clouds above. We walked slowly along the paths between the plants' homes. The upturned soil overwhelmed my nose. Earth had a strange scent, one of both life and death, fresh greens and rotted carcass. "Abha told me of a traveler you met years ago. The one who gave you the frankincense. Tell me about her."

Confused, but willing to aid his god in any way possible, Nakon said, "Yes, she was different from other women. She spoke in a strange tongue, but she knew enough of my own to barter." Nakon paused to clear his throat. "It was at the port near our borders. I go once a season to trade. Even more the last few years. I went to exchange our clothing and jewelry for food."

"Where does this port lead? Are there many traders?" I asked.

"The port goes many places, and there are many traders from those places. Though I see several familiar faces when I visit, there are always new ones." Nakon smiled a curious smile. "This woman was far from her home. She never said a name, but the description sounded similar to my wife's homeland."

"Where was your wife from? Abha didn't seem to know."

"She never told me. In the end, all she would say was, 'It was a magical place, but a hard one to live in.' One she didn't want to return to."

"What did the traveler look like?" My fists were clenching and unclenching in anticipation.

"Beautiful woman. Ivory skin and green eyes. That's another reason I suspected she was from the same place as my wife. They looked like kin, just as our village does."

"Did she have red hair?"

"My wife? Yes, bright as fire."

"No, the traveler," I pushed.

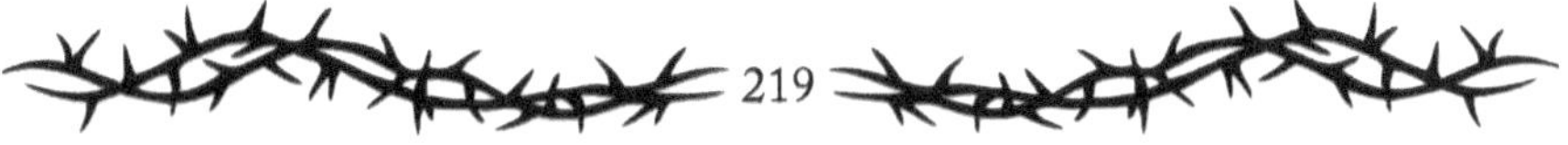

Nakon looked to me with an apologetic face. "I am sorry, I didn't see her hair. It was pulled back into her shawl." I wiped at my face in frustration, wishing the beard was gone. "Is that blood, Sun God?" Nakon asked.

I looked to my hand and realized I had forgotten to remove the vampire's blood before returning. "Yes, I was hunting this morning."

Satisfied with my answer, the chief offered, "Should we be searching for this woman, Sun God? We are at your beckon call. Ask us anything, and we will do it."

I smiled.

Leaving the chief to organize his people, I sought out my shelter and found the mirror Abha had shown me before. The coarse blonde hair clung to my face, even longer than it had been when I first saw it. It was not normal for hair to grow so quickly. It was not normal for me to have facial hair at all. It was new and strange.

A change. I was not supposed to change.

Though the skin beneath the beard was young and vibrant, it was unnerving to look at a different version of myself. He was unfamiliar. Unwanted. But I had felt that way previous to the change. Even before I leapt into the volcano, I had refused to look at myself for ages. When I drank from a stream, my eyes remained closed. When I walked past protruding ice, I glanced the other way. I didn't want to see the face *she* rejected. That *she* continued to run from.

Ever since the day she split Earth and disappeared, I've been ashamed of my defeat. She had won because I was weak. A tear landed on my hand. I bowed my head, unwilling to look at my reflection once again.

No. She would not win.

I raised my head and fell back, startled by the man in the mirror. He was just as young and strong, but he was not me. His face was wider, his jaw squarer, his skin and hair were as dark as the Maya people, and a short, black beard covered his cheeks and chin. But the most drastic change was the eyes. Bright emerald eyes stared back, wet from unshed tears.

I smiled. It looked warm and friendly.

What was this? Had I somehow lost my mind?

Had she finally taken that piece of me?

A gasp sounded from the doorway. Abha stood in the entrance holding a plate of food. It clattered to the floor as she drew a small knife from under her robes and said, "Who are you? You are disturbing a sacred place."

So, I hadn't lost my mind. This was real. "Lower your weapon, Abha. It is your Sun God."

Confused, Abha looked me up and down, noticing I wore the same clothes as the man she longed for. Then her gaze unfocused as she watched my golden soul twitch with irritation. "How?" she asked, lowering her knife only slightly.

I wished she hadn't found me during this time. I had no idea how I changed myself, let alone how to change back. "I have many powers you don't know of." Looking in the mirror, I forced my new face to hold a neutral expression as I tried to alter my features. Soon, my hair was dark blonde, my eyes dirt brown, and even a monkey's tail grew from me, though this was trapped beneath my clothes where Abha could not see.

I stared at Adam in the mirror. *Lilith created this face from nothing.*

What did this form have that mine did not?

"My Sun God?" I didn't respond, but Abha came close anyway, the knife sheathed beneath her robes again. "Which one is your true face?" she asked.

In an agonizingly familiar voice from long ago, when there were waterfalls and children, I said, "I am the sun incarnate. I have no face."

XXII

Conquer

This could not be. If I had the ability to change my appearance, then Lilith did, too. All this time, and I had sent out so many different creatures to search for a woman with red hair and green eyes.

All that time and effort was wasted!

She could appear as anyone she wished. The more I experimented, the angrier I became. I could change nearly everything about myself: race, gender, species, but not my age. I could not alter the young adult I was.

What could I tell my subordinates? Search for a fully grown human or animal? It gave me nothing to work with. Nothing at all. I returned to my original form but smashed the mirror before I could fully see my face. The glass scattered across the room; my knuckles bled red sand only a moment before healing. Abha ran. I bellowed in despair, "Lilith! Where are you?"

The walls were next. Then the ceiling collapsed on me. Nothing was immune to my strength. The shelter was but dust when I was done. I ran up the mountainside, hitting and clawing at anything in my way. When I had no more trees and boulders to torment, I attacked the black ground, daring it to bury me. The clouds overhead darkened, blocking the sunlight.

The sky howled in pain, as I beat the mountain until its cooled lava was nothing but shattered glass.

When the black glass was gone, I beat on the solid ground with both fists, bringing them down hard, unable to release all the fury I felt. It only grew the more I attacked, but I couldn't stop.

How could she do this to me?

How could she leave me alone on this world with nothing but my hatred?

Why did she make me hate her when I wanted to love her?

Lifting my arms high, I brought them down with force I hadn't exerted in eons, creating a split in the mountain. It continued toward the rim of the volcano, the ground thundering along with the skies. Then, it was hot.

Beneath the earth was lava. Just as it had woken me from my sleep, I had woken it. From the great split in the volcano, fissures appeared. They split in different directions, allowing the roused lava to escape and fly down its side like a mighty dragon come to exact its revenge.

At the thought, those dragon's souls pushed and tore at my light, wishing for release. Thousands upon thousands of them resided in me. Still, I was too strong. So, I used them to save me now. I wasn't ready to go back to sleep.

Rain fell heavy from the clouds. I willed the earth at the base of the volcano to rise, creating a wall. I rose with that wall and stood at its peak. I was high in the sky, directing the lava with powerful gusts of wind. The molten earth was endless and angered by the beating I had given. Earth battled for its freedom fearlessly, but it would not win.

It was nearly sunset when I regained control of the land. The ravines created during the process were deep, and the lava merely trickled down the mountainside now; rain and snow slowed its descent. Some parts of the mountain turned black again, though it was far from solid.

The temple was lost.

Tired, I leapt down from the wall on the opposite side. The sun was shining over the village because I had stolen every cloud I could to use in the battle. I laid down, struggling to catch my breath. The orange and amethyst hues, which waded across the darkening sky, calmed me.

I raised a hand to find that my soul had dimmed. I dropped the hand, feeling weaker than before. The dragons, which had been harassing me during the entire battle, were quiet. I felt for them, wondering where they had gone, but nothing answered.

Footsteps approached with haste, as they traversed the rock-covered ground. "My Sun God, are you hurt?" Abha asked. Finding where I lay by the new wall, she knelt beside me and brushed the hair from my eyes.

I removed her small hand from my face and said, "I cannot be hurt. I am a God." Pushing her aside, I stood and swayed on my feet.

Abha reached out only to retreat and said, "You need to be fed."

"Food is not my problem." I took another unsteady step.

"No, your light needs to be fed."

I refused to look her in the eye because she was right. Somehow, after all these years, I never understood what it took to use the magic. I was no different than my children. Now, I knew my magic came with a cost. Souls for power. And I had used too much of what I had collected over the eons.

Did I burn away my own? Looking to my soul, I knew I hadn't, but it had come close. *What would happen if I did?*

"This way, Sun God." Abha reached out instead of grabbing me as she had done before. She waited for me to take her hand. It was difficult to allow, but I was in pain. It was as she said before, *My light needed to be fed.*

The chief's daughter led me to a section of woodland where there was shade from the heat. There was also a fence bordering the forest's edge, and looking deeper into the darkness of the trees, I could see the other side.

"There are at least twenty goats within the pen, bred specifically for you, Sun God. Please heal yourself," she begged. I looked into her emerald eyes and pretended, for just a moment, that it was Lilith caring for me. But my eyes unfocused, and I could see the gold light surrounding her. It remained calm, too calm for someone who was supposed to be worried.

Instead of jumping over the wood-lined barrier, I walked through it. The wood splintered and snapped, causing Abha to step back and the goats to run in fright. But I didn't need to catch them.

I made my way to the center of the pen and reached toward their souls. So many colors and so many different qualities in those lights. They were mine now. I absorbed all of them. So much that even their carcasses became dust and disappeared into the grass. I took a deep breath, and the pain ebbed just enough for me to focus.

I needed to be the one who found her.

No one else would be able to see her if she changed her appearance. I knew what I had to do. "Abha, bring your father to me. I need to have a word."

"My Sun God—," she began.

"Now!" I ordered.

Abha ran as fast as she could past the village and into the opposing woodland. The chief evacuated his people when the volcano erupted, but they couldn't escape fire. If it wasn't for me, they would have burned alive.

I continued to drink in the souls around me. Plants and insects died one by one as my magic grew. Nowhere near satisfied, I departed the deceased goats' home and followed Abha's footprints. She was no longer in sight, but I heard her harsh breathing as she ran to her father. Five hundred breaths later, there were two sets of feet running toward me.

Yes, I knew exactly what to do.

If Lilith was still roaming the planet, trading and interacting with our children, then she would hear of a place with so much power she could not ignore it. A place where, when its ruler's names were uttered, the speaker trembled in fear, because they knew it would mean death if they misspoke. A place with vast bounty and riches. A place and people that destroyed all others in their path. A place Lilith could not resist to subdue.

If she wouldn't stop running, I'd make her run to me.

"We leave now," I ordered.

"So soon, Sun God?" Nakon asked, his breath lost from exertion.

"There is no more time to waste. My orders from before will take effect immediately." I straightened my back, realizing I was still hunched over in pain. "Ready your warriors."

"Sun God, we will do anything for you—"

"Good," I interrupted.

Nakon struggled to finish his thought, "But we are not ready. We will be massacred."

"What are you talking about?" Abha questioned, her face pinched in frustration.

I ignored her and continued, "Your people won't be destroyed. I will be there to guide you through battle. No one who has fought in my name has lost." I thought of Asher in that moment, and a sharp pain shot through my chest. *I still hadn't recovered from my battle with the volcano.*

Chief Nakon, though worried, said, "It will be done." The Maya man turned on his heel and shouted orders to the warriors as they entered the farmlands, knowing they could return without fear of the raging mountain.

Still weak, I turned my face away from Abha's curious gaze. The sky was pitch black now, and only a sliver of moonlight cast light upon us. "Weapons," I muttered.

"Sun God?" the chief's daughter inquired.

"Where are your weapons kept?" I demanded. Quietly, Abha nodded and walked to the shelter I had slept in. The home was nothing more than rubble now.

The woman made her way to the center of the ruins and began pushing aside debris. Abha's hands were small but strong. Her bare arms flexed, revealing muscle I hadn't seen before. She was not an idle woman.

Soon, the ground was cleared enough for her to grab a wooden handle protruding from the soil. Pulling, it opened into a small, dark hole in the ground. "In here is where we keep our most treasured weapons and jewels. Ones forged by the most skilled of our people over the generations." Stepping aside, she added, "It is all for you, my Sun God."

Slowly, I approached the man-made hollow. It was as if the night itself was stuffed into the ground and left to fester. Even I, with perfect night vision, could not see the bottom. Sensing my discomfort, and watching my dim, wavering spirit, Abha dug through the debris again. She raised a thick, short stick. It had plant fibers wrapped around its peak. I recognized the sweet scent of yucca immediately; it grew in abundance on this land.

Abha was searching for the right rocks to start a fire with when I allowed my weakened soul to reach out and light it myself. The flame was small, but it grew as it burned through the yucca. Soon, it blazed bright and strong. With a small smile, Abha placed the torchlight in my palm, making sure to run her hand along my forearm before stepping away, distracting me from the mocking flames. "You are taking us to war," Abha stated.

"Yes."

"For *her*?"

Surprised, I answered, "Yes."

"Is she worth the pain? The death?" The woman bowed her eyes, readying herself for my answer. But I merely stepped into the small opening, falling with the fire blazing beside me, unknowing of what waited below.

When I landed, it was not graceful. I crumpled to my knees, barely able to hold the torch upright. As I recovered, I watched the flame slowly lick its way down the stick. *The fire wouldn't last long.*

I shined the light over the tunnel. There were stone pedestals lining the walls. Each one held a shining black and grey weapon. I approached the one nearest to me. It was a small, curved knife made of stone. I could see the reflection of the fire in its gleaming obsidian handle. I ran a finger across the blade, allowing it to cut me. *Always curious.* My wound healed as quickly as it had been made.

I moved on to the next, where a spear, the length of two men, stood erect. I could tell its stem was sycamore wood due to its subtly sweet scent. The spearhead was obsidian, and the base of the rock was wrapped carefully in beads and colored threads. I longed for my own spear. The dragon bone was now a rare thing. As well as the meaning behind it.

I moved on.

It wasn't until half the torch had burned away that I reached the very back of the tunnel. Glittering jewels were lined up on a long table. Coarse red cloth rested beneath them. There were many pieces made from bone, obsidian, and gems. The gems were common, but they were bold, bright, and beautiful. I didn't see much beauty on Earth, but the Maya people had managed to create it.

I thought of Lilith wearing such things and huffed out a small laugh. *She would hate it.* Too extravagant. Too unnatural. But of course, these lovely creations would look gruesome beside her own beauty.

Near the stone table stood another pedestal. What rested there captured my attention, and I lifted the strange weapon up high to admire the artistry.

Macuahuitl. Macana.

This weapon was built long and wide. The wood's scent was strong—maple. Different versions of the sky was etched into the flat surface. At the top, the sun shone down on the land, as the etching moved downward toward the ebony handle, the sky grew angry with clouds and lightening—I could almost hear the thunder—then it was rain and snow, and finally, nearest the handle, the nighttime sky. The moon shone down on the land. Shards of obsidian were placed among the skies to accentuate the trees, lightening, and rain. But the obsidian soon transformed from decorative to deadly. From the sides of this instrument stemmed sharpened points of black rock, so each blow made by the wielder was a deadly one.

Putting the torch upon the pedestal, I waved the macana slowly through the air, enjoying the weight of it in my hands and relishing the comfort it gave me after so many centuries of being weaponless. My soul thrummed because of it. Though, I realized too late, I had spent too much time exploring the cavern. The fire was now small. I tried to light the torch again, but I had not yet recovered from battle.

I had no more to give.

Grabbing what was left of the torch and my new weapon, I ran for the entrance. I searched for the light above, but it was night and difficult to find. When the very last flame vanished, along with my composure, a sliver of white light appeared. I followed it to the skyward entrance. I leapt into the hollow tunnel, gripping the soil with the macana and my bare hand, pulling myself up and out of the blackness. Once I reached the surface, I stood to face Chief Nakon, who said, "Sun God, we are ready."

I watched the moonlight reflect against the obsidian edges of my new weapon and acknowledged I had an army ready to fight in my name, yet I couldn't find it in myself to smile.

The Maya men were ready to travel quickly, leaving the women and children behind to tend the fields and homes, though a few young males stayed to protect them. I secured the earth-wall before departing. The lava still flowed on the other side, slowly now, but nature was unpredictable.

On the journey, we walked slower than I was used to. I wished to feel the wind on my face, the natural flex of muscles between strides, and to command the ground to harden as I ran. But alas, hybrids did not inherit such abilities. The sun seemed to move quicker across the sky than we could walk by land. The men behind me were fit for their species and kept any complaints to themselves. I respected this quality, but they couldn't hide their pounding hearts and labored breaths.

Night soon covered us in its dark blanket, and my army was falling far behind. "We stop here for the night," I commanded.

Chief Nakon nodded once, no expression on his face, though there was sweat along his hairline. With only a few words from their chief, the men collapsed where they stood, not bothering to make fires or proper shelters. They rolled out their furs, drank from their waterskins, and lay down to sleep.

I thought of my first army, before the land parted, and wished I had the chance to raise and train these men for myself. *They would be much stronger if I had.* With Asher at the front, the first ones had traversed miles and miles of dense forest in only a few days. A feat that managed to impress even me. A half-smile appeared, remembering my lost children, but my eyes were wet.

"You are sad," Abha said from behind. She had insisted she come with as my personal caretaker. I didn't need one, yet I'd allowed it.

I tilted my head in her direction and said, "Sad?"

"You grieve for something lost."

"I told you to keep your eyes focused on the physical realm."

Placing herself in front of me, Abha responded, "I don't need to see your light to know you are in pain." The woman boldly took my hand in hers, and to both of our surprise, I didn't pull it away.

"Lay with me tonight," I said. My gaze met hers, and I allowed myself a rare moment of pleasure by pretending they were someone else's.

"As you wish, my Sun God." Walking a short distance from the rest of her people, Abha took the furs from her sack and laid them out neatly, planning to share her bed since I hadn't carried one of my own. The land we were on now was nothing but desert. We passed through the Maya woodlands quickly, forcing us into hot sand and a cruel sun. I willed the clouds from the distant mountains to cover us, but it only lasted so long before they, too, dissipated.

It was still colder than a volcano.

After a moment, I could no longer hear the silent chattering of people, but slow, relaxed breaths as they slept. "Please, lie down, my Sun God. You must be exhausted."

I walked to where Abha stood and removed my robes, leaving only a small fabric cloth hanging from my waist. Reluctantly, I permitted the woman to take the macana from my hand, its obsidian edges glittering in the moonlight, and set it down gently beside our bedding. I followed her lead as she situated herself on the soft jaguar fur.

Abha raised her hand to move the gold strands from my ice-blue eyes, then stroked my bare cheekbones. "You don't like hair on your face." Again, Abha did not ask, she simply knew. It had been a day and night, still the growth had not appeared as the other men's had.

"It is too warm for such things."

She pinched her lips, considering her next words. "You are very handsome with such things."

"If you don't enjoy my face the way it is, you don't have to look at it." It wouldn't have been the first time a woman preferred another's face over mine.

"*She* hurt you, didn't she?" she whispered.

Slow to answer, I said, "Yes."

"Then why search for her? If she does not want you as you want her, why do you seek her out if it only causes you pain?" Abha kept her voice low, but the urgency in her tone was undeniable. She wanted to understand me—understand what I was doing with her people.

"No more words tonight." Misunderstanding, Abha reached for my waist, stroking the skin there. I grabbed her hand and brought it up to rest over my empty chest. "Just look at the stars with me," I clarified.

Her green eyes finally turned upward and gazed at the nighttime sky. Knowing what was to come the next day, my mind drifted as I remembered a similar moment in the beginning when there was no one but The First Man and Woman.

The sun rose and cast its light over the Maya people, the sky a mix of cobalt and saffron. There were groans of protest as it roused the men, but it was quickly snuffed once they remembered where they were and what they were about to do.

"Are you sure?" Abha asked as she lay beside me. While we slept, I had wrapped my arm around her shoulders, bringing her closer. The woman's arm still laid across my chest.

"It's the only way to help your people."

Abha shifted her head, and those familiar green eyes scanned my expression. However, she didn't say anything because she knew this *wasn't* for the sake of her people. And there was nothing she could do about it.

I released Abha and replaced her with the macana. As I stood, I looked out over the men while they ate their morning meal. Some couldn't stomach the rations, their nerves defeating them. I made sure to commit these weak men to memory. Some men scarfed down as much as they could. *Good. They would need it in the hours to come.*

The neighboring tribe, the K'iche people, were blocking our path to the port Chief Nakon had spoken of before. Nakon confessed to me that he needed their permission to cross the land. Their conditions to cross were unreasonable, forcing the chief to leave most of his warriors at the border, as well as, forfeiting most of his trading goods to them as payment.

Unacceptable. "Nakon, where do we travel from here?"

The chief, already well awake and fed, rushed to my side to answer, "Not much farther to the border. Their patrols pass by every hour." He paused. "Should we not try speaking with them first? They have caused us no harm."

"They are bigger in number, yes? More land marked by them?"

Nakon nodded.

"It is in a human's nature to expand and conquer. The difference between them is merely a matter of who does it first." Meeting the chief's gaze for the first time since speaking, I said, "We will be first."

Nakon bowed his head, acknowledging I knew better. I didn't blame him for his reluctance to fight, but this was the first step in creating the most powerful civilization in the world.

One Lilith could not resist.

"This will be a quick battle." I placed my hand on Nakon's shoulder. "You have sacrificed your nourishment and your loved ones to me so I could rise. And I am asking you to sacrifice even more so my power can flourish. With this, your people will not only be protected, but strong and respected. They will have a power of their own that no one will be able to ignore."

Chief Nakon smiled, imagining the kind of life I described. One without hunger or fear. One with riches, land, and happy, fulfilled people. *What else could a hybrid want?*

"Will we be like you?" Abha asked. I had forgotten about her as soon as I stood to face my army.

"No one can be like me." Abha turned away before I could see her expression, but her soul thrashed in frustration, a frustration I couldn't comprehend.

"It's time." The men were up and moving before I said another word.

After crossing the desert land, we came upon the border to the K'iche people where a small woodland stood. The patrol's scent was weak, indicating that another one would be passing by again soon. The smell of tobacco was prominent in the distance. They must have been a prosperous people if they had such things. I recalled an elderly man in the Maya village offering me his stash of rare tobacco leaves. I refused, unsure of their purpose. Scenting the burning plant on the breeze, I now knew it had a relaxing effect. A quality I was sure every hybrid craved.

"The patrols are to be taken first." Pointing, I said to Nakon, "Lead your men to the east, I will take the west. We will meet in the heart of the village. Abha, you are to stay here until we come to retrieve you. Stay in the trees and out of sight."

The woman bowed her head in submission. The Maya were surprisingly agile in the trees. I could barely hear their footsteps on the dry ground. "Stay safe," Abha ordered, a strange look in her eye as she raised her head. An expression I wouldn't associate with concern.

"Save your well wishes for the men who need it."

At that moment, when I stepped into the tree line, I was transported to another time in my existence. When my daily activities consisted of hunting and killing. A time when I was as close to being an animal as I ever would be because Lilith had no interest in what I had to offer. My mind emptied as instinct took over. Every sound and smell was a sign, signs that would lead me to my prey. A torn leaf, a trampled path, a musky scent, a beating heart. *I found you.*

My magic was growing, but still too weak. However, it didn't matter because my natural abilities were more than enough. I ran without assistance from the wind and earth. My muscles flexed and stretched, following the scent deeper into the woodland.

Two herds. Twelve animals. Twelve hearts.

I was on them in minutes. Weapons were drawn and then detached, the limbs with them. Blood poured onto the thirsty plants. Only one creature was able to scream before it was, too, dead and gone. My appetite grew as the hearts slid down my throat.

The other herd drew close, beckoned by the sounds of the hunt. I smiled. Their hearts and souls were mine in seconds. Blood dripping from my face and hands, I ran again, following a fresh trail. It led right into the heart of the prey's home. They were surprised to see me. I laughed. The creatures screamed, fleeing.

The hunt began anew. I took dozens of hearts, devouring them where their masters had fallen. Soon, I heard the sounds of stone clanging. I turned to find that more prey had entered the clearing, battling their own kind. I wondered at the oddity of it but merely continued my hunt, savoring the souls that entered my light.

"Put down your weapon or she dies!" A man's body collapsed at my feet, his heart still pumping in my hand, as I looked to where the voice came from.

"Release her!" A familiar voice said. I found two men, one holding a woman in his grasp, a knife at her throat. The other was standing near, a spear aimed toward them.

"Leave and you can have her! We have done nothing to you, yet you attack. Leave now, and all will be as it was." The man cut into the woman while she struggled, and blood trickled down her neck. "I know how important she is to you, Nakon. She is easy to recognize, she looks the same as your dead wife. Go now, and you can keep your daughter."

Nakon took a step forward.

"Stop! One more step and she is lost to you."

As I watched this event unfold, a man charged at me with a knife in his palm. His head was removed before I could think. I looked down at the hand that had done it only to realize a weapon lay there; the macana. The once smooth, dark wood was now soaked in crimson blood, the etchings drowned. *I hadn't even noticed it was in my hand before now.*

I looked up to the struggling woman again and met her gaze. "Sun God, please help me!" she cried. Tears ran down her dirt covered face, and it blended into the blood that dripped from her nose.

Abha.

My mind woke from the trance. A trance I hadn't experienced before. I'd relied on instinct in the past, but never had I lost my humanity—my mind.

I was in front of the captor before he could blink. The knife was turned and shoved into his own chest, but not into his heart. *No need to waste.* Not fully released from the trance, I consumed the heart in front of Nakon and Abha. Once I was finished, I realized the horror of what I had done. No one knew this side of me. Not even Lilith.

Unsure of what to say, I stood there, watching the battle rage on. It was only when Nakon approached a freshly killed body and started cutting into its chest that I met his gaze. Holding the organ in his palm, the chief brought it to dry, cracked lips and took his first bite of life. "You said we will have our own power. If this is the way, so be it," Nakon said.

With a warrior's cry, he raised the heart up so his men could witness the ritual for themselves. One by one, the Maya people killed and con-sumed their enemy's hearts while gaining their power. Both Abha and I watched the souls of the deceased enter the killer's light. The murderous spirits grew both brighter and darker the more they consumed. And the more they took, the more they tried to take from each other.

"What have you done?" Abha whispered.

With the tang of iron on my tongue, I said, "I've created an empire."

XXIII

Gold

Surrender to what lights your way, but
don't ignore the darkness that ensues.
-S

The celebration for the victory of the Maya people was short and consisted of pillaging the K'iche's valuables and women. When all were rested, I ordered them to execute the survivors. The K'iche were the only ones blocking our path to the port. Now that they were gone, we could accomplish what we came to do.

Abha hadn't said a word since she watched her father and brothers devour the K'iche people's hearts, but now, she begged as one of the warriors raised his spear to stab a young woman. "Please, spare her! Let us bring the survivors back to our village. They can serve us in the fields. Please!" Acknowledging that he wasn't going to listen, she grabbed the spear and fought to take it from the man's grasp. He threw her aside and raised his weapon again.

"Stop," I ordered. The spear was lowered.

"Sun God, please spare the women and children. They can be of use to you." Abha stayed where she had been thrown on the ground but moved to face me on her knees, her head bowed. The woman's soul thrashed in frustration, not fear. She thought herself safe from cruelty.

"We don't have the time or men to spare to take the prisoners back to the village," I said, my voice unwavering.

"Please," she whispered. "They are innocent. The women only followed the men. Those men are gone now. And the children will be grateful for a new home. I will take them back to the village myself."

I was about to concede, against my better judgment, when the K'iche woman reached for the knife hanging from the warrior's side. Successful in unsheathing the small weapon, she aimed it toward me and said, "Cursed are those who take what is not to be taken." Before the warrior could grab the knife from the woman, she turned it on herself and plunged the obsidian into her own heart, knowing we would not be able to take it from her now.

Nowhere for the soul to go except down, I absorbed the woman's jade light, refusing to be robbed by Earth. "Do you see now, Abha? They do not want to be saved."

Defeated, Abha stood and walked into the forest, unable to watch as her kin killed and then devoured their newfound power.

We soon reached the opposite border of K'iche land. From the dense tree line, we watched the port bustle with traders. The men and women gathered on the beach were all different from one another: there was a man with ebony skin, earth-colored eyes, and tight-curled hair; a small, fine-boned woman with angled eyes and darkened skin which held a sunlight warmth; and a tall man that looked as if he lived and breathed winter, his hair and eyes mimicking the falling snow.

Without thought, I altered my own appearance. I was once again the man I had changed into before. I was a Maya man with emerald-green eyes. Chief Nakon did not waver when he saw this power. He knew he had barely begun to witness what I was capable of.

It was strangely intriguing to watch this time's hybrids. They had changed and adapted to the land around them: their appearance, words, mannerisms, and clothing. They traded not only food, furs, and weapons, but beautiful, needless things such as jewelry, colored cloths, and scented sticks.

Why create such things? Why did they hold value to the hybrids?

"Creativity is highly regarded because it is what separates us from nature." Abha whispered in my ear.

Refusing to tear my eyes away from the port, I said, "Why would you want to be separate from nature?" *From life?*

Without hesitation, she said, "Because we are stronger alone." I turned my head toward Abha, surprised by her answer. I had only ever heard the opposite from Lilith. Abha possessed the same *sight*, yet she saw something different.

I was distracted by the falling of sails. I turned to look behind the hybrids, where more creations floated in the water; the most useful I had seen so far. Most of the boats were only big enough to fit a few traders and their cargo. I observed supplies being unloaded and loaded. Then my gaze reached one uniquely built creation. This boat could hold at least fifty hybrids, but I suspected there was space beneath the deck, allowing for more. I could appreciate this creation, for it would be of significant use to me.

"The big one is similar to the boat I purchased Abha's mother from. It could very well be the same," Nakon whispered. My army was hidden in the trees, the shoreline being only a short sprint from where they stood. I heard leaves rustle and dry grass crunch behind me. I glanced to the traders, concerned they would become aware of us, but they continued what they were doing; bartering for better deals. There were traders with other hybrids beside them, translating what the ones across from them were saying. Language had been separated, torn apart, and pieced back together again to create the combination of words each unique color of person spoke.

We are stronger alone. Abha was not the only one with these thoughts.

"Then you will take that one, Nakon," I said. Abha retreated deeper into the forest and climbed up a tree to hide. The sun was high above us, lighting our path. I raised my hand and brought it down. That was all they needed.

Hundreds of Maya men charged from the trees, their warrior's cry piercing the air. I didn't move a muscle. I let the warriors flood around me in a sea of pain and power. I raised the macana to eye level, enjoying the glint of light along the sharp edges. I had rinsed the weapon in a stream, but the blood refused to leave the maple wood. It was now dark crimson, the same shade as *her* hair.

The traders scattered, fleeing for their boats and abandoning their livelihoods. Nakon was a force to be reckoned with. He cut a direct path to the biggest boat. The slave traders were working in haste to flee and sail away before losing their lives, but they soon realized that this wasn't an option. The chief reached their walkway, and the crewmen armed themselves. Some flew forward wielding swords made of stone and metal, while others stayed behind shooting arrows from a bow. Screams could be heard from below the ship's deck as the slaves contemplated their fates.

The smaller boats were taken quickly along with its traders, though I caught some hybrids sneaking back to the shoreline to gather valuables. The men ran toward the tree line in hopes to escape. Faster than they could take a breath, I was in their path. "Surrender. There is no other option." One of the men held a sword and stepped forward to attack. I heard something breathing heavily behind me in the thicket. I didn't move. "Surrender," I repeated.

"Get out of the way!" The winter-skinned man said. I stared into those eerily similar eyes as he pierced my middle, the blade not quite reaching my spine. Red sand poured onto the beach, adding to the shimmering particles.

"Surrender," I said calmly. The traders watched as the hole in my body healed before their eyes. The man and his companions dropped their weapons and bowed so low their heads were partially buried in the sand. One of the men held colored clothing, the fabric smelled of flowers; flora was the main ingredient for creating such bright colors.

Bright gold caught my eye to the right. Small sunflowers were facing upward along the woodland's edge. Reaching out my soul, I gripped the flower's light and stripped its color, leaving white petals. The gold was mist in the air as my experiment began.

"Hold still," I commanded. Though the hybrids did attempt to listen, they shook with fear. Stepping forward, I gripped the man who stabbed me and lifted him up, stripping him of his light cloth shirt. The flower's essence floated toward his neck and dug into his skin, moving through the small pores.

The man screamed, "Stop!"

"Silence."

The trader screamed again.

I placed my hand over his mouth as I concentrated on the intricate design. Thick swirls of gold sunrays lined his throat. Once I was done there, I moved to his wrist and ankles. Before long, he was the first to receive the Sun God's Mark. A mark that would tell the world, *This man belonged to the Maya Empire, an empire led by the very sun itself. And doomed to be a slave for the remainder of his life.*

Stealing from the sunflowers, I began again, while the first man lay crying on the ground. I was nearly finished with the third hybrid when the last of the group ran. Unwilling to leave my project, I broke the man's neck without touching him, my golden light quick to retrieve the frightened hybrid.

I would have to find a better way to recover the ones who ran; I shouldn't have wasted the resource. The K'iche were different, they had been inhabitants of this land and an obstacle, but these travelers were useful.

Once I had mastered the marking technique, I went to Nakon, where the battle still raged on the large boat. Though the slave traders fought ruthlessly, fear could be seen in their blood-spattered faces. They were unprepared and outnumbered.

Calmly, I walked to where Nakon fought and placed my hand on his arm. He spun to defend himself but immediately bowed in submission when he realized it was his Sun God. The crewman paused, confused.

I raised my hand and said, "You will surrender and join the slaves below deck."

Predictably, they attacked.

One by one, I disarmed and threw the men into the pit of the ship. While I did this, the Maya pulled the ladder up and discarded it, so those below could not find their way back out. Tossing the last one in, I listened to the groans and cries of the traders. The fall was not fatal, but it would have broken some bones.

"Chief Nakon," I said.

"Yes, Sun God?"

"Did you recognize any of the traders? Had any of them been on the ship when your wife was aboard?"

Certain of his answer, he said, "Yes." For the first time, Nakon's expression was angry, and he motioned to the last man I had overpowered.

"Wait here." I ran back to the woodland's edge, knowing what had watched me mark the hybrids. "Vampire, reveal yourself."

Heavy breathing could be heard from the thicket. "The sun… I can't."

"Do not struggle. The pain won't last long," I said. Without another word, I grabbed the night creature and ran it as quick as I was able to the ship, dropping it in the darkness of the pit.

Screams erupted upon the creature's arrival. I couldn't blame them; vampires were one of the ugliest creatures on Earth. I followed the colorless monster and landed silently on the wooden floor. The vampire was as frightened as the hybrids, cowering in a dank corner to hide from the sunlight that peered through the cracks in the wooden planks above.

Adjusting my sight to the dark hull of the boat, I could see the slaves were tied to the floors and each other. They were covered in grime and sweat. The putrid odor of waste filled the small space. I searched their faces and saw nothing of *her* in them. The crew stood behind the starved hybrids, and as far away from the Sun God as possible.

"Nakon."

"Yes, Sun God?" he responded from above.

"Gather all the food you can find on this boat and lower it down. These people are hungry."

Perplexed, Nakon said, "Right away." Several footsteps hurried away to find what I asked.

"Vampire, come. You are frightening them," I ordered.

"Yes, Creator." The creature crawled to my side, skittish of the few spots of light in its path. Although, a little light would not harm it, the creatures had such a severe intolerance for the sun that their fear of it had grown out of control.

Soon, a basket was lowered down by a rope; it held bread and cheese and waterskins. I untied the basket slowly, taking notice of everyone's reaction. The slaves' stomachs groaned, and the crewman tensed—still selfish, even now, after they had been defeated.

A child peered out from behind his mother. I approached him and crouched down to offer him a piece of bread. "You will not be hungry again, my child." Patiently, I waited, and the child reached out with his dirt-covered fingers, plucking it from my hand. The bread was gone before I could stand.

"You are all slaves of cruel men intent on selling you to the highest bidder." I walked and placed the food and water in the hand of every slave

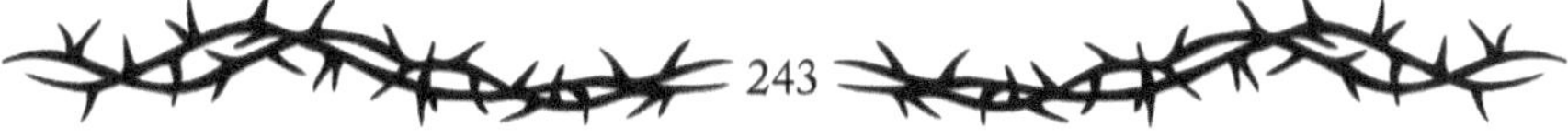

there as I spoke. "That ends today. I am Kinich Ahau, your Sun God and savior. The power I wield is vast. Powerful enough to protect you from harm and starvation." I moved to stand below the deck's opening where the sun shone, the basket empty at my side. "You are now a part of a mighty empire, at the heart of Maya land. You will contribute to the construction of The City of Gold." I smiled at the name that came to mind. "Here, you will be protected. But if you should attempt to leave the city…"

I looked to the white vampire. His eyes connected with mine, and I knew he could hear my command. The vampire, faster than any hybrid could move, ran for one of the crewmen cowering behind the slaves. His screams were intense and filled the space with panic. I merely held my position and raised my hand in silent command. The slaves obeyed but huddled together, as far away from the carnage as possible.

The screams faded as his blood was drained. The blood was stark against the creature's pale complexion, making it even more terrifying. "As you witnessed, these creatures are much more powerful in strength, speed, and agility than humans. You are outmatched. You have no chance of surviving." I took a step into the dark. "But I leave your fate in your own hands. If any would wish to flee, now is the time." Nakon lowered the ladder, anticipating what I wanted. The Maya freed the slaves from their bondages. And I waited.

None moved. The first boy I had given food gazed at me with great reverence, his blue eyes sparkling. *Smart child.* I smiled at the young hybrid.

I had Nakon and his men gather them on the beach to await their marks. Most of the crew agreed to join, those who didn't made the vampire very happy. Only one remained in the darkness. "Nakon, will you join me?"

The chief followed me to the back of the underdeck. The vampire had the last man trapped in the corner where the waste was kept. "Do you remember this man?" I asked the slave trader.

He peered around the monster to examine Nakon. The man nodded, and his dark, waved hair fell into his brown eyes.

"You remember what you sold him, so many years ago? A light woman with crimson hair and green eyes."

"Yes," the man whispered.

"Where did she come from?" I demanded.

"I don't know… I found her wandering my homeland," he stuttered.

"Vampire." Hearing my thoughts again, it raked its long claw down the man's forearm, and blood poured to the floor. "Enough," I demanded. The vampire struggled to resist the blood, but it did once it heard my most recent thought.

"You must have tortured her. What did she tell you?" I questioned.

"Nothing! I swear!" The man clutched his arm, though it didn't do much to slow the bleeding.

"Think hard." With another order to the vampire, it forced its eyes upon the bleeding man, hearing any and every thought that crossed his mind. *If only they could hear memories as well as current thoughts. That would be most useful.*

"Nothing Creator, he speaks the truth."

"Did he torture her? What did he do?" Nakon interjected.

The vampire moved its gaze to Nakon and delivered what he learned into the chief's mind. Nakon fell back a step, and a tear slipped down his dark cheek, seeing things no mate should ever have to see.

The man screamed again, but the creature had not laid a finger on him. Only its eyes gazed upon him. "No more. Let him keep his mind intact. I am sure Nakon would like him aware for what is to come." I nodded my approval to the chief and placed the macana in his palm. "Do what you must." Ignoring the ladder, I leapt and landed on the deck, grateful for the fresh air. The sun was fading into the distance now, and crimson hues cascaded across the darkening sky.

"Creator, what of me?" the vampire hissed.

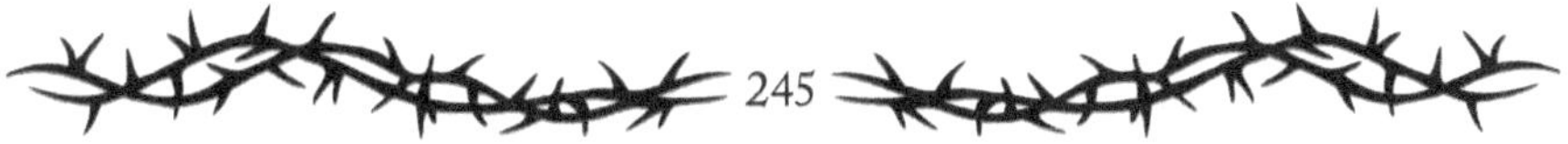

Looking down into the darkness, I said, "You will tell your kin this: Abandon the search for Lilith. Come here to serve me instead. There will be plenty of food, and your kind will have power on this land, so long as I am obeyed." *There was no point in searching anymore. She would come to me.*

"It is done, Creator."

"Good." I abandoned the vampire, knowing it would wait for full darkness to leave its dank sanctuary. Until then, it would have to be content with the slave trader's screams.

The slaves were fed and cleaned when I found them resting on the beach. The Maya people were guarding them, awaiting my orders. My men were exhausted, but there was not one complaint. The hearts from their kills would sustain them for a time. Abha played with the same boy I noticed before, creating strange shapes in the sand.

I looked to the woodland's edge and admired the gold flowers. "Line up. You will now be bestowed the greatest honor of your lifetime, the Sun God's Mark." The hybrids did as I instructed. I motioned for a Maya warrior to bring me the first of the marked. The winter-skinned man no longer looked upon me with anger, but with submission. *It was too easy to break hybrids.*

"You see the gold upon his skin. This will mark you all as citizens of The City of Gold, and the *honored.* This mark will protect you and prove to others that you have been blessed by Kinich Ahau himself." I released the slave and beckoned one of my warriors. "To show you there is nothing to fear, I will demonstrate on my own men."

The warrior dropped his weapon and shed his shirt, prepared to receive the same marks. As I looked at the man, I realized the Maya people had covered their bodies in black designs of their own. Not much of their skin was left for me to work with, and the gold would only be dim in comparison. "For my warriors, you will receive the mark of the *fearless.*"

I reached out with my soul and took the sunflower's hue. Its essence floated through the air in waves of shimmering gold until it landed upon the man's forehead, swirling and integrating into his skin, and creating the first *fearless* mark—a jaguar's head. Its teeth were bared, and its ears lay flat in defiance.

The Maya man had suffered through many markings before and was able to disguise his pain, but he could not hide the sweat dripping from his skin, which made the gold shimmer in the rays of the fading sun.

I continued this process with all my warriors before moving to the traders and slaves, making them into citizens of The City of Gold. Nakon was last, for him I gave the mark of the *wise*, assuring everyone that he was to be respected and obeyed. This design was simpler, involving only a vertical line crossed by a shorter horizontal line between his brows. Nakon returned the macana to me afterward. The chief was covered in the slave trader's blood, and I was sure the vampire was enjoying the remainder of the man's body before it would depart into the woodland to await its kin.

The boats were searched and stripped of food and goods. Small carts were made to carry the bounty back to the village, now known as, The City of Gold. The dead were burned. The boats were left with a few guards which would warn us of visitors. I explained how to use the vampires as a form of communication.

We would repeat the process until we had gained all the knowledge the world had to offer, all the people I needed to serve the empire, and all the power I needed to attract Lilith's attention. As I watched the hybrids work, a familiar feeling warmed me. It was the same emotion I had when I watched Cainadra speak her first words and Asher spear his first kill.

Pride.

"You are happy," Abha said. She stood at my side, not close enough to touch, but closer than I thought she would stand after her protests earlier that morning.

"You are not?" I asked.

"I am happy because you are happy, my Sun God." Her golden spirit was calm and controlled, not a flicker of emotion revealed itself.

"You should be. You are alive to witness a great rising of your people. The Maya will be known across the world as the richest and most powerful of humankind." I reached out and took her hand. "With you at the center of it all." I willed the flower's gold to us, and it hovered in the air, an unanswered question.

Abha met my emerald gaze with her own. "It would be my honor."

My hand slipped from hers and reached for the neckline of her robes. Though the stitching was beautiful, it was in my way. With nothing but a gentle tug, I ripped the covering until her chest lay bare. Her breath hitched, but she did not run.

The gold floated over her chest, merging with her skin. She swallowed a scream and clutched my arm for comfort. The process was quick, and a shining crescent moon now rested above her heart. Abha looked down at her new mark, her aura shifting in confusion.

"Mark of the *spirit*. For you are a Seer and must be treated as such."

The sun had completely faded now, and the waning moon had risen, its ivory light reflecting against the water's calm waves. The warriors were making camp with the furs they had pillaged. Fires were crackling and meat was roasting. The citizens had bedded down for the night, the children were already fast asleep in their mother's arms, knowing they were safe for the time being.

Abha released my arm for the first time since I started marking her, and I grabbed it before her skin left mine. I led her into the trees where I heard a creek flowing. This woodland was not the same as the one from the beginning; the trees were smaller, and the leaves were shaped strangely. The forest of my past would not have allowed such light to bleed through its canopy, but the moon fell to this woodland floor, comfortable in its reach.

I stopped at the creek's edge, reassured by its sound. Though, it was not the same as the waterfall. I looked to Abha; her emerald eyes sparkled, her crimson hair was bright in the night, and the white rays from the moon lightened her skin. I couldn't remove my gaze. *Lilith.*

"My Sun God—"

"No words," I said. I would not wish to break this trance ever again. It had been so long since I laid eyes on my mate and felt her skin against mine. Loneliness clutched my chest and refused to let go. Still, I did not move.

Abha stepped closer, running her hands up my chest. She pulled the clothing over my head and laid it in the dry grass. Her golden aura was bright in the darkness and blended into mine easily; I could no longer see the difference in shade. She clasped the two folds of fabric along her neckline where I had torn it. She continued to rip the seam down until it fell from her body. The only thing she bore now was the golden mark I had given her.

I raised my hand and allowed my fingers to drift through her hair. *It was almost the same.* I leaned forward, and for the first time in millennia, touched my lips to a woman's. Abha was shocked at first, despite her eagerness before, but she calmed, and there was soon an understanding between us.

The night was quiet besides the sound of our breaths and the flowing creek alongside us. Abha was not *her*, but she was her descendant, and I would need the chief's daughter if I was to find Lilith's kin, perhaps even Lilith herself.

And it felt good to take, simply because I could.

I never returned to Lucifer's form. His name was no longer uttered into the air of this world, and it wouldn't be again until I found The First Woman, for she was the only one who knew my true name. I was now Kinich Ahau, Sun God of the Maya people, founder of The City of Gold and the Maya Empire.

Earth was mine, and I looked forward to seeing Lilith again, knowing she would greet me when I sat upon the world's throne.

XXIV
Threads

Desperation will be your path to destruction.
-E

19 Years Gone

The temple was beautiful. It was made of stone and stood as no structure had stood before. From its wide base to its narrow top, where I now lounged, was glorious. Thousands of steps were built along its sides so those who wished to worship could visit the shrine at its peak. A shrine dedicated to the Sun God, Kinich Ahau.

The stones were painted in gold and blue designs, depicting the Sun God's Mark: the *spirit*, the *wise*, the *fearless*, the *admired*, and the *honored*; seers, leaders, warriors, mothers, and slaves. Titles to distinguish roles and placate minds.

The temple was surrounded by vast fields of golden flowers, a sacred plant that represented the city. The breeze caused petals to fly up and over the wall to the west where lava still bubbled and tore angrily into the packed earth, but I kept the barrier strong. Only when I wished for it to fall would the lava ever be freed.

The Maya had expanded their farmlands as far as the eye could see.

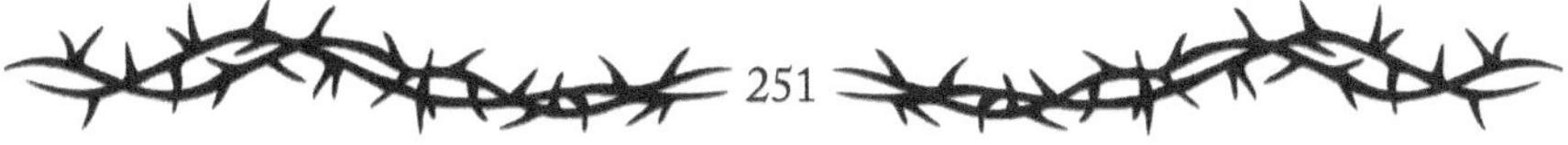

There were slaves working in each field, preparing for the harvest. The cold season was approaching, and there were many mouths to feed in the coming months, but there was plentiful meat and vegetation to spare. Thousands of hybrids now lived on my land. Travelers, traders, slaves, and the like were collected from the port and given a choice: Become a citizen or be fed to the vampires that dwelled in the shadows of the city.

There were a few who valued freedom above their lives, and I could not condemn such a choice. *If I were the weak one in the same position, would I choose freedom over life?*

I didn't have an answer.

The sun was disappearing over the horizon. The slaves were returning to their huts, kept in the same place the original Maya housing used to be. I scanned the fields, the glimmer of gold attracting my gaze to necks, wrists, and ankles. No matter the color of the hybrid's skin, the gold was dominant. I was about to turn away to admire the city's new god-depicted statues in the east when another glint caught my eye. It ran the opposite direction of the huts, quickly disappearing across the fields and into the woodland beyond. *Another traitor.* The vampires would scent the deserter soon, but I had become bored.

I needed to hunt.

I leapt from the temple's peak and landed in a field of sunflowers. Careful not to trample them, I made great leaps from one step to another, crossing full fields in only a couple steps. Soon, I came upon the woodland and stopped, raising my nose to the breeze.

I followed the trail until I heard the hurried footsteps of the slave. He was quick and agile, careful not to make a misstep and attract attention to himself, but he didn't understand that no matter how quiet he was there was no masking his scent or the sound of his pounding heart. I was upon him in moments. "Though you are fast, there is no escaping the city." I clutched the man's thick arm and he turned, blue eyes expectant.

He dropped to his knees, and I released my grip. "I'm not trying to flee, Sun God."

I chuckled. "Lies won't save you now, boy." The runner was a young man, the same age I appeared.

"No lies, I promise you, Sun God. I am…" the man failed to finish his words.

"My patience wanes."

"I am training my body. I wish to be marked as the *fearless*." His heart sang to the vampires surrounding us. The blood coursing through his veins was a great temptation to the monsters.

"Look at me," I commanded.

The man rested his blue eyes on my emerald ones.

"You are one of the first *honored* ones," I stated, remembering the small boy I had fed on the slave boat. "A warrior risks his life to defend our city. You are safe as an *honored* one. Why would you wish to abandon this role?" I asked.

"Your generosity is great, Sun God. I will forever be in your debt for saving me from those men, but I wish to fight. I was not made to tend fields and build structures." The man bowed low, his forehead touching the dirt beneath us. "Please, Sun God, allow me to serve and protect this city as a warrior, for I am fearless."

The man was determined. He risked his life just by being in these woods at night. He knew as well as any other citizen what creatures dwelled here. Still, his will to train in the dense greenery and nurture his skill was more important than his safety. Perhaps he *was* fearless.

"Prove yourself."

The man raised his head slightly. "How?" he asked, eager for my response.

"The vampires have found us. They scented your blood the moment you entered these woods. You may have evaded them before, due to your

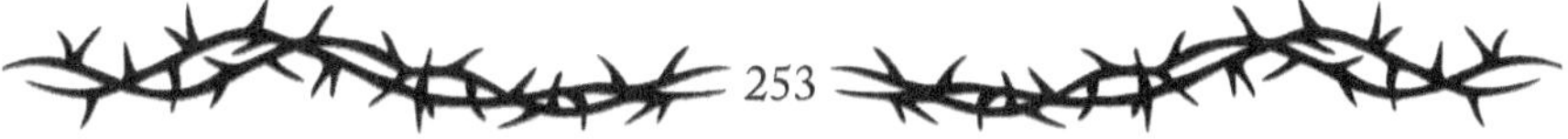

speed, but there's no running now." I held out the macana. "Take it and fight your way out. Prove to me you are truly fearless." I paused, as he had not moved from his submissive position. "If you do not wish for this test, I will accept that as well. I will take you back to your hut, and you will return to the fields in the morning with the rest of the *honored* ones." The man didn't move. "I won't wait forever," I prodded.

The man reached up and clutched my offered weapon. "I accept your challenge, Sun God. Thank you."

"I hope to see you by morning." Before he could speak again, I was gone. The vampires had heard what I said and knew the man was fair game. At least he had a small chance with a weapon. If he hadn't taken it, I would have left him to the monsters without one. He disobeyed a city rule: No one is allowed in the woods.

When I reached the first field, Nakon was waiting for me. "We found her," he said.

Lilith? "Who?" I asked.

"The woman trader from my wife's homeland. She was captured at the port, lured in by temptations The City of Gold could offer." The *wise* one smiled, his symbol glittering in the dim light of the evening.

"Well, we will have to show her exactly what the city is made of." Nakon and I followed the path to the temple where the woman waited for us at its base, locked away in the catacombs beneath.

Nakon unsealed the heavy stone doors. We stepped through the archway and into darkness. The tunnels were long and turned in odd directions, so if a prisoner managed to free themselves from the bindings they could not find their way out. The tunnels were added upon from the Maya's original catacombs. And their treasures were now kept in the light and at the top in the Sun God's temple where they could shine and display the wealth of the city.

We turned down several passages before reaching a dank room that smelled of waste and molded bread. Most of our captured were willing to tell us anything we needed to know and adapt to their new lives as slaves. But there were a few who were spiteful. Even with the vampires hearing their thoughts, it was difficult to accumulate all the information we needed to know. The difficult ones would not even think of revealing their land's secrets. So, here they remained, rotting away until they starved to death or died from their injuries.

The woman was tied down and had blood seeping from her nose and lips. A vampire lurked in the corner, its eye swollen. "Her mind is strong, Creator," the creature whined.

"I see that," I said. The woman spit in my direction, just missing my feet. I approached and stood above the aged hybrid. Her hair was still red, but it was streaked with silver strands. I knew the moment Nakon said they had captured the woman that the traveler had not been Lilith; only another being like herself could restrain her. "Where are your people?" I asked.

"Nowhere you will ever find. It is a place of peace. A place without men." The woman sneered. She spoke unique words, ones I had not heard in many eras. Nakon could not understand her, but the vampire could. Vampires lived in all lands, and with their minds linked, they shared all human languages. Still, the monsters could not find what I searched for.

Despite his lack of knowing, Nakon interjected after hearing the tone with which she spoke, "Watch your mouth, you are in the presence of the Sun God, Kinich Ahau. He will be treated with respect." The woman only smiled. Clearly, she spoke more than one language.

I raised my hand to silence his protest. "No need, Nakon. Peace is something to be cherished and protected. This woman is only trying to hide her loved ones from a harsh world."

"Do not speak down to me! You know nothing of the world. God or not," she stated.

"What is your name?" I asked.

"Naavah," the vampire said.

"Stay out of my head, monster!" Naavah ordered.

"An old name. One from an age now gone and buried." I paused. "How long have your people stayed hidden from the rest of the world? Why do you risk exposure by traveling?"

"She fights it, Creator. She knows of my kind and what we can do," the creature explained.

"Maybe a little encouragement would help." I signaled to Nakon to continue where he ended earlier. The chief unsheathed his knife and rushed to Naavah. He flattened her hand against the wall where her wrists had been chained. He was quick, but the point was made. Her little finger fell to the cold ground, blood pooling around the appendage.

Naavah's scream could have shattered Nakon's eardrums. The vampire laughed, his eye swelling even more from where the woman had hit him. "Where are your people? How long have they hidden?" I demanded, unwilling to move from where I stood.

"She imagines all of our deaths," the colorless creature relayed.

"Again."

Another finger was lost. Another scream sliced the air, reaching down the winding tunnels.

"I see green grass and towering trees, great fires, and women without faces," the vampire said.

"Again."

"Blue paint covers their bodies. They dance around the fires. Still, I do not see faces."

"Again."

Her screams were constant now. The tunnels were filled with her pain.

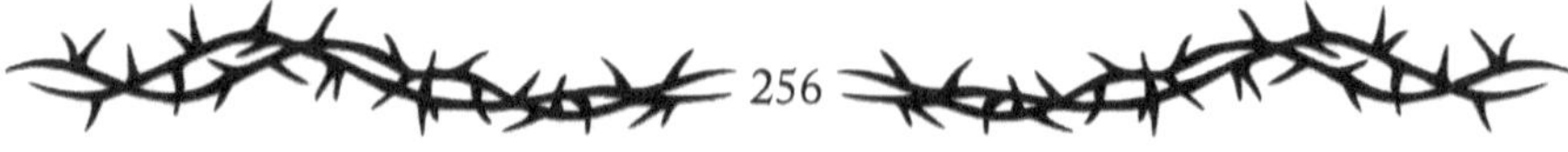

"There is only fire now," the vampire whispered, wary of my reaction.

"Stop," I ordered. Nakon stood and sheathed his knife, still coated in blood. If we continued to cut pieces of her off, she would bleed to death before answering my questions, which was exactly what she wanted. "My turn."

Naavah glared, but was too weak to fight, as I kneeled beside her. I held her head between my hands and stared into her green eyes. "Where is Lilith?"

"I don't know who that is," Naavah spat.

Perhaps not, but she knew something. I reached my soul outward and wrapped it around Naavah's silver one. *If I could create creatures that could infiltrate minds, then I must have the ability as well, buried deep in my spirit.* I reached into her soul and tore it open.

Naavah screamed again, startling Nakon because he was unable to see what was being done. I ripped her apart piece by piece, leaving her light tethered together, as to not kill her. I reached inside her soul and felt for her mind. *Where was it?* Her heartbeat was too fast, and blood was flowing from her wounds. Her soul withdrew from my touch. I reached and reached, but it would not obey.

"Let me help." Abha appeared and kneeled beside me, her golden light already reaching out to assist. I was grateful for her presence because I was desperate for answers; the ones I had been waiting for since I woke. Her light touched my own, and together we learned the intricate weaving of the spirit. There were millions of threads within one soul, and it was nearly impossible to untangle them.

But finally, we found the one that led to her mind—to her memories. "Where are your people?" I asked with both words and spirit.

This time, with Abha's help, she answered, "Across the water, in the land of sprites. We are the Picts, the painted ones. Beside the North Sea you will find us dancing around the fires, worshipping the magic of the

Goddess."

"How long have you hidden?"

"For all time. The triple goddess guided us to our sanctuary and there we have flourished. We leave once a year to mate, but we always return to our land and defend it from invaders. None have been able to conquer us." Though Naavah was being forced say the words, she still said the last sentence with pride.

"Why do you travel?"

"I am the chosen one. The shaman. I watch the world as it changes and bring back what I learn to my people." *A Seer.*

Lilith must have been helping them; no one people could defend themselves for that long. It was equally as strange that Naavah possessed the name of Lilith's firstborn child. *She* had to be there. "Where is Lilith?" I asked again.

"I don't know who that is! Stop!" Naavah broke from her trance and struggled against my grip. I let go, disappointed with her answer.

Abha did not. She latched onto Naavah's soul and asked a question of her own, "Why did you cast out my mother? Mirren. Why did you banish her?"

Naavah stopped struggling and looked into Abha's eyes, the tears she shed were of a greater pain now. "Mirren," she whispered. "Before me, she was our shaman, but she never returned."

Abha didn't pause to absorb what she'd heard. "Your people sent her to her death. Just like they did you," the chief's daughter said calmly, though her spirit was thrashing, wishing to be released. Abha unsheathed the knife she kept on her hip and plunged it into Naavah's heart. Naavah was gone and her tortured soul was now Abha's.

Nakon said, "You need to consume your enemy's heart if you are to grow in power."

"I don't want her tainted heart, and I don't need it to be powerful," she replied, rising from her place beside Naavah's corpse. "You found what you needed, my Sun God?" she asked, unable to look me in the eye.

"Yes."

"Then I will prepare for travel." Abha left without my permission, and I listened to her steps echo down the halls and out the heavy doors into the night.

Orders were sent ahead to the docks to prepare for travel, using a raven to deliver them. The hybrids were too slow to deliver something as simple as a message, but I was impressed by the creation of the written word and use of the birds, nonetheless.

I felt no need to take anything but my weapon on the journey, which I would retrieve soon enough. Nakon would stay behind to lead in my stead, but he had reservations. "Sun God, you have not left us before. Without you, who will defend our city from attack?"

It was true, after waking in the obsidian soil, I had not left this land. I had been building the city to what it was now, a rich and prosperous empire. One that stretched across the land. Of course, there was still territory to be conquered on this continent, but it would happen soon enough. I was hoping Lilith would have made an appearance by now, but that was why I had to leave and find the place Lilith's descendants called their home.

"The vampires will still be here."

"Sun God, they are useless during the day. Many know this. It is only a matter of time—"

"As you wish, Nakon," I interrupted. "I will not leave you unprotected." The Maya asked for more every day. They had a massive army of men and vampires to protect them, still it was not enough. *Greed only grows, never wilting in its need for more.*

We stood at the outskirts of the city, the wall a looming force above us. The world quieted around me as I said the words that would concentrate my magic and will it into being:

Earthen strength and skyward reach
These new monsters will fight and die for heat
Each step is one of power
No one person will ever be able to counter
Rise Giants
Reach! Reach! Reach!

From the soil of earth and lava, came a creation the world hadn't yet seen. The monsters towered over the wall. Souls from the roots left behind by deadened greenery gave life to these beings, the roots were now buried in their soil-packed bodies. Lava flowed from their eye sockets, as if they were weeping. A mouth formed soon after, where wood burned and caught flame. These monsters would only stay alive if they had kindling, and it didn't matter what it was, so long as it burned.

Knowing I had written my will into the three giant's simple psyches, I turned to Nakon. "They will guard this city. So long as they are fed and their fire continues to burn."

I expected Nakon to cower from such power, but his smile was bright, and his eyes were full of greed. He bowed low and said, "Thank you, Sun God. Thank you."

I nodded, unconcerned. Rustling from the woodland's edge distracted me. I then found myself smiling, enjoying the sensation of surprise—it didn't occur often. "You have done well." I approached the young man who crawled on his hands and knees out of the trees. Once he reached my feet, he stopped, and looked upward to his Sun God, eyes glistening with unshed tears.

I kneeled beside the man and carefully removed his tightly curled fingers from the macana, dark hair falling irritably into my eyes as I looked down. His body was shaking from pain and shock and adrenaline, the only way a man could truly feel alive. Crimson blood coated him in a uniform of honor. "Sun God," the man whispered, unable to speak any louder, "I am fearless."

As I looked into the eyes of this man, I determined that he spoke the truth, even after the battle he'd endured. "Yes, you are."

The man screamed.

Little by little, as to not shock his body further, I removed his slave markings and gathered the gold to his forehead where a fierce jaguar was now etched, the blood making the design even more menacing.

The man smiled, and his blue eyes closed.

Abha approached, a small bag hanging from her side. She looked to the new creatures lingering near the wall and the bloodied man on the ground. She said nothing.

"Nakon, this man is to be a warrior." I took one last glance at the blue-eyed man. "If he should survive his injuries of course." Nakon immediately ordered two of his guards to take the man to the temple where he would be healed.

"Are you prepared, Abha?" I asked.

She nodded, but her spirit thrashed at my question.

Worried, I picked her up, unwilling to wait for a carriage to carry us to the port, and ran. It was difficult not to think of Lilith during this time. When I had carried her through the forest, her long red hair blowing behind us, her hands clutching my shoulders, her lips unable to leave my skin as we ran for the waterfall—for home. *We were content in that moment.*

I gazed at Abha, wishing for the same emotion again, but she refused to look at me. The woman held her hands close to her chest, relying on me to hold her weight. Despite this, I needed her, so I would give her whatever she asked for.

I looked away, concentrating on the heat of the sand beneath my feet and the call of the ocean ahead.

The port was quiet. There was no trading here, not anymore. The Maya empire took and gave nothing in return. The only boats leaving the harbor were mine, and they offered only death and destruction to those in the sea and lands beyond. They would bring back riches and knowledge to the Maya people. There were ships that never returned, but it was rare because I was the one who trained the new generation of warriors; much stronger men then those of their forefathers.

Warriors now swarmed the docks and tree line, always waiting for another unsuspecting ship to approach, ones that never returned home. The other lands had not yet grown suspicious, because if the city was as the rumors said then who would ever want to leave?

I placed Abha on her feet just inside of the ship we were to sail. It was my first time using the contraption instead of swimming, and though swimming would be faster, Abha had to be considered. I needed her to find Lilith. *I needed her by my side.*

"When you are ready, Sun God," the ship's captain said. One last look toward the volcano had me eager to leave and begin this long-awaited journey. Though, the thought that Lilith could take advantage of my absence worried me. But I looked ahead anyway, taking the chance.

The sails of the grand wooden ship fell and allowed me to admire the sky-blue fabric, which was embroidered with an intricate golden sun. Those who knew the emblem would be tempted to attack and steal, as they had been these last two decades, but I could hear the sirens even now, singing their song to the pirates and luring them into storms and monster infested waters. They sang and sang, laying the path ahead of us bare. As the wind carried us forward, I felt a lightness in my body, a glimmer of an emotion long forgotten.

Hope.

XXV
Sprites

Colors give meaning to that which has none.
-M

The night was moonless. The chill from the sea seeped into my bones. The ground was rough, and the rocks stabbed the soles of feet. Still, I felt wonderful. The man I chased was skilled in the art of evasion. His steps and breath were unheard, and his scent was masked. If it wasn't for the steady beat of his heart I wouldn't have been able to find him.

We reached shore only one moon cycle after we departed and merely chose a land along the North Sea where one of my personal ports were kept. The waters had been kind, and the sirens had done their job. Once I set foot on the new soil, Abha and I began our search. We moved from village to village and town to town, interrogating any hybrids we could find.

Word had spread across the land of our endeavor, and soon, a young woman told us of a forest across the sea. None had returned from this forest, none except one man. She told us where to find him: in a nearby town swarming with thieves and murderers. The woman warned us to not underestimate him. He was ruthless and surviving an encounter with the creatures across the sea was a terrifying feat. I merely smiled and gave her a small piece of gold to pay for her travels, offering her sanctuary in my city.

I hunted that man now. We were in the center of town, and buildings made of crumbling stone, wood, and mud were packed together, leaving only small pathways in between. I scented the air again. It was rare to come across such an intelligent hybrid; he covered himself in mud and earth to disguise his scent. Rumors traveled quickly of my power, though, how he knew to disguise himself was a mystery, and one I looked forward to solving.

Abha lurked in the shadows as well, using her *sight* to detect any hidden hybrids. She had been quite helpful these past weeks. She had honed her skills by manipulating others' souls. She could force information from the most ignorant and docile of hybrids, giving details they weren't aware of before.

How could I have done this without her?

Soon, I came across mud marks on a wall. They traveled up and over the edge of the flat roof. The man had used the loose bricks to climb. *Clever.* I leapt and landed quietly on top of the structure. I peered into the darkness, knowing my eyes were much sharper than those of my prey. A dark shape moved swiftly across the rooftops, just a few homes from where I stood.

The wind bit my face as I ran, and I caught the man just before he jumped down to the street below. With his hair in my hand, I pulled him back over the edge toward me. Without saying a word, the man gripped the arm restraining him, placed his feet, and threw me over his shoulder to the alley below. I was in such shock I didn't bother trying to save myself. I allowed my body to fall, smiling as I did so.

Eons had come and gone, yet not one of the hybrids had managed to surprise me as much as this man did now. Turning in the air, my feet were on the ground for only a moment before I leapt back onto the rooftop. I stood at its edge, scanning the darkness once again. *Three homes away.* This time, I didn't allow him to move. With one swift blow to the back of his head, he was asleep and thrown over my shoulder.

I met Abha at the edge of the dark town and began our ascent from the pit we had come from, while moans of misfortune echoed behind us. The town was where the worst of the hybrids dwelled, treating each other as if they did the grime beneath their feet.

Eventually, all of humanity would be the same.

"It took you longer than usual to find this one, my Sun God," Abha stated, a small smile on her lips.

"This one is talented. He has seen much of the world." I looked back to the fading town. "And many of its monsters."

"Perhaps, but he has not met a god," she said.

I merely nodded, wondering if there was a difference between the two.

Night came and went as we found our way to the edge of the sea. The sun had risen, and its light shimmered in the blue-green water. It was a drastic change from the pitiful town. A place so plagued with misfortune it had no name, for to give it a name would be to acknowledge its existence.

I dropped the mud-covered man in the lapping waves. He woke quickly, coughing from the salt water that entered his lungs. Before he even rose from the water, a knife was revealed and thrown toward Abha. I blocked its path, the handle now protruding from my chest. Once it was removed, I looked to its wielder: he was halfway down the beach and running at full speed.

"This man may be more trouble than he's worth," Abha commented, her long, dark red hair following the breeze that passed us by. A few strands of silver interlocked with her curls, reminding me just how short the hybrid's lives were.

Angered, I caught the man for a second time, disarmed, and bound him. I dragged him back to where Abha stood watching the sea. "Enough.

You can cooperate or die." I paused to meet the man's green-eyed gaze. "No matter your talents, you will not defeat me. I am the Sun God, Kinich Ahau. You will tell me what I want to know."

I signaled for Abha to begin. She gripped the man's face between her delicate hands. Her brilliant golden soul latched onto his vermilion spirit, prying it apart with her will. "What dwells in the forest across the sea?" she demanded.

Fighting, but unable to resist, he answered, "Nothing good. It is only pain and suffering." There were tears along the edge of his soul. *What could have caused such damage?*

"What is the source of your fear? Tell me what is in the forest," she demanded. Abha saw the tears in his spirit as I had and used it to her advantage, clawing at them and forcing her way into his psyche.

With a cry of pain, he said, "Monsters!" His bindings pulled tight and split his skin, but he refused to submit. His soul pushed back and forced her out, the golden light unwelcome. They struggled in a battle of will, and I watched in fascination.

"Submit!" Abha demanded.

"Let me," I said, my hand now resting on her shoulder.

Abha broke her eye contact with the man just long enough to meet my gaze and said, "No! I will conquer him!" The anger in her eyes forced me to release her and take a step back.

Soon, she did as she promised, and the man let her in so she could take what she wished, though not by choice. "The women we seek are in this forest," she told me, "but there are creatures that live in the trees and lure humans to their death."

I looked at the man's soul once more and realized the marks weren't tears. They were bites. *The Land of Sprites*, Naavah had said. It had been so long, I'd forgotten about them. The creatures I created after Lilith disappeared, the ones who dwelled in the forests and fed on human souls.

"Sprites. They will be no issue," I assured.

"The women are formidable warriors. They have managed to keep men out of their land for centuries, perhaps longer."

"How did this one survive?"

"Talorc. He is a child of the Picts, but only daughters are kept. The sons are given to the sprites to feed upon." Talorc lashed out again, but Abha had complete control of him. "The night after he was born, his mother came for him where he was abandoned in the forest and tore the feeding sprites from his soul. She laid him in a basket and set him out to sea, hoping someone would find her son."

A tear streaked down Talorc's cheek. "Stop," he whispered.

"Talorc was found and sold as a slave until he was thirteen years of age, and then fled across the sea, back to where he was born, unsure of why he did so. He fought his way through the forest until the women found him, but he was met with rage. He was hunted by the Picts for years but escaped across the sea again when he was nineteen."

"Why didn't he cross sooner?" I asked. Talorc was an impressive hybrid, and I wanted to know how such skill was created.

"His choices were either slavery or prey. At least in the forest he was near family, though he didn't know it until now." Memories were unlocked and revealed to us when we tore open souls, even ones forgotten by the soul bearer.

"Does he still know the way?" At my words, Talorc lashed out with his red light and managed to free himself from Abha's hold. The bindings fell to the sand-covered ground.

"No more!" he shouted, another weapon in his hand.

"Yield," Abha ordered, ready to battle again.

"No," I said, halting her attack. "Talorc, lead us to your people and you will be rewarded with your weight in gold." I wanted to see what a male descendant of Lilith could do.

"They are not my people! I don't know what you did to me, but these thoughts are not my own. Those women hunted me for years. I will never return to that place!" Talorc gripped his knife tighter, expecting another fight.

"What you saw were memories. Locked away for years, yes, but they are your own. Your mother saved you from a cruel fate. The sprites are vicious creatures. Your death would have been slow."

"She saved me from nothing! I was a slave! Beaten, raped, and worked until I bled. I would have preferred the sprites." Tears streamed down Talorc's angered face. Old memories were now fresh. It was impressive he still stood upright; most people broke and lost control of their mind completely.

"You wish for them to suffer?" I asked.

"Yes," he answered, not skipping one heartbeat.

"I can make that happen. We wish to conquer the Picts. I promise a painful death to those who harmed you," I tempted.

"My Sun God..." Abha began, but she didn't dare finish her thought, not in front of a stranger.

Talorc glanced between Abha and me, contemplating. "How do I know you won't kill me the moment we arrive?"

"You don't." I shrugged, indifferent. "Perhaps the real question is this: Can you live in a world where they exist?" Talorc lowered his knife. "Will the anger ever calm on its own? Especially now, discovering they are your own family. A family that abandoned you. That tried to kill you. Simply because you were not the right gender. Can you live in a world where they exist?" I asked again.

"No."

"Our boat is not far. Follow me, and I will grant your wish."

Talorc followed.

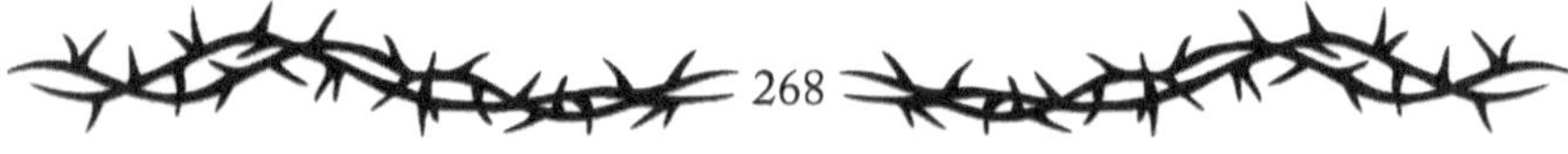

"We can't trust him, my Sun God," Abha said as we lay in our bed, the ship swaying gently. She straddled my hips, her body free from clothing. "If you would allow me to search his soul further, I could find what he is hiding." Abha's lips grazed my jawbone, and her hands rested at the base of my neck, stroking the skin there.

I groaned with pleasure and said, "Do not worry. I won't let him harm you." I nipped at her shoulder, and she withdrew, sitting erect and allowing me the full view of her breasts.

"It is not my life I am worried about," she whispered.

"Nothing can kill me, you know this. Why must you obsess over my safety?" Her skin was soft, and my long fingers traced her hips downward until she gasped.

"You once said, 'There is only one thing on this Earth that can kill me.' What is it, my Sun God? Let me protect you from it," she whimpered. Abha's soul shone in the dark space, and it comforted me. It was as if the sun had been given life in this mortal woman. Ever since we met, it had only grown in brilliance and color.

"Abha," I whispered, "there's no need to think of such things."

"Is it *her*? Can she hurt you?" I traced the lines on the woman's face, familiarizing myself with the new ones that had appeared in the recent years.

I threw Abha onto her back and plunged deep inside her. I thrust hard and fast, ignoring the ache in my chest. I fixed my gaze with Abha's, concentrating on the emerald green. Her pupils dilated and blackness overwhelmed, allowing my reflection to appear. A Maya man with dark hair stared back, Kinich Ahau stared back.

I left Abha on the bed, unable to finish. "I am here to serve you, my Sun God. What do you need?" she asked. I dressed and stepped outside into the cold, ignoring the woman. I looked down into the waters below the ship. No matter how hard she tried, Abha could not give me what I needed.

"Can't sleep?" I turned to find Talorc leaning over the boat as far as he could go while holding a small white candle, the flame flickering aggressively.

"If you're trying to escape, at least wait until we reach shore. We are far from land and these waters are dangerous, not to mention freezing," I suggested. Though the first snow had yet to fall, winter was upon us.

"I am well aware, but no, I was trying to catch a glimpse of those glowing fish. I saw them the last time I crossed. Staring at their strange, beautiful bodies was the first time I had ever felt anything but pain. Their light seemed to bleed right into me, giving me life."

I chuckled.

"Laughing at another man's pain is a sin, you know," Talorc snapped.

"I am not laughing at your pain. I merely know how you feel. It is a strange emotion to be captured by a light that's not your own. You are no longer in control of yourself." I gazed into the dark depths of the sea, wishing for the light he spoke of.

"You describe the light as if it causes you pain, but it's supposed to take it away, not add to it," he remarked, unaware of what he had said.

"I agree."

"What about that woman you keep around? She cause you pain? If so, I believe it." Talorc pulled out a small cigar. He used the candle to light the end and breathed deep.

"What makes you think so?" I asked, enjoying the scent of tobacco.

"I've seen her type before, she can change faces as fast as the sky." He took another deep inhale of cigar and caught me eyeing it. He offered the herb-packed leaf to me, and I paused in surprise. "I thought it best to share, you being a god and all," he explained.

I laughed again and accepted his offer. I inhaled and allowed the fire to swirl inside my lungs. I blew out the smoke, savoring the warmth on my face. The effects would only last a moment, but it was nice just the same. "Abha is the same as you." Another smoke-filled inhale was taken. "She is a direct descendant of the Picts, but she was raised elsewhere." I handed the cigar back to Talorc.

"Makes sense," he said.

Before I could ask what he meant, hundreds of lights appeared in the water. Glowing sea creatures floated near its surface. Their mushroom-shaped tops and trailing tentacles were weightless. The smile on Talorc's face was one I wished for—one of pure happiness. We stood at the edge of the boat until the lights disappeared and the cigar was but smoke in the sky.

Only a few days had passed when we reached land. Talorc hadn't tried to escape, but instead, led us near the Pict's shoreline, staying out of sight. Precautions were taken when it came to unknown peoples. My ship was at the women's mercy if it was discovered, and I would not be around to defend it.

I was unsure if I was going to allow the Pict son to live. He was an interesting hybrid; strong, but uncontrollable. "Stay close," I told Talorc. The sunlight shone on his dark hair, and streaks of red appeared. I signaled to the crewman to wait for our return. Abha joined us at the forest's edge. She had many weapons strapped to her lithe body, prepared for battle, per my orders. I was equipped with my own weapon. Though the macana fit well in my hand, it would never be the same as my spear.

We entered the forest, and I immediately felt them—my creations. The sprites had one job these past millennia: Find Lilith. If they were harboring her during that time, their existence would come to a swift end. "Reveal yourselves sprites. Your Creator has returned." What would sound like the whispering of trees to mortals were really the tinkling laughter of sprites. "Reveal yourselves!" I ordered. I was losing patience. I was so close to finding Lilith. I could not waste any more time. *What if she ran again?*

"Yes, Creator?" A sprite peered from behind a leaf, her blue eyes the same as her ancestor's.

"You remember me?" I asked.

"In a way," she giggled, and her long, white hair shifted with the flutter of her wings.

"Don't test my patience. I am in no mood for your mockery."

The smile disappeared, but she opened her mouth slightly to reveal the small sharp teeth with which she had devoured many souls. "We feed on the souls of our dying sisters. That is how we remember our past. We keep their memories with us, generation after generation." Talorc gagged, and the sprite turned to him and grinned, displaying all of her deadly bite.

"So, you remember your purpose?"

"Yes, Creator, though we haven't found her or else we would have told you."

"Lies! She must be here! Her descendants gather on this land." I forced myself to calm and remembered Lilith could have been disguising herself all this time. "Is there anyone on this land with a crimson soul? One as red as human blood?"

"There is one," the sprite flirted, looking to Talorc's scarlet light.

"Where?" I demanded.

"Deep in the forest with the others of her kind." The sprite flitted her wings in exasperation, clearly unhappy I wasn't playing her games.

"There is only one other of her kind," I corrected.

"I can take you to her," she offered, uncaring.

"Yes, but make certain she does not know I approach."

"Of course, Creator." With those words, the three of us followed the sprite through the dense forest. The fog was thick, and the sun had long disappeared behind the clouds above. I could hear the sprites whispering to one another, and I suspected Talorc could as well because he shifted uncomfortably, as if his soul ached from the memory of being feasted upon.

Soon, I could smell smoke. The chanting came next, and it was not the forest spirits this time. We hid in the thicket and gazed out to a clearing where red-headed women danced around a fire wearing nothing but blue paint. The paint was crudely used to draw symbols, ones I could not understand.

"What do the symbols mean?" I asked Talorc.

With vengeful eyes boring down on the frolicking hybrids, he answered, "From what I remember, they represent Samhain, which celebrates the end of the harvest season." He looked on bitterly. "It looks like they had a good season."

"What are they saying?" Abha asked. She gazed at her kin in wonder, and it was hard to imagine she wished them dead with an expression such as that.

"Praise the goddess. The one who creates life. The one who gives nourishment. The one who blesses them with strength. Blah, blah, blah. It's all made-up in my opinion. Gods just give terrible people an excuse to do terrible things." Talorc grimaced as he watched the women take turns drinking from a waterskin overflowing with blood. Animal or human, I could not tell. I expected Abha to interject on my behalf, but she remained silent, focusing on the women in front of her.

"You have a rare wisdom, Talorc. One that will keep you alive in the future." I turned and smiled at him. "Or get you killed." The smile startled the man, and he looked away, despite this face's improvement over my own. I turned my attentions back to the celebration. "Abha, now is the time to make yourself useful."

She finally looked to me, and I caught the beginning of a glare before she morphed it into indifference. "Yes, my Sun God."

"They will see you as a blessing from the goddess if you reveal yourself now. Tell them Naavah found you. She was bringing you home when you were attacked, and she was lost. Make them believe you are one of them. Find out everything about their culture, and most importantly, look for a woman with a red soul. When you find her, call out to the sprites, and tell them to find me."

"What will happen when you find her?" she asked.

"Your god will finally take back what was stolen."

XXVI
Comforts

There had been no sign of a woman with a red soul. *Did she know I was here? Was she hiding? Or had she already run?* I could not smell her sweet night pollen scent anywhere in the forest.

They were hiding her. They had to be.

"You promised their suffering. Instead, I am forced to watch as your concubine feasts and dances with those monsters." Talorc had been difficult these past few days. He never left my side and harassed me constantly about killing the Picts. I almost wished he would run again.

"They have something I need. We will do nothing until it is found." I followed the border we'd created around the women's camp, the fallen leaves were damp and clung to my bare feet.

"You mean the woman? This one isn't enough? But you're a god, I am sure you can pick anyone you want."

"Do you ever stop talking?" I asked.

"Only when it benefits me," he responded with a smile.

"Does living benefit you? If so, remain silent."

Talorc didn't speak again until we had circled the perimeter twice and then rested in a tree behind one of the huts. The Pict village was underdeveloped compared to the city I had built. Its foundation lacked stability, and its walls were without proper insulation. Despite this, they had amassed a trove of items from across the world: weapons, arts, manuscripts that depicted the histories of lost peoples, and etchings of their own history was written on animal skins. They kept all this hidden underground, but I had found it easily. The smell of woman was prominent beneath the structure resting beyond the village. It was comparable to the shrine the Maya had erected for me as I grew from the ashes of the volcano. "Is this woman really worth the trouble?" the Pict descendant questioned, baffled by my obsession. Clearly he had never loved a woman.

For the second time, someone had asked me that question, and once again, I didn't have an answer. "Listen," I whispered, hearing footsteps enter the adjacent shelter.

Abha's voice sounded through the thin walls of the hut while she spoke, "We must come together. It is the only way."

A second voice responded in the Maya's native tongue, "If what you say is true, we are in danger. I cannot risk my people, especially on the word of a stranger."

"I am one of you. I am Mirren's daughter. Men tortured and killed her. Men are not to be trusted, and the only way I can defeat them is with your help." I could hear Abha pacing in the small space, her skirts brushing against the soft skin of her thighs.

The second voice sighed. "Have you been told the legend of the triple goddess?"

"There is no time, wise one. We must—"

"There were three women who fled man's hold. A crone, a mother, and a maiden," the wise one began, interrupting Abha's pleas. "All three could see into the hearts of man, just like yourself. Each one they came across would be executed, knowing they were ridding Earth of a disease." The woman took a deep intake of breath, as if she was in pain. "Time came and went. Few men were left in the world, and children were a rare thing to behold. The crone did not have long left, the mother had grown weak from war, and the maiden had a heart full of sorrow.

"One day, the maiden was hunting in the same forest we thrive in now, and she came upon a man huddling in the thicket for warmth. She immediately grew angry and prepared her weapon. She stood above the man, but just before she plunged the spear into his back, a small cry sounded from his chest. At first she thought the man was crying, but she soon realized it was not the man, but a baby. A baby girl was tucked tightly in his arms. The man was giving all the warmth he could to this child, even at the expense of his own.

"The maiden watched the man for a time, pondering, until she saw that his hands had gone limp, and his breath no longer clouded the air. The child began to wail, growing colder by the moment. Without another thought, the maiden gathered the child in her arms and left the man to rest for eternity in the forest."

"What does this story mean?" Abha asked.

"Listen and see." The woman continued, "The maiden returned to her camp. She showed the child to her mother and grandmother and explained how the man had sacrificed himself for the baby girl. They were shocked but knowing this warmed their cold hearts. They vowed to only kill men when women were threatened and allowed the girl to join their clan, marking her forehead with blue paint to symbolize her new family by the sea.

"For years they gathered women in need of a home. They were brought to the forest and trained to fight and hunt. Year after year the clan grew, and before long, the crone's time to pass was upon them." I could hear the smile in the wise one's next words. "As she breathed her last breath, the mother and maiden used their power of *sight* and joined their souls with hers. They moved into the spirit realm together, forever watching over the clan they had created. *The Painted Ones.* Their daughters."

"The Triple Goddess," Abha whispered.

"Yes, she is three and one and none. She is our goddess. She is the one who decided to spare men. She saw goodness in their hearts, and here we flourish and defend, but we do not conquer. Our people forget that sometimes."

"I understand, but now is the time to defend. He is here, and he wants you dead."

"Why?"

"He is a monster. He searches for a woman who is not here, one he wants to conquer. And he will kill you all if he does not get what he wants," Abha said, her voice full of anger. "With your help, I can kill him. I know it."

"If he is as powerful as you say, why do you think you have a chance against him?" the wise one asked.

"He is weak now. I have learned to take from him without his knowledge. I have uncovered power our people have yet to master. I have manipulated his thoughts and actions. I am strong enough to end this. To end him," Abha explained.

A long while passed, but the wise one answered, "Very well. What do you need?"

I turned my face away from the hut, though I couldn't help but hear the rest.

"From the look on your face, I can tell there's trouble. What are we going to do?" Talorc asked. Although he had been unable to hear the conversation that took place in the hut, his face lit up with a smile, because he knew he just got exactly what he wanted.

The nighttime sky was dark, and the moon was bright. It guided me through the unfamiliar trees toward the place I was to meet Abha. The macana swung with ease at my side, and the smell of trees cleansed my lungs. The rush before battle was what I existed for, even if this battle didn't involve weapons. It was when my mind was the clearest. I could sense everything around me, and my thoughts were precise, sharp. Still, a cloud seemed to hover over me. Clear thoughts were created and cast away with the next.

What was wrong with me?

"My Sun God." Abha rushed to me and flung her arms around my shoulders. She kissed me with vigor, and I returned it, knowing this would be the last kiss we would share. As we melded into one another, I paid attention to my spirit, knowing what Abha would try to do. Her golden light blended with mine, disguising her, as she seduced the ancient light that allowed her in. She caressed my psyche, nudging trust and devotion for her to the forefront of my mind. I allowed it only so my plan wouldn't be revealed, but it was difficult to hate her when all my thoughts were consumed by Lilith's descendant.

Abha had been doing this for years, and I never realized. I had allowed myself a small comfort. And it was a weakness that I would not succumb to again. "Abha, did you find her?" I asked, finally removing my lips from hers.

"Yes, she is at the edge of the village. Her soul is as red as blood. It must be her," she said, excited for the next step in our journey. "Finally, after all this time, you have found her, my Sun God."

"Bring me to her," I ordered.

"Of course." Abha took my hand and led me through the trees, toward the hut she had spent many hours in while discussing traitorous things with the wise one. "Beyond this hut, she wanders alone in the trees."

I listened to the sounds of thundering hearts in the distant thicket. The last time I allowed the hybrids to trap me, I had been imprisoned under water with a spearhead lodged in my spine for days. *I would not return to the darkness.*

"Go without me, I will be right behind you," I said, a small smile on my lips. Confused, Abha nodded and walked the path she had created for me. Whispering commenced upon her arrival, but it died down as quickly as it sounded.

Lilith was not here. I had known that as soon as I stepped onto this land. It was just as empty as the rest of the world, but I could not lose this piece of her. If it was thousands or even millions of years before I saw her again, I needed this place to exist. However, they had to be controlled, and they would not listen to a man no matter the torture involved. These women were bred to die for their freedom. I had only one choice if I wanted to keep them.

Limbs thinned and tightened. Hair grew down and past my waste, curling as it did. Sun-kissed skin lightened, matching the moon's ivory shade. Every detail was perfect because I had trapped this memory of Lilith deep inside myself to use when I truly felt alone. Now, she would give me what I wanted, in one form or another.

I willed the leaves from the trees to cover Lilith in a dress of emerald to match her eyes, so long, it trailed behind her as she walked, which also disguised the obsidian weapon hanging at her side. Branches reformed to create a crown which lay upon her crimson hair. She was a goddess in human flesh. Night flowers bloomed as she passed. Her footsteps quiet, she followed the path before her.

At the end of the trail, an old woman was perched on a fallen tree, looking away from Lilith. Her hair was crimson and silver, and her soul was as red as blood. This was the woman the sprite had spoken of, and I knew the instant I saw her that it was not Lilith. We could transform into many things, but we could not age. That power was beneath us.

"My child, why is there such sorrow in your heart?" Lilith said, her voice more beautiful than even the sirens.

The woman turned, surprised. "Who are you?"

"I suppose you would not recognize me. I am three and you are but one." Lilith took another step, and then there was rustling in the tree's canopy where the Picts were waiting to attack Kinich Ahau. "You may tell your sisters to come down and join us. I know I have not appeared in many lifetimes, but I have been watching, and you need my guidance now more than ever."

"Cailleach, The Triple Goddess," the wise one whispered to herself.

"Yes, I have returned. Please make peace and surround your goddess with love." Lilith motioned her arms outward and in, as if she could take it from them by force.

The woman nodded her head, signaling to her people, but her hands shook. She was unsure how to feel about the appearance of her goddess, especially when she was expecting someone much different.

Pict warriors fell from the trees, wearing nothing but blue paint and weapons. It was strange how two completely different cultures could give such significance to a color. "My daughters, for centuries I have longed to speak to you and hold you in my arms. I am so sorry I could not before. I could only watch from afar as you fought tirelessly to protect this land— our land." A tear fell down Lilith's cheek. "But a grave misfortune has come upon you, and I fought to return from the spirit world to warn you."

"What has happened Goddess?" the wise one asked. "Is it the man who hunts us? Is he here?"

Slowly, I shook my head. "My dear daughter, there is a trickster among you. She has lied and killed to get what she wants. Though she is Mirren's offspring, men have tainted her heart."

"Abha? No, Goddess, it cannot be." The wise one stifled a cry, overwhelmed.

"It is. She tortured Naavah for the location of our people and then killed her when she obtained it. She is not to be trusted. Naavah knew as much."

"No!" Abha appeared from behind one of the painted women. "Lies! This is the man who wishes for your death. This is a trick!" She had learned enough of the Pict's language in her short time here to understand what Lilith said. Abha met my gaze and her pupils dilated, seeing a soul she had come to know intimately.

"Abha only wishes to use you. She wants you to be as bloodthirsty as her. Her heart was broken by a man, and she believes all of them should suffer for it." Lilith turned away from Abha, ashamed of her daughter. "But I will not allow an outsider to corrupt my clan. If you were to hunt men as I once had, our race would be doomed. You must stay in this forest. You must continue to defend and cherish it. It is a sacred place and one that will withstand the test of time, if cared for."

"What of this man she spoke of?" a woman near me questioned. Her long crimson hair was knotted with blue and black paint, and intricate braids were woven within the mass of curls, which pulled her skin back, making the bold charcoal outline of her eyes look fierce and deadly.

"Yes, I know of whom you speak. His name is Talorc. He was captured and forced here against his will. Abha did this so you would believe her story." Refusing to look at Abha, I motioned to the thicket behind me. "Come, they will not harm you."

Talorc revealed himself and kneeled at my side, submissive and covered in mud. "It is true. She kidnapped and beat me. She said if I didn't play the part she wanted, she would kill me." Talorc managed to sound frightened, but perhaps he was. The man was in the presence of those who hunted him for years. Though it had been decades since, and I doubted any would recognize him.

Abha ran at me, her golden light reaching out to mine, vengeful. But my soul was as strong as stone. She would not enter again. There was no Seer here; Naavah had been the last and another had yet to be born. No one could see what was happening or stop it.

"Abha, daughter of Mirren and my descendant, you are banished from this land. You will not be allowed to return ever again. You have disgraced us and nearly started a war that would kill your sisters." I clutched Abha's soul tight and ripped her open. Her screams unsettled the quiet night air. I cocooned her psyche with my light and locked her within her own body. She collapsed, unable to move.

The wise one approached Lilith and sank to her knees. "Goddess Cailleach, please forgive us. I allowed us to be swayed by lies and hatred. Please, what can I do to repent?"

"My daughter, you are a noble and brave woman. I accept your offer of penance. Come with me, it is time to join your lost sisters." Lilith offered her hand.

The rest of the women sank to their knees, crying and shouting for one of them to be taken instead. "Please, do not be sad. The place she is going is one of peace. Reinforce your clan with stories of the maiden, the mother, and the crone, knowing I will always be watching over you. I am sorry I could not stay with you longer. The spirit realm calls for my return. Farewell, my daughters." Lilith did not smile as she left but wept in sadness for having to leave her daughters again. Talorc carried Abha over his shoulder, and the wise one followed close behind, her mind not her own.

We reached the shoreline, and Lilith looked out to the boat floating in the water. Flames licked its sails. The Picts had found it while we were in the forest. There was no recovering the creation or the hybrids on it.

"Where do we go now, Goddess?" the wise one asked.

"What is your name?" Lilith said.

"My name? It is Deidre. You know this..." she said, the trance faltering.

"Diedre, I have an arrangement with Talorc. He wanted you in exchange for his cooperation." Lilith met Deidre's gaze. "I believe you owe him a debt." Lilith nodded her head to Talorc, and he dropped Abha in the sand.

"It's been a pleasure, Sun God. I hope we don't meet again." Talorc bowed in false submission and took Diedre's hand, pulling her down the beach. "Come, there is much I want to tell you, Mother."

Confusion, then realization crossed Diedre's face as she took in Talorc's familiar features. "No, it can't be."

"You should have left me to the sprites," Talorc said, an ugly grin plastered on his face. It was very unfortunate for Deidre that Abha had unlocked Talorc's memories.

Lilith watched as their silhouettes faded into the rocky shoreline. The sun was rising and cast eerie shadows along the cliffs. Ignoring Abha's still form, Lilith peered into the waves at her feet, absorbing the reflection there. Her emerald eyes shimmered with tears.

Alone. I am alone.

Lilith's face disappeared, revealing the monster beneath. That monster lifted Abha from the ground and waded into the sea.

XXVII

Sacrifice

You lack a very important thing.
-A

The journey was long. I didn't swim back across the sea. I went south, toward the ocean, the stars mapping my route. Abha rested on my back as I swam, her mind still trapped but very much aware. I didn't go ashore to eat or drink. I didn't use magic to assist my travels. I completely relied on my strength and stamina. And it felt good.

Abha's light was fading quickly, her mortal body unable to handle the elements. The waters were freezing, and only the warmth I provided kept her alive. *I could leave her in the middle of the ocean to drown.*

No. That was too easy. Too peaceful of a death for her. She needed to suffer for what she did to me and what she failed to do.

I kept a steady pace. The sirens swam to me often, sharing news of the world, but I wasn't interested in hearing it. Weeks passed before I reached the Maya shoreline. I crawled onto the sand, not tired, but done. I had worked my body enough. It was time to return to the city.

The port was a short sprint down the beach, but I merely sat and waited for the warriors to see me. They ran to their god and bowed low in the sand, grateful for my safe return.

"Take Abha to the city's dungeon. Feed and bathe her." The warriors looked to one another in confusion. "Now!" I ordered.

The Maya men lifted Abha's starving form with ease and carried her to The City of Gold. I released my hold on her psyche, but she didn't move. The sand burned my skin. The life here was dry compared to the land we had come from. It was hot and miserable. I felt trapped, as I had in the volcano.

"What has she done, Sun God?" Nakon said as he ran to me. I had just passed the city's borders, my hair dark and eyes green.

"Nakon, your daughter has betrayed our people. She has betrayed your god." I placed my hand on his shoulder. "The only contribution she can make to our people, the only way she can repent, is to be sacrificed."

Nakon collapsed and grasped my bare feet. "Sun God, I beg you to reconsider. She is all I have left." Tears were streaming down his face and nourishing the desert plants below us.

"There is no other way, Nakon." I placed my palm atop his head and said, "Please, do know, that I understand your pain." Cainadra's face shown in my mind for the first time in eons. Her dark curls bounced as she ran, a smile shining on her young face. Then there were ice-blue eyes glaring at me with hatred before they crumbled into ash. "There is no other way," I repeated.

The giants I created months ago stood vigil along the earth-wall, the fire burning in their eyes and mouths. I walked the perimeter of the farmlands, inspecting the slave's work. There was something different in the air, a taste that hadn't been there before. *Fear.*

I approached a young girl tending to the corn. "What ails your people? Have you not enough food and water?"

The girl looked to her feet, unable to speak.

"Answer your Sun God at once, girl."

She raised her head, and the blue of her eyes made me flinch. "Yes, we have enough food and water, Sun God," she whispered.

"Why do you cower? Have the warriors been harsh to you?" I asked.

"No...Yes..."

"What have they done?" The slaves were an important part of the community. The city flourished due to their hard work.

"It is not what they have done, Sun God. It is the giants. We are sacrificed so they may live." The girl looked down again, her body shaking with fear.

Why not use the excess lumber to feed them? The waste even? Anything could be fed to them. "Who made this order? Who is feeding you to the giants?"

"Chief Nakon, Sun God. He is there, watching as it happens." The small child began to cry.

"No more tears, child. Return to your work." The girl ran to the opposite end of the corn field to do so.

I created The City of Gold and raised the Maya people up so they could conquer and take more than their share. It seemed I had accomplished just that. But too much, and they would destroy themselves before Lilith had a chance to intervene.

One problem at a time.

Abha sat in the corner of her cell, chains tight around her wrists and ankles. She was thin from hunger, still, the woman had nearly escaped twice, controlling the minds of those guarding her. Kinich Ahau watched her now, the sacrifice taking place at sunrise.

"Why so quiet, my Sun God. Have you nothing to say to me?" she mocked, revealing her true self. Weeks trapped within herself and even more days imprisoned in this cell had given her ample time to contemplate

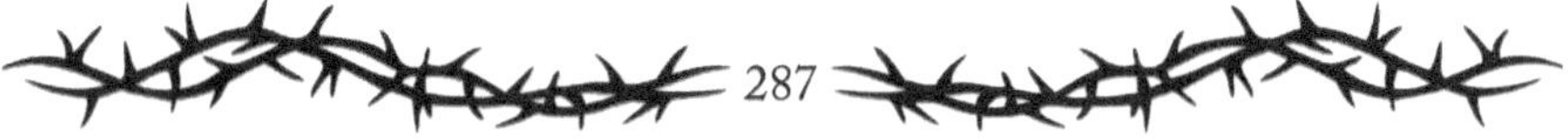

her actions, yet she did not regret them.

"There is nothing to say. You betrayed me, and now you will pay with your life." I wished to know her thoughts, to know why she did what she did, but to ask such a thing from her would mean that I cared. It would mean I was weak. Abha's light reached toward mine, caressing its surface, taunting. "Enough," I said.

"You enjoyed it. Letting go, trusting someone. You reveled in the freedom it gave you. I would know." Her light attempted to penetrate mine again but was met with a wall of strength.

I grimaced.

Retreating, she said, "I would have defeated you. You were weak. I only needed the Picts to trap you, then you would have been mine."

"Doubtful."

"Don't you want to know why? To know, after all these years, why I tried to kill you?" Abha pulled on her chains, and they pulled her backward, so she fell against the stone wall.

"I don't care."

"You forget, Sun God, that I was in your mind for years. I know you. It's eating at your soul. It's festering. I can see it." Abha smiled.

"It sounds like its festering within *you*, but please, if you need to confess, feel free to do so."

Abha's smile disappeared, but she continued anyway, "You killed my mother."

"Your mother was dead long before I woke. Do not spin tales. It will not save you."

"I am not lying!" Abha pulled at her chains, ignoring the bruises it gave her. "She was sacrificed to you when I was a young girl. The crops were dying, the rains were nonexistent, but we did have *you*." Her emerald glare pierced me, and I had to control a flinch. "We had a dead man in the ground. One we sacrificed our much-needed food to. A dead man who took and took from the life around him. I watched as you killed everything that dared to be nearby." She paused, wiping a tear from her cheek. "I told my father what you did, but he did not listen. He could not *see*."

I looked away as if I wasn't listening, but I couldn't stop myself. She had caused a unique kind of pain, one I thought I was immune to, and I wanted to know why I must suffer through it.

"One day, my people decided animals and crops were not enough. In order to awaken you, we must sacrifice our own." Abha wept freely now. "They took her from me. They forced her to lay at your side, and it was only a moment before your greedy light attacked her. She screamed and begged for help, but Father held me back and looked away as her life was taken."

"That was your people's doing. Not mine."

"Keep telling yourself that, perhaps another lie will get you through the day." I could feel Abha's gaze, but I could not meet it. "But one thing is for certain: though they were misguided, you took a peaceful people and turned them into monsters." Chains rattled. "You made them like you!"

"I gave your people power. They were nothing before me. They were starving and weak." My fists clenched.

"You are the weak one," Abha whispered. I finally met her gaze, and a glare was shared between us. "You lack a very important thing."

"What is that?" I asked.

"A heart."

Stone crumbled to the ground as my fist penetrated the wall.

"I suppose I can die happy now, seeing you in as much pain as me." Abha smirked.

"To that end, let me give you closure on another topic. A question, now answered." I extended my fingers, red dust coated them. "You asked me years ago, 'Is *she* worth the pain? The death?'" Abha leaned forward, eager for the answer, and I said, "Yes." I allowed my arms to fall, hanging limp. "She is worth every death. Every second of pain I endure."

"Why?" Abha's heart was thundering.

"Lilith is the only one who can save me."

The sun rose, however, I couldn't see it from the dungeon where we waited. I could feel it. A burst of energy and warmth came over me, even in complete darkness. I knew, so long as the sun returned every day, I would survive.

Guards came to collect Abha, and I trailed behind. I wanted her focused on the path in front of her. I wanted her to feel what I felt. *Pain.* We were indeed similar in nature, just as our colors were.

Abha flinched from the sun as we exited the catacombs. We began our ascent to the top of the temple. The citizens surrounded its base. There were expressions of both fear and excitement.

It was easy to participate when it wasn't your own life being taken.

The gold paint on the steps shimmered, and I traced their designs with my gaze as we walked. The breeze was still cool from the night and chilled my skin. The sun had difficulty keeping me warm today. Once there were no more steps to take, I looked to where the sacrificial altar rested. It was built when the temple was constructed but was only ever used for the yearly animal sacrifice. No human had lain upon it and bled. Until now.

Abha tensed. I prepared for her to flee, but her father laid a hand on her shoulder and said, "Please don't." She looked into her father's eyes, not full of hate as I had expected, but pity. Though she saw him as weak for submitting so easily, he was still her father and knew he had been corrupted by something beyond either of their control.

She nodded and kissed her father's cheek. Nakon looked to me for permission, and I granted it. He unlocked the chains from her wrists and ankles, trusting she would not run. There was nowhere *to* run. Abha approached the altar and climbed atop it, her back cringing at the cold stone. Her long, flowing azure dress clung to her sweat-dampened skin.

I stepped forward and spoke loud enough for the citizens standing at the temple's base to hear. "Abha, daughter of Nakon, holder of the *spirit*, you are to be sacrificed for your people. You have proven to be dishonest and hateful. You have no place among us, but you will contribute to our power." The gold moon that was etched into her skin was removed and cast into the wind. She cried out in pain but refused to meet my stare.

A guard bowed, offering me the sacrificial dirk. When I looked into his eyes, I realized it was the same man who had fought the vampires and won, scars covering nearly every inch of his skin. *He had come far from being the small, starving boy on the boat.* I took the weapon from his outstretched hand. The knife's blade was long and gleaming. I raised it above my head.

"Stop," Nakon begged.

"Nakon, you know—"

"No, please." Nakon held out his hand. "Let me. She is *my* daughter."

Surprised, I gave him the blade and stepped aside. "I love you, Abha," he said. Nakon kissed his daughter's forehead, and a sob escaped her while tears cascaded down her cheeks.

With a quick and precise stab, Nakon pierced Abha's chest. He waited until she had passed before carving farther, and it wasn't long before he held her heart in his hand. Blood dripped rapidly to the ground, resonating with the stone floor.

Nakon turned to me and said, "For The City of Gold," before taking a bite of power. Abha's light abandoned her body and drifted to Nakon as expected. But just before they joined, the golden soul slipped away and toward me. I took a step back, shocked. Nakon's spirit fought to take her, but she was too strong. She found my light and tore it open once more, except this time, she stayed within and closed the door behind her. I could only feel uneasiness knowing she had been strong enough to choose what vessel would carry her and what that could mean for me in the future.

Nakon raised the heart in the air, and the citizens cheered because of it. Their leaders had gained more power, and that meant more for them as well. However, the giants in the distance proved this was untrue. The Maya would flourish, and they would grow in power, but they would also throw their city into chaos getting there.

I thought of Lilith and what she would have done.

The Maya could take all they wished. Lilith would come before their fall.

900 Years Gone

The city was crumbling. Waste littered the streets. The farmland was barren. All the Maya's advances had been lost or left unfinished. I was particularly fond of the calendar they had created to track time, but they had abandoned that as well. There was no point when they could simply bask in riches, feeding their fat bodies with spoils and lounge safely in their temple with walls that had been erected for the sole purpose of keeping the slaves out.

The slaves had stopped working because the guards didn't care to enforce them. The guards didn't follow orders because the leaders were unwilling to share their wealth. But that wealth would run out. Time would make fools of them.

I had allowed them to govern themselves and they did as Eve predicted. Lilith had not shown herself, despite this. It made me wonder if she cared anymore. Perhaps she had abandoned Earth as she had me. I sat atop the earth-wall while the volcano rumbled. The giants stood still, waiting to defend the city from attack. They were fed daily, and the slaves had nowhere to flee. It was either wait to be sacrificed or run and be sucked dry by vampires. Or worse yet, scale the temple walls and beg for help from their leaders. That fate was the cruelest of them all.

My hand sank into the soil I sat upon, the earth weak. Instead of reinforcing it, I dug farther, wishing I didn't have to maintain it. I flinched and raised my hand. My fingers had been sliced open. I watched as the wounds closed, sealing in the dirt. Looking into the small hole, I realized what had cut me. A small bone was revealed.

I raised it up, willing the clouds to scatter and allow the sun to shine down on the object in my hand. It was such an unbelievable find that I didn't truly trust my eyes.

My spearhead. The dragon's fang from ages ago.

I traced its contours, relishing the feel of my long-lost weapon. A genuine smile appeared for the first time since the beginning. "Old friend, how nice it is to see you." It brought back memories of hunting and the old forest. Looking at the woodland now, it was incomparable. The beauty was sucked from this land by heat. The old forest had been lush and full of life.

It's time.

I walked the peak of the wall until I reached the giants. I whispered commands into their ears and ran, prepared for what was to come. As I ran, I remembered ancient words from an ancient daughter: *It's only a matter of time before it no longer wants us and sends out a flare.*

The Sun God sent out a flare, leaving the macana in the dirt.

The earth-wall was knocked down and the ground beaten by the giants until the volcano flared in anger. Lava poured from its peak as well as the cracks in the ground. The giants walked away from the mountain, traveling south to live as they pleased until I returned. The farmlands disappeared first, then the huts, then the stone wall surrounding the temple. The temple began to crumble, though its structure was strong and would most likely survive the river of fire. But those inside it would not.

The City of Gold was no more. It would become legend as it passed from ear to ear, then myth, and eventually it would become nothing at all.

None would believe it to have existed. A city so rich, the very structures were made of gold, at least that's what they would say.

I reached the Maya shoreline and the abandoned port there. I took a small, rotting ship and began my journey. East, toward a divided land, and one that needed a strong hand to guide it to greatness. I would try again. It didn't matter how long it took to find Lilith. Time had come and gone. Eras and peoples had become nothing but distant memories. And the longer she ran from me, the angrier I would be. But I was stronger than time. I would outlive time. And finding Lilith was inevitable.

XXVIII

Weak

1224 BCE

I watched the man while he waited in the center of the square. He held flowers in shaking hands and nervously paced back and forth only to sit upon the edge of the water fountain. Then he would repeat the process over again, the flower's stems being crushed in his too-tight grip.

He waited. It had been over an hour now, but still he would not leave. This man was determined, and I had a good idea of what he was waiting for. A woman.

Yes, always waiting. Always pacing. Always searching. I empathized with the young man. I had been waiting for eons. Eras had come and gone. Hundreds of thousands of my children had lived and died. But still I waited. Growing more impatient and bitter by the moment.

But she would come back to me.

The lilies the man had picked from the meadow on the outskirts of the city were near their end when a woman's voice called out. "I'm here! I'm so sorry I'm late!" This woman ran to the man who waited for her and embraced him. Their kiss was one for the ages. I had only seen a few whose souls mingled, whose didn't fight to take from the other but gave freely. This couple was rare indeed.

The man's blue eyes mimicked my own, proving our relation. I lounged in my ebony tunic with my spear at my side. The bench I rested upon was old and had supported many of my children throughout the long years. I could almost feel them sitting beside me.

"It doesn't matter how long it takes for you to come to me, so long as you do." The man released the woman from his embrace and gave her the wilted lilies. *The action reminded me of a different time in my existence—in the beginning.*

Though the flowers were less than satisfactory, the woman didn't take notice. She only saw how kind and thoughtful her love had been to bring her such a gift. But the man wasn't done. "My dear Hecuba," the man lowered to his knees and held her hands, "I am nothing without you, and I wish to be with you for the rest of our lives."

Hecuba let a tear slide down her rosy cheek, "Priam, you are not nothing. You are quite more than something. You are the Prince of Troy. Do not ever say you are less than the great man you are."

The man smiled, "But don't you see? What is a future king without his queen?"

Hecuba nearly dropped the lilies, if it hadn't been for Priam's grip on her hands the ground would have ended their small lives.

Priam cleared his throat before continuing, "So, what I am asking is, will you be my wife and queen to this great city?" The young woman gaped at him, so he said, "I know you love seeing me on my knees begging for your love, but the ground is quite uncomfortable." He smiled.

As if coming out of a daydream, Hecuba gasped and said, "Oh, my love, rise from your place on the ground. There will never be a reason to do it again, for I will give you my answer."

The young man stood, and that's when Hecuba swung her arms around his neck and gave him another kiss, though this one was unique compared to their previous ones. Their souls had danced and tangled in one another's before, but now they were one. The crimson soul of Hecuba and the royal blue soul of Priam merged until they were no longer existing separately. Both had attained a violet aura as deep as the setting sky.

They could no longer be apart now. It would be too painful.

The rich ebony curls of Hecuba blew softly away from her face as the breeze passed by, revealing her shining, joyful face. I couldn't help but envy what they had. Even when Lilith and I were happy, our souls never aligned.

Were we ever happy?

Suddenly, a man with a knife ran at the couple from the other side of the fountain. I had noticed him lurking before but swiftly dismissed him— he was no threat to me. Then I saw who his target was. With faster reflexes than anyone could see, I threw the spear from my sitting position on the withered bench. The dragon fang impaled the assassin just before his knife pierced the young prince in the back.

The force behind my throw was strong, and the man landed in the fountain. I watched as a statue of young Apollo poured water onto the assassin's corpse from his hands. Though the purpose was to offer water to his subjects, it looked as if he was attempting to drown the man who threatened his land's future king.

Yes, I remembered Apollo vividly. He was a rebel by nature and wished to obliterate all my arduous work by bringing kindness and joy to the world. Though he proved himself a skilled warrior, his sister, Artemis, had too much to lose if his philosophies spread. She enjoyed hunting humans greatly and needed them weak and afraid. Despite the early demise at his sister's hand, Apollo's words were passed down, and his memory remained intact.

In a way, he was just as immortal as I was.

Realizing what occurred, Priam rushed to me and said, "Brother, I thank you for your swift and accurate hand." The young prince took in my relaxed position on the bench. "I am morbidly curious to see how well you fend when you stand."

I couldn't help but smile. "Hopefully your curiosity will never be satisfied, because my skill brings nothing but suffering to those who come in contact with it."

"A warrior of Ares himself," the prince observed. I chuckled. If only Priam knew most of his gods were merely twisted versions of my past, given new life by my descendants.

The prince cleared his throat nervously but stood tall. "Well, since there is no need to display your skills further, perhaps you would like to do something less perilous and come with me to meet the king. Surely he will want to give you a reward for saving his only son and heir to the throne." I was glad then that I had changed my form so the prince would not recognize our relation in my eyes. I thought of the emerald irises that now shown from my face and lowered my guilty gaze.

I stood and walked across the small clearing to the fountain. Apollo looked down on me disapprovingly as I yanked my spear from the assassin's chest. "I am in need of no such reward." I paused. "But I thank you for the offer. Perhaps we will meet again one day."

"If you don't want gold and jewels, then what?" the prince asked. He signaled to his unworthy guards to remove the dead body from the fountain, as onlookers were gathering. Priam quickly found himself by Hecuba's side and held her protectively. Lowering my gaze again, I answered, "Penance."

Penance. I wanted Lilith to atone for what she did to me.

"If penance is what you seek, then look no further. You will be my protector, and guard against those who wish to hurt me and my family." He gripped his future wife tighter. "You have done awful things in your life?"

The prince's gaze darted to the corpse being carried away.

I met his gaze, boring the ancient grief into my offspring, begging him to understand.

Slowly, he said, "Then use the skills the gods gave you for good and protect those in need."

I twirled my spear as I thought on what the young man said. Though Lilith's penance was the one I wanted, perhaps this would be an acceptable way to pass the endless amount of time I had.

"Very well."

"What do we call you?" Hecuba asked, reserving a kind expression for her beloved's savior. I couldn't help but notice the striking resemblance Hecuba had to my firstborn.

Only pausing a moment, I said, "Achilles." *Pain now defined me, and only when I saw Lilith would the name Lucifer be uttered again.*

Satisfied with my answer, the future King and Queen of Troy led me through the city and into the home of the king where I was to guard the royal family. Never, in all my years of war and destruction, had I been someone's true protector. *Not since Lilith.* The pain in my chest eased as I stepped through Prince Priam's doorway.

20 Years Gone

"Achilles, my friend, how do you do it?" Priam slurred. The King of Troy was having his third child. Hecuba was in labor and had been all day and night.

"Do what?" I finished my drink in one gulp and relished the burning sensation slipping down my throat. The intense odor of honey was prominent, but it was the only drink that affected me without having to consume gallons of it. I was pleased when Priam had the winemakers experiment with different ingredients. He was determined for me to relax and enjoy myself. But he also wanted a chance to learn more about my past. *Always an ulterior motive with hybrids.*

"Stay young! Did you pray to the gods for eternal youth? Did you drink from a magical spring?" He paused and moved close enough I could smell the mead on his breath. "Or have you bathed in a virgin's blood?" The king moved back so he could take another swig of his drink. There always seemed to be one in his hand or in his gullet, unable to handle the pressures of ruling.

I snickered. "I think you've had too much to drink, *my king*. Delusions are regaling you with many absurd theories."

Priam nearly spit. "I will discover your secret one day, and on that day," more drink was poured down his throat, "you will have to share."

Amused by the way he swayed, I said, "And why would a king with everything want more?"

He shook his head. "It's not for me. It's for my dear wife, Hecuba. She wouldn't want to ride an old man. That would be torture, wouldn't you agree?"

"You are hardly an old man, Priam. You are a mere child of forty, and I doubt Hecuba would mind, so long as you were the old man she was riding."

Priam smiled. "Yes, I suppose so." The king was easily convinced.

"Just enjoy the time you do have with your family," I said. A melancholy emotion washed over me, and my amused smile disappeared.

Noticing the change in my mood, Priam held up his glass and said, "To family."

I raised my own glass. "To life." That was the last drink Priam had for the night. The king slumped down in his fanciful chair, the man's snore louder than a tiger's purr.

Relieved to be alone and free to sulk as I wished, I put down my glass and went to check on Hecuba. But not before I shifted the king onto his side against the throne so he wouldn't drown in his own fluids. This caring deed of mine happened more often than I liked to admit.

They would all die eventually anyway. Why did it matter when?

Still, I couldn't stop myself. They were my children after all.

I thought of Cainadra, Abel, Seth, Asher, and many more. The memories of them plagued my thoughts often. Before I agreed to be Priam's guard, I was able to ignore such weak thoughts. *Weak emotions.* But Priam and his family had revealed something to me.

I wasn't alone.

So why did I feel alone?

I knew the answer, but even thinking *her* name had become too painful. My night lily still ran from me. Not a trace of her had been seen or heard from in eons. I didn't even know the exact number of years. Time blended together and the order was often lost to me.

Still, I allowed myself to hope. My creations were scouring Earth for my beloved. The sirens and sea monsters searched by water, while the sprites and vampires searched by land. I added more and more until I wasn't sure how many abominations truly existed in the world. And they had brought me nothing but disappointment. Lilith could change her form as I could, and it gave them little chance of finding her. Lilith would have to be the one to slip up. She would have to reveal herself, accident or not, if I was to see her again.

But I would not rest. *She would be mine. I would be loved.*

"Father! Achilles!" Hector called. The eldest son of the king came crashing through the doorway of the throne room. Seeing his father was asleep, he looked to the next man he trusted. "Achilles, Mother is not well. The midwives say she won't last much longer." Tears were pouring from the boy's eyes.

I took a furtive glance at the sleeping king. He had been so happy just moments before, a smile still rested upon his face. "Let me see her," I said.

Hector went to rouse his father when I put my hand on his shoulder and said, "He is no use to us at the moment." Understanding, Hector led the way to his parent's bedchamber where the queen lay unconscious on the wool bedding. The bed's frame was a modest metal. I knew they could have had gold or silver, but the King and Queen of Troy believed in only taking what they needed. The rest was for the people.

Earth had an odd way of rewarding kindness.

I watched Hecuba's breathing hitch as she had another contraction, her damp, dark curls splayed around her on the pillows. Her blankets were soiled with blackened blood and sweat flowed like a river over her pale skin. *She didn't have much time left.*

"Hector, take your brother, Alexander, and tend to your father. I will assist your mother."

"But—" he began.

"All of you need to leave." I looked to the three midwives who blotted the queen's sweaty forehead with damp cloths and massaged her spasming muscles. They took too long to move. "Now." The expressions on their faces gave me hope that people still feared me. I had become lax in my authority these past couple decades due to my connection with the royal family.

Once the room was empty, I looked to the dying queen. In my existence, I had killed more than I could count as well as created, but never had I *healed.* I had thought it unnecessary until this moment. *Why did I feel the need to protect them?* I asked myself, remembering an ancient time when I held my dead, unborn child in the palm of my hand.

I stopped thinking of the past and prepared for what I came here to do. I sat upon the soft bedding and brushed a stray curl from Hecuba's face. I knew I was capable of healing. All I had to do was will it to be and it would be.

I rested my hands on her womb and sensed the life within. The child had a strong heartbeat. I felt a connection with the creature. As if the trapped spirits of my children existing inside me wanted to help their kin.

They wanted her to live.

I allowed my lost children to guide my power. My golden spirit wrapped around Hecuba's violet one, and I spoke the healing words:

Mother to be
You are not lost to me
The child inside you
Wishes to be—

Hecuba's eyes flew open, and she screamed. Women's cries of pain during childbirth were unbearable, but this scream was of one of utter torment. This scream was from one who wanted to die.

"Make it stop!" Hecuba begged. I still held her womb in my grasp, and she clutched my hands. The strength behind her grip nearly hurt. The surprise from the act forced my release, though I knew the spell wasn't complete. The connection I had to her child was dulled, and the spirits that dwelled within my body withdrew, abandoning me, leaving only my own spirit to guide the magic.

Alone, I was not strong enough. My soul burned away little by little until, finally, I let go of the connection, unwilling to sacrifice any more of myself. Loneliness weighed on me a hundred fold. All at once, emotions broke through the walls I had built for myself. Each brick crumbled and fell onto the cold, hard ground of my psyche.

Hecuba's cries grew, and I fled. Though it was slight, I couldn't help but notice a stinging sensation, like a tether had been detached. My soul weakened upon the disconnection. A bloody tear streamed down my cheek.

I exited the doorway to find Alexander waiting there for me. The young boy of seven years looked up at my distraught expression and immediately began to cry.

I forced what remaining magic I had to assist me. "Forget, child." Upon the touch of my palm to his forehead, Alexander stopped crying and walked away slowly, as if he didn't remember where he was.

The next place I found myself was in the throne room where Hector sat beside his blissfully unaware father. The midwives were nowhere in sight. The boy didn't say a word when I walked in the door; my grim expression said it all.

Hector didn't cry as his brother had. He knew he had to be strong for his family now. I sauntered across the throne room. When I reached the stone chair etched with design and gems, I placed a palm on Hector and his father's forehead, saying this last word to them with a small, grieving smile, "Forget."

The king remained unconscious. Hector stood and departed the room, in the direction of his dying mother. I took advantage of this solitude to adjust the king's position one last time. His breathing returned to normal. *For both our sakes, I hope it's the drink that kills you.*

When I tried to heal the queen and her child, I had a taste of true connection. One that the animals shared, as well as the mortals when they found their soulmates. I had a taste of what it could have been like if I had been willing to sacrifice myself.

I had wanted that connection my whole existence, but the only emotion I felt during that touch was *fear*. Fear for what that meant for me. Fear for what I would become. The way I had been existing for eons, miserable and alone, was preferable to the unknown spiritual bond. I had created these beings for a reason. Their succubus nature would drain the planet of its energy, and in turn, destroy *all* the bonds.

If I allowed myself to join the masses, then what would become of The First Man and Woman?

Despite the horrific experience of the night, it had reminded me of my purpose. I abandoned the royal's home in need of solitude. The darkness outside was suffocating, and I looked to my golden light for comfort. Though the light I relied upon wasn't displaying its usual brilliance. Grey was what encased my spirit now, the spirits of Earth and my own children hiding within its core. I had burned away too much of myself. This sickness had hold of my soul, and I didn't know if I'd ever be able to rid myself of it.

I passed by my ancient son's crumbling monument. His hands were black with mildew, however, they still allowed the water to flow downward. The pool Apollo fed froze upon my passing, and the sound of the ice-water's groans echoed loudly in the small clearing. My ears rang with pain following the wrathful noise. The darkness turned the pretend-god's kind expression sinister, and I knew it was because he was my son.

Ancient words echoed in my mind: *You will destroy yourselves.*

The city was quiet. The hybrids slept peacefully, unknowing of the tragedies unfolding in the king's home as well as their front steps. I quickened the pace as I clutched my heartless chest. The buildings vanished from my sight, and the beach's sand tried to pull me down. I knew this sickness would cost me dearly, but it would cost these people just as much.

As I boarded a ship to sail away from the once great city, a newborn's cry sang from the royal's home.

As the boat carried me forward to Greece, the water rippled in strange patterns. I looked deep into the darkness below, searching for the cause, but even my acute vision could not penetrate its depths. Curiosity beckoned me to the edge of the boat anyway, wondering what dwelled beneath. My light reached out, and just as my soul touched the water's surface, it retreated. Still wounded, the spirit clung to my body, unwilling to expose itself again.

Instead, what I saw in the water was a man with gold hair and ice-blue eyes. He looked young and strong, but also old and lonely. His aura barely shone in the reflection of the sea. The man tried to smile, but the ripples shuddered in distaste and he disappeared.

I'm never going to see Lilith again.

Forgetting what had drawn me to the water, I looked up at the stars above, wishing as the mortals did, for answers to the unknown.

XXIX
Found

A heartless man can still break.
-C

1194 BCE

The dragon bone pierced the wooden target with ease, directly where the heart would have rested. Though I wouldn't have wasted the vital piece of life if the prey was flesh and blood. I retrieved my spear, thinking the man-shaped training tool was laughable. The object should have been for young children to play with, but I watched as grown men, ones who had seen many battles, still struggled to master it. The hybrid beside me leapt and threw his spear at the adjacent mark, missing the imagined organ.

I sighed in disappointment. *Hybrids weren't the same warriors they used to be.* No, they had become soft, too comfortable to be true warriors. But it was not them I blamed, it was their leaders. The leaders used the warriors the same way they handled their imported treasures, women, and clothes; abused without mending, and tossed away without a second thought.

How could one expect the warriors to care when the kings did not?

It was only a matter of time before the fighters were tossed away as well. After watching them train only a short while, I could see it would be sooner rather than later.

The scent of roasted meat wafted on the warm breeze, making me turn and walk into the king's home. The training grounds were insignificant compared to the massive structure, so the trek was short. It didn't tire me to travel a greater distance, but it was agitating to wait for something as basic as food. And, of course, I had to walk at the pace of a hybrid, as to not raise any more suspicions about Achilles; Demigod and Great Warrior of Greece. I would have chuckled at the title if it had not been for my rumbling stomach. But this was the existence I chose. Perhaps Lilith would appear to reprimand the greediest of humankind if I was nowhere to be seen. But if she hadn't appeared by now, she wasn't going to.

I heard a slap as I approached the dining room. "Silence woman!"

Agamemnon's dim brother must have been summoned. There was no bigger fool than that man. He could abuse all the women he wanted, but he would never stand against the true monster dwelling in this house.

"I see you have been giving away secrets, Menelaus," Agamemnon said. "Would you risk a Trojan becoming aware of our plans? Shame, brother. Just because you fancy this woman does not mean you have to speak to her."

Greece's plan to attack Troy was a well-known fact by most of the land. Agamemnon only acted as if it was a secret to keep his true goal from reaching his brothers' ears. The king planned to sign a peace treaty with Troy and gain their trust, goods, and warriors. He would then use them to take over the entirety of Greece, dethroning his brothers; all six kings. When all was said and done, he would turn his vast army against Troy themselves, knowing full-well King Priam was an over-trusting drunk. Ten years without his soulmate had only made matters worse. If anyone wanted to take Troy, the time to do it was now, while its leadership was weak.

Distracting myself from the thought, I concentrated on the food being carried in by the servants. I motioned for them to set my place at the head of the table, wishing to see Agamemnon's calm demeanor crack, if only for a moment.

"Ah, Achilles. The great god Ares has blessed us with your presence at last," the dark king said as I entered the dining room.

"Indeed, he has," I replied, a smile threatening to appear.

"What is he doing here?" Menelaus whined.

"Why, he's just here to discuss strategy. Aren't you, Achilles?" Agamemnon lied smoothly. The king knew very well that I came and went as I pleased, but he couldn't allow his brother to know that; it would ruin his illusion of control.

I nodded, concerned more about my starved middle and the steaming food in front of me.

"Strategy? For what? You said the matter was ended? That there would be no more discussion?" Menelaus bellowed.

Savoring the taste of my meal, I tried to ignore the brothers' squabbling, though I couldn't help but notice Agamemnon had switched tactics and told his brother there would be no more efforts to attack Troy. It was almost entertaining to watch the hybrid's lives play out. Lies, secrets, and greed were all their existence amounted to.

"Brother, there is no harm in discussion, as I also said. Man to man. King to king," Agamemnon cooed.

"He is no king!" Menelaus cried.

Tiring of their banter, I said, "I have no desire to be king, and I have no desire to discuss strategy with you. Attack or don't attack. I could care less. I simply came here because you have the best food." I took another delicious bite. "When you decide to attack, then and only then will I respond to you. And that response will depend on if I feel like fighting that day or not. Lucky for you, that is most days."

Finally, there was silence, and I could enjoy my meal, though it was

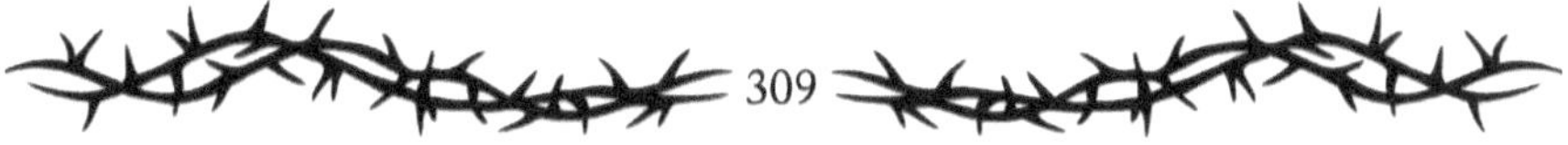

almost gone by then. I motioned for the servant to fill my plate. My energy was waning, even as my stomach was filled.

Thinking of Troy had brought unpleasant memories to the forefront of my mind. Two tearful sons, a dying woman, an unborn child, and a golden soul misused and damaged for the remainder of its existence. I felt the edges of my soul now, grey and crumbling, and struggling to contain the restless souls within. It was made even more difficult by the blood moon that appeared a few days earlier; its arrival weakened me, though I hadn't seen the crimson orb since the land-split. Still, if I concentrated very hard, I could make the grey disappear by shining my golden core outward, even so, what was the point when there was no one to see it but me?

"May I be excused? I need to use the lavatory," a woman's soft voice whispered. I looked up to see Menelaus nod angrily in the woman's direction. I hadn't taken the time to notice the other person sitting at the table. *Probably a concubine.*

I lifted my fork, a steaming chunk of chicken awaiting me, when an ancient scent reached my nose. I dropped the utensil, my body frozen.

Had I finally lost my mind?

Was it in this moment, among fools, I was to lose my senses?

The kings paid me no heed as they bickered. I could feel the eyes of the servants on me, wondering what had happened to cause my reaction, but they wisely stayed silent.

Just before the woman disappeared around the corner, her crimson core flared. Her movement caused the stale air in the room to dance, bringing with it the scent I had chased after for ages but could never catch. The scent of night pollen, of the moon and stars, of The First Woman.

After all this time, all I could do was sit and wait for her to return, so I could see for myself if I could truly trust my senses. The seconds ticked by, slow and agonizing. As I waited, I thought of what I would say to her. After billions of years apart, what could one say? The emotions ran through me in intervals, each one a dagger to the chest. Fury, betrayal, hope, sadness, longing, loneliness, but the last one forced me to stand, the strongest—pain.

The feeling heightened my senses, and I could hear her delicate footsteps circling the halls. *Would she run again?*

I couldn't risk it. Slowly, I took the first step. The closer I came to the doorway, the faster I was, and it soon became difficult to keep the mortal's pace. Once in the hallway, her scent enveloped me, and I knew for certain that it was merely a disguise she had worn.

Just as I had been in the beginning of this existence, I became feral and followed her. She would not escape me, no matter how far she ran. I quickly caught up with the small, blonde woman, keeping my distance, stalking, and waiting for my chance.

After she had circled the hallway once more, I stepped into an open room, knowing she would circle again. I had expected her to turn and search for me, as my scent was now in the halls with her, but she was lost in her thoughts—that much had not changed.

After all this time, she hadn't even twitched her nose in recognition of my scent, while hers was rooted in my memory. The sharp pain returned, and my shoulders hunched to protect my chest. The instinct to hunt was strong, but the pain my prey had caused was overwhelming.

Look at what she had done: I was now a wounded creature, no better than an animal limping away to lick its wounds. *But what could be done about it?* The damage was done. Nothing she could say or do would ever heal The First Man. The mind, the body, or the soul. I looked to my light now, the grey was growing inward.

I didn't know what I'd expected after all this time. My goal for centuries was merely to find her, but what then? Even if she had changed completely and wished only to be with me for the remainder of our existence, she could not erase the hatred I had formed and clung to all these years.

It could not be as it had been.

Lilith passed by the room I cowered in, still circling, still thinking, and still unaware of my nearness. *She had not changed.*

Fury consumed the pain in my chest, burning it away.

What could be done? What could be done?

If she could not erase the pain she'd caused, she would feel the same pain. If she could not return all the time gone from our existence, she would sacrifice her own in turn. If we could not be happy together, we would suffer together. If we could not love, we would hate. If we could not forgive, we would fight.

One thing was for certain: I would not lose her again.

I would no longer be alone.

Lilith's footsteps grew close. I stood in the door's archway now, my breathing ragged, but I managed to shine my core bright, and the grey was all but gone.

I stepped into the hall. Lilith turned the corner. I felt her strong but equally soft body collide with mine. Her intoxicating scent drowned me in temporary bliss, knowing what was to come. The woman was dazed for a moment, but she eventually looked upward and into my gaze for the first time in eons.

"Hello, Lilith. Nice to see you."

The Creation of Eve

A grating voice summoned me to the clearing. I always felt safer in the foliage, but I couldn't stop myself from responding. However, I wasn't worried because whatever dwelled there would have to face me—a deadly predator of the land.

One bite, and they would be mine.

A challenger resided in my territory. I had become familiar with its scent a long while ago, but I never had the chance to see it—it was too fast. Though I anticipated the day I would finally have the chance to subdue it. The golden fur was all I saw as it passed by me, hunting *my* prey.

I slithered along the ground, relishing the warmness of the grass. My eyes darted from one movement to another in the woodland. I saw a bird fly down from its hiding place in the trees and snatch a blood-colored butterfly in midair. A shrew scuttled by, unaware of my presence. My tongue instinctually licked the air and tasted the scent of the rodent. I could hear its rapid heartbeat when it saw me, and it darted for a hole in the ground.

Despite my want to go after the underling, I moved toward the clearing instead—toward the voice that called to me. I crossed into the open area confidently. Though I knew this was a terrible vantage point; I could be seen. I raised myself up and extended my hood. I hissed when I noticed a monkey traveling alongside me. The ignorant primate gazed at the red-furred animal that spoke to us, oblivious to the predator beside it.

Irritated that I was being ignored, I opened my hood even wider and spat at the red-furred creature. It didn't take notice of my challenge, so I prepared to attack. My muscles tensed, and the ebony scales that shone on my skin gripped the soil. Right before I sprung, I was lifted into the air by an unknown source. At first, I thought the foolish monkey had grabbed me, but there was nothing to bite when I turned my head to and fro.

I fought for freedom to no avail. I turned my sights to the red-furred animal as it continued to speak to us, but the sounds were foreign. For the first time in my life, I felt fear. Especially when I started to understand the sounds coming from its lips.

The monkey floated toward me as the strange words were said, ones that would alter us indefinitely. Soon, we weren't a snake nor a monkey. We were a *human*. I felt the power that willed me to be. I had instructions, but every fiber of my being was fighting against it. I wouldn't allow this creature to join with me, if I did that would mean we would be one.

We would be *Eve*.

But the monkey's soul was stronger than I thought it was. It wouldn't bow to my will.

The challenger I hunted before entered the clearing, barking sounds at the red-furred one. I wanted to attack, but the being that shared this body with me wouldn't allow it. I pushed and prodded against its soul, hoping to take control of this form. But to my surprise the monkey's spirit had control of the limbs and ran to the creature that did this to us.

It said to us, "I am sorry. Everything is going to be all right. I just need to make a few changes." Our limbs moved once again, and we stepped back, submitting to the red-furred woman.

I coerced and whispered to the spirit, but it only pushed me to the very borders of this new mind. My silent scream filled the void while another spell was being said, however, it was not for me. The monkey's soul was released from this vessel and I was left to suffer alone.

Little had I known that without the will of the monkey, I was lost to the spell that intertwined with this body, in the very blood itself. I was at its mercy. The fight was over before it had begun.

Now, all I had was the faint memory of what I had been and the realization that my freedom no longer existed.

21 Years' Gone

The years passed slowly and agonizingly. I was aware of my actions and my unnatural feelings, but still I could not fight. My spirit had not completed its turn as a snake. It was ripped away by her—Lilith.

Two conflicting personas plagued me. My natural one: the one that wanted to strike Lucifer with my bite and watch as the poison slowly killed him. And the unnatural one: the woman that wanted to care for him and bare his children, despite his cruelty. Every time I fought against the unnatural one *her* words pounded against my skull. Again and again, the curse repeated itself: *You will be Eve. You will be Eve. You will be Eve.*

But I fought through the pain just enough to make subtle changes to Lucifer's life. The damage I made was not immediate as I wished, but damage it was. I manipulated Lucifer's emotions when I could. I said small comments here and there to his children. I planted ideas in their heads, which was exactly what he didn't want. Lucifer wanted his children mindless, but they would rebel. *It didn't take much.*

I watched the seeds I planted throughout the years blossom. I sat comfortably from Lucifer's burrow above the waterfall. Lucifer seemed calm and collected in the presence of his children, despite the fact that his eldest daughter was encased in ice, and the rest questioned him. I wanted to smile, but the curse wouldn't even allow that. I would be a dutiful mate and mother until the end.

Just as I predicted, Cainadra broke free from her prison. I had suspected she inherited such qualities from her father, but I never approached her about it. If I knew the truth, then I would have been obligated to tell Lucifer. And I couldn't spoil the surprise for him.

I watched triumphantly as Cainadra treaded her way across the frozen pond, only to see her face fall and all the aggression dissipate. She had unintentionally struck her twin brother, and he collapsed, bleeding and fatally wounded.

I managed an angry sigh. All my hard work was gone in an instant. Cainadra would not be strong enough to fight her father now. But I looked to Seth and saw how he glared at Lucifer. *Smart boy. He knew this was his father's doing. I could rely on my descendants to continue what I started.*

And so, I waited and watched as Lucifer dug his grave deeper and deeper with his own words and actions. I realized, at the very moment when Cainadra became nothing but ash, that I needn't had worried. The man's hand shook slightly after Cainadra was carried away by the wind.

Lucifer would destroy himself.

I didn't bother saying goodbye to my offspring. Naturally, I should have left when they were born. Snakes were much stronger than humans. They didn't need parental guidance once they hatched, but alas, I never had the pleasure of creating true offspring. I left my grieving children without another glance in their direction. The smell of Abel's burnt flesh was prominent and only when I entered the dense greenery of the forest was I free of it.

I followed *his* scent until I came upon the human's sad form. He lifted his nose to the breeze, and I watched as his face fell.

"She won't come," I said.

Lucifer turned toward me. Though I was aware that he asked me questions, and I answered them in turn, I couldn't concentrate on the meaningless conversation. I wanted only one thing, and he could give it to me.

I knew little about Lucifer and Lilith besides what I had seen. Their power over the natural realm was vast, but surely they could not control me after death.

That would be too much power for any being to wield.

I could have waited for death to take me naturally, but I had many years left, and I could not suffer one more moment. Knowing that I needn't be alive for Lucifer to suffer was freeing. I could stop fighting.

So, I revealed my ploy to the human and mocked him about his own impending downfall. Though, he was not as angry as I expected.

Perhaps he already knew.

Still, he granted me a kindness, which was very unlike him. I found myself in his embrace, his hand caressed my cheek, and though I had been repulsed by his touch all these years, it was nice to know I wasn't alone.

There was a moment of agonizing pain in my chest, but my death was quick. I found that only upon my demise could I finally breathe. I was freed from the curse Lilith had placed on me. I was no longer tethered to Eve. I found the line that led to the rest of the natural spirits. I could hear their call and feel the warmth and comfort they would provide.

I followed the tether as quickly as I could, but soon, a strong grip had hold of my soul, and I was made helpless once again. The tether I clung to was snipped, and I could feel the pain of the separation. As much as I fought to go to my family, I was forced to Lucifer and into the golden aura that I could now see. I was forced to feed his starving soul. I should have known better than to think the man was capable of any form of kindness.

If I had a body, I would have cried out, but even that privilege was lost to me. Though my senses were gone, I understood perfectly well. The humans had won.

But perhaps their victory would also mean their defeat.

Acknowledgments

I want to acknowledge my family for their undying loyalty to me and my dreams. Thank you, Brandon, my husband and book designer. Your skill and patience with computers astound me, and your keen eye for design grows each day. I am grateful to have you as a partner in both work and life. You are a rare soul. You are my heart.

Thank you, Mom, for your dutiful eyes and ears. I made you read chapter after chapter and not once did you complain. I couldn't have written this book without you.

Thank you, Dad, for your constant flow of ideas and opinions (even when I didn't want to hear them). A lot of your persistent words made their way onto my pages.

Thank you, Conner, for your endless amount of wisdom on every subject imaginable. Your talent for debate keeps my mind sharp and my writer's muscles toned. You're an amazing brother.

Finally, thank you, readers. The First Man and Woman's journey is long and unforgiving, but it is the difficult experiences in life that prove how strong we truly are. Like these struggling immortals, you all have a voice. And all of you have inspired *my* voice.

Follow Lilith's undying story in
book two of
The Creations Saga:

Red Soul

*The determination of an immortal
can save Earth or destroy it...*

About the Author
Anne MacReynold

Anne MacReynold believes our universe holds magic that we have yet to comprehend, and she wields this power of thought in her writing. Not only do her philosophical views weave themselves into her stories, but her life as well. Anne continues to find happiness with her family and animal companions in Alaska, a place that still displays the natural beauty that is the Earth, and a home that allows her to spend time with those she loves. Anne proves that sometimes the simplest of lives can be the most fulfilling.

Keep up with Anne's book releases and other writings by following her website, annemacreynold.com, or connect with her on facebook.com/WriterAnneMacReynold, twitter.com/AnneMacReynold, and instagram.com/AnneMacReynold